INVISIBLE scars

JANE AND BURT BOYAR

ALSO BY JANE AND BURT BOYAR

Yes I Can The Story of Sammy Davis Jr.
With Sammy Davis, Jr.
Farrar Straus & Giroux (1965)

Why Me? The Sammy Davis, Jr. Story
With Sammy Davis, Jr.
Farrar Straus & Giroux (1989)

SAMMY: The Autobiography of Sammy Davis, Jr.
A compilation of the above. Edited by Burt Boyar
Farrar Straus & Giroux (2000)

H.L. & Lyda - Growing up in the H.L. Hunt and Lyda Bunker Hunt Family.
With Margaret Hunt Hill
August House (1994)

World Class - a novel set in the world of international tennis
Random House (1975)

Hitler Stopped by Franco
Marbella House (2001)

Photo by Sammy Davis, Jr.
Judith Regan/HarperCollins (2007)

Jane Boyar passed away in 1997. *Invisible Scars* is the last book on which she collaborated with Burt.

Marbella House Los Angeles

ISBN: 0971039259
ISBN-13: 9780971039254

For ALINDA HILL WIKERT
our inspiration for this book

Prologue

It was an easy landing, and America Harvey taxied to the parking area until ordered to stop. She cut the engines. It was 3:30 P.M. on Sunday, June 10, 1982, at the *Aeropuerto Internacional de Málaga* in the south of Spain.

America went into the cabin, lowered the back of the rear seat of the Learjet and removed her new suitcases from the luggage compartment.

"Permit me to help you, Señorita." A Captain of the *Guardia Civil* was standing at the entrance to the plane. He wore the traditional *tricornio*, the three-cornered black patent-leather hat that came down from Napoleon's time in Spain, and patent-leather shoulder belts and holster over his olive-green trousers and shirt. He saluted. She knew it was the same courtesy that would be extended had she approached a policeman to ask a question, or if he had come to arrest her.

Two more *Guardias* stood behind him. He did not seem surprised that the bags she had no choice but to hand over to him were weightless. Other than by his presence he gave her no reason for fear. What could he possibly know?

The Captain helped her down the two steps to the ground. "Thank you," she said, speaking to him in English for anonymity. Another tourist pilot. Chilled by fear the hot Mediterranean air did not warm her.

He replied in English. "You are Miss Harvey?"

"Yes."

He snapped handcuffs onto her wrists.

She had been born and raised to have her wrists encircled with silver and gold. Unable to take her eyes off the stainless steel that now pinioned her hands together she asked, "What have I done? Why are you arresting me?"

"You are not being arrested. You are being detained."

"In handcuffs?"

"Required procedure. Once inside they will be removed."

"But on what charge am I being detained?"

"None. As yet. Under the law you can be detained for forty-eight hours without a charge."

"But there has to be a reason."

Cynically, world wearily, he replied, "Oh, yes, there's always a reason. Perhaps your papers are not in order . . ." He stopped and looked at her with eyes that had seen just about every scheme that mankind had devised and now he spoke to her in his own language. "Let us end this farce of forcing me to speak English, Miss Harvey, when we know you speak Spanish as easily as I. My orders are to be courteous. Please return the favor."

The room in the offices of the *Guardia Civil* was comfortable enough. The officer had removed the handcuffs and told her that someone would bring coffee.

Seated on a hard wooden bench she was staring at a blank, whitewashed wall that might have been a screen on which she watched the last twelve years of her life pass by in detail. From castles in Spain to a Spanish prison.

PART ONE

America Jane Harvey: she was what Cecil Beaton, Lagerfeld, Diana Vreeland, Avedon and Selznick, the Supreme Court on Beautiful Women, would call alluring. At twenty-two she was a professional jet pilot, five feet, ten inches, tall, broad shouldered, slim waisted, a strong, healthy Texas beauty with long blonde hair and eyes too brilliantly green for her to wear emeralds.

The family fortune had begun with her mother Margaret's grandfather's ranch that included what is now known as downtown Dallas. Then in 1943 reserves of petroleum were discovered below her father's ancestral home, a large agricultural property in San Antonio. As he owned all the land for many miles around, he did not fear that other landowners would drill wells and draw oil out of the same pool, not even by slant drilling, so he was able to protect the livestock and farm by drilling on only one acre, from which he produced fifty thousand barrels a day.

When not in school America and her brother, Albert Galatyn Harvey, Jr., whom she called Gat, enjoyed sitting with their father in the twin-engine plane he flew over the thirty thousand–acre Harvey Ranch, inspecting what was happening in the sectors below. Gat was two years older than his sister, six-foot-three, also fair haired and green eyed.

Al Harvey taught them about farming, about growing things, about their responsibilities. "This ranch on which we and four generations of our ancestors were born has fed us and cared for

3

us. This land gave us everything we have; the oil reserves under it, the soil, the grass, and those trees down there. So though it's accurate to say that this land belongs to us, it's equally a fact that we belong to this land and we have an obligation to return the enrichment and protection it has given us. But life isn't a piece of cake. Never was. My grandparents nearly starved because of a two-year drought. 'Most everyone around sold their ranches, cheap, but Pops and Moms were tougher'n the back wall of a shooting gallery. They believed in the land and they guts'd it out 'til it came back. And so y'all and I are here today. In my parents' time cattle prices went up and we were rich, they went down and we were broke. Then we got lucky and struck oil. We're better than comfortable now, but in this life you don't take anything for granted. Play your cards close to the vest because every time you wake up there can be a surprise."

And he taught them how to walk through their privileged world. "With what your mom and I can give you, you're going to be spoiled. But if I ever catch you *acting* spoiled I'll wring your necks. You are to treat the cook and ranch hands with the same respect that you treat your mother and me."

As they flew over their lands a source of special pleasure for America was in looking below at an orchard of five thousand pecan trees her father had planted for her. A small silver plaque on a post bore her name and date of birth: America Jane Harvey—1943.

He had also planted five thousand trees on the day Gat was born, as his own father had done for him in a tradition begun by America's great-grandfather.

Working days began at six A.M. Lunch was served at eleven-thirty at the ranch house. The four Harveys sat at the end of a long dining table and after them the foreman and fifteen hired hands. The food, most of it home grown, was served on large platters placed along the length of the table. The ranch produced beef, wheat, barley, pecans and corn.

San Antonio is extremely hot in the summer so they owned a home at the Garden of the Gods Club in Colorado Springs. Their closest neighbors in San Antonio, the Jaspersons, who owned Jasperson Oil, followed them to Colorado and bought the house next door. Sam Jasperson was a successful wildcatter who had started off as a roustabout in the oil fields before going out on his own, risking everything he had and striking oil. Their son J.J. was Gat's best friend. He was a year younger than Gat and a year older than America, and he had a romantic interest in her that was emphatically returned. The three were constantly together. Gat and America, and also J.J., were encouraged to become competent in sport. In the summer it was water skiing. The Harveys owned a speedboat, and they hired an instructor for two hours every day except Sundays. Gat skied well. But J.J. and America, similar in nature, wanted to excel. Gat always skied with them for the first hour then watched from the boat as they worked at becoming adept at doing handstands on their skis, then abandoning the skis altogether and skimming along behind the boat on their bare feet.

Christmas holidays were celebrated at the Harveys' ski lodge in Vail. There, too, the Jaspersons had bought the lodge next door. The Harveys liked them. Though a bit rough around the edges they were good people.

At sixteen, America was among a dozen finalists in tryouts for the United States Olympic Ski Team but she didn't make it. She had dreamed of wearing the flag and skiing all over the world for her country. J.J. stroked her hair. "Don't let it get you like this. Those people made the team because they are totally dedicated to skiing. While they travel to Vermont and Canada to work on the snow almost twelve months a year you're here working to get straight A's. I think it's fantastic that you came as close as you did."

That same year she got her pilot's license. People could get one at any age at that time, and from then on Gat and her father sat behind and beside her as she flew over their lands.

Margaret recognized that there was more in the world than was to be found in San Antonio, Dallas and Colorado. She told her husband, "In the summers we should make trips to Europe and begin exposing the kids to new and different places, people and customs."

They started with France. America hated to go and leave J.J. and almost refused, but she wouldn't defy her parents in anything, let alone in their attempt to educate her. They stayed at the George V in Paris and did the Louvre, the Eiffel Tower, the Arch of Triumph and had meals at Tour d'Argent, Lasserre and Maxim's.

If Albert had thought about it he would probably, but not surely, have bought some conventional Eastern city-type clothes rather than feel himself being observed with amusement walking through the Palace of Versailles in his western-style suit, string tie and comfortable cowboy boots. America bought a phrase book and for a while Albert tried to order meals in French, but he went back to English rather than suffer the smugness of the Parisian waiters openly tolerating his inability to pronounce French words and condescendingly taking his orders while speaking what they mistakenly believed to be excellent English. As has been said, Paris would be the most wonderful city in the world if not for the Parisians.

After a few days Albert gathered his family in the living room of their suite. "Here's the truth, folks. I'm as tired of all these foreigners as they are of me. And I'm aware that *I* am the foreigner. But they are unkind, inhospitable except to our bucks, and they even eat differently than we do. This morning I saw a guy eating a sandwich with a knife and fork. And they hold the fork and knife in the wrong hands. Or maybe it's me who's got it wrong. Doesn't matter. I have got acceptable manners for where I belong, which isn't here. Also, this famous French cuisine may be God's gift to the world, but I miss our own cooking."

Gat needled him, "Dad, you're educating us, remember?"

"Son, I do not drink more than a few beers every now and then, I do not smoke, I do not chase after women and I don't even take up much closet space. Give me a break! And tell me the truth. Are you enjoying yourself?"

"Well . . . it's educational . . . they say."

"The education you need is how to run your ranch and look after your inheritance." He turned to America, "Are you enjoying yourself?"

She was, immensely, as she wrote to J.J. every day, missing him, describing the places they'd been, what they'd seen and what it felt like to be in a foreign country. She did not want to upset her father, but he read her clearly. "Okay, darlin', I'll tell you the new plan. Instead of just doing Paris and the French Riviera this year and other countries in the coming years, we are going to stay over here and do it all in one go: London, Rome, Berlin, Switzerland, anyplace your mother says. Then we are going home to San Antonio, Texas, which is situated in the blessed United States of America and I am *staying* there. You will all be free to return here, as my guests, any time you like, but the Old Man is a country boy and he knows when he's in the wrong country."

Al Harvey was comfortable wherever he wanted to be comfortable and among those places was the White House. Being a Republican Eagle, someone who contributes ten thousand dollars a year in support of the party, he and Margaret were invited to all dinners the President gave for the Eagles. On one occasion she suggested, "Take America with you this time. She'll enjoy and benefit from the experience."

More than was imagined, for at that dinner she met the girl who was to become her best friend, Marisa Tarancón y Domecq, whose father was the Spanish Ambassador to the United States. Raised by a Scottish nanny, Marisa was fluent in English, and she and America took to each other immediately, attracted by differences: Marisa by Texas oil, ranching, cowboys and cowgirls, modern architecture and technology; America by Spanish history, the tragedy of losing three older brothers in the Spanish Civil War, bullfighting, castles, and knowing a direct descendant of Queen Isabella. That weekend Marisa flew to San Antonio to visit the Harveys, and the girls spent the days talking, on horseback and seeing the ranch from the small plane that America piloted, a Piper Cheyenne 400 SL her father had given her for Christmas.

The weekend together was followed by others alternating between the Harveys' ranch and the Spanish Embassy, one of the loveliest homes in Washington.

When Marisa's father retired from the diplomatic service and the family returned to Spain, the girls kept in touch by mail and springtime visits by America to Madrid and Marisa to San Antonio.

America followed Gat to Texas A&M, where she majored in "Ag-Sci," agricultural science. As J.J. was away at Harvard Business School, she was undistracted and free to work hard enough to make the dean's list every year and ultimately graduate summa cum laude and valedictorian of her class. J.J. was doing equally well at Harvard. When he returned to San Antonio for holidays and the summer, she, J.J. and Gat still skied and played tennis together, but they were no longer a constant threesome. America and J.J. always managed to get off by themselves.

One day J.J. showed up with a swollen lip and a black eye. "My dad got mad when he saw my grades. I wasn't number one this year."

"He *slugged* you for your grades?"

J.J. shrugged it off. "He means well. It's just that I've got to be the best."

They took long walks together, talking about school and what they hoped for out of life. "I've got to work hard," J.J. said. "I'm on my own after college. My dad makes no bones about it, 'Nobody remembers who finished second' and 'I made mine, you make yours.'" He stopped walking. "I will, too, Ame. I'm going to be rich."

Chapter One

Whenn J.J. finished school he went to work in the downtown branch of a national brokerage house. Quickly he displayed a workaholic's drive, and an uncanny talent for anticipating that entertainment and computer companies were going to make it. He was the first to convince the Texas "heavy hitters" to back Apple and Disney. They went in big and earned millions, winning him a vice-presidency at age twenty-three and a tremendous income from salary and commissions. Within sixteen months J.J. was promoted to head the Oklahoma City branch.

Before accepting, he went for a walk with America through the orchard of pecan trees on the Harvey ranch. "They want me to go next month. I've spent too many years away from you at school, Ame. I'm not moving to Oklahoma City without you. I'd like for us to get married."

When the newlyweds returned from their honeymoon in Acapulco and prepared to move to Oklahoma City, the President of J.J.'s brokerage firm counseled, "Buy a house in River Pine, it's the most exclusive area there, which means that your neighbors will be among the most affluent and therefore potentially your best customers. Join the country club, socialize with them. The firm will pick up the initiation fee and dues. That's a perk. So is the Mercedes you need to drive. Your house should be important and expensive. The firm will advance whatever you need to buy and furnish." He waved off J.J.'s gratitude. "We're merely equipping you to make money for all of us. Take command of that office, J.J. and sell a lot of stocks and bonds. Spend and do whatever you need to make sales. That's what it's all about. Sell, sell, sell."

The Jaspersons bought a mansion in the best section of River Pine. As they decorated it and added an indoor-outdoor swimming pool and every conceivable luxury, America worried, "This is awfully extravagant."

"I agree, but it's what the Big Daddies want me to do or they wouldn't be advancing the cash."

Their home was located on a private airstrip, and the garage was built to accommodate their two automobiles, an S500 Mercedes sedan and a bright red convertible and America's plane, the Piper Cheyenne 400 SL. The airstrip served their house and their neighbors, who enjoyed similar opulence. Several had Lear jets, and Falcons. The Jaspersons had an indoor-outdoor swimming pool that started in their living room and extended into their yard.

Shortly after they had settled in they were invited to dinner parties on consecutive Friday and Saturday nights, as a welcome from their neighbors. Seven couples. The food and wines were superb and impeccably served by a houseman named Ralph. The conversation was easy and fun. They were all south-westerners, all around the same age and all of them motivated to be major achievers in their fields, none of which was competitive.

By the end of the dinner America and J.J. were marveling at having lucked into such a homey situation. They were enjoying coffee and cognac when two of the men started disagreeing over the merits of collecting and restoring antique cars. The other neighbors began taking sides and it accelerated into brisk combat. Not with rapier-like wit but with fists; punch-outs resulting in cuts and bruises while the women urged them on like cheerleaders. America and J.J., too new to intervene, remained on the sidelines, astonished.

On their way home in J.J.'s sedan he gasped, "What was *that?*"

"I can hardly believe it happened. I was amazed when none of the wives tried to stop it."

"Me, too. I sure hope they patch it up by tomorrow night or it's going to be awfully uncomfortable."

"It would be more peaceful. We'd be the only guests."

However, on Saturday night the friends were all there, one with a black eye, another with bandaged knuckles, but it was a lovely evening of joking, good business talk and not a mention of the fray.

On the following Friday, during coffee and cognac in the living room, Bo Pearson, the Jaspersons' next-door neighbor, said, "I've been thinking that the bunch of us should coordinate our summer vacations and charter a hundred and fifty– or a two hundred–foot sailing yacht for a couple of weeks of cruising."

There was immediate enthusiasm. "We could do the British Virgin Islands."

"Why not the American Virgin Islands?"

In short, it came to disagreeing, pushing and shoving, then punching and wrestling until it was finally stopped by Ralph, who buttled at all of these young couples' dinner parties.

At home America said, "I have a terrible fear that the first dinner wasn't the rare exception, that every Friday is Fight Night."

"Obviously they enjoy it. The wives, too." He took her in his arms, and they stood in their bedroom feeling alone except for each other in this strange environment.

They began undressing for bed. "I'm sending regrets for next week."

"We can't, Ame." He was removing his necktie. "It would be perceived as judgmental. 'You don't like me? Okay, I don't like you.' And we'd be out. We can't afford that. I'm still a kid with a big hat but no cattle. Now, I've already got half of them as customers. And they're all heavy hitters. I mean *really* heavy hitters. My commissions this month are triple what I made in San Antonio. The office is having its best month in five years. That's a gold star for me."

In bed she asked, "Are you sure you couldn't do it without the parties?"

He put his arm around her and they lay side by side staring at the ceiling. Downhearted, he said, "Logically, it's related: 'Give your business to your buddy.' Besides, this group is our entree to everyone like them in the state. Stocks-and-bonds is too competitive not to use every angle available to you. 'Sell, sell, sell. That's what it's all about.' And the firm is ruthless. I'm a hero today, but if my bottom line doesn't keep looking good then my other bottom gets booted out and they'll bring in someone else. Let's hope the fights will be fewer rather than more. Please, Ame, hang in. It's going to be worth it."

She nodded glumly, then asked, "J.J.? Why put so much pressure on yourself? You're making a ton of money, we're living real well, I have a trust fund and your father will one day leave you a fortune."

"I can't bet on that. He told me plainly, 'Make your own dough. Don't expect me to leave you a bundle. You make your own Easy Street.' My mom thinks he says those things to keep the pressure on me. It's logical that I'll inherit *something* someday. But I can't count on it. I've got to make it on my own."

"But you've got talent and brains. You earned a quarter of a million dollars after only a year in the brokerage business. Forget what I said about inheriting your father's money. It's not necessary to be as rich as your father."

"You don't understand, Ame. I've got to be *richer* than my father."

She sat up and put on the light. "Richer than your *father*? Why?"

He seemed confused. "I don't know. It's just that all my life it was him pushing me, 'Get top grades; win letters, medals; be number one.' The winning-is-everything syndrome. Why else did I spend four years freezing my tail in Cambridge when I could have been with you and Gat? And now that I'm out in the world I agree with Dad. Why be less than the best if you can make it? And I can. I'm going to be the biggest. Not only in Oklahoma City. This is just a stopover until I'm Chairman of a major investment banking house in New York."

"In New York?"

"That's where it's happening. That's where they finance entire cities, even countries; where they buy and sell in the billions. Everything else is just bush league."

* * *

America's vague interest in fashion and clothes took a giant step forward when J.J. urged her to be the best-dressed woman in Oklahoma City. "Spend whatever it takes. Ridiculous or not, with your gorgeous body, how well you dress will be a major business asset."

Encouraged by the pleasure of doing something that was important to her husband, as well as enjoying the effect she had on their neighbors, America became extremely welcome in the best shops in Oklahoma, Dallas and Houston. She wasn't a frivolous person but in this one matter she was having a wonderful time looking quite fabulous in Valentino, Oscar de La Renta Galanos and Traina-Norell.

The eight couples were an insular group that began their weekends with cans of Coors on the country club tennis courts in the morning, followed by bourbon and iced tea on the club's veranda and in their swimming pools, where floating bars were standard equipment. America did not mix beer and tennis. She enjoyed an occasional after-the-match bourbon and iced tea, but the group of friends ritualistically began their weekends this way, leading into evenings with cocktails and dinners with an abundance of fine wines, all of which were older than they, and as they did not have the sophistication to appreciate their elders appropriately, they wasted, by getting smashed on Haut Brion, Chateau Latour, Cheval Blanc and the like. By the time they came to after-dinner cordials there was nothing cordial about the men who concluded the evening by brawling.

The reason the group retained Ralph and paid him three times more than any other Oklahoma City houseman was attributable not to his buttling but to his refereeing, which was indomitable—he had been a Marine Corps hand-to-hand combat instructor. And they relied on his judgment. If a fight broke out he did not stifle his employers' pleasure, but he kept it down to minor injuries.

Probably a psychiatrist could explain what would cause friends who were privileged, formally educated, accomplished people repeatedly to begin drinking and laughing together until an argument was deliberately provoked and ultimately settled gleefully with brute force. But America and J.J. couldn't begin to understand it.

A few days after a dinner at the Jaspersons' resulted in Bo Pearson going home through their picture window, America told J.J., "This is madness. Apart from the physical danger the cost is astronomical. I just got the estimate to replace that window. Eighteen hundred dollars!"

"Sweetie, it's just a pimple on the prick of progress. This morning Bo placed an order for two million-three worth of electronics stocks. For my commission on that order alone he can go through our picture window every day."

She despaired, "I can't relate to these people. I've never known violence before. I'm a peaceful person. My parents are. I never heard my father raise his voice in my life."

J.J. said, "Why don't the two of us go back to Acapulco for a long weekend? I know how you feel about these parties and people. This business I'm in . . . the pressure . . . I've lived under pressure all my life, but it seems like it's getting worse and it's making us lose touch with each other."

Removed from that environment J.J. was again the loving, thoughtful, amusing young man she had gone with all her life.

The following month, some very special news from her doctor consolidated her happiness. As she drove home that afternoon in her little red Mercedes with the top down allowing the wind to play with her hair, she excitedly planned how to help J.J. enjoy it the most. Seated in a red leather love-seat in their library savoring a before-dinner glass of wine she challenged, "Let's see if you can tell me the major 'young couple cliché'."

J.J. liked games and puzzles and eagerly sat forward, staring at the floor, ticking off the possibilities. "'I haven't got a thing to wear.'" She shook her head. "'I can't, I've got the curse.'" Again, negative.

'Aw, honey, I've been working all day, I'm too tired to go out.' Then his mouth fell open, his eyes widened and he looked up at his wife with a tentative smile, "'I went to the doctor . . .'?"

"You've got it."

He leaped up. "I can hardly believe it."

"Me either."

"It's the icing on the cake. We're really going to have everything."

America planned a barbecue for her husband's twenty-fourth birthday. The coup de grâce was that she was able to hire the Mamas and the Papas to do a "club date." It cost thirty thousand dollars, but she knew that J.J. would appreciate it, charge it to the firm as business entertainment and consider her a great corporate wife. And he did. He whooped, "That'll be an all-timer, darlin', even for River Pine!"

Marisa came over from Madrid for five days and helped with details. America had bought an unconscionably expensive Christian Dior dress. On the day of the party she called each of the guests and implored, "This is a special occasion. Please, let's not allow it to end as the usual Fight Night." They all emphatically agreed. Sitting with her, hearing the extraordinary plea, Marisa said nothing.

The party was planned to perfection. She had hired the family from Louisiana that her parents used, and they brought an oven that, buried three feet into the ground, cooked ribs and sides of beef for twenty-four hours, and they were finger-lickin' luscious. For non–barbecue lovers—an offense punishable by loss of your "South-westerner Passport"—America provided a tank of lobsters and a chef to prepare them any way her guests desired. Her bar scotch was 21-year-old Chivas Regal, and there was perfectly chilled Taitinger Blanc de Blanc. The champagne glasses, engraved with J.J.'s name and the date of his birthday, had been ordered from Steuben as souvenirs for the guests to take home.

But after the Mamas and the Papas had enthralled everyone, the jokes and then the arguments and the fighting began, and America found herself watching just another of the "fun" weekend evenings. The men were hilarious, including J.J., and the other wives were delighting in the action. Marisa escaped to her room. Two of the wives were twin sisters; beautiful, black-haired oil heiresses who drove twin red Ferraris and whom America thought of as "the tigresses." They were both dressed in oh-my-gawd necklines, one showing cleavage in front, the other in back, and were cheering for J.J. against their own husbands. America couldn't write off their partisanship as a tribute to J.J.'s birthday. She had previously observed them boldly in pursuit of him.

Undressing for bed she asked, "Did you enjoy this evening, J.J.?"

"I really did, Ame." He took her in his arms. "I love you and I appreciate you."

"What I meant was, you are really coming to enjoy these insane weekends, all the drinking....the fights?"

He thought about it seriously. "It's the fast track that's going to take me where I need to get." He saw her disapproval. "I enjoy the 1.4 million dollar bonus I got last week from the firm and the hundred and twenty grand Aston Martin I was able to buy for you to zip around in, which I notice you don't exactly hate."

"I like it very much. But I don't *need* it. *You* do. That car is for *you,* for the J.J. Jasperson image."

"I appreciate your accurate insight into my character."

"Well, I definitely do not appreciate the 'friendship' of the tigresses, cheering my husband on over their own husbands."

"Why not?"

The callousness of the question shook her. She hesitated, "Have you . . . had anything to do with the tigresses?"

He was piqued. "Hey! These are the Sexy Sixties. Don't go Patty Puritan on me. Like you've forgotten we made it before we said 'I do.' We could've said 'I did.'"

"But we were in love and got married. And there has never been anybody except you."

"This conversation is assholian. Look, tell me something: how does it effect our marriage if once in a while they come by the office and we fool around a little?"

"You 'fool around a little'?" Despite her vague suspicions she was genuinely stunned. "I need a definition of that."

Reluctantly he said, "It's nothing. They come by the office every day or two and if the stocks I've put them into have gone down . . . well . . . then I do, too."

"On them?" It was rhetorical. Wanting to erase that mental picture she asked, "And when their stocks go up . . . ?" And she was immediately sorry she'd asked.

He shrugged. "Right. Of course. Hey, what's the big deal? It's a game." He made it sound like a coffee break. "Ame! It's business." He became impatient. "They're rich, rich, rich! And they buy, buy, buy! When they whistle, I waltz. Haven't you learned yet that 'It's not how you play the game, it's winning!' isn't just a slick line? It's real life."

She sat down, willing herself to think clearly. *He's my husband. We've been in love nearly all our lives. I'm carrying his baby. He's going through some kind of a stage. He says it's meaningless. Okay, he made a mistake.....*

"But, J.J., now that I tell you I can't live with this, will you promise that it's over?"

He saw tears clinging to her eyes. "Does it mean that much to you?" He sat down beside her and put his arm around her shoulder. "Of course it's over." Gently he put his hand on her enlarged stomach and said, "Open your mouth. Wider." Then, speaking into her throat he called out in a whisper, "Hello, down there. It's me, Daddy. How are you feeling? Don't worry. I won't do anything to make you or Mommy unhappy."

The months passed slowly for America, who wasn't exempt from any of the usual prenatal sicknesses and discomforts but accepted them with joy, with incredulity that a baby was growing within her body. She could hardly wait to see the child she already loved, could hardly wait to hold it in her arms, to take care of it, teach it, help it, protect it. She had beautiful maternity clothes made, and though she felt that she'd somewhat lost her glamour when she looked like she had a watermelon under her dress, she enjoyed the way she looked, she loved being pregnant and was happy to be seen. But suddenly the weekend parties made her nervous. The tension had always been there, but now the possibility of an accident, of someone bumping into her, was terrifying.

"It's dangerous for the baby, J.J. I don't want to go anymore until after the child is born."

"You're right. They'll understand."

She was amazed that he considered it important that they would "understand" about his baby's safety.

He said, "As long as I show up it won't matter."

There was only a month to go, and she had taken it for granted that he wouldn't think of leaving her alone at night on Fridays and Saturdays. But she didn't say anything. She couldn't bear to hear even one more time that it was ". . . business. 'Sell, sell, sell.'"

On Friday she sat up reading, waiting for him until two A.M., the hour they usually returned home. But by three, unable to keep her eyes open, she fell asleep.

Saturday was the same. She was lonely, but she had her baby for company. It kicked her often, and she talked to it about all the fun they would have together, yet again by around three o'clock she fell asleep.

She was awakened when the lights went off. She smelled a familiar perfume. Both of the tigresses wore it. She did not move. She felt J.J. easing himself into bed, trying not to awaken her. Or *hoping* not to wake her? Why? So she wouldn't see the hour? The luminous dial on the clock at her bedside told her it was a quarter past four. The perfume was such a cliché. She wasn't about to make anything of it. The whole group often kissed hello and good-night. Maybe one of the tigresses had rubbed a little too close. He had promised her that was over, and she believed him. Yet what had he been doing for the two hours after the party had ended? It couldn't be that he and the tigresses played with each other. What about their husbands? It was different when they visited him during the day while their husbands were in their own offices. But they wouldn't tolerate their wives staying on with him after a party. Or would they? Though they were oilmen their drilling was financed by their wives' money. How much could they "not tolerate" when they were almost kept men? She threw it all out of her mind. She wasn't going to let her imagination work up a case against him. She continued pretending to sleep. Her mind was moving fast. She rationalized that he had not rushed home to be with her because they couldn't do anything together; she wasn't exactly the best bedmate, so what was the rush? They must have all sat around drinking, keeping him company.

She mentally told her baby, "First you're going to learn to walk and talk and then to ride a tricycle and then a bicycle and a pony at Grandpa and Grandma's. I don't care if you're a boy or a girl we'll do everything together. We'll go roller-skating, and in the winter we'll ice skate and I'll teach you to ski. You're going to love skiing. It can be pretty cold but we'll have you all bundled up, we can't let an angel feel cold. Oh, angel, I love you, I *love* you, I love you. Maybe you can't understand that now or maybe you can, but someday you will for sure. I love you. I love you more than anything or anybody in the world. I love you . . ." and she fell asleep thinking as if singing, "I love you, I love you, I love you . . ."

The doctor said, "You are the mother of a healthy, gorgeous, green-eyed, golden-haired girl. She weighs six pounds and she's two inches longer than the average child, which means she'll probably be even a longer stemmed beauty than her mother." He handed her the baby and America held her to her bosom, adoring the infant's delicious smell, stroking her little wisps of flaxen hair. She felt so soft and wonderful. America thought that nobody in the world had ever been good enough to deserve being as happy as she was at that moment and she said, "Thank you, Lord, thank you."

The doctor agreed. "I have delivered a lot of babies, but He made yours very special. Instead of crying when I slapped her to wake her up I could swear she laughed. She's a little angel if ever I saw one." Aware that America was tired he gestured to the nurse to take the child.

J.J. was sitting in the room, waiting for her to wake up. When she did, he kissed her, "Thank you. Our daughter is gorgeous, not as gorgeous as you but maybe someday..."

The Harveys and Jaspersons came in together. Margaret said, "Our granddaughter is an angel. We all looked at her through the glass and while the others were either howling or red faced and grim, I tell you she smiled at us."

Albert asked, "What are you going to name her?"

J.J. said, "We never decided on a name, not knowing if she'd be a girl or a boy. We discussed naming it after one of you, or you, Mom and Dad, but we were afraid that could hurt someone."

America asked her husband, "What would you think of calling her what everybody's been calling her: Angel. I know that whatever her name is, I'll always call her Angel."

"Then that's her name. We have a beautiful, wonderful angel named Daughter." He laughed with everyone else. "I guess all that waiting for her got me nervous and worn out. I'll try again: We have a beautiful daughter named Angel."

When a few days later America was released from the hospital at noon, J.J. couldn't come to take her home until the market closed. Gat and her mother and father waited with her.

Her brother, characteristically, spoke his mind, "How many times do you get to bring your first baby home? So he loses a sale. So what-the-hell what?"

"It's business, Gat, 'sell, sell, sell, that's what it's all about.' I don't mind. I love this extra time being with you all before you go back home."

When J.J. arrived he said, "Ame, before we leave let's get a list from the hospital of really good governesses."

"No. I'll have the nurse they're sending for the first weeks until I know what I'm doing. But when she goes I'm bringing up our own child."

J.J. came home with a new stuffed animal every day, and he left work earlier than in the past to be with Angel before she got tired. Whenever he reached into the bassinet he melted as he looked at her and touched each of her little fingers, marveling over her.

America said, "Darling, forgive me, but please don't baby-talk. You know what the book says."

"You're right, except it seems funny not to have anything to say. I can't tell her I just sold two million shares of Tandy at a 30 percent profit."

"Yes, you could. I don't think she'll be impressed, but she'll hear her father speaking to her like a person."

"Okay. Well, now, Angel, I'd just like to tell you that things are going fine at the office and whenever you're ready you've got a job as my assistant because anyone who looks as good as you will have people emptying their pockets just to get one of your smiles."

Angel smiled up at him.

"Wow! I was right. She's a killer."

When Francine, the nurse, was having dinner he said, "Ame, I know it's been only a couple of weeks but do you think you'll feel up to going to the dinners this weekend?"

"I'm up to it but Francine goes home after Angel is sleeping. We can't leave our baby alone for four or five hours."

He nodded his head impatiently, "I told you we need a governess. Not only for her, for us. Also, it doesn't look good not to have an elegant governess. Maybe English or French. All of our friends have them. You don't have to waste your time pushing a baby carriage when you can be at the club enjoying yourself with your friends."

Firmly, quietly, she said, "J.J., those are not my friends. They are your customers and I'm willing to be a hypocrite to further your business . . ."

"*Our* business."

"Fair enough. Our business. But I'm not going to have anyone coming in here and instilling her values in our child. Angel is going to be brought up with what you and I believe in."

"I hear you. It's sound. But you can't mean that we never go out again until Angel is sixteen."

"Of course not. I'll ask Francine if she would like to make extra money baby-sitting on weekends. Or, if she'd prefer to be with her family I'm sure she'll help me find a registered nurse who'll do it."

"Great." He kissed her. "I love you. And I love our kid. Wow! Who's got it better than us? And if someone has, I'm happy for them."

Chapter Two

A year and a half after Angel was born, Marisa called from Spain. "I am going to marry my childhood sweetheart, as you did. He is Carlos Izcaya y Williams, the Count of Avila. I would be grateful for you and J.J.to be members of the wedding party."

"I'd love it," he said, "but there's no way I could leave the office."

"Well, there's no way I can refuse to be one of Marisa's bridesmaids."

"But you've got a daughter who needs you."

J.J., what would you say if I brought Angel to my parents? I'll be gone less than a week. Mom and Dad will be the dotingest grandparents in the world. And it would be a great present for them."

"Perfect. The fact is, even if I had the time I wouldn't have a clue how to change her or fix her meals. I'll call your folks every day."

Marisa and Carlos met her at the airport in *Sevilla* to drive her to *Jeréz de la Frontera* in the south of Spain. After lunch, seeing that America was jet-lagged, Marisa suggested she take a siesta.

Fatigued, America was relieved to see that her bags had been unpacked and her clothes hung in the armoire. Her suitcases were stored out of sight. The bed was turned down; draped on the covers was one of her nightgowns, she smiled at how it had been puckered in at the waist, and her bedroom slippers had been placed on the floor beneath it.

The wedding would be a three-day fiesta in *Jeréz*, Spain's sherry country. Marisa's mother was a member of the large Domecq family, and no one had the flare for the spectacular, as did the Domecqs. There were visits to the *bodegas* and tasting of sherry that was over a hundred years old. Late afternoons were for bullfights and dressage performed by the Domecqs' Lipizzaners, horses often painted by Velázquez and described as "suitable for a King to ride." There were banquets every night followed by flamenco tableaus that lasted until daybreak.

Following these late and liquid nights many of the Spaniards began the day with a mid-morning glass of *fino*, a young dry sherry. Carlos told America, "One of the uncles of Marisa, Manuel González Gordon, wrote a verse about mid-morning *copitas*. It goes:

> 'I must have a drink at eleven,
> it's a duty that must be done.
> If I don't have one at eleven
> then I'll have eleven at one.'"

Carlos was cultured, handsome, kind, and mature. She was happy for Marisa, and for herself for having them as friends.

At all of the parties America gazed at women wearing exotic, long, colorful gypsy dresses, some of them with small children Angel's age in matching outfits.

"Marisa, what do you call those dresses?"

"*Faraleas.*"

"I just have to have two of them. For me and for Angel. I'll take my measurements, Angel would be a size two, and I'll be so grateful if you'll have them made and send them to me."

"It's much easier than that. There are probably twenty shops in town that sell them ready-made. We all wear them to *ferias*. I have a dozen or more. From since I was a child."

America browsed through racks and racks of the colorful polka-dotted dresses with long ribbons hanging down the back, exaggerated puffed sleeves and skirts that came in tight above the waist and then billowed out voluminously in layers and layers of ruffles. They were all beautiful. She chose one of red and white polka dots because there was a size two in the same model. Marisa was as excited as America. "And you need some big gypsy earrings for yourself and smaller ones for Angel. And plastic bracelets, lots of little ones for her and two large ones for you. And red bead necklaces, and flowers for the hair for you both. Also, the low-heeled shoes with the bands across the instep . . ."

Back in Texas again America retrieved Angel from her parents, flew her home and taking her by the hand rushed up to her bedroom to unpack the dresses. She laid them side-by-side on the bed.

Angel went straight for the small one.

"Yes, darling, that's yours. Come on, let's get dressed." She unbuttoned Angel's pinafore and helped her into her *faralea*. Then she rushed into her own. She put on Angel's little black dance shoes and then her own. She clipped red and white plastic earrings on her lobes while the child waited, hopefully. America clipped the smaller ones onto her, put bracelets on their wrists, flowers in their hair, hung the beads around their necks, and then they stood in front of the mirror dazzled by how fabulous they looked.

"Wait a sec and we'll dance like the gypsies did in *Jeréz*." She put an audiocassette that Marisa had given her into their tape deck in the bedroom. As the music began playing America raised her arms over her head, trying to assume the flamenco dancers' posture.

Angel lifted her hands over her head copying her mother. America tried to move in time with the music. So did Angel. For a minute. Then she fell down, flat on her bottom, amidst yards and yards of polka dot fabric. America dropped down beside her, and they laughed until their stomachs hurt.

J.J. returned from the office, rushed to kiss his child goodnight in her bed, and then he and America had a glass of wine in their library.

"Congratulations," he said.

"Thank you. For what?"

"For being invited to be a Member of the Board of Intercontinental Electronics and Entertainment."

"Me? On the Board of I.E.E.? I don't know anything about electronics or entertainment. I don't qualify."

"Wrong. They have large food subsidiaries, and you have an agricultural background. You were a shoo-in."

"Who 'shooed' me in?"

"My pal Bob Perry, who's Chairman."

"J.J., this is ridiculous, I have no time . . ."

"All you need to do is attend two meetings a year, vote the way Bob does and listen carefully. All board members receive an honorarium of $25,000 per meeting. The check will be at your seat when you arrive."

"$50,000? For doing nothing?"

"Correct. Just listen carefully, and when you're alone, make notes so you'll be able to tell me everything that's planned for the future."

She felt a whir in her stomach. "J.J., you're talking insider trading."

"You're not going to be trading anything."

"Oh, no. Hey, listen, this is serious. It's illegal. It's one thing to be a workaholic, to butter up obnoxious clients, but J.J., please, this is dangerous."

"Danger, schmanger, it's done every day by everybody."

"I don't think it's done by everybody. And I'm positive it won't be done by me. And I really think you should clean up your act. I implore you."

The next morning America bathed and fed Angel, and after breakfasting with J.J. she put on Levis and a blue gingham bandana.

"You going, Mommy?"

"To visit Grandma and Grandpa for lunch."

"Me, too?"

America plopped a small white cowboy hat on Angel's head. "Of course, you too. What do you think? That I'd leave my best friend behind?"

They went to the hangar. America buckled Angel into her seat, buckled herself in and taxied to the end of the runway, her hands on the stick. Out of the corner of her eye she was touched to see that Angel had her hands forward, holding imaginary controls. And as they left the ground and settled into flight, Angel continued copying exactly what America did, flicking switches, speaking into a radio.

America said, "You know something?"

"What?" the child asked eagerly.

"You're fun."

"Fun?"

"You sure are. And there are not that many people I know who are fun."

"Mommy fun!"

"Thanks, Angel. That's why we're friends."

As she landed on the strip at the ranch, her parents were waiting to drive them back to the house. Albert lifted Angel out of the plane.

After lunch he told his granddaughter "Let's go pick some pecans."

She giggled. "I too little, Gramps."

"Not at all." He picked her up and sat her on his shoulders, holding her feet to steady her.

"Gramps fun, Mommy!"

After the pecan picking America took her riding, holding her on her lap, walking her horse, looking forward to buying her a pony so they could ride together.

A year or so later America was invited to the baptism of Marisa and Carlos' twins. The Harveys were thrilled to host their three-year-old granddaughter. America missed Angel desperately, and she called home every day to hear her voice. She had to admit to herself that she honestly did not miss J.J. as much as she imagined she should. She and her friends passed four restful, happy days in a palace that one of Carlos' ancestors had built three hundred years before.

Life in Oklahoma City wasn't restful, not happy. On her first night home J.J. announced, "I've hired a governess for our child. Miss Nolan. She worked for the British Royal Family and came over here for the Rockefellers. Are we lucky she just became available! She's class! And, boy, is she demanding: Miss Nolan must have her own room connecting to the baby's, she must have a kitchenette where she can fix the child's food. We have to hire a baby's maid because Miss Nolan does not do laundry and ironing or clean, and she won't let our regular help have anything to do with the baby's quarters. She supervises the cleaning. We'll convert the small guest room into the kitchenette. Miss Nolan will start as soon as the renovations are done."

"Oh, really?"

"Yes, you're-damned-right really! I missed my daughter. Angel could have stayed here with me instead of being shunted off on her grandparents."

"Shunted off? She loves them and they adore her. You think that's not better than being with a woman she doesn't know, who doesn't care about her?"

"The group made comments on you working so hard as a nursemaid that they never see you at the club during the week. It's embarrassing. Like I can't afford to hire a proper governess."

"Well, I'll tell you how to solve that. Buy yourself a $100,000 C.D., make seven photocopies and send them to your friends with a note explaining that you're really solvent and could afford . . ."

"Very funny. But I'm not laughing."

"And I'm not having anyone else in this house to look after my child, let alone a woman such as you've described, who'll tell me how she'll discipline my child, and tell me when I may or may not see her. Have you lost your mind? My greatest pleasure in life is being with my child. We have high quality, responsible babysitters. That's as far as I bend. Period."

* * *

Carlos had business in New York so he and Marisa came over from Madrid, looking forward to visiting America and meeting Angel.

J.J. said, "I'm real glad you're here over a weekend. Life is quiet during the week. We get up early, work late, and we don't have the luck to take siestas and three-hour lunches like y'all do over there in *España*. We're workin' folk. But on Fridays and Saturdays we howl. We don't often have a real life Count and Countess visiting Oklahoma City and our friends have all said they hope you'll be able to join us."

America was distressed that her best friend and her husband were going to be exposed to what she lived with.

Marisa came into the bedroom while America was dressing for the dinner. Angel was standing beside her. As America turned to look at her profile Angel turned to look at *her* profile. As America fluffed her hair Angel fluffed *her* hair. America blotted her lipstick with a Kleenex. Angel plucked a Kleenex out of the box and blotted *her* lips. Then the child smiled up at her mother, "I'm fun, Mommy, right?"

Marisa was delighted, "America, she's you. In small."

Friday's dinner was at Bo Pearson's and he took Carlos and Marisa on a tour of the house, showing them his gym, indoor squash court, hunting trophies from African safaris, and his Lear jet in the garage-hangar. They appreciated his genuinely warm hospitality and tried to appear as impressed with everything as they thought he wanted them to be.

But what they saw from the beginning and more so as the evening wore on was that America was out of place and not happy in this environment. The dinner ended with only loud arguing among the friends, no fist-fighting, in deference to the foreigners.

Bo Pearson invited J.J., America and their guests for Sunday brunch at the country club, which America deftly sidestepped explaining that Francine was off on Sunday. J.J. went by himself.

Lunch was served at home before Marisa and Carlos' six P.M. flight to New York. While Angel was napping, America confided, "J.J. has totally changed since we left Texas. He's growing down instead of up. Or was he simply standing still and the immaturity more apparent on a grown man? No. He was another person when I married him: thoughtful, kind, considerate, warm. Where did that warmth go? When had the tenderness turned to toughness; the ambition to immorality?"

It helped to have Marisa there, someone on her own wavelength who was saddened and understanding as America confided her disenchantment with J.J. and her despair over their lifestyle.

Marisa said, "Normally, I believe that everyone would be happier if they were Catholic, but in this case I think you are fortunate not to be bound by the restrictions of our faith."

It was an accurate forecast of the inevitable.

America continued being J.J.'s corporate wife, good window dressing for him, living through the weekends, overlooking the blatant interplay between her husband and the tigresses. He had given her his word, she accepted the theory that he had to butter up his big customers and she convinced herself that it ended at looks and innuendoes.

On a Friday when it was their turn to be hosts, America kissed Angel goodnight and tucked her into bed. "Sweet dreams, darling. Mommy and Daddy are just going to be downstairs." She left the door open for the hall light to come in.

By midnight, as the rowdiness had accelerated, it seemed to America that the sound level was more horrific than ever, and she went upstairs to close Angel's door. Halfway up the stairs she saw her baby in her nightie and bare feet staring through the safety gate at the top of the staircase down toward the noise, frightened, crying. When she saw her mother, she continued crying, but out of relief. America opened the gate, lifted her into her arms and stroked her, speaking to her softly, comforting her as she walked into Angel's room and put her back into bed. When she got up to close the door Angel clutched her hand. "I'm not leaving you, darling, I just want to close the door." She returned and sat on the edge of the bed, soothing her baby, telling her the story of "Alice in Wonderland" until the child was calm and fell asleep. America remained seated next to her in case she should have a nightmare from all the noise and awaken crying.

Over an hour had passed when the door opened. There was no sound from downstairs. J.J. came in and looked at their sleeping child. They left the room together. "Where the hell were you? How dare you walk out on your own party, on your guests?"

America said, "That was the last party that will ever be held in this house. Our child will never again be exposed to that madness; people screaming and shouting and scaring her to death."

He shrugged, "The world's a noisy place. She needs to get used to it."

"She will. But by the time she hears it, she'll be prepared to handle it."

Once in bed, she knew he had not put up a fight because he didn't believe she meant it. But as God was her witness he would come to believe it.

On Saturday night, driving to the Tom Cornells' house, they did not speak a word, her distaste for the parties compounded by her unhappiness at having to leave her child to attend another one.

As they got up from the dinner table America saw one of the tigresses clutch J.J.'s behind, and she did not see him appear surprised or displeased or even make a face warning her not to be so obvious.

At home America asked, "We've never lied to each other have we?"

"Never."

"Then am I right that you haven't been able to keep your promise to me?"

"I did for a while." He looked up at her, "I really meant it when I told you it was over. But then I felt them reacting against me. It wasn't good business. Changing partners is the name of the game here."

"A game! But what about fidelity?"

"Frankly, sexual fidelity isn't meaningful. It's irrelevant. Sex is just a physical exercise that's more fun and less effort than squash."

"But when you and I have sex it's 'love'?"

"No. It's still fun and exercise. Love is my fooling around but coming home to you. Love is looking after you. And you looking after me. Love is our wanting to have more kids together, to grow old together . . ."

More children with J.J. was now the last thing she wanted. Lovemaking between them was suddenly onerous.

Wondering what to say, where to go, she sensed something and looked up. The man who had become a stranger was grinning lasciviously, his arms extended, his hands beckoning for her to come to him. "Hey! What've I got in common with a Mexican wetback?"

She was afraid to ask.

"We're both dying to get into America."

She left the room, bundled Angel into a blanket, gathered some of the child's necessities and went downstairs. J.J. was standing in the foyer. "May your husband ask where you think you're going with our daughter in the middle of the night?"

"I'm going to the Hyatt Regency, and I'm going to do my best to think of some way that I can possibly continue to live with my husband."

He wanted to object but the steel he saw in her eyes changed his mind. He walked her to the door leading to the garage, opened her car door for her. With Angel in her safety seat she started up the engine. "I will call you to let you know that we have arrived safely. After that please do not contact me. I need time."

America paced the floor all night. Though she couldn't bear the thought of going on with J.J., as he was unwilling to change, except for the worse, still she was willing to accept an unhappy life for herself for her baby's sake. She had made a mistake and she would pay for it. She looked at her sleeping child. How could she deprive her of a father? But what kind of a father was he? Granted, he acted loving toward the child. But what kind of an example was he for her to follow?

At eight A.M. the phone rang. "I know you told me not to contact you, but I'm calling to ask you to come home. I love you, I love our baby. Please come back."

"J.J., can you tell me honestly that anything is going to change?"

There was silence. "Look, Ame, I never said that you weren't free to have a little fun on the side, too."

"That isn't what I married you for. Nor is it the only issue. The problem is I cannot find peace with your immorality and its effect on the upbringing of my child. I need more time. I'll be flying to San Antonio today."

* * *

America's father looked her in the eyes and said, "His dishonesty toward you and toward the law, his lack of scruples—it's plain disgusting."

"I can't decide what's worse, a child growing up without a father? Or with a father who grows more amoral every day?"

"I can answer that one in a minute."

The days, the weeks took on a pattern: Angel's asking for her father; his calling every day to beg America to come home but never giving her a hope that there was a reason to come back. She knew only that she had to do what was in her child's best interests. Yet, she felt like a quitter.

Walking with Gat among their forest of pecan trees, she said, "I'm such an idiot. I made a horrendous failure of my first adult decision."

"I don't buy that. Like Dad says, 'The only time you fail is when you haven't learned from the experience. You're beating yourself up unfairly. I grew up with J.J. too, I don't consider myself slightly stupid and I chose him as my best friend. I loved the guy. He was bright, loyal, fun. You did not make a mistake. He did a one-eighty on you. He went nuts. Lost his values. Never did I see a sign of a rivalry between him and his old man. But I guess if you obsess somebody with the idea that they've got to be the best it becomes a mania, and suddenly J.J.'s got to be bigger than his father. My own opinion is that I'd rather grow up without a father than with one who might end up in jail." They stopped walking and Gat put both hands on her shoulders, "You are not quitting. I think you are wisely adjusting, turning away from a life that wasn't what he promised.

"You're too young and too desirable to sacrifice your future in order to keep your child with an undesirable, unfit father. You're a healthy, normal woman and eventually nature will cause you to become interested in continuing your life with a man. Only this time you'll know what to look for and you'll end up with a man who will be the solid father that Angel should have."

Chapter Three

When J.J. received the letter from America's lawyer, he called her and snarled, "You can dump me if you want. You've been a puritanical bore. But don't think for one second that you're taking my child with you. I'm suing for custody."

"You're talking through your hat, J.J. The mother always gets custody unless there's a tremendously strong reason why not. And you wouldn't dare go to court. You? Go public? Implicate the wives of half your customers? And I would sure as hell name names. How would the 'Big Daddies' at your firm enjoy reading about a nice messy divorce?"

A long silence. "Well, at least I get to see her on a very regular basis."

America dreaded having to tell Angel that she wasn't going to have a full-time father anymore. She put it off for days but one morning when Angel asked, "When are we going back to Daddy?" she bit the bullet and sat down on the bed with her. "Darling, I have something important to tell you." The little girl looked at her intently. It was a serious tone of voice she had never heard before. "Daddy and I have decided not to live together anymore. He will come and visit you and spend the day with you but not every day."

"Why?"

"Because we are getting a divorce. That means we will no longer be married to each other. But he'll still be your daddy."

"But why? Don't you wanna be married to Daddy?"

"No, darling."

"Why?"

"I stopped loving him."

Angel looked confused and frightened. Her lips quivered. The child looked into her mother's eyes, deeply disturbed. "Mommy . . .?"

"Yes, darling? What is it?"

"Will you divorce me, too?"

America hugged her tightly to her breasts. "Oh, my darling, no…I'll never stop loving you. Never in a million, billion years. We will always be together. You're my whole life . . ."

"As long as I'm fun?"

"Oh, my Angel, you don't have to be fun."

"I don't?" she asked, still frightened.

"You don't have to do anything. You're my heart and soul, I will never stop loving you, never, never, never . . ."

The lawyers settled on a Saturday afternoon visitation every two weeks. And it was agreed that considering that he had not seen his daughter for three weeks, the first Saturday after the papers were signed he would have visitation rights from ten A.M. until five P.M.

J.J. called America on the day before he was to visit Angel. "Look, I know you're not exactly disposed to doing me favors but I'm going to ask one anyway. I'd really appreciate it if you'd fly Angel here. I don't want her to forget my home. After all, it's her home, too."

She landed on what had once been her landing strip and taxied to what had once been her house. She climbed down from the plane, carrying Angel. The man who had once been her husband was waiting at the door of the hangar, staring meaningfully at his watch. "You're twenty minutes late. So don't come back until five twenty."

No "thank you," no "hello," no smile even if it was false for the benefit of his daughter.

She parked the plane in the hangar, took her car and drove with no goal in sight except to pass seven hours. She did not have a friend she wanted to see. She had no desire to visit the boutiques she had frequented in order to be the Best Dressed Woman in River Pine. How ludicrous! She wanted to forget everything of that period of her life except that it had brought Angel to her. As the minutes dragged by she regretted not insisting on it being only once a month.

By four o'clock she had walked through a whole shopping mall and eaten a lunch she did not want. The only pleasure she had was buying some cowgirl boots for Angel.

At five o'clock she began driving toward the house, slowly, to avoid an early arrival and a snarling confrontation. Two blocks away she stopped the car at ten after five and waited. At eighteen after she began driving again. Two red Ferraris that she recognized sped past her.

As she turned the corner onto their street she saw police cars and a Paramedics ambulance in front of J.J.'s house. She ran from her car. The front door was open and she rushed in. There was nobody in the foyer or living room. She saw people out at the pool. She ran outside. J. J. wearing bathing shorts was sitting at one of the round lunch tables speaking to a policeman who was writing down what he was saying. She looked around for Angel.

"Where's my baby?" she screamed.

No one had noticed her arrival but all turned toward her. J.J. was ashen.

"Where is my baby?" she demanded at the top of her lungs.

J.J. did not move or speak.

"For God's sake, please, someone, tell me, where is my baby? Angel! Angel! It's Mommy. Are you hiding? Please come out so we can go home."

Another policeman asked, "Are you the mother?"

"I'm the mother of the little girl who was visiting her father today. Where is she? Where is my Angel?"

He turned to J.J. who nodded, confirming who she was. The officer tremulously forced out the words, "I'm deeply sorry to have to tell you this, ma'am, but your child died twenty minutes ago, by drowning in the swimming pool."

"I don't believe you. You're lying. J.J. what are you doing to me? Where is Angel? Please! Where is my Angel?"

J.J. couldn't speak.

The policeman's voice was tremulous, "I'd give anything for it to be a lie, ma'am. I swear I would. But it's not, ma'am, it's a tragedy." He pointed to a body bag made for an adult. In its center was a small bulge that would be made by a three-year-old child. The officer's eyes were glazed as he forced himself on. "Your baby was dead of drowning when we arrived. The paramedics did everything they could to resuscitate her, but she was gone."

Dizzied, half stumbling, America ran over to the body bag to open it, to see that it was all a lie. The paramedic standing with it looked at the police officer who nodded. He unzipped the bag and America saw Angel, her eyes open, unmoving, her delicate body bloated with water, her face black from lack of oxygen when her lungs had filled.

America knelt and picked up her baby. "Angel, speak to me, speak to me, darling, say something. *Anything*. It's me! Mommy! Please speak to me. You'll be all right if you'll just try. Please, darling, Angel, my life, please try, speak to me . . . speak to me . . . ."

The policeman touched America's shoulder, "It's impossible, ma'am. I know it's unbearable but you have to accept the fact. Your Angel isn't with us anymore."

America felt herself about to faint but she refused to allow it to happen. J.J. had not spoken a word. She looked into the misty eyes of the policeman. "How? Why?"

"The father was . . . occupied with some lady friends and did not notice that the child had wandered to the pool and fallen in. She floated from the living room out to the yard. By the time he was aware of her absence and pulled her out of the pool and called us, it was too late."

America knelt down by the side of the zipped closed bag and put her arms around the small, lifeless body inside, gone, dead, drowned, killed. Inaudibly she sobbed, "My child, my Angel, my flesh, my life, my love, my everything . . ."

* * *

She left the church behind the tiny coffin, her father and brother by her side, her mother behind her. Gat drove them to the family burial ground on the ranch. No one spoke. America had not stopped crying since it had happened but after the first day the tears had dried and she cried internally, constantly, by day, while she slept. Her sunken eyes concealed by the black veil she wore, she was thinking, *If I hadn't left him this could never have happened. If I had stayed on, stuck it out, this couldn't have happened. I would have been there. But I wasn't. I wasn't there for Angel. I wasn't there for her when she needed me . . .*

The minister finished speaking and the little coffin was lowered into the grave and everyone filed away.

J.J., facing indictments on criminal neglect of a minor and manslaughter, approached the family, tears in his eyes and spoke to America for the first time. "I'm so sorry, Ame. I'm sorry, Gat."

Gat took him by the arm and walked him out of America's hearing. He stared into J.J.'s eyes. "You murderer! You couldn't forget your ass-kissing whoring for seven hours? If you ever address me again, if you ever make contact with Ame or my folks, I'll find you and break your face. I might kill you like you killed your daughter and my sister. Stay far away. Don't test me."

He returned to America and his parents and they drove to the house. Close friends came by and sat with them in silence, unable to console the inconsolable. It wasn't a case of "ninety-two is a ripe old age" or "at least he's out of pain." There was no possible solace. They could give only their physical presence and lessen their own grief with slugs of the liquor that had been put out in the dining room with sandwiches and coffee.

When the last of the friends had gone, the family remained together in the living room, still unable to say anything that would alleviate anyone's pain. After an hour Gat said, "Mom, Dad, why don't you get some rest?"

America urged, "Please do. You need it. Thank you for everything."

After a while she put her hand on Gat's arm and squeezed it. "I love you, I don't know how I could have survived without you and the folks, but you could use some rest, too. I'll be okay. I'm going to take a walk."

She knew exactly where she was going. She walked past Gat's pecan trees, past her own, and she stopped at the saplings her father had planted for Angel. She stared at the silver plaque engraved "Angel Jasperson—1968." America touched one of the young trees and continued walking until she arrived at the burial grounds. She was alone. She fell to her knees and lay down on her child's grave. "My darling, I'm sorry, I'm so sorry to have taken away your beautiful life. I should have stayed on, I should have known, I didn't have the intelligence I should have had. Oh, my Angel, I know you're in heaven, I know that God will take care of you. I only hope he lets me come to you soon. There's nothing for me here without you. I don't know how I can face the days without you, without seeing your beautiful face, your beautiful smile, without hugging and kissing you and telling you I love you and knowing that you can hear me. I think I know it now but I can't be sure. Oh, my Angel . . ." As dizziness came over her she prayed that she was dying, that God was calling her.

Gat had followed at a distance. When he saw her head roll to the side and her body seem to deflate, he knew she had passed out and he hurried over, picked her up and carried her in his arms. She was breathing easily and steadily. He realized that after the faint she had slid into a tremendously needed sleep and he thought, *why bring her back to reality any sooner than necessary?* He carried her back to the house, upstairs to her room, and put her onto her bed. He took off her shoes, loosened her clothes and sat down in a chair watching her until she awoke.

* * *

America had not slept more than an hour or so at a time since her child had died, and without exception she dreamed that Angel was standing at the side of her bed, waiting to play or to be bathed, and she forced herself awake only to find that Angel wasn't there and would never be there again.

Her mother brought her meals on a tray and sat with her. Margaret cooked everything America liked, but she could only pick at her food. She had no desire to eat anything but she made the gesture for her mother.

She went to the burial grounds every morning and sat by Angel's grave, talking to her, crying, hoping God would have mercy and take her to her baby. Gat always stood out of sight for an hour or more until, fearing for her sanity, he would take her by the arm, "Come on back to the house, pal, it's almost lunchtime," and she rose and went with him. She began sitting at the table for meals with her family and the ranch hands, who had been instructed to talk naturally about the cattle, the crops, and the work that needed doing. It was her father's hope that something someone said might stimulate her interest, but it did not happen.

Television, books and magazines were insufferable. The least painful moments were when she could stare at the ceiling and imagine seeing her child in the hundreds of ways she could remember her: being bathed, dried, powder-puffed, dressed in her cute little flamenco outfit, mimicking her. She could envision their singing together, driving in the car with Angel securely in her safety seat. She listened for Angel's voice, her laughter. But finally, each time, as if coming to the end of a film, the screen went blank and she did not see her baby, only the white plaster ceiling. Every day was the same: breakfast; Angel's grave; Gat taking her home for lunch;

staring at mental images of her baby; then dinner; then trying to sleep and succeeding only in patches.

Friends called and asked her mother if they could visit. Margaret wanted urgently to say yes, but she knew that trying to have conversations was painfully futile and America was, for the time being, better off in lonely silence.

America forced herself to write to Marisa, ending, "I know you will think of coming over here to comfort me, but I implore you not to. Nothing can help me now, except to be alone."

Three weeks had passed when she looked across the dinner table and suddenly focused on what her agony was doing to her parents and her brother. They hardly ate, they had all lost weight, their faces were haggard from little sleep. They had supported her in every possible way, and she realized that they would continue until it killed them and that she had to snap herself out of this, haul herself out of the emotional quicksand into which she had been allowing herself to drown. She knew that she needed to do something. She thought of helping out at children's hospitals and orphan homes but the idea of seeing young, living faces—it was unbearable.

"I think I should go to work."

That simple, positive statement had such a powerful effect it brought tears to her father's eyes. It caused her mother and brother the same elation.

Gat groaned, "Oh, could I ever use some help! I tell you what, with the oil business and the farming and with Dad loafing around and hardly working anymore, and you being a top agriculturist . . ."

"I have to think. I'm going to do something constructive. I'm so sorry for what I've done to all of you."

She deliberated. The ranch was really Gat's domain. And he was only being generous saying he needed her. She remembered the happy hours she had spent flying over the Harvey properties. Being in the air, her mind occupied with the controls and the air currents, was cleansing.

At dinner she told her family, "I think my future is in aviation. I think I'd make a good jet pilot."

Normally one can only learn to fly jet aircraft at the expense of the Air Force. The machinery and the quantities of fuel are too costly for the average student pilot. But her father could afford, in fact was delighted, to send her to a school for jet aviation. Gradually, she earned her first license to fly small jets, working toward her instrument, multi-engine and commercial ratings, all toward the final goal: an Airline Transport Rating. She continued studying logging the airtime and gaining further licensing until she was qualified to fly a Boeing 727. Working that hard was easy, it was a blessing because when she wasn't studying and concentrating on the controls of a plane, her mind went immediately to visions of her baby. She forced away the memory of seeing Angel in the body bag, in her coffin, and concentrated on her work.

Hardly planning to have spent all this time, money and effort to fly aimlessly through the air like a seagull, although the bird at least was hunting for food and not spending more than five hundred dollars an hour on jet fuel, America applied for work as a copilot at three airlines.

She promptly received letters from the personnel managers of each, congratulating her on her certifications and asking her to come in for a job interview.

Showing the letters to her parents and Gat she was, they felt, normal for the first time since Angel's death.

She entered the personnel manger's office at the first airline and handed him his letter to her. He looked at her curiously, then, remembering his manners, he stood up and shook hands. "Sit down, please." He looked at the letter. It was addressed to A. Harvey, the way her application had read. He shook his head slowly, "I'm sorry. I didn't imagine you were a woman. Our company policy does not provide for female pilots."

"But I'm qualified for the job. You said so yourself in your letter."

"I know, and you're entirely right. But as much as I would like to, I cannot hire you."

"May I know why you have such a policy?"

"The public. The passengers. It's tough enough to fill planes on our routes, which have aggressive competitors. The company is afraid that the public simply wouldn't have confidence in a woman pilot and wouldn't fly with us."

"But these are the seventies. Women are proving they can do most things men can and just as well, often better."

He nodded grimly and held out his arms in a gesture of futility. "What can I do? Stand in every plane you fly and tell the passengers, 'Don't worry, she's as good as any man?'"

It was the same at the two other airlines except at the third the personnel manager leered at her body and wise-guyed, "However, I'd be glad to audition you for our Flight Attendants Program."

Her anger at the reason for rejections had therapeutic value. Night and day she pondered the problem of how to put her skill to work. She spoke with her father, "I'd like to start up an air courier and charter service. I've checked with several big courier companies, and they farm out work their own planes can't handle. I'd need to buy a jet. A medium-size Lear would do it. I'm hoping you agree that it's a good idea and that you'll let me use some of the principal from my trust. I would need three million dollars for the plane and for overhead to carry me until I begin to break even."

"I definitely agree that it's a good idea. I think there's a big future in air courier and charter services. However, in even the best business idea there's risk. You have a ten million dollar trust fund. I'm inclined toward making a distribution of the three million you need, but before I do I want you to seriously analyze what you are proposing. First of all, you will reduce your net worth by 33 percent and you will lose the interest the trust has been earning on those three million dollars. Hopefully you will be successful and begin earning money, so the lost interest will be moot. But you must recognize that you will be betting almost one third of all you have in the world.

"You're a wealthy young woman today. If your project does not work out you will want to put in more money in order not to fail and lose your initial investment. With bad luck you could eventually wind up bust. Give it some heavy thought. Few people start off in life financially secure. That doesn't mean much when you're young and have dreams, but as you grow older you will come to understand and appreciate it more and more. You will always have your portion of the ranch's income, but it will never be sold in your or Gat's lifetimes, or ever, unless some descendant manages to break your mother's will and my own. I'll abide by whatever decision you make. I only ask you to study it very thoroughly."

She spoke again with some of the successful air courier companies and was given assurance of approximately how much business she could expect from each of them. It completely filled the normal hours a pilot flew. But she was willing to work as long as she was able to. Thus, the numbers balanced favorably against her investment.

America named her business "Jetways" and rented space in a hangar at Love Field in Dallas that included maintenance service for her new Lear. The immense new Dallas–Fort Worth International Airport would soon be opening and Love Field would be used strictly for private and charter-courier aircraft. She used her Piper Cheyenne to commute between Love Field and home in San Antonio.

As promised, the courier services gave her contracts to fly packages for them. They started with small amounts. Quickly they recognized her reliability and were especially impressed by her willingness to fly in bad weather, through storms no other pilot would risk. America never said no. She was fearless, feeling she had nothing to lose. If she went down it would only reunite her with Angel that much sooner. In the first year her customers were so pleased with her performance that they began increasing her contracts. As her father had anticipated, she needed another four million dollars for a second, larger plane and for hiring other pilots to fly for her. She went to several banks, but they were not interested in lending a young woman four million dollars with a plane worth just two and a half million dollars as collateral in a risky, competitive business. She went back to her trust fund.

Her father commented, "But at least you are not reducing your trust in order to make up for losses. You're using your money well, for expansion based on success and signed contracts with reliable companies."

Within another year she needed seven million more for further expansion, and this time the banks were willing to bet on her. They put up four million in loans both collateralized by her aircraft—now worth seven million dollars—and justified by her contracts and track record. She took the last three million from her trust fund.

"Well, you're broke," her father smiled. "But you own a first-class, profitable airline, and a lot of equity."

Jetways was off and running, operating two Lears, a 727, and a large helicopter capable of deliveries and charters to small cities where jets couldn't land. And she continued to take package flights and charters in weather that nobody else would risk.

She worked night and day, seven days a week, and all holidays. Soon Jetways owned a large hangar that also maintained and serviced other private planes. America found herself with more than a full-time job. She needed someone to take part of the administrative load off her shoulders, so she consulted with her father and together they interviewed four potential general managers. America was strongly impressed by Jerry Gottlieb, a financial man with aviation background. They asked him to return for another interview and after two hours of intense conversation America invited him to be Executive Vice President of Jetways

Later, when she and her father were alone, America looked to him for confirmation of what she had done. Albert said, "If Jerry Gottlieb tells you a rabbit can pull a freight train I'd say you'd better hook him up."

America laughed. "You really hate being a Texan, don't you?"

Her father threw another Texas cliché at her, "You can always tell a Texan, but you can't tell him much."

American Airlines sent a notice to all of their better customers, explaining that AA often flew needy children to cities with hospitals they couldn't afford to reach without help. The notice explained that AA couldn't handle it all by themselves and asked for contributions of some of their AAdvantage Miles to the children's program. She donated generously, as the plight of a child in need brought Angel to mind. And she put herself in touch with the director of the program. "Whenever you know of a child you can't help, call me. I'll always make a plane available, or borrow one, and I've got a long-range helicopter for out-of-the-way places without landing strips."

America bought paramedic intensive care equipment and a bed that could be installed in either a jet or the chopper. Soon Jetways was ferrying sick children from poor homes to hospitals in big cities. America made a point of flying these missions herself whenever she could. They were her happiest hours in the air.

Jetways was in the right place at the right time. The economy was up, more and more people were flying privately. The business had grown to own eight jet airplanes and employ twelve pilots, twenty maintenance people and five secretaries and bookkeepers.

Forbes Magazine ran a story about the growth of the air courier business and focused on the success of Jetways. This time being a woman and beautiful worked in her favor, and they used a photo of her in her pilot's uniform on the cover. *Fortune* did a three-page profile on "America Harvey, Pilot-Entrepreneur" that was picked up by the *Financial Times* in London.

Such favorable publicity in such prestigious publications, read by almost every American and European businessman, banker or professional money manager, drove her volume higher and higher and Jetways enjoyed continuing growth and prosperity.

Time ran a story on her with a "Woman of the Year" format, covering her outstanding business success and disclosing the fact that she had lost her own child in a tragic accident and in the past two years had flown hundreds of children, gratis, to hospitals they couldn't otherwise have reached. *Time* ran her picture on a full page captioned "The Angel of the Airways." The title made her happy, and sad.

On her way home, on the day the *Time* spread appeared, America stopped at Angel's grave. She lay flowers on the small marble stone engraved with only "Angel Jasperson—1968-1971" America had discontinued the daily visits, understanding that it was debilitating, even destructive. Sobbing, she pulled herself away and went to the house.

Sitting in their living room waiting for dinner, the *Time* article open before him, Gat smiled, "You've earned every bit of it. You took the risk; you did the work. Oh wow! have you been working!"

"I've been lucky."

Her father said, "And the harder you work, the luckier you get."

She had not taken a day off in the three years since she'd founded Jetways. "I'm pleased to be successful but it's not nearly the joy of holding your baby's hand." She stopped. When she had control of herself she shook her head, "I should never have left J.J. If I had only hung on, Angel would be six years old now, in school. I should have tolerated him and my baby would still be alive."

Gat was emphatic, "That's hindsight and it's not 20/20 vision. What I do think is that you are worn out. You have just shown me that burying yourself in work isn't the answer to forgetting. You need a change. The business is in good hands with Jerry. Why don't you think about taking a trip somewhere? Maybe a different place, different faces, some distance will make you see this in its true perspective and help you to stop dwelling on the idea that you made a mistake. You didn't. J.J.'s a cheap conniver. He even managed to wriggle himself out of an indictment. You made a decision with which we all agreed. Nobody could anticipate what happened."

She looked at her father, who continued, "My advice will be worth about what you pay for it, and it's free. But if I were you I'd take a vacation."

Suddenly she craved to get away from familiar surroundings, to ache less, and to expose herself to the possibility of being stimulated by the unknown. She placed a phone call to Marbella, a town on the southern coast of Spain. It was July and that was where Marisa would be. Marisa insisted that she come over immediately and spend the summer, or as long as she could, with her and Carlos.

* * *

Looking out the window of an Iberia Air Lines flight to Spain, on July 25, 1973, at the lights of New York City fading as though being dimmed by a rheostat, it couldn't have occurred to her that this visit was going to change her life. That she was going to meet a man of a style, background, of a world she would never have imagined, who would so strongly affect her life that she, a patriotic, totally American girl was going to cut her roots and never return to live in the United States again.

PART TWO

The man in the parachute being towed through the air by the mahogany speedboat had black, shining hair. His deep tan was the result of a Latin complexion and year-round exposure to the sun.

America was at the pool of the Marbella Club with Marisa, who was wearing a rumor of a bikini, causing America to feel dressed for winter in her Cole of California tank suit. The girls were a head-spinning combination: Marisa, supermodel slim and long-legged, with waist-length gleaming Spanish hair the color of ebony and dark vibrant eyes; America, equally long-limbed but stronger, more athletic, her wheat blonde hair cascading below her shoulders, with bangs ending above deep green eyes.

Marisa's olive-toned skin was tan and accustomed to the powerful rays of the semi-tropical Mediterranean sun; concerned, though, she gave America a bright orange Marbella Club towel. "Cover up. You have had enough for the first day. Have respect for the sun, eh?"

As the man in the parachute floated low over the beach his face was serene. Marisa said, "Alfonso is good looking." She observed America: "I see that you agree."

The man on the flying trapeze signaled to the sailor at the wheel of the speedboat, which veered to the right, taking him out to the deeper water, then turned, towing him parallel with the beach. They could see him unbuckling the harness with one hand while suspending himself from the support bar above his head with the other. Then the harness fluttered free of his body and he was held in the air a hundred feet above the water only by the strength of his arms. As the parachute passed directly in front of the Marbella Club he jackknifed his body into an excellent swan dive into the sea.

America was impressed. She thought nothing of flying thirty thousand feet above the earth's surface, but when she did it she had a machine with the power of seven thousand horses holding her up. Freefalling a hundred feet into the unknown was something she wouldn't have dared.

Surfacing, the man tilted his head backwards, causing the water to comb his hair, and waited as the boat neared. He took the wheel while the sailor hauled in the parachute and the ropes. As the boat came as close to shore as it could without the propeller becoming fouled in the sand he cut the engine and stood on the bow. He appeared to be in his late forties and had an athletic physique. He dove over the side and swam until he could stand then strode the rest of the way to the beach, pushing against the resistance of the water, then continuing to stride even after he was on the sand.

He walks, America thought, *as if he were wearing a sword.*

He came out of the dressing room in trousers and a shirt and walked to the swimming pool area of the Marbella Club, splendid posture, head erect, not looking at anyone unless they called out to him, as many did. Everyone appeared to know him and want to be seen greeting him as a friend. Without stopping he went to a table where a man was seated. The man handed Alfonso his wristwatch and a heavy gold chain with a jeweled cross gleaming from the sun. He put it around his neck, touched the man affectionately on the shoulder and left the club.

Marisa said, "I'll tell you about him during lunch."

It was three o'clock and a Mediterranean buffet was being offered. The girls filled plates with paella, langosta, langostinos and sat at a table.

"Alfonso is one of the most charming men in Europe. We call him *El Inmortal* because in Spain, a Catholic country, we believe that when we die we go on to a better life. This man was a renowned war hero at sixteen; he's handsome, titled, wealthy and has eight splendid children and a beautiful, aristocratic wife who overlooks his indiscretions. He's a scratch golfer, eight-goal polo player and wonderful at water sports. He has a delicious personality that exudes experience and wisdom. Men as well as women adore him. That is why we call him immortal: he'll never die because there cannot be a better life to go on to!"

The joke over, Marisa reflected, "There's another, terribly sad side to him. Alfonso had a tragic childhood. We all did because of the war, but Alfonso's was even more ghastly. He lost both parents, horrifically. During the battles he became known as *'El que no son-rie, nunca'*: 'He who never smiles.' And though he's charming and entertaining, the fact is I can never remember seeing him smile genuinely. Out of courtesy, yes, but never of happiness. You will meet him at my party for you. His full name is Alfonso García de las Arenas y de Beltran El Bueno. The title he uses is *el Duque del Castillo de Tarifa*, the Duke of the Castle of Tarifa. He has inherited many other titles and is several times a *Grande de España*. He inherited vast lands. He's a banker and industrialist."

"The businesses also inherited?"

"*¡Que no!* A Spanish nobleman of the old school would feel humiliated to be in business. And banking, worse! A moneylender? But Alfonso does not care what a nobleman is expected to be like. He makes his own rules." Marisa's face took on a tender look as she thought about him. "The joke about *El Inmortal* isn't entirely true. Alfonso's life lacks one major element. Love. Yes, he has a wife and eight children, but he and Magdalena have never been in love."

America's attention was drawn to the man who had held Alfonso's watch and chain. His build was the same though less muscular. He also had black hair, good teeth, with the dark eyes and the large aristocratic nose. Carrying two plates from the buffet he put them down at a table at which an extremely attractive woman had just arrived. She had similar coloring and features, except for the nose, and she had a three-inch long scar on her left cheek. Yet, it did not detract from her good looks.

America commented, "He and Alfonso could be twins."

"They are half brothers. His name is Francisco. We call him by the diminutive, Paco. Paco Moreno Ortega. He is a Count, el Conde de Los Escalones. He's an important lawyer in Madrid. The woman is Alfonso's sister Cristina, Paco's half-sister and wife." And in response to America's expression of shock, Marisa said, "Yes. It's a sad and complicated story." She put her hand on her friend's. "Tragedy finds us all. Nobody escapes."

Marisa's house was on the beachfront grounds of the Marbella Club, a privilege she shared with Prince Alfonso Hohenlohe, The Duchess of Alba, John Davis Lodge, who was the recent American Ambassador to Spain, and a few others, among them Baron Hans Heinrich Thyssen-Bornemisza and Baron Guy de Rothschild, both so civilized as to overlook that some forty years earlier the family of one had financed Adolf Hitler while the other had been forced to flee from him.

The party for America had been planned for a week after her arrival to allow her to recover from jet lag as there was a seven-hour time change between San Antonio and Marbella. She took advantage of the time to develop a reasonable tan and become accustomed to the Spanish hours. Though the guests were invited to arrive at ten-thirty, few would appear before eleven and dinner wouldn't be served until midnight.

Marisa took America to the Marbella club's *peluqueria* to have their hair done. At eight-thirty it was bustling with striking women still in their bathing suits and *pareas*. America enjoyed the atmosphere. "At home by this hour dinner is over and most of the country is staring at prime time."

"We have longer days here. Spain has daylight saving time all year round and then in the spring we advance the clock an hour more with the rest of the world. As you have seen, it doesn't get dark in summer until nine-thirty or ten, so people play tennis or stay on their boats or the beach until quite late. By the time they get home, rest, bathe and dress for the evening it's ten or ten-thirty at the earliest."

It occurred to America that she had not been to a hairdresser in three years. She thought of Alfonso, the man on the flying trapeze. It wasn't the first time he had come to her mind since seeing him at the Marbella Club. He had not returned since the first day, or at least she had not seen him. No, he definitely had not returned. He was a man who gets noticed.

Leaving the beauty shop they walked down the road to Marisa's house, *La Gaviota*, the seagull. America confided, "I feel odd. On one hand I'm looking forward to seeing Alfonso, yet it's wrong, he's a married man."

Marisa was overjoyed to find her friend looking forward to something, and she hoped she could convince her of the truth. "He isn't married in the sense that Carlos and I are married. He and Magdalena could be brother and sister. They love each other but as I told you they have never been in love with each other."

"Never? How strange."

"Yes. Nevertheless, it's a fact."

They passed through a centuries-old door. The house, like all of its waterfront neighbors, was new, but Spain has many abandoned farmhouses and churches that lost their fabulous doors and old roof tiles to antique dealers. The girls walked through a high-walled outdoor patio. Texas, with its Spanish history, has many of them. They had originated as a form of security obliging visitors or intruders to pass through an extra locked door before reaching the house. But in 1973 in Marbella few people locked their doors or removed keys from their cars. The banks did not employ armed guards. One could prosper selling suntan oil but starve vending burglar alarms. America appreciated the palpable freedom from fear of robbery and assault. In Dallas, New York and other large American cities it was known that the police could address themselves only to crimes of violence, as drug crime was on the increase and there wasn't enough police personnel to cope with simple robberies. But there was no drug problem in Spain because of a mandatory throw-away-the-key seven years in prison for anyone caught entering the country with even one marijuana cigarette.

As she dressed in a strapless yellow gown, made of clinging silk, her mind passed over the people she had met in the last week. All Spaniards, they had been extremely welcoming. If on any given day at the beach club she had accepted a drink with every man who invited her to have a *copita* she would, in the words of Dean Martin, ". . . be speaking to you from a jar in the Harvard Medical School."

Knowing that in an hour she would be seeing Alfonso, she applied eyeliner with extraordinary patience; it occurred to her that ten days ago she wouldn't have believed that she would ever again be inspired to make an effort to look attractive for any man.

Chapter Four

Hoping she looked as good as she wanted to, America joined Carlos and Marisa on the terrace, which faced about twenty yards of lawn and then the beach and the Mediterranean. Flaming torches lit hundred-foot-tall palm trees, the grass and the border of the sea. Tables for eight with umbrellas to fend off the night dew were spread around the lawn. The moon was new, the sky flecked by a billion stars, and there was a gentle breeze.

To Marisa's surprise and America's delight Alfonso was the first to arrive. He was beautiful, even taller and more dramatic looking than she had remembered. He wore black trousers, a shirt of heavy white four-ply silk with black pearl studs and cufflinks and a black cashmere sweater over his shoulders. He kissed Marisa, not on both cheeks in the Spanish custom, but in a hug that lifted her off the floor as one would a favorite sister. Then he greeted Carlos with an *abrazo,* the hug and pounding of the back that Spanish men exchange.

"Alfonso," Marisa said, "thank you for being punctual."

"Do not thank me. I have waited five days for this moment." Turning to America he raised her hand almost to his lips and said, "I am Alfonso. I risked my life for you the other day and you did not even throw me a kiss."

"I apologize. I thought it was a performance for everyone to enjoy. I didn't know that you'd seen me."

"But how not? A goddess seated next to Marisa, who is also a goddess, but as she's the wife of my friend I look at her differently. I was sailing through the air and I saw you and was absolutely certain that I had to know you. I calculated that first it would be clever to impress you with my courage. In fact, such a dive is rather dangerous."

"I thought that, and now I'm sorry you didn't come by to receive your well-earned applause."

"Unfortunately I had business in Madrid. But I knew that I was invited to this party to meet you. Anticipating this moment has provided me with five days of exquisite pleasure. And now, the sublime realization." He took her by the elbow and guided her to a sofa in a corner of the terrace.

America asked, "Do you fly in the parachute because you feel happier when you're in the air?"

"Absolutely not! The wind bothers my eyes and tickles my nose, and it's a terrible strain on my arms. How could I possibly be happier hanging from a parachute than I am at this moment sitting here and gazing at you?"

Oh, wow! Nothing she could think to say could equal him, so she said nothing, a fact that went unnoticed as Alfonso clearly intended to entertain her. A waiter stopped with a tray of champagne and America took a glass. Alfonso asked for ". . . *whisky con soda.*" America had noticed that in Spain when one wants scotch they ask for "whiskey," rye, bourbon and Canadian whiskies being virtually unknown.

She sipped her drink. "I don't usually like champagne but this is delicious."

Alfonso asked the waiter if the champagne was Spanish.

"Sí, Señor Duque, it's *cava*, Ferret Guasch. But there's French champagne if the Sr. Duque wishes."

"*¡Que no!*" To America he said, "We make excellent sparkling wines. The Spanish word for them is *cava*. The only reason to drink French champagne in Spain is *esnobismo.* Further, the French are not friends of Spain, nor of anyone for that matter, but especially not of

Spain so I will go considerably out of my way to avoid their products if I can do as well elsewhere. Not always easy. But with *cava,* yes, especially the mark Ferret Guasch, which has a small production."

She looked at the glass in his hand. "You didn't specify Spanish whiskey."

"*¡Hombre!*" he exclaimed. The word for "man" is employed affectionately to a man or a woman, as if to say pal or buddy, "I'm the most Spanish Spaniard, but not a madman. Spanish whiskey has nothing to do with whiskey from Scotland. The British stand alone in the making of Scotch whiskey. Also, they are our friends. True, there remains the matter of them holding on to Gibraltar but that will be resolved one day so it isn't reasonable to sacrifice drinking the best."

America observed a gorgeous woman arriving. "Could that be Ava Gardner?"

"Yes. She has been living in Madrid. Frank Sinatra came to visit her, they had a public disagreement. The 'disagreement' was Luis Miguel Dominguin, our most famous bullfighter. Ava fled, leaving Sinatra, behind and is staying down the road here at Los Monteros with the Count and Countess of Romanones."

America stared at a group of spectacularly attractive, tall young men and women, "My goodness, the Young Lions!"

One of them, a slender girl, six-feet tall, with long blonde hair and enormous vivacity was wearing elasticized blue satin jeans over a figure that was a gift of happiness to all men who saw her.

"That is Princess Gunilla von Bismarck. A Marbella personality. She's with her brothers and sisters-in-law. They are descendants of the Iron Chancellor."

Behind them was another exotic blonde woman dressed in a skin-tight, blood-red leather jumpsuit. Her escort was substantially younger. "That is my eccentric sister Cayetana. She's building a house in the hills near here. I'll introduce you at another time. Tonight I share you with no one."

As they spoke America felt that he was absorbing her, everything there was to see or sense about her, reading her, memorizing her. His intensity was creating an intoxicating intimacy. He touched her face with his fingertips. "You're even more lovely than I had expected."

The noise of the party, the sound of glasses and conversation and laughter all around them seemed to be moving away from them, or they from it, until it was merely a drone in the background and the two of them were enclosed in a bubble separated from the rest of the world.

She felt a hand touch her shoulder and looked up. It was Marisa. "The seating will remain the same, only the venue will change. Come, dinner is served."

Alfonso entertained America continuously, giving only enough attention to the lady on his left for politesse. Carlos felt touched with pleasure just looking at America's face. Following Angel's death Marisa had made frequent telephone calls to Gat and had spoken in depth with him about America's state of mind. What he had been able to tell her had left her deeply fearful that her friend might never come out of her grief. Also what struck him as extraordinary was Alfonso. Carlos had never seen him so animated.

As dessert was being served guitarists strolled the lawn at a distance, strumming romantic Latin music. The dinner ended at around two in the morning. As they were getting up from the table Marisa came over and whispered, "Ava Gardner just left with my *mayor domo*." She rolled her eyes. "Should I fire him or congratulate him?"

Alfonso took America's hand and led her to a gazebo with a fountain and a lovely ceramic floor, all enclosed by a trellis with climbing flowers and night-blooming jasmine. Curving around its perimeter were upholstered benches. He chose a spot for them and they rested against the cushions.

"Tell me about your unusual name."

"My father always believed that the most beautiful thing in the world was the American flag. Then, when I was born, he kinda fell for me so he named me America. I like it, I like it a lot, but some people think it's corny and flag-wavey, like, 'It's a good name—if you're a boat.'"

"And what's wrong with waving your flag? I love your name and I love your father's patriotism. I love everything about you."

"That's pretty. But you know little about me."

"Not so. When one's business is money, as mine is, it's prudent to keep current on everything about it. I read many financial and business publications, among them *Forbes, Fortune, Time,* and *The Financial Times.* I knew of your tragedy from Marisa, but that was several years ago, when it happened. Recently I have been reading of a young American entrepreneurial woman of extraordinary accomplishments and generosity. I know of your courage, your strength, your humanity . . ."

The sound of the guitars in the background blending with the music of the water falling from the fountain, the strong perfume of the jasmine, this man at her side, his shoulder lightly touching hers, attacked all of her senses, causing her to feel slightly dizzy. She thought she must be going mad. Ten days ago she believed she would never sense any emotion but sadness, or at best moments of numbness, and now she was feeling as if she were falling in love— with a total stranger.

"I want to dance with you," he said.

In his embrace their bodies moved tightly together, and she felt the strength of him, his arms and legs, and she knew she really was falling in love with him, and he with her.

She understood her own value, knew who she was and what she had accomplished, yet here was this bigger-than-life man, this Knight or Prince, reacting to her as she was reacting to him. There was a feeling of unreality about it. Yet she knew it *was* real, and she was slightly afraid that he was so experienced, so accustomed to beautiful women that seeming to be in love was his way of conducting himself and tomorrow she would wake up still in love with someone to whom she had been just another amusing evening.

Alfonso said, "Let's join the others," as if he, too, felt it was almost too much, too fast.

They followed the sound of Spanish music to another part of the grounds where Marisa and Carlos had put up a large tent. Inside were tables and chairs for the hundred or so guests and a raised platform, a stage on which eight gypsies performed, singing and dancing *Sevillanas*.

Alfonso took her hand. "You are sad. Why?"

"My daughter. I bought us twin dresses like the entertainers are wearing and we tried to dance. It was a lovely time . . ." Changing the subject she said, "I'm quite hopeless at grasping this rhythm that I like so much."

He did not pursue the subject of Angel but explained, "For an American to quickly understand the *Sevillana* is difficult, nearly impossible. You must grow up with it, like a first language. It has a unique beat and emotion."

At three in the morning the gypsies were just warming up and the guests were served *ajo blanco,* a delicious cold white soup made with garlic and pulverized almonds.

By five o'clock the gypsies were enjoying themselves, the show was in full swing and continued for another hour. For those guests who stayed on till the end, hot chocolate was served with *churros*, a Spanish breakfast staple that is neither bread nor toast nor a donut, yet has something to do with each of them, being a circle or a stick of deep fried batter that isn't sweet, just delicious.

Slightly before dawn Alfonso led her to a secluded corner of the terrace. "This is my favorite *rincon*, 'nook' I believe you would say in English. Let us sit here and wait for our first sunrise together."

Looking to the east, toward Málaga, the sky was not still dark but not yet light - it was that moment when night is first being softened by the not yet visible sun.

In the distance large commercial fishing boats were at work. On the beach local fishermen were pushing a rowboat into the water, dropping nets, then struggling to haul in what they hoped would earn them a living for the day. As America and Alfonso watched, the men divided their catch into wooden boxes and plastic buckets, then tied them onto the backs of motorbikes and rushed off to a municipal market where they would sell to the dealers who had stalls there.

"We used to have many more fishermen like these when we were poor, until the fifties, when we became industrialized, more profitable employment became available and fewer people needed to make their living so tenuously as by the luck of the net."

Abruptly he gestured toward the east. The sun had just appeared at the horizon, a sharp red line swelling into a half-round.

"Good morning," he said, taking her in his arms and kissing her lingeringly.

As he held her, as he caressed her body through the thin silk dress, Alfonso had an overwhelming desire to make love to her. *Impossible. Too soon.*

And America was thinking that the touch of his hand on her back was almost all of the pleasure in the world and she longed for the rest. She remembered with craving the firmness of his arms and legs as they had danced together. But she knew that she would go no further.

Alfonso ended the moment. "What would you like to do this afternoon?"

She wanted to reply, "Anything, with you," but she said, "Alfonso, you're married and I've never admired 'the other woman.' I can't believe I've gone this far. I understand the unhappiness it can cause."

"You will be hurting no one. Yes, I'm married. My wife is a superb woman and we have eight wonderful children. In Spain divorce does not exist. It's illegal, as well as contrary to my religious belief and to my own desire. But though my wife and I are forever, if not constantly, we are not in love with each other, nor ever have been. Apart from raising our children together we have separate lives. For example, she's spending the month of August with our younger children in Paris and Mallorca, whereas I'm here. But we will always remain married. So when I speak to you romantically, and I mean every word, you and I must understand from the beginning that we have no future, only whatever happiness we can draw from the present. But I promise you we will be hurting no one."

She agreed, without the foresight to understand that she was stepping onto a merry-go-round of love, laughter and euphoria that one day would make her cry and feel like a widow.

Alfonso kept a thirty-five foot cabin cruiser at the new marina Puerto José Banus. When he picked America up at Marisa's house at one-thirty P.M. and drove toward the port, he handed her a plastic shopping bag. It contained a green visor decorated with daisies. She put it on immediately.

"What do you think?" he asked. "I'm not experienced at buying presents for ladies. I thought the green would go well with your eyes."

"I love it. Thank you. I love that you took the trouble to do it."

Pleased, he handed her another package, "Then maybe this, too, will be agreeable."

It was a purse made out of cork. "It's rather Spanish. Cork comes from the bark of Mediterranean oak trees."

"Thank you. It's lovely."

"And practical. If you happen to fall into the sea it will float."

She laughed because she thought it was funny, and then for the sheer joy of laughing. "But when did you have the time to do this?"

"I woke up thinking about you. As I couldn't sleep I went to town and tried to do something that might make you happy, as you make me by being in my thoughts."

A sailor standing on the dock, seeing Alfonso's car hurried over.

"Manolo, la Señorita Harvey."

As they boarded *La Primavera,* America asked, "What does it mean?"

"The Springtime."

Manolo carried on coolers from the trunk of the car that were filled with iced *cava,* soft drinks and beer.

Alfonso began putting an array of *tapas* onto a large lazy Susan: slices of *chorizo,* or Spanish sausage, *manchego* cheese, *jamon serrano,* and a Spanish *tortilla,* an inch-thick soft pancake made of potato, egg and onion. He put it where the sun would keep it warm.

Watching him setting it all up America was disappointed. "Are we expecting others?"

"Unthinkable! We are alone. But after a few hours we will want a little something until lunch. And to want something and not have it would be *fatal,* no?

Delighted, she said, "Well, I don't think it would be really fatal. But I appreciate your going to so much trouble for me."

"Our use of the word *fatal* is less literal than in English. However, there's no such thing as too much trouble to please the woman with whom I'm falling in love."

He went to the cabin below and took off his shirt and trousers. His bathing suit revealed his excellent physique. America removed her skirt and blouse. She was wearing a one-piece black lastex tank suit. "I'm sorry I don't have a bikini, they're not worn in San Antonio, but I'll get one here."

"I think the most elegant, the most beautiful sight in the world is a body like yours—a very dangerous body—in a one-piece black bathing suit."

Manolo steered the boat out of the port, and as they reached open water he turned westward, toward Estepona and Gibraltar. Alfonso asked, "Do you water-ski?"

"Yes. As children we spent our summers on a lake."

"Do you prefer two skis or one?"

"I'm comfortable on one."

He picked up their skis and threw them overboard with towlines attached to the boat. They dove over the side. Manolo navigated toward the deeper water, slowly, allowing the lines to become taut.

When they were both up and skiing without mishap, Alfonso shouted with delight, "I assumed you might need a few starts to get up. The sea is different than a lake."

America called back, "It's different but it's different-easier. The ripples in the sea don't bother me and the salt water gives buoyancy. Staying up on this is a piece of cake."

He was amused by the expression. They skied for five minutes, exhilarated by being side by side, by the air against their faces and bodies and the spray they caused on both sides. Then Alfonso lifted one leg in the air so that he was skiing on one foot. He looked to see if America was entertained. She did the same trick. Pleasantly surprised, he veered to his left to do a crossover in front of her, leaping over the wake. America veered to the right, and they crisscrossed back and forth over the foamy, churning water. America thought of more spectacular tricks that she could do, but she decided not to perform any of them. She wanted to be sure where the fine line was between being impressed and preferring to be the impresser.

Behind them, but further out to sea, steering another speedboat was a twenty-three-year-old boy named José Maria, his younger brother Luis, and two of Madrid society's best-looking girls. "Look," he said with delight, pointing to the water-skiers, "it's Papá," and he steered inland to come abreast of Alfonso's boat.

America swam with cultivated strokes back to *La Primavera*. Helping her aboard, Alfonso hugged and kissed her. "You're a mermaid. And what a skiing partner! What fun! What joy!"

Using a freshwater hose he washed the salt off her body and out of her hair, and wrapped her in a large towel.

José Maria steered back out to sea.

Alfonso suggested, "Go below and change into a dry bathing suit."

When America returned, a cassette deck was playing Mari Trini's currently popular album as Alfonso opened a bottle of *cava*, poured them each a glass and offered her the *tapas*. He had been right; she had a healthy appetite.

"Now I will take you to a *chiringuito*. They are small restaurants on the beach where they prepare fish that have just come out of the sea. You will enjoy it." He called out to Manolo, "*El chiringuito* Marisa. But do not hurry."

America commented, "I always thought Marisa's name was unusual."

"In a Catholic country there are many Marias, so there are many diminutives: Marisa, Marita, Mari, Mavi for Maria Victoria, and there are many combinations with Maria: Mari Sol, Mari Luz, Mari Paz, Maria del Mar, meaning Maria of the sun, light, peace, sea . . ."

They stretched out on a large mat at the front of the boat to take the sun and sip the *cava* and nibble at the *tapas* as they were nibbling at life and enjoying every bite.

Alfonso sang to her:

"TODOS DICEN QUE ES MENTIRA QUE TE QUIERO,
PORQUE NUNCA ME HABÍAN VISTO ENAMORADO . . ."

"What does it mean?"

"It might have been written for me. 'Everyone says it's a lie that I love you, because they have never seen me in love.'"

She had the feeling he was telling the truth, yet found it incredible for such an attractive, romantic man. But she was happy to believe it and luxuriate in the moment. J.J.'s infidelity had not bolstered her self-confidence.

He gazed at her as she lay stretched out in the sun. "*¡Que buena facha!*"

"I'm sure that's flattering. I'd enjoy knowing exactly what."

"It means that in addition to having a beautifully formed body your skin is delicious looking, appetizing."

In half an hour they passed the marina from which they had begun this wonderful day and continued past it toward Marbella. As Manolo began cutting the throttle and steering toward land Alfonso got their shirts. "We can not go in closer or we will foul the propeller. We must wade in."

They were alongside an anchored yacht on which a group of six were having lunch on the upper deck. They all waved and one called out, "Alfonso, come aboard with your beautiful friend and have a drink. Or lunch." He called back his thanks and declined.

Holding their shirts above their heads they waded onto the beach, where, up on the terrace they saw a man with a handlebar mustache, white trousers held up by colorful suspenders, but no shirt, a bronzed torso, and wearing a Panama hat. He greeted them as they stepped off the sand. Alfonso introduced him to America, "La Señorita Harvey, this is Antonio, the husband of Marisa."

It was four-thirty, the perfect hour for summertime lunch in Spain. They were taken to a table from which they could view the sea, the beach, the girls in ribbon-sized bikinis, sailboats gliding by in the distance, multimillion dollar yachts, speedboats hauling water-skiers, others anchoring to allow their owners to wade ashore for lunch, all with abandon and gaiety as if none of them had a child who had died, a friend who had betrayed, a fortune lost, a marriage in despair, or a relative crippled or killed in their Civil War.

A beautiful woman of around forty, with vivid blue eyes, colorfully dressed in beach clothes, kissed Alfonso hello. He introduced Marisa to America and ordered a bottle of white wine. Then they listened to her describe the dishes available, *chanquetes, calamares, bogorones* . . . and as the food began arriving America found herself delighting in things she had never tasted before. Like everything that had been happening to her in the last twenty-four hours.

When they returned to the port they bought ice-cream cones and strolled along the docks. The panorama was spectacular. Berthed along the outer wall was Adnon Kashoggi's two-hundred-and-seventy-six-foot boat "Nabila."

Looking at the helicopter it carried, America said, "That's an FB 25. It cost him around two million dollars."

And then there was a row of the "lesser" boats: ninety- to one-hundred-and-thirty-foot sailboats and cabin cruisers, and then rows and rows of smaller craft.

He brought her back to *La Gaviota,* then picked her up at ten P.M. and took her to dinner in the *pueblo,* the old part of Marbella, to a small Italian restaurant called Don Leone owned by a young man named Paolo, who took their orders, cooked and also served the meal.

After dinner they strolled the narrow cobble-stoned streets lined with whitewashed houses with potted geraniums everywhere: on terraces, windowsills, hanging from hooks on the outside walls. They went to a bar, the living room of a private house owned by a vivacious woman named Menchu who moved about the room speaking to her customers in three or four different languages.

As they were leaving there was a window-rattling clap of thunder and ten-carat sized raindrops began bursting on the sidewalk. Menchu had walked them to the door. "Wait a moment, darlings. I'll give you an umbrella."

Alfonso's car was parked several blocks away so they splashed their way through the downpour, arms around each others' waists, holding tightly together to both fit under the umbrella and to avoid slipping on the wet cobblestones. Their thighs touched with every stride and America wondered if Alfonso was feeling the same sensations that were producing a tremulous excitement within her. As if in answer he dropped the umbrella and took her into his arms. It was a tender kiss, a question. When she responded he drew her closer, and the kiss was long and deep and the rain continued falling on them.

Alfonso drove to his cottage on the beach. Leading her by the hand he opened the front door, and they were inside a cozy living room. He lit the fireplace, then left her and returned with two large, white towels bearing the monogram "T" under a ducal crown.

Unbuttoning her soaking wet blouse he peeled it away from her body. He unzipped her skirt, and she let it fall to the floor. He unhooked her bra, and then rolled down her bikini underpants.

He pulled a fur rug up to the fireplace, covered it with a towel and she lay down on it. With the other towel he gently began rubbing her dry. His hands heated her more than the fire. He towel-dried her hair. Then, holding her face in his hands, he kissed her, tenderly.

Alfonso removed his clothes and then she was enfolded within the strong arms she had longed to have holding her. They kissed hungrily. Her body was held tightly against his and again she felt the hardness of his limbs, and the gentleness. The only illumination was from the flames. Alfonso ran his hands along her sides, touching the skin gently but firmly, up the outside of her thigh to the curve of her buttocks, then her waist, up her torso to her back, just avoiding her breasts, caressing the smoothness of the skin all over her body. Then he touched her breasts and his hands told her that he loved her.

Afterwards he brought them each a pair of his pajamas and a bottle of *cava*. America put on the pajama top. "That's all you need," he said gazing joyfully at her long legs extending out of the racing-green silk.

"And you don't need to bother with your top," she said stroking her hands across his chest.

They sipped their wine without speaking. In a while he reached for her and they put aside their glasses.

Later, in bed, planning only to rest, they fell asleep in each other's arms.

At daybreak, again watching a sunrise America mused, "Marisa won't miss me because she and Carlos were getting up at seven to sail to Gibraltar. But for me to return home and be received by their maid, still wearing the clothes she pressed for me last night . . . tacky!"

"Impossible. But easily solved. Why would you return until this evening? By then my *casera* will have ironed your clothes and it will be the appropriate hour for you to wear them. As for what you will need to wear during the day . . ."

They were together day and night. Constantly she asked herself, *What am I doing having an affair with a married man? I should run, flee, end this!* But the joy of being able to experience happiness again, and such happiness, caused her to look only into his eyes.

She asked him about his marriage. He saw through the question. "I told you, and truthfully, you are not threatening my wife and our marriage. Ours was a marriage of convenience clearly understood by both of us. We have never been in love with each other."

"Never? Why would you marry someone without being in love?"

"That is a complicated and long story. I'll tell you one day. For now you need only to be assured that my wife and I are good friends and we try to be good parents and kind to each other. But our marriage ends there. As I pointed out at the beginning, I'm summering in Marbella and Magdalena is in Paris and will pass August in Mallorca. That isn't a marriage you can hurt."

It was the absolution she had needed.

They went horseback riding in the hills, drove through mountains, stopping at whitewashed *pueblos* burgeoning with hospitality. Almost all of the women they saw were dressed in black. Some men were missing an arm or a leg. "The war," Alfonso said. America had noticed that when Spaniards spoke of "the war" they meant the Spanish Civil War, not World War II. Loathing the subject Alfonso lurched into something else.

Other *pueblos* were semi-deserted as the new generation chose to move to the cities, or down to the coast and a more modern life. "In Guadalajara," Alfonso said, "there are *pueblos* completely abandoned. One could buy an entire town for nearly nothing." He said it with sadness that the old Spain—*pueblos* isolated from the rest of the world, without cars, electronics and electrical appliances— wasn't good enough anymore. "The young moved to big cities, the elders remained, expired, and then there was none."

Wherever they were, either Saturday night or on Sunday he went to church and heard Mass. Though she wasn't a Catholic, America accompanied him. After Mass one Sunday, she asked, "Alfonso, you're a married man, running around with a shameless

73

woman, yet you unfailingly go to church every week. Isn't there a contradiction somewhere?"

"Not for me. Yes, I'm a sinner. So I repent and ask God to forgive me."

"But can you ask to be forgiven the same thing every week?"

"I can ask. I'm hoping that God, who is all-knowing and all-understanding will forgive even me." He added, "If not, it's better than doubling my sins by not going at all. Jesus wants us to come to His house."

They drove to the north of Spain and stopped in the medieval town of Santiago de Compostela, in the heart of Galicia. They checked into adjoining rooms at "*Los Reyes Católicos*," a restored 15th-century convent, the oldest hotel in Spain and one of the loveliest. America unpacked and bathed.

Alfonso's door was open. He looked at his wristwatch. "The dining room is excellent but it won't be open for another hour."

"Great." Her eyes flashed. "Let's have explicit sex." She began unbuttoning his shirt. Their hands touched every part of the other's body, and when Alfonso entered her America felt that he was reaching to her soul.

Afterward, he looked at her stretched out along the bed. "I remember telling you that the sexiest look in the world was a body like yours in a black one-piece bathing suit. I was wrong."

Again their souls touched and there was nothing else in the world for either of them, nothing but the exquisite passion being fulfilled.

America asked, "Don't you worry about falling too much in love?"

"When one does not love too much, one does not love enough."

"How beautiful."

"Blaise Pascal wrote it centuries ago."

Hours had passed when Alfonso looked at his watch. "I think the dining room is closed."

She responded by rolling over, this time stretching out her body on top of his.

In bed, resting, she said, "Tell me about having eight children. That's a whole day camp." She joked, "Do you remember all of their names?"

"The eldest is José Maria, then Luis, Rafael, twin girls Maria del Mar and Carmen, Alfonso, Elena and Trinidad. José Maria is twenty-four and Trini is ten. I also remember the exact day, hour and minute when each of them was born."

"Do you have fun with them?"

He looked at her quizzically, considering the question. "No, not really. I love them, I often enjoy them, but I don't see myself as having fun with them. That's not my role. I see myself as their protector, their friend and instructor who is responsible for preparing them to navigate safely, and I hope happily, through life.

"José Maria, being the eldest and male, according to Spanish law and custom is my heir and will take over the bank and administer the family fortune and titles. I'm lucky to have three more boys giving me back-up successors. Men less fortunate than I have had a single son who turned out to be a disaster and the family ended up in ruins. Therefore I have been firm with my sons, insisting that they work hard and earn good grades." He was amused, "It can be expensive. I told José Maria that if he graduated from university among the top three in his class I would buy him an automobile. He graduated number one and told me he wanted a Porsche Carrera. I said I had been thinking in terms of a small Renault or Seat. He out-negotiated me, pointing out that I had not specified what level of car. So he drives a sensational Porsche.

"When he was fifteen I took him to the bank every Saturday. When he was eighteen I gave him his own office and opened an account for him with one million pesetas to invest, around ten or twelve thousand dollars then. I offered to help him if he wished and he frequently asked my advice on a given security." With obvious pride Alfonso recounted, "Six months after he graduated from Pamplona he gave me a check for the exact amount I had paid for his Porsche. He works in the bank and receives a modest salary but this was more than five million pesetas he had earned by investing cleverly."

"And the girls?"

"Magdalena tries to instill a sense of social consciousness, she teaches them manners and how to dress. I spoil them to death at every opportunity. We both keep on top of their religious upbringing. I go to Mass with the family every Sunday and religious holiday when I'm in Madrid. If I'm not, they go without me."

She mused, "Four boys and four girls. One more and you'd have a baseball team."

"There are many large families in Spain. Latins are a passionate people but also it was a matter of patriotism. In our war Spain lost nearly an entire male generation. General Franco appealed to the people to have large families in order to rebuild our population . . ." As he spoke of the war he seemed to be leaving her, his face darkening.

Then he became aware that with only momentary exceptions America's presence in his life had kept his mind off the past as nothing or no one before. He stroked her hair and the width of her shoulders. "We will awake from this dream in September. I will need to be back at the bank and with my family Mondays through Fridays. And you will be returning to Texas?"

"I can stay on a while longer—if you like. I don't want to complicate your life."

He hugged her. "We both know this isn't a summer romance. I'll fly here every Friday as long as you will stay."

* * *

Watching a bullfight, America was overwhelmed by the beauty and the power of the "brave bull" as he charged into the ring, so much stronger, larger and fiercer than the bulls on the ranch, but then she was appalled by the *picador* on horseback jamming a lance into the bull's neck, and then the *banderilleros* stabbing barbed, metal-tipped sticks into him, weakening the magnificent animal before he had even seen the bullfighter. "It seems like such an unbalanced, unfair sport."

"The *corrida* has nothing to do with sport. We are here to see a tragedy. The bull will almost surely die. This is a spectacle of life and death. There are among us those who consider it a national shame. I have read: 'The bullfight is indefensible, yet irresistible.' The novelist Vicente Blasco Ibañez wrote that the only beast in the bullring is the crowd. Still, it's a part of our culture. I do not know why we Spaniards are so involved with death, but we are. In Portugal it's different, there it's a sport, or a ballet, because they do not kill the bull. But we Spaniards kill. For centuries Spaniards killed Spaniards. Killing is a part of our nature."

They drove to the Rioja region and then to Ribera del Duero, where they sat in the cellars of the greatest Spanish wineries and ate *jamon de Jabugo* and local cheeses and became euphoric on love and stunningly grand wines. Wherever they were, Alfonso's total attention was focused on America. He was there to dine with her, to amuse her, to become intoxicated by her eyes, to cherish the glow of her skin, to feel profound pleasure in knowing that he was helping her through the pain of Angel—and as summer came to a close, to fall more deeply in love with her, while at the same time causing her to become so enamored with him as to lose track of reality, of that corner into which she was allowing them to paint themselves.

On September 1, Marisa, Carlos and the children left for Madrid, giving America use of their car, the house and the *caseros*, Juan and Maria, the husband and wife who looked after it. Juan spoke good English, having worked for Marisa's father during the ten years he was the Spanish Ambassador to Washington.

Alfonso, too, had to return to the bank and his family responsibilities during the week.

On Monday morning she walked along the beach, and when she returned Juan was standing on the lawn with a nun in the traditional black and white habit. "Señora," Juan continued in English, "this *hermana* is from Málaga, from a home called *Hogar San Carlos* and her work is to go to the houses on the coast asking for money to help the sisters in their work. She comes here every six months. I always give her five hundred pesetas. If you would be so kind, a thousand or two would help to feed and buy clothes and blankets for the little girls who have nobody."

"You mean it's a home for orphans?"

"Yes, little girls without parents."

"Juan, ask her to wait a moment while I go inside." She returned with her checkbook and asked him to write in the name of the home. Then America filled in the amount, a hundred thousand pesetas, around twelve hundred dollars.

Looking at it with incredulity and joy the nun began saying thank you in Spanish, asking God's blessings for her. America hugged her, stopping her. "Juan, please tell her there's nothing to thank me for. It gives me pleasure."

On Friday afternoon America met Alfonso at the airport. He was the first one off the plane. She stood where he could see her, and when he had she turned and went outside. Only within the privacy of the car did they venture a greeting. As she drove up the coast, following the curves of the beach, he sang to her,

> "Y VOLVER, VOLVER, VOLVER,
> A TUS BRAZOS OTRA VEZ.
> LLEGARÉ HASTA DONDE ESTÉS,
> YO SÉ PERDER, YO SÉ PERDER,
> QUIERO VOLVER, VOLVER, VOLVER."

"What does it mean?"

"'To return, to return, to return to your arms again. I'll arrive wherever you are. I know what it is to lose, I want to return, to return, to return . . .'"

Leaving for the office the following Friday, Alfonso kissed Magdalena on the cheek. "I won't be home for the weekend." She did not ask why.

That evening the dining table was set as always for Magdalena and Alfonso and their children. On Saturday and Sunday the dinner table was still set for ten though the place at the head remained unoccupied.

In the past Alfonso had been absent on occasional weekends, but Magdalena had kept his place waiting in case he came home early from minor indiscretions, and always he had. Now it was the second full weekend. None of the children had commented, and Magdalena wondered if it might be less awkward to acknowledge that he would be gone until Monday. Yet, she couldn't bring herself to tell the butler not to set Alfonso's place as she was hoping he would return.

Their second youngest, Elena, asked "Where is Papá?"

José Maria, the eldest, said quickly, "He's away on business."

Magdalena continued eating as if she had not just learned that her son knew that his father was unfaithful to her. And, distressed, she wondered how he reacted to it, did it hurt him? And how many others must know?

On the following Friday at dinner, again Elena asked, "Where is Papá?"

And again José Maria silenced her. "He's looking after one of our *fincas*, Elena. We have a lot of them. Obviously he can't be away from the bank during the week. He will be back on Sunday night."

In late October they were going to a *pueblo* near Seville to a *cacería*, a partridge shoot. Magdalena was playing golf in a charity tournament and wasn't fond of shooting. Alfonso advised America, "Dress warmly and do not wear bright colors that would frighten away the birds."

She brought a long, brown leather skirt and vest and a long, matching coat, a wonderful ensemble made for her by the famous

Spanish couturier, Mitzou, when she had been in Madrid for the baptism of Marisa's twins.

The shoot for wild quail, partridge and also pheasant that would be released from cages would start at nine A.M. and, with *Sevilla* being a four-hour drive from Marbella, they left the evening before, stopping to eat and to sleep at a grape growing *finca* that Alfonso owned. Dinner would be served by his *caseros*. It would be a simple meal, he told her, food grown on his land. And it was. Pork chops, green peppers, fried potatoes and a young local red wine. Nor was it formally served. It was homey and good. She sipped her wine, enjoying the peace and quiet of the *finca*, and as often happened, she couldn't help contrasting the life she had led in River Pine, where it was mandatory that everything always be the best. There was no pressure here. They had the best when it was appropriate and the not-so-best when it was not.

America was seated between a window and an open door. She wasn't yet aware of feeling a chill when Alfonso got up, closed the door and put his sweater around her shoulders. He lightly caressed her hair.

Wherever Alfonso was, there was a fire burning. He stood the logs on end so they would flame more, though they would burn out faster, what the simple Spaniards call a rich man's fire. And, as always, there was music. He had brought his cassette player and the tapes he had made of the popular songs he enjoyed most, those by Maria Dolores Pradera, Mari Trini, Rocio Durcal and Nino Bravo. Then, as if he felt they couldn't give America enough, he turned off the music and sang to her, romantically, and then amusingly about a little bull that had fallen in love with the moon.

As, she thought, had she.

In the morning Alfonso dressed in olive-green knickers and argyle socks with richly brown weatherproof shoes. He wore an olive shirt, necktie, jacket and cap. The muted color was standard for *cacerías* because the shooters blended into the foliage and therefore did not alert the birds. A *cacería* is an organized shoot whose members know exactly where the other guns are. It differs from American hunting, where there might be twenty independent hunters stalking game in the same woods without knowledge of the others, which makes it prudent to wear a bright shirt and cap.

They drove a few miles and came to a farm building, a large, once-white barn that appeared as if it would contain farm machinery and a hayloft. A few windows on the second floor had iron bars. America was surprised when Alfonso stopped and parked the car. It wasn't what she had expected as the seat of something so posh as a partridge shoot.

A woman, also in olive green, was standing outside as they arrived. Alfonso introduced, "My cousin Isabel, the Duchess of Viña Arcos. Miss Harvey, America Harvey." It was Isabel's shoot and she welcomed America in cultured English. "I'm sure you would like some coffee. The only negative factor of the *cacería* is the dreadful hour we must begin."

"I'd love some coffee, if it's not too much trouble."

Inside, the transformation was stupefying. The furniture was of museum quality. Everything had a patina of having been cared for over centuries. Windows of antique hand-blown glass had not been visible from below because the walls were a yard thick and the windows were mounted on the interior wall.

In a large salon were two paintings by Velázquez and one by Goya. Such art is catalogued by the Spanish government, considered national treasures and illegal to remove from the country. America expressed her surprise at the sharp contrast between the interior and exterior.

"The best security is no indication that wealth exists." Alfonso's face hardened. "In 1936, just before the war it could cost a man his life to be seen on the street while looking prosperous. In Spain today only the young, the newly rich and the imprudent show their money by driving Mercedes-Benzes and Rolls-Royces. The people you will meet here drive simple cars."

"Like your Renault."

"We cannot forget the bloodshed of '36. It's more comfortable for us to blend in with the masses and not be noticed."

Seeing that the subject pained him America turned to the paintings. "It's unbelievable to have such treasures hidden out here in the country."

"Isabel has more and better in her palace in Madrid. All the old Spanish families have them." Gesturing toward the Goya he explained, "That is an ancestor of Isabel. In the late 1700's and early 1800's, before he became the Court painter, Francisco Goya couldn't support himself selling the paintings that today are among the treasures of the *Museo del Prado*. So he took commissions for portraits. People seem to wish to immortalize themselves on canvas and as Goya adjusted his standards of artistic integrity to meet the demands of his stomach, he developed the reputation for being an excellent portrait artist. Velázquez was in much the same condition before he was appointed the Court painter for Felipe III." Looking at the woman in the Goya, Alfonso became mischievous, "She appears to be attractive, no?" He lowered his voice. "In fact, the then Duchess of Viña Arcos was the homeliest woman who ever lived in the entire nineteenth century. There's an expression in Spanish that was invented to describe her: *'la anti-dota contra la lujuria.'* The antidote to the sin of lust.

"Curiously, both Goya and Velázquez were willing to compromise their art for rich patrons, such as the Duchess, but never for the Kings and Royal Families that they later painted without flattery, in fact often with dangerously unerring harshness. Presumably they had a sense of history, they knew that their major works would become a part of our culture and with this they would not tamper."

He took her to the *comedor*, where breakfast was being served by white-gloved, liveried waiters, at a table that comfortably seated twenty. It had a damask cloth and centerpieces of silver sculptures of pheasant and partridges. It was set with silver serving plates and extra large breakfast coffee cups. Texas-sized. America was half-humiliated, half-amused as she remembered saying "if it's not too much trouble" for a cup of coffee. She had assumed the Duchess would have to go to the kitchen and ask the cook to make her a cup of coffee, as her own mother would have. What another world this was! As she was introduced to other guests she noticed that she was the only person there without a title, the only Miss. Everyone else was el Duque, la Condesa, la Marquesa, el Barón.

She realized that except for brief visits with Marisa she had never really been in a foreign country. When her parents had taken her to Europe they had seen Big Ben, the changing of the guard at Buckingham Palace, the Louvre, the Eiffel Tower, the Coliseum. But for all that she learned she could have watched travelogues. With Alfonso she was *meeting* people, she was exposed to different customs, she was *living* inside a foreign country.

A waiter passed a silver tray offering several kinds of sausage, ham and two rows of fried eggs, one of which had a crisp browned edge around the white of the egg, looking like lace, *encaje,* the others not. Taking two *"con encaje"* she planned to learn how to make eggs like that. Another waiter followed with a tray of *migas,* crumbled breadcrumbs soaked in milk then fried in olive oil with diced ham and garlic. Scrumptious! Another dish mandatory to learn.

Out in the field she stayed with Alfonso at his first post, a blind made of branches of trees and shrubbery to hide the shooters from the birds. The beaters chased the partridges ahead of them until they took off into the air. As they appeared overhead Alfonso fired with the first of three exquisite English-made shotguns loaded for him by two men called *secretarios* who sat behind him, loading, handing, loading, handing. He never looked down, keeping his eyes focused on the prey, firing both barrels, handing down the gun and having the next put in his hands as a scalpel is given to a surgeon. When the shooting at this post was over, at a signal from the approaching beaters all guns were lowered and the *secretarios* rushed out to collect the fallen birds.

While they were waiting, a fly landed on Alfonso's hand. He shuddered and made a violent, frenzied, finally successful effort to kill it. How strange, America thought, it was just a fly.

The birds were counted and all put together. Other than a few presented to each gun to take home they would be sold in the market.

They traveled in Jeeps and Range Rovers to the second post. There some of the vehicles provided trays of sliced *serrano* ham, *chorizo, manchego* cheese, and beer and red wine. After the fourth post they returned to the house for lunch before the final two posts.

Everyone removed their sturdy, waterproof boots. America looked at her fragile Robert Clergerie boots covered with mud, and her leather suit full of bramble scratches. But it had been a memorable morning.

At dusk, the shooting over, they gathered again in the house. In the main salon men and women sat together at card tables to play *Mus*, pronounced "moose," a Spanish game requiring a special deck and a lot of poker faces and bluffing. Sitting with Alfonso at a table of four were Carmen Franco, the only daughter of General Franco, and her husband, Cristóbal, the Marqués de Villaverde, a prominent heart surgeon. Like Alfonso they were among the best guns in Spain.

Later, seated at a fireplace with two other women, America observed Alfonso joking, winking at his partner, indicating he'd lied, a major part of the game. He always spoke to America in not perfect but charming English. Now, listening to him chatter on with his Spanish friends she understood that it cost him to communicate with her in a language that wasn't his own. She also felt badly that whereas in Texas she had a good sense of humor, in Spain she couldn't contribute anything. Her companions conversed with her in good English, but American slang or nuances wouldn't have been understood. They both had been among the "guns" and had shot expertly. One wore hunting-green breeches with sturdy knee-high leather boots—ideal against the brambles; the other had worn a suit with a cape, and they had wonderful green hats with small medallions on them from other *cacerías*. The meal, the ambience, the camaraderie were delightful. She planned that when she got home she would become expert with a shotgun and buy a fabulous outfit for the *cacería* if ever she came back to Spain.

When I get home! The thought struck her like so much buckshot. In three months Alfonso had become her home. Leaving him was unthinkable. Yet she had to go back. Jetways was her company, her responsibility. Though Gat and her parents had encouraged a change of environment, during recent phone calls she had begun to sense an attitude of when-are-you-coming-back?

Her airline ticket had the following week's date on it. She could change that. Stay on another week or a few more weeks. But that wasn't the point. She had no desire to leave, ever!

"Yesterday" seemed as though it had never been and she was desolate at the possibility that it would come again. She couldn't fathom that this wonderful movie she had been living was to end.

Yet she clearly understood the failure in logic. Everything she knew, had loved and been raised to understand, was in the life and the place to which she was due to return. To stay on was to abandon all that for weekends with a man who was married and would never divorce his wife. And with him came a different civilization, a foreign culture. Presumably she could learn to speak the language but could she ever learn the people, ever become at home in their ways, their centuries-old heritage? How could she ever understand growing up in Spain during the Spanish Civil War? Being titled, being a Monarchist? Moreover, she had her own heritage. By American standards America Harvey ranked as a Duchess. And she had always been comfortable with what she was, with knowing who she was and being adept in her natural role.

It was their last day together. They were on Alfonso's boat. Drifting, lying side by side in the sun Alfonso sang to her. She wished that Manolo were not there and that they could spend their last hours alone, out at sea, two bodies and souls becoming one again and, far more than that, remaining so forever.

They docked and were having lunch on the sidewalk terrace of Antonio's at *Puerto José Banus*. Not one of their more animated meals together. Loving the tenderness of the song he had sung to her she asked him to translate.

"It says 'there are times in life when we lose hope, and our boat and our love are shipwrecked; that for every smile there's always pain. To live: sometimes is to laugh, sometimes to cry.'"

"It's been the best few months I've ever known."

"That I do not urge you to stay does not mean it isn't what I would like more than anything in my life. It means only that I love you so profoundly that I give you your happiness at the cost of my own."

"I doubt that my former life is the way to my happiness."

"I would be wrong to influence you. Nor will I write to you. But I will love you always."

A family passed by with a screaming infant. Alfonso wondered aloud, "Why do children cry so much?"

She stared after them. "I guess we'd all cry a lot more if we weren't schooled against it. Every time you'd get hungry you'd cry. Every time you got tired you'd cry . . ." Looking at him her eyes were filling with tears.

"Every time you must say goodbye."

Chapter Five

America visited Angel's grave, her heart hurting as much as ever for her child and the life she could never have. She felt that God had given her Alfonso to lessen the pain, but then Alfonso was also impermanent. She rattled around in the sky above Texas, but all she was accomplishing was a waste of jet fuel. There was no happiness in the air anymore. She flew over her parents' ranch, hoping for the sight of the land to draw her back to her roots. She looked down at her pecan trees, and though she appreciated them they couldn't sing to her, they couldn't make her laugh, or cry, they couldn't stroke her body, they couldn't tell her they loved her.

She taxied to Jetways and went to her office. There was a ten-page expansion plan that Jerry had prepared for her, the sort of work she had always relished. She couldn't get into it.

The mail came in. For the eighth day she searched for an envelope with a Spanish postage stamp and bearing an engraved ducal crown with the letter T over it. Nothing. Understanding why, she missed him all the more.

She sat at her desk, thinking over the most exhilarating time of her life. Why shouldn't she have more? Why was she treating it as a lifetime decision? Though Angel had never been long out of her thoughts in Spain, here in the familiar surroundings the sadness was crushing her. She needed to be with Alfonso. Jetways was thriving under Jerry. Why not let him take over for a few more months? She called in her secretary. "I need a ticket and reservation to Málaga, on November third. Leave the return open."

The girl grinned, "Did you leave your toothbrush or something, boss?"

America gave her a look. *I sure did leave something there.*

"But you just got back," her mother protested.

Her father intervened, "Apparently a mite too soon." He looked at his daughter. It was a question.

"Yes, Daddy. Though I wouldn't have dreamed it possible, I was having a wonderful time and frankly I'd like some more. I'm not quite ready . . ."

They were at the dining table at the ranch for a family Sunday lunch that the Harveys had not anticipated would be their last together for quite a while.

Her brother interjected, "It's a man. You met a guy over there." He was smiling hopefully.

"That's right."

Eagerly he asked, "Is it serious?"

"Not really. He's married, he has eight children, he's a devout Catholic and he'll never get divorced."

Gat put down his fork and knife. "I can hardly believe you."

"I was pointing out that there's no danger. I'll be back. I was hoping that you'll look in on Jerry once a week."

"While you're off in Spain with some gigolo."

Albert looked at his son. "Careful, boy. When you put your foot in your mouth you'll find that leather's hard to chew."

America retorted, "I deserve better than that from you, Gat. He's no gigolo. He's a distinguished Spanish nobleman. A gentleman. Something you will agree with in five minutes if you meet him; someone you would admire and be delighted to have as your friend."

"And you're in love with him."

"Are you asking me or telling me?"

"I'm telling you you're nuts, is what. What are you doing, Ame? Okay, you had a surprise with J.J. and you were smart and extricated yourself. Fine. So now you've spent three months with a Spaniard, away from your family, your business, your friends, your own language and culture, everything in the world that a lucky person has. Have you forgotten: '*This is my own, my native land*'? I guess you have because now you're going back to bury yourself deeper into something with no future. I'm jubilant that you're able to fall in love. But Ame! There are *two hundred and fifty million Americans!* Don't you think that with the same effort you might find a terrific guy *here?* Granted that your friend over there's tops, first class. But I'm talking eligible. Someone you might make your life with. Not a foreign, married Catholic with eight kids."

America looked at her parents. She settled her eyes on her father's.

"Darlin', when you came back last week I told your mother, 'The kid hasn't looked this good in too many years.' I'm not keen on hooking up with foreigners, certainly under the conditions you have described, but I sure do like you looking happy again. However, take care of yourself and quit the game when you know you should. Even if it means taking your losses. Don't go for broke."

Her mother said, "I cannot agree with your father. I rejoice knowing you have found a reason to smile again. But I worry about a no-win emotional involvement. Be careful, child. Look at this warily before you fall into something that could hurt your heart."

"I have to go for a while. I'll be back for Christmas."

America understood that she was fortunate not to have become pregnant. There had been no thought of contraception, nor would it have been easily available in a Catholic country. But now, anticipating two months with Alfonso, not wishing to push her luck she went to a gynecologist and had herself equipped with an intrauterine device.

Alfonso was in his office in Madrid when his secretary, Mari Sol brought him a cable. Opening the envelope he unfolded the blue paper.

Y VOLVER, VOLVER, VOLVER,
A TUS BRAZOS OTRA VEZ.
LLEGARÉ HASTA DONDE ESTÉS
YO SÉ PERDER, YO SÉ PERDER
QUIERO VOLVER, VOLVER, VOLVER!

He could hear her voice, "I want to return, to return, to return to your arms . . ." and he put his head down on his desk.

The sky was sapphire blue, without a cloud, and the air felt soft and warm on her face as she stepped out of the front of the plane in Madrid. Alfonso was standing on the tarmac. An Iberia car brought them to the terminal building of Barajas Airport. He did not kiss her until they were alone in a private lounge. His looks, his arms, his mouth were even more than she had longed for.

While they waited for their flight to Málaga, America took Alfonso's hand in hers, "I understood but hated that you didn't write."

"I wrote a letter to you every day. I told you everything I did and thought of, how lonely my heart and body were for you."

"But I never received even one."

Alfonso handed her a packet of un-mailed envelopes.

Holding them, loving them before she had read a word, she said, "Darling, I'm only planning to be here for two months, so I'm not going to waste a minute of it. I'm not going to hem and haw . . ."

"Hem and haw?"

"Beat around the bush. What I'm saying is, I've got sixty days before I turn into a pumpkin."

"Stop!" He had both hands in the air. "Now *you* translate for *me*."

"Wow! There really is a culture gap! Okay, let me put it simply: if it had been me, instead of flying commercial to Málaga I would have hired a small jet and we would have joined the Thirty Thousand Feet in the Air Club."

"Believe it or not *that* I understand. I have heard of that. And I wish that I had thought of it. Since you left I have imagined you beside me every morning, every night. During business meetings you penetrated the matters at hand and I craved you. It cost me all the strength of character that I could summon to resist my desire to send you gifts, to mail the letters, anything to lure you back to me." He furrowed his forehead, "But I'm quite sure that in Spain we have no private jets available to rent."

Thinking how much she loved his seriousness reminded her of J.J.'s overly slick ways. She snuggled against him, "It was just a way of saying that I missed you and I love you and I'm so happy that I came back."

"If you had not, despite my incredible attempt at strong character, soon I would have gone to Texas to see you."

"That'd shake 'em up in San Antonio. 'I'd like y'all to meet my friend here, the Duke.'"

"Would I be funny there? Out of place? I'm something of a Texan, you know."

She tried to understand the joke.

"My family used to own Texas. Not all of it, but a large part. One of my ancestors was Pedro Menéndez de Aviles, who founded San Agustín on the northeast coast of Florida in 1565. It was the first colony in North America. He continued west, raising the Spanish flag as he went. Spain ruled what is now Texas until 1821, when we accepted Mexican independence. Then Mexico lost Texas to the United States when the two were at war in the 1840s..."

She was nodding her head, remembering the history of the discovery of North America. "You were there before we were."

"Of course."

Her eyes flashed merrily, "You'd hardly recognize it, Alfie. It's changed a lot."

On the flight to Málaga, America was seated at the window. Looking down at the terrain, she remarked, "There's a whole lot of undeveloped land down there."

"Yes. Much of it is mine."

America turned to him. He was entirely serious. She remembered Marisa telling her his full name and title: Alfonso García de las Arenas y de Beltran El Bueno, Duque del Castillo de Tarifa, and that he'd had a tragic past.

She said, "I know you as the man I love. But there's so much I do *not* know about you. Who are you? Where did you come from?"

Chapter Six

Alfonso's family blood did not begin turning blue until the year 710. Before then his ancestors worked the soil. But an extraordinary happening made it possible for them to begin accumulating the tracts of land, the castles, the palaces, and the noble titles that he would inherit twelve centuries later, in the 1900's. It began with a peasant named Beltran who worked a piece of land near the village of Tarifa. He kept a few animals and grew the food on which he and one son subsisted. Beltran had lost his wife during her second pregnancy and had never remarried. He delighted in his boy, teaching him everything he knew, squirreling away every coin he could in order to provide for his son's future.

Tarifa is the point on Spain's southern coast that is closest to Morocco. Thus, it was there that the Moors chose to land their invasion of Spain.

Though he was a farmer, Beltran was known to be a brave man, a natural leader with an extraordinary love of King and country, so he was put in charge of the Spanish troops and the Castle at Tarifa.

During one battle the Moors held up a white flag, the fighting paused, and their leader called up to the fort, "Beltran! We have your son. Surrender or I kill him."

Looking over the turret to the ground, Beltran saw his boy in the grasp of two Moorish soldiers. Holding a dagger high, their leader called out, "You have until the count of ten. Open the gates, lay down all arms or the boy dies by my hand."

There was silence. Then Beltran called out in a powerful voice. "Say your prayers, my son, you are my life, may God take your soul and love you. And God bless our beloved King and country." Then, drawing his dagger from the scabbard at his waist he threw the weapon to the ground and shouted, "If murder him you will, then use my own steel. But the Castle of Tarifa will never surrender."

The leader of the Moors seized Beltran's dagger, slashed the boy's throat, then plunged the blade into the child's stomach and ripped upward. Seeing this the Spaniards stormed out of the fortress. Fighting with superhuman strength born of the passion of rage they crushed the invasion and every Moor was killed or driven back into the sea.

Peace was restored. One day, while he was listlessly working his land, a royal courier arrived and addressing Beltran, a peasant, with extraordinary respect presented him with a letter from the King. The salutation was a term used among royalty, and by a monarch to a most trusted and high-ranking nobleman.

COUSIN,

I HAVE JUST BEEN INFORMED OF YOUR LOVE FOR ME AND OF THE TERRIBLE SACRIFICE YOU HAVE MADE IN MY DEFENSE. FOR THIS I GIVE OVER TO YOU AS YOUR PRIVATE PROPERTY, IN PERPETUITY, THE LANDS AND THE CASTLE OF TARIFA AND I WELCOME YOU TO MY COURT AS THE DUKE OF THE CASTLE OF TARIFA. FURTHER, BECAUSE YOU ARE A GOOD MAN HENCEFORTH WHEN YOUR NAME IS SPOKEN IT SHALL BE BELTRAN EL BUENO.

PLEASE COME TO SEE ME, AS I WOULD LIKE TO KNOW YOU PERSONALLY AND BESTOW UPON YOU OTHER GIFTS TO PROVE MY APPRECIATION OF YOU.

KING

Thus it began. The newly created Duke of the Castle of Tarifa married a noblewoman in a match made by the King. The marriage bore sons. Through centuries of wars the now-noble sons and descendants of Beltran El Bueno, "The Good One," fought at the sides of the Kings and Queens of Spain, which is to say quite a bit in front of them, and accumulated more royal gratitude, more lands, more privileges and noble titles all with *grandeza,* that rare and extra honor for special service to the crown.

The story of the patriotism of Beltran El Bueno was published in Spanish history books and taught to Spaniards in the centuries that followed and into modern times. Perhaps it inspired General Moscardó to make the same supreme sacrifice when his son was held outside Toledo's Alcázar during the Spanish Civil War.

A long line of male heirs ensured that the family name was passed along without interruption until some thousand years later when the final male "de Beltran El Bueno" failed to produce a son, and, instead, his daughter, Esperanza (Hope), inherited his estates and titles. She married an appropriate nobleman, a Baron named José Maria García de las Arenas y Montalban, but as hers was the more important title he became the Duke consort. However, as Spain was a patriarchal society he was for all intents and purposes the Duke of the Castle of Tarifa who would receive and care for his wife's inheritance and, in fact, have more power over it than she. In Spain even into the 1970's a woman couldn't sell a piece of property without her husband's consent, nor, technically, could she travel without his written permission.

In the autumn of 1922 Alfonso García de las Arenas y Beltran El Bueno was born in the palace that his parents, the Duke and Duchess of the Castle of Tarifa, occupied in Madrid, along with the Duchess' mother, the Marquesa del Olivo, who chose to use her own title rather than Viuda Duquesa del Castillo de Tarifa, the widow Duchess of the Castle of Tarifa.

The infant Alfonso took his father's family name of García de las Arenas, and in the Spanish custom honored his mother by using her family name as a second last name, thus Alfonso became García de las Arenas (for his father) y Beltran El Bueno (for his mother), which is the reverse of the Portuguese custom of putting the mother's name first because the child comes from the mother, this is sure—but who knows about the father?

The Duke was thirty, the Duchess twenty-three. They were both dark haired, tall, slim and strong. He had a ten-goal polo handicap and played the crucial number three position on King Alfonso XIII's team until Don Alfonso went into exile in 1931. The Duchess was one of Spain's better guns, a scratch golfer, a splendid horsewoman, the first Spanish woman to drive a car and one of the country's few woman bullfighters. Of course she did not fight in public, she did it for her own pleasure and to entertain friends on the ranches that raised Spain's brave bulls.

Alfonso, their first born and a male, under the Spanish law of primogeniture would one day become the thirty-second Duke of the Castle of Tarifa. He would inherit all the family titles as well as administer all the lands and properties, which—after twelve centuries of continuous accumulation and virtually no taxation—were incalculable.

Together the Duke and Duchess owned so many *fincas* throughout Spain, in Tarifa, Granada, Cordoba, Alicante, Seville, Toledo, Bilbao, Valencia, and San Sebastian as well as half of Guadalajara and much of Extremadura, that many of them had not been seen by a member of the family in centuries. The reason was the lack of roads: most of their farms and ranches had to be reached from the nearest town by paths so rough and narrow that they were suitable only for a person riding a donkey. Dukes and Duchesses did not ride donkeys and one wouldn't endanger a good horse on such treacherous footing.

There was usually a main house kept in readiness in hope that the master might one day hazard a visit. The peasants who worked the land, the shepherds and their families lived in *chozas*, huts they made of thatch, cardboard and anything they could find that would block out the elements. They had no running water or electricity, and in winter their only heat was from smoldering charcoal *braseros* placed under a table with a heavy cloth that reached to the floor and held the heat within the area where they could keep their feet and legs warm.

As the Castillo de Tarifas (one's title is often used as the family name because it's easier than a mouthful like . . . los García de las Arenas y de Montalban y de Beltran El Bueno y Sánchez del Castillo) did not visit most of their *fincas,* once a year the tenant farmer from each of the family's properties would journey across the country and arrive in Madrid's oldest residential section at the palace of the Duke of the Castle of Tarifa, ride up the long driveway to the front entrance and, while still mounted, call out, *"Señor Duque! Aqui estoy!"* "Duke, I'm here."

The Duke was delighted to receive the tenant in one of the palace's salons because the farmer's mission was to pay his share of the income, and for that purpose he had brought with him a canvas moneybag as plump as a pumpkin, filled with coins and bills. He had also brought, on a second donkey, apples, cheeses, a baby lamb or suckling pig, olive oil, wine, depending on what the *finca* produced. The Duke then listened to the ritualistic excuses of lack of rain and poor market conditions, intended to justify the *finca* producing less income than what it should have been. The Duke knew very well that the farmer was cheating him, as the farmer's father and grandfather had cheated the Duke's father and grandfather, but it wasn't a bad living for doing nothing, and it was better than making that miserable journey and staying on for months in isolated, primitive farm areas, to oversee the work about which he knew nothing anyway. The Duke, like his father and grandfather before him, had more money than he or the generations to come could possibly use and he wanted to enjoy it, thus he saw no logic in devoting his life to working for still more money that he would have no time to spend. An alternative was to hire a knowledgeable overseer to travel from *finca* to *finca,* but though the overseer would protect the Duke from the farmers, who would protect the Duke from the overseer? One financially sophisticated man in control of twenty major properties would eventually be stealing even more than twenty simple farmers. It was a case of the thief you know being better than the thief you do not know. Besides, it had been done this way for centuries.

While the Duchess rode and golfed and pursued a busy social life with her husband, her mother, the Marquesa del Olivo, managed the palace. No noblewoman would be seen stirring out of her quarters before noon. But at that hour every morning (in Madrid, twelve o'clock noon was still morning) the Marquesa went to the courtyard, where the servants were assembled for inspection. They were maids, manservants, chefs, kitchen workers, seamstresses, ironers, nannies' maids (Nannies obtained from the Britannic Nanny Registry in London, as well as its French and German counterparts, did not wash clothes or do housework) coachmen, grooms, gardeners and the floral designer with whom the Marquesa worked daily in the flower cutting room. A house of that size—it was set on a square city block—needed someone akin to a general to run it, and the Marquesa was equal to the job. Perhaps she inherited her ability to command and to act decisively along with her title, which dated back to the year 712, when the Moors first occupied a part of Spain. During the resistance her ancestor decapitated three hundred and sixty Moors, using the stump of an olive tree for a chopping block. The King thought that dispatching three hundred and sixty of his enemies was an awfully good show and rewarded him with the title of Marqués del Olivo, the Marquis of the Olive Tree.

The butler, Calixto, who was in charge of the staff, required no inspection: he was reliably perfect. He stood at the Marquesa's side. All of the manservants had to be approximately six feet tall, slender but strong, and attractive. Their uniforms were made to measure by the Duke's own tailor in the house colors, racing-green and yellow. Their vests were of green and yellow stripes and their jackets and tailcoats dark green with yellow velvet collars, their trousers black. Dressing servants in the house colors was done by all the noble families. The maids wore traditional daytime and nighttime uniforms with white lace caps. When they served food or beverages all servants wore white gloves.

The Marquesa, carrying a jewel-headed walking stick that she used as a pointer, scrutinized the uniforms for missing buttons, shoes that did not shine, shirts and gloves that were not sparkling white, and she wouldn't hesitate to say, "Juan . . . your shoes . . . oof! They smell terrible. Don't you wash your feet?"

"*Sí, Sra. Marquesa,* often."

"Then wash them *more* often. And throw away those shoes. Go to the Duke's quarters and have his man give you two pair of his shoes and change them twice every day . . . Ramón, your shirt is wrinkled. Take it to the ironing room . . ." There was no unkindness intended or taken in these orders. Rather, in the early 1900's in Spain it was good fortune to have a position in a palace like that. The house of the Castle of Tarifa never lost a servant they wanted to keep, and there was a long list of applicants for every job.

During meals the Marquesa kept a pad and pencil at her side and made a favorable or negative comment on every dish. She had three chefs, one trained in Madrid, one in Segovia, the other in Barcelona. They were sent to France, Germany, Italy and Switzerland to learn the cuisines of other countries. When one returned, another traveled.

The Marquesa lunched promptly at one-thirty, very early for Madrid; the Duke and Duchess at three-thirty, a more likely Spanish lunchtime, because he was occupied with polo practice almost every morning and she with riding or playing golf.

Other than for a good morning and good night kiss it was the custom among these Spanish families for their children to be raised entirely by governesses, but the Castle of Tarifas were among the exceptions. They often invited their children to lunch with them and took them riding or shooting.

The Marquesa adored her grandchildren and when they were not with their parents she invited Alfonso and his younger-by-one-year twin sisters Cayetana and Cristina del Mar, to lunch with her. Often she would take them on her daily carriage ride along *El Paseo de la Castellana,* Madrid's main artery, a modern, broad boulevard on which were the city's new, palatial homes.

Her son-in-law owned two Rolls-Royces, both painted racing green with black roofs and fenders, his *escudo,* or shield, bearing his coat of arms painted onto the doors with his ducal crown and the letter T for his title, under it. But cars were a new thing in Madrid and even those who could afford them preferred their horses and carriages. Though the Duke had many carriages, the Marquesa kept her own and a team of four matched dark bay horses. Her daily trip across town was for the purpose of calling on friends, though she never descended from the carriage. She would tell the coachman which houses she wished to visit and upon arrival give the footman her calling card, after having bent down one corner of it that meant "I'm thinking of you," or a different corner that meant "I wish to have a visit with you one day soon." After an hour or so of this socializing she returned home and rested.

The children had their own wing of the palace. When not invited to lunch with their parents or *abuela,* grandmother, they and their governesses were served the midday meal in their own dining room by two manservants. There were three governesses, "Miss," "*Mademoiselle*" and "*Schwester,*" who spoke to them in their respective English, French and German. The children never saw the inside of a school or a barbershop or a haberdashery. Everything came to them. The whole family went to Madrid's Cathedral of San Isidro every Sunday. Their palace had its own chapel and the family priest, Padre Tomás, came by every morning so they could hear Mass. Often their parents slept through this theological exercise but the children's religious formation was taken most seriously.

In their playroom was a spring-powered carousel of four carved wooden horses with saddles and manes and tails. A strong footman wound it every day. It had been popular with them until they were old enough to ride real horses. But one plaything that continued to delight the girls throughout their childhood was a gift from the King, a table-sized music box with six ballerinas, each a foot high. They had wardrobes of embroidered dresses and a repertoire of ten dances, each with its own music.

Alfonso had male schoolteachers, and Cayetana and Cristina had female instructors. The girls did not study arithmetic because they would never need to know about money and accounts. They learned French, German and English in conversation with their governesses and were taught Spanish grammar, literature, history and art appreciation, though the latter would have come naturally in a house in which all furniture, paintings, porcelain collections, rugs and silver were of museum quality.

Ski resorts had not yet been established in Spain and as travel to Switzerland was difficult that sport wasn't a part of their curriculum. But the children had professional instruction for golf, tennis, and riding, and all of them were taught to shoot from the age of eight.

Alfonso was an adept pupil with shotgun and rifle. His father guided him. "You must practice and practice until you can hit the animal exactly where the bullet will penetrate and he'll die immediately. Generally this is in the head. Or, if the skull is dense, as in the case of a *jabalí*, a wild boar, then through an eye. If you are not that accurate then the animal, though wounded, may live to kill you." He made targets and practiced with the boy until Alfonso could hit coins tossed in the air.

Frequently the Duke took him on a shoot, occasionally for wild game, and was rewarded by his son's nerve and expertise. More than once, the young Alfonso faced a *jabalí* thundering through the brush at him, but he stood his ground, firing at the animal's head until it fell, more than once as close as only a yard away.

One craft was taught to Alfonso alone, by his father: the sewing of leather. Not to Cayetana and Cristina, only to Alfonso. No reason was given as to why this noble child must know how to sew leather—as if one day he might need to repair his own saddle—but the leather sewing lessons were mandatory. Once a month the Duke visited the children's quarters and asked to see Alfonso's stitching and they would work on it together.

When they had finished their daily studies they and their favorite nanny, "Miss," would get into a *tonneau* drawn by a single horse with a coachman and ride along La Castellana, stopping here and there to play with friends. There was little automobile traffic, and in the center of the broad boulevard were two wide expanses of grass on which the children played, tended by their nannies, who wore long plaid uniforms with stiffly starched white cuffs and collars.

In the afternoons, when not with their parents, they went by car to a *finca* just outside Madrid owned by their bachelor uncle, Guillermo. Tio Guillermo had a steeplechase course and the three children rode horses over it for hours. They also shot clay pigeons there. Today the *finca* of Tio Guillermo still stands as a residential property though it's surrounded by industrial complexes. This valuable land on the outskirts of a world capital remains undeveloped because Tio Guillermo felt that a gentleman wouldn't sell his land to have it defiled by factories or paint shops, and it was thus stipulated in his *testamento*.

Weekends for the Duques and their children were almost all spent outside of Madrid, visiting the properties that amused them. They held a *cacería* once a year at each of these during the fall shooting season, inviting from twelve to a maximum of twenty guns. Though they loved to shoot and be hospitable to their friends the Duke and Duchess put a high priority on conserving the game, giving the birds and animals a chance to recreate. Never would they have a second shoot on the same *finca* in any given year, unless the King requested it. But, of course, the King would not.

Among the Grandees, entertaining at home in Madrid was the mainstay of social life. Good restaurants did not exist and nightclubs were only for whores and those men who wished to meet them. During the week it was dinner parties, exclusively Spanish society that was small and impenetrable. They were all Grandees, almost two hundred of them, Dukes and Duchesses because Dukedoms automatically carried *grandeza,* plus various Barons, Counts and Marquis whose titles had been given *grandeza* by the King who had bestowed them. The table seating was always according to Court Protocol, the importance and age of a title being the arbiter. A Count whose title dated back to the year 1100 would go ahead of a higher title, Marques, whose title was only a few hundred years old. The Grandees respected rank; they liked knowing where they belonged. Place cards would have been superfluous. Arriving in the dining room everyone went directly to his and her proper seat. The result was that one almost always sat between the same persons. This explains the serving of meals as rather more rapid than lingering because the moment the guests rose from the table for coffee and cognac they were free to mingle with whom they chose.

The late Duke of Windsor, while still the Prince of Wales, visited Spain frequently for the shooting, and he would have enjoyed his meals while seated between a pair of ravishing *señoritas*. However, the inflexible Court Protocol always placed him between the same two elderly most important Duchesses, who, to his dismay, had inherited their titles in the previous century, rather than perhaps six months ago, at the age of eighteen following "the untimely death of the mother Duchess." The Prince of Wales eventually forsook the marvelous shooting that Spain offered. The price was too high.

During May and June every great palace in Madrid gave a ball, the last of which finished the social season—to say nothing of the socialites. As the Duke did not work and as the children did not have to wait for school terms to end the family did not remain in Madrid after the social season, when it became hot and uncomfortable. The palace was closed in June and the family boarded a train to San Sebastian in the north of Spain en route to their favorite property, *Los Escalones*. The most privileged left Madrid in June. The slightly less privileged were able to get away in July. None of the aristocracy remained in the city during August. They all had beach homes in the north and south of Spain or the Balearic Islands. Some summered at the Palace Hotel in Biarritz for the gambling.

The Castillo de Tarifas did not travel within Spain enough to warrant owning a private railroad car. Many years before, to prevent the French from invading Spain by rail, the Spanish trains had been built with a wider wheelbase than French trains, and consequently Spanish trains couldn't be used on the French railroad tracks. So, unable to traverse the Continent, it was hardly worth the trouble of furnishing, decorating and maintaining what was, in effect, another home. When they traveled they rented a private railroad car.

The servants went to the station in advance of the family so the maids could remake the beds with the house's own linens, put out the towels, the rugs, the virgins, crucifixes, framed pictures and other comforts, much as if the Duke and Duchess and the children were in their own bedrooms in Madrid.

The manservants prepared the dining area the family would use, setting the tables with their own linens, flatware, crystal and china brought aboard in wicker hampers, along with the foods and wines they would serve. All luggage was dark green leather with yellow stripes and bore the ducal crown above the letter T.

When the train arrived in San Sebastian automobiles, which had been driven ahead for the purpose, were waiting to take them to the *finca* forty minutes away. There was a good road between the city and *Los Escalones*. As automobiles were a rarity in Spain, repair stations did not exist. Therefore one traveled with a mechanic, which explains why even today in Spain one's driver is called a *mecánico,* except for the pretentious, newly rich who have "chauffeurs".

Los Escalones was a property of fifty thousand hectares. On its highest ground was a castle built in the sixteenth century by an ancestor, a Count, whom one could argue to have been either an eccentric or a pragmatist. For security he wanted his bedroom six stories above the ground. The Count excessively enjoyed drinking, as well as he enjoyed drinking excessively. Who, then, in that end-of-the-evening glow would like to nullify it by hiking up a few hundred stairs to his bedroom? As riding a horse was the Count's natural state, something he could do safely in whatever condition, he wished to be able to ride his horse to his bedroom. Therefore he had a staircase built with each stair six feet deep and easily climbed by a horse. Thus the name: *Los Escalones,* the stairs. The castle had since been modernized with plumbing and electricity. A kilometer away from the castle was the family burial place.

When it was hot the children were driven to the beach of San Sebastian. They played in the sand but swimming wasn't one of the sports taught them. They loved the ocean but after a one-minute dip in the surf the nannies, clad in their dresses and stockings (in those days Spanish women bathed in below-the-knee swimsuits and hose), waded out, extracted the children from the water, bundled them up in robes and braced them each with a shot of quinine.

In the summer of 1933, when Alfonso was thirteen and Cayetana and Cristina were twelve, though the girls rode as well as he and he enjoyed their company, he began ducking out on the governesses whenever possible. Alfonso yearned to protest, "Stop telling me to say this or that. I have a thousand years of manners in my blood," but he wouldn't be rude, and he was wise enough to know that the future Duke of the Castle of Tarifa wasn't yet out of danger of being turned over someone's knee. Alfonso could listen endlessly to the history of his country, or of his family; he would work for hours with his golf pro; he practiced daily with both shotgun and rifle. But the nannies' harping and reminding was tedious, so while he had the freedom of the *finca* he would take a horse and get away. In Madrid, for security, he and the girls couldn't leave the grounds without a nurse and a coachman or footman, whereas on the *finca* the family was completely safe. If any stranger set foot on the land without having business there the peasants would run them off.

As Alfonso rode his horse past a *choza* the shepherd's wife curtsied and the shepherd, a short, powerfully built man removed the beret he wore and threw it to the ground. Alfonso wasn't surprised nor did he like or dislike the exaggerated gesture of respect. It was how life was. He rode on. But what did surprise and please him was seeing a boy who appeared to be about his own age. He looked familiar yet Alfonso had not seen him before. He was obviously the son of the shepherds. Eager for another boy's companionship Alfonso dismounted.

The shepherd rushed over, "Can I do anything for the Señorito?"

The "young master" replied, "I would like to greet your son. May I?" It was a rhetorical question.

Astounded that the Señorito would be interested in speaking to his son he commanded, "Paco," and the boy ventured forward.

"Hello, Paco. I'm Alfonso."

Timidly Paco accepted the outstretched hand. They each smiled and their hands gripped firmly.

Alfonso loosened the girth on his horse, tied him to a tree in the shade and he and Paco sat on the grass and talked about the *finca*, its animals, the vegetables it grew. Steadily Paco gained confidence and he spoke in detail about the *finca* of which Alfonso knew little and was therefore impressed.

They threw stones for distance and accuracy, and the result was pretty much a draw.

From then on they were inseparable except on those days when Alfonso's father took him shooting, and at lunch and at night, when Alfonso, back at the castle, was served a six-course meal by two manservants and fell asleep in a linen-covered, canopied bed, while Paco ate goat cheese and slept on a pallet of straw on the dirt floor of the *choza*.

"What do you and the Señorito talk about?" the shepherd asked, awed by his son. "You have nothing in common, he's a nobleman, we are people of the soil."

Paco told him the varied subject matter they touched on but he couldn't convey why two boys of roughly the same age but with such different backgrounds would have developed such camaraderie. Paco had come to love Alfonso as a friend and he told this to his father, which he saw made the older man uncomfortable.

Alfonso, meanwhile, told his father, "Papá, I have a friend on the *finca* and I was amazed to see that the *choza* in which he and his family live has no electricity. And it has a dirt floor. What do they do in the winter when it rains?"

"They get wet. They are accustomed to it. They have never known anything else."

"And we live in a palace. Papá, why couldn't we provide better homes and electricity for the people who work our lands? We have the money, no? And they must have terribly uncomfortable lives."

The Duke was interested in this child of his who was almost surely the first of their family in a thousand years to have a social conscience. "Most of the people in the world have uncomfortable lives," he replied. Yet, he had been thinking lately, the current unrest in Spain surely was caused by the disproportionate distribution of the nation's wealth. There were a few very rich and many, many painfully poor, a situation that had, historically, been dangerous for the very few. He did not fear the people who worked his lands, indeed he had a warm feeling for them and he wanted them to feel the same toward him and his family. But giving them homes with stone floors and electricity . . . and what then? Radios and electric heaters?

"*Alfonsito*, you're a nice boy with a good heart but if we were to fix your friend's *choza* we would have to do the same with twenty-five others on *Los Escalones*. Nor would it work. If we gave them cement floors they would be colder and less comfortable on the stone than on the soil. And if we gave them electricity and electric heaters that they have never known they would sweat while they are inside then go out into the cold and become ill. Don't change their lives. They are comfortable, for them, as they are."

Cayetana also liked to take a horse and gallop across their lands. But her reason was different. She was a free spirit. On a warm day, as she rode, confident that she was nowhere to be seen by anyone, she unbuttoned her shirt and, enjoying the breeze against her skin and her recently emerging breasts, she forced her horse into a canter despite the heat and the sweat that was curling the animal's hair. Her first interest always was in what she desired and through force or guile she always got what she wanted.

Breaking into a clearing she saw a boy picking vegetables. At the sound of the horse's hooves he turned and looked up. Cayetana was about fifty feet away. It was too late for her to cover herself, and surely he would look away and she could simply gallop past.

But the boy stood transfixed. He had never seen anything so beautiful as this woman child on a galloping horse and it did not occur to him that he shouldn't look. He knew only that he should remove his cap, which he did at once, throwing it to the ground as a mark of respect.

Outraged to be discovered thus, Cayetana pulled her horse to a halt beside the boy. Her face burning red, her riding crop in her hand, she leaned down and whipped him across the shoulders with all her athletic strength. He yelped in pain, and, as he did Cayetana sensed something warm and distinctly enjoyable within her. The boy started to run away. Cayetana followed him on horseback, easily overtaking him and again she leaned down and whipped him across his fleeing back. She shouted, "Halt. I order you." The boy obeyed. As he stood still she walked her horse in a circle around him. She knew that she should leave, that she had acted unpardonably, but she had an overwhelming desire to see the damage she had inflicted. "Remove your shirt." The boy hesitated. She raised her whip. He tore at his shirt, breaking the buttons loose, and let it fall to the ground. Cayetana gazed at two burning-red welts, one across his shoulder, and the other across his back. They exhilarated her. Excited her.

Fearing what might happen to him next the boy looked up.

"How dare you! How dare you stare at me? Bend over."

The boy shook his head pleadingly.

"Bend over or I'll whip your face."

Believing she would, knowing he couldn't outrun her, the boy bent over. "Don't dare move," she ordered, and circled her horse until she was on his left. Cayetana raised the whip and brought it down hard against his buttocks. He stiffened from pain. She warned, "I forbid you to move." She dismounted, and placing herself in a better position to punish him, she lashed at his behind, crisscrossing the blows, imagining the pain she was inflicting through his thin trousers. She guessed he was too poor to be wearing underwear, that he would feel it all the more, and that made it all the better.

She mounted her horse again. "Now you may look at me." The boy was too afraid. "I command you."

He looked at her face, trying not to focus on her body, but she knew he couldn't help but see her bare chest. She remained silent, forcing him to see but not look at her nakedness. Finally, knowing that she dared go no further, she said, "If we meet again, and if again you display your ill manners, it will go much worse for you," and she turned her horse and galloped away.

Paco did not tell Alfonso of this meeting. It would have outraged his friend and embarrassed them both. Alfonso had told him he had two sisters. She was, obviously, one of them. What a difference! Better to forget it. He and Alfonso continued to spend happy days together.

Alfonso regretted leaving Paco in order to go home for lunch. He again spoke of his friend to his parents. "I've been teaching him to ride and he's doing incredibly well. Even to his posture on the horse. He may be a peasant but after only a few days he looks like a *caballero*, a gentleman. I feel uncomfortable leaving him at midday. I imagine they have little to eat. Mamá, may I bring him home to lunch?"

"Of course, *querido*. Bring him tomorrow."

That night Alfonso foresaw a problem. Paco's clothes. His shirt and short pants were made from the cloth of flour sacks and his shoes were *alpargatas*, sandals the poor made out of a strip of rubber cut from an old bicycle tire, or lacking that, of woven cord. Paco would walk in looking like a peasant, he would feel like one and he might be treated as one.

In the morning when Alfonso arrived at the *choza* riding one horse and leading another for his friend as he had been doing all week, he also had a package and he was nervous.

At the sound of the horses Paco came running out. He tightened his horse's girth and mounted in a single fluid movement. Alfonso was silent.

"What's wrong?"

"Nothing. My parents have invited you to come home with me to lunch today."

Delighted, he said, "Thank you."

"There's nothing to thank me for."

"Who gave them the idea to invite me?"

"Well . . . we're friends aren't we?"

"Of course."

Alfonso paused. "I'm hoping that we are good enough friends so that if I say something clumsy or stupid you won't be offended."

Paco laughed at the impossible idea.

Without any of his normal poise Alfonso blurted, "Would you mind very much if I made you a present of some clothes? We're the same size and I have a great many more than I need."

Paco's instinct, his intelligence, caused him to understand exactly. He realized what it had cost his friend to do this. "I'm grateful to you. Why don't I wear them today? In fact, what would you think about us having a wash before I get dressed?"

They rode to the lake and removed their clothes.

Alfonso held up a cake of soap and two towels.

Paco stared curiously at the oval-shaped white ball. "What's that?"

"Soap."

"Soap?"

"You get yourself wet then rub it on your skin and in your hair and it helps to make you cleaner and to make your hair shine and smell nice."

Paco took it in his hand, held it to his nose and inhaled deeply. "Like the flowers in the fields all in one."

As neither knew how to swim they waded around the edge so that Paco could wash. Though a nanny had bathed Alfonso just a few hours before, he made a point of washing himself thoroughly. They dried themselves with towels from the castle, thick terry cloth that caused Paco to smile at the amazing way in which it absorbed the water from his body. The clothes fit as if they had been made for him. Remounting their horses they galloped toward the castle, across the fields and the boundaries of social classes.

Alfonso worried that Paco would be insecure, even servile, and he feared that his family might possibly be cavalier. Especially Cayetana, whom he knew to be unpredictable. He hoped for the best.

"This is my sister, Cristina del Mar. Cristina, this is my friend Paco."

Cristina kissed him on both cheeks. It's the custom in Spain for children to kiss friends when they enter or leave the house on the theory that if they were not family friends they wouldn't be there. Cristina thought Paco was the handsomest boy she had ever seen.

Introduced to Cayetana, despite the tremor in his stomach, he said, "I'm happy to meet you."

She offered her hand to shake, looking at him coolly, yet, as only he could understand, relieved that they had avoided the necessity of explaining how they knew each other.

Alfonso introduced Paco to Padre Tomás, who always summered with the family and took his meals with them.

The Duke and Duchess of the Castle of Tarifa kissed Paco hello, and Alfonso thought, *How could I ever have worried about my parents? He could have come in his own clothes and they would have treated him well.*

On the other hand, though they had greeted Paco with warmth and sincere welcome, the Duke and Duchess couldn't refrain from looking at him curiously, as if they recognized this boy whom they had never before seen.

Seated across the table from Paco, who was at his mother's left, Alfonso suddenly knew why his friend had looked familiar. He was the image of Alfonso's father.

What Alfonso couldn't know was that the boy he had been drawn to and had befriended was his half brother, the product of a union between the Duke of the Castle of Tarifa and the shepherdess, Paco's mother.

Being a Grandee of Spain carried numerous privileges, among them the convenience of a Diplomatic Passport and the right to wear a hat in the presence of the King. There were others, long out of use but a bit more imaginative. Some nobles were granted the *Derecho de Entrar a Caballo con Espuelas de Plata,* the right to enter a church on horseback while wearing silver spurs. But the more widespread privilege that caused Paco to have noble blood in his veins was the *Derecho de Pernada,* the right of the master to sleep with all the virgin peasant girls of his *finca*—not indiscriminately, only on their wedding eves.

This right derived during the fourteenth century—Spain had not yet been united into one nation by *Los Reyes Católicos,* the Catholic Kings, Ferdinand and Isabella—when the King of Castile was informed that one of his most valued subjects, the Duke of Pernada, had been badly beaten by a peasant who had caught the master trying to bed his fiancée. The King knew of his friend Pernada's appetite for young virgins and worried that once recovered from this beating he would again be on the prowl. And now that a peasant had established the precedent of rising against his master, the King had to take steps to protect his friend, and to avoid the necessity of punishing other justifiably indignant peasants who beat up their masters. Therefore, the King decreed *El Derecho de Pernada,* making it the legal right of the master of a Dukedom or even of a major *finca* to sleep with any maiden on his land on the night before her wedding. As his friend owned vast lands populated by a thousand families, consequently as rich in young virgins as in cattle and wheat, his appetite could surely be satisfied without further danger of uprisings. The King also did a clever bit of marketing, making it known that it was an honor for a peasant girl to be introduced to adulthood by the master of the land that had weaned her and that she would faithfully serve throughout her life. And so it was that young couples in Spain expected these prenuptial visits, and even came to feel somewhat blessed.

El Derecho de Pernada flourished during the fifteenth through the eighteenth centuries. But by the late 1800's the peasants were beginning to see themselves less blessed than fucked. Thus, no longer feeling entirely welcome, fewer landowners were invoking this privilege. The Duke of the Castle of Tarifa was one of the last still claiming his rights as late as 1922.

Looking across the table at her husband and at the boy who was his replica, the Duchess deduced that 1922 was when it had occurred, the summer when she was carrying their first child and when they had been at *Los Escalones* before Alfonso's arrival in September.

"Paco, dear, when is your birthday?"

"May tenth, Sra. Duquesa."

"And what year was it?"

"In 1923, Sra. Duquesa."

The Duchess smiled at the Duke. Daggers.

The Duke was remembering the night Paco had been conceived. He was fascinated. This boy who lived in a *choza*, brought up by peasants, clearly had the characteristics of a nobleman, everything except what even a noble child had to be taught, such as the use of a knife and fork. The boy had innate nobility in the way he sat, the way he moved. There was nothing peasant- like about his figure. His torso was long, his legs strong yet slim. He wasn't built close to the ground as the result of ancestors whose bodies were for centuries crushed down from trudging under heavy burdens. No, Paco had escaped his mother's genes; the blood running through his veins was from his aristocratic ancestors, who had ridden through time on horseback.

The Duke was saddened that he couldn't acknowledge his son, that the boy couldn't bear his name, that he couldn't give him one of his titles. But that was impossible! It would humiliate his wife, and it would disrupt the family for his children to suddenly learn they had an illegitimate half brother. He had inadvertently given Paco a lot, and now he would find ways to discreetly give him more tangible help.

Cristina had an immediate crush on Paco and hoped that Alfonso would let her come along when they went riding. She was a fine horsewoman and had a craving to impress Paco.

Cayetana wished she had never met him and that he would disappear. This was all too close for comfort.

Alfonso was relieved that the meeting had gone so well. He sensed a chill running from his mother to his father, but the Duchess was genuinely warm toward Paco and clearly the Duke liked him. It did not occur to Alfonso that the similarity in appearance had anything to do with family, was anything more than a coincidence.

Paco was exhausted. Entering the castle he had understood that he knew nothing of this life and he yearned not to embarrass Alfonso. Until they had met, Paco had never imagined a life other than the sheep and the *choza*. His family had no radio as cheap ones made with transistors did not yet exist, they were not educated and able to read newspapers, nor could they afford to buy magazines and look at the pictures. They knew only what they saw around them. Paco had seen *el castillo* in the distance every day of his life without ever wondering about it. The castle had never had anything to do with him. He knew that the owners of the land they worked had complete power over their destinies but it was a benign domination.

Though the experience was exciting it was difficult. He had never eaten with a knife or fork. He and his parents used their fingers to take food from a common eating bowl, which his mother filled at mealtimes for the three of them. Fortunately the Duchess, Padre Tomás and the two girls were served first, and as the Duchess said, "Start eating or the food will get cold," he had the opportunity to observe them remove food from the silver tray the butler passed, then pick up their cutlery. When the tray was offered to him he successfully served himself but then he picked up his knife and fork in the wrong hands.

Gently, the Duke said, "Hold them in reverse, Paco."

Embarrassed, he apologized.

Alfonso explained, "You have nothing to apologize for. There are a lot of things I wouldn't know how to do unless somebody showed me. Papá wanted to help you, to teach you, as Cayetana and Cristina and I were taught."

Paco looked at the Duke, "Thank you, Señor Duque," but he was really speaking to Alfonso. He watched the others, trying to copy what they did and he handled the fork and knife remarkably well considering that he had never seen flatware in his life. By the end of the meal—though he had not eaten as much as he would have liked, and he was drained from the effort of trying not to embarrass Alfonso, though it was all foreign, all strange, though he was tense—he had enjoyed it. He had a sense of belonging, and the feeling that he would be there again.

Chapter Seven

In Madrid, on June 2, 1936, at seven-thirty in the afternoon the Duke and Duchess of the Castle of Tarifa entered the quarters of the Marquesa del Olivo to wish her good night. They were dressed formally for the wedding of a daughter of the Condes de Valdepeñas. The Marquesa was frantic. "I beseech you once more not to go. I beg of you, call them, make an excuse."

"Mamá," the Duke said gently, "they're our best friends."

"They are fools. A lavish wedding at this time is akin to insanity. Suicidal."

"There's no danger, Mamá."

"There's nothing *but* danger. There are militiamen all over Madrid. You know very well there isn't a day without them killing and robbing. You know that they murdered poor Padre Tomás only a block from here. He had nothing worth robbing. What could that good man have done to them except to have been a man of God? Gathering all the Grandees together for a wedding is utter madness. And, as the parents of three children, it's irresponsible of you to go."

Four months before, in February of 1936, it had been expected that the national elections would retain the conservative government, the National Front. The Communist and Socialist parties couldn't bring out enough voters to win. Thousands of potential leftist votes belonged to the Anarchist Party, but as anarchy was in opposition to the "tyrannies of church and government," it

117

was against their principles to participate in an election, and they never had.

But at the last hour the Anarchists surprised everyone by voting en masse with the other parties of the Left, and a Popular Front government was elected in Spain as it had recently been in France. This had been accomplished by Soviet Russia's Comintern (Communist International whose mission was to make Spain the first Iron Curtain country.)

In the months that followed, Spain became embroiled in a wave of anarchistic revenge against the church, military officers, and the upper classes. Simply being a nobleman, or carrying a copy of *ABC*, the conservative Madrid daily, could get one killed as a "Fascist." Churches were burned, priests were murdered, nuns were raped.

The Marquesa said, "We should have left Madrid months ago."

"Mamá, you know that the Valdepeñas would have been offended if we hadn't stayed. Now, please, calm yourself. Should we allow ourselves to be frightened off the streets of our city by hoodlums?"

"It will be a miracle if a mob of those hoodlums does not surround that palace and rob and kill all of you."

Since the election of the Popular Front the government had armed all members of the Anarchist Party, legalized them as a militia with the power to make arrests and allowed them to roam the streets, stealing, looting, beating, killing at will. The municipal police looked the other way. But despite all the Duke had heard, his background of an all-powerful landowner and friend of King Alfonso XIII, though now in exile, made it difficult for him to fear a working man, even one with a weapon. Or was it a matter of pride that caused him to ignore or minimize the danger?

Resignedly, the Marquesa said, "At least do not go in a carriage. Use one of your cars. The militiamen are on foot. They would be hard put to stop an automobile."

The Duke and Duchess kissed the Marquesa goodnight and descended the grand stairway. The steps, as in the Royal Palace, *El*

Palacio del Oriente, were only three and a half inches high, half the standard height so that ladies attending dinners and balls, wearing long gowns could more easily ascend and descend. They also made it more comfortable for the men, who carried the weight of good living plus their medals, swords and heavily braided uniforms.

At the bottom the three children watched their parents approaching, their father in black tailcoat and white tie, a blue and gold sash across his shirt and decorations on his left lapel; their mother in a royal-blue taffeta ball gown with golden pumps matching her silk shawl and evening bag. Kissing her goodnight, smelling her perfume, Alfonso said, "You look beautiful, Mamá."

She kissed him again, "Thank you, *querido.*"

Their favorite carriage was prepared and awaiting them but deferring to the Marquesa's wishes they were driven to the Valdepeñas' in a Rolls-Royce sedan. Looking through the windows along the way the Duchess observed, "Not a one of them. It would have been so much lovelier to have used the carriage."

Upon arrival they noted that the Valdepeñas had taken the precaution of hiring enough armed guards to surround their palace at close intervals. The wedding was a spectacular affair and the party lasted till dawn without a sign of trouble.

At five in the morning, as the couple was returning home, their car made a choking sound and stopped a few blocks from their palace.

"What's happened?" asked the Duchess.

Their *mecánico* replied, "The engine seems to have died, Sra. Duquesa."

She asked her husband, "In all of your life did you ever hear of a horse dying before returning the carriage home?"

The Duke anticipated teasing his mother-in-law about this one. "We can walk the rest of the way."

"It's a beautiful morning," agreed the Duchess.

The *mecánico* locked the car doors. "Allow me to accompany los Sres. Duques."

The Duke waved away the idea, "Not at all necessary. Take care of the automobile. We can look after ourselves."

The *mecánico* persisted, "I beg los Sres. Duques to allow me to accompany them. The streets are not safe. The *milicianos* are everywhere."

Feeling too good to belabor the point, and appreciating his loyalty the Duke said, "Very well, my friend, come along and escort us home. Attend to the automobile tomorrow."

The streets were deserted. Then, a block from the gates of their palace they heard footsteps behind them, and looking back they saw figures in the first light of day. Unruly, crude sounding men carrying rifles. *Milicianos.*

Then, another group of militiamen materialized, coming toward them. In front and behind were a dozen militiamen, laborers who now held the power and wanted revenge for all the years when they had been poor, sweating and servile, while others were rich, comfortable and, too often, overbearing and abusive.

They were face to face with six men carrying rifles who blocked the sidewalk. Meanwhile the six others in the rear had reached them and they were boxed in.

While the Duke and Duchess stood still and silent the obvious leader of the band of militiamen walked slowly around them, inspecting their clothes, their faces, their jewelry. Speaking to his companions he sneered, "I'm offended by the necktie this *caballero* is wearing." He grabbed the Duke's white bow tie in his fist and yanked it off, obviously hurting the Duke's neck, but getting no cry of pain to satisfy him. On the contrary, the Duke swung a fist at him but the man ducked and the blow grazed his cheek. He jammed the butt of his rifle into the Duke's stomach, doubling him in half, then brought it up hard under his chin knocking him to the ground, unconscious and bleeding from the mouth.

The Duchess fell to her knees to help her husband. The leader roughly pulled her to her feet by her hair. "Stand aside. Your turn will come, *guapa.*" Outraged that he had the audacity to call her good-looking she started to protest but a hand was clapped over her mouth and she was held firmly by two subordinates.

The head man bent down and tore the gold medals off the Duke's lapel, ripped at his shirt, plucking the sapphire studs from it and pocketing them along with matching cufflinks. The Duke's bare chest revealed that he wore a cross. "Ah, a man of religion." He spat at the Duke and yanked off the gold chain and jeweled cross.

He searched the unconscious Duke's clothes for a wallet and was disappointed to find nothing. Carrying cash had not been a necessity for the Duke of the Castle of Tarifa. But the militiaman did find a diamond and sapphire ring on the Duke's finger that he removed. Then he looked at the right hand on which Spaniards wear their gold wedding bands. The Anarchist pulled at it but it wouldn't come off. The Duke had not removed it since the day his wife had placed it on his finger. Experienced, the militiaman produced a chisel, placed its sharp edge on the Duke's finger and with a single blow with the heel of his fist he severed the finger from the hand. He pulled the ring off and dropped the finger in the gutter.

Finished with the Duke, the headman approached the Duchess. "His whore wears sapphires and diamonds around her neck, on her ears, on her wrists and on her fingers," and he began to strip them off, carefully, not to lessen their resale value. "In the name of the *Frente Populár* I'm confiscating this property of the people, taken from our sweat and blood."

The *mecánico,* also held tightly by two militiamen, could only cry out in rage to leave her Excellency alone.

Laughing at the helpless *mecánico* he said, "We will see how excellent she is." Turning to the Duchess, opening his trousers he removed his swollen male organ and waved it at her. "Did you ever see one of these, Excellency?" The Duchess looked away. Pointing to the unconscious Duke the militiaman shrugged, "I don't know what that one's got between his legs, Duchess, but all real men have one of these." He gestured to his group, all of whom opened their trousers and displayed themselves. "Now Excellency, you are going to lay down on the street and get fucked like you have been fucking us all your life. If you have any sense you can enjoy getting fucked, whereas it was never any fun for us."

The two men holding the Duchess forced her to the street. Two others pulled her legs apart and the headman tossed her long silk skirt up over her waist. She was wearing underpants and stockings supported by a garter belt. After a few rough tugs the underpants broke apart and came off. God is good. The Duchess had fainted and was unconscious to what was happening to her. While one after another raped the unconscious woman the head man sat on the curb watching until his feeling of lust returned.

Her eyes were closed. He slapped her face back and forth and she awakened. "That's better," he said. "It's time for breakfast, Excellency." Crouching over her face, he pried her jaws open and forced himself into her mouth. "Lick my prick, cunt, lick it good, suck me dry."

With all of her strength the Duchess bit down on his hardened member. He screamed. Blood poured from his penis that he held in both hands. He bellowed the worst obscenity: *"¡Me cago en tus muertos!"* "I shit on your dead!" He wrapped his bleeding penis in her torn underpants and, holding it to quell the flow, picked up his rifle with his free hand.

"Get off her," he shouted to the last man, who had been enjoying her while this had gone on, "get off the fucking whore!" The man rolled off the Duchess. "Keep her legs apart," the head man shouted to the others and taking the muzzle of his rifle he placed it at her vagina and pushed it in, roughly, twisting it vengefully. "You like fucking better than sucking eh, cunt Excellency? Well, let's see how you like this?" and squeezing the trigger he fired the gun within her body. The bullet crashed through her organs and a field of blood appeared at her rib cage where it tore through the skin and left her body.

The *mecánico* moaned in agony. The headman looked at him and withdrew his rifle from the Duchess. "You could have had the gift of your life, but you turn out to be a lackey and a traitor," and he shot the man to death.

Then he attended to the Duke, placing the rifle exactly between his unconscious eyes and firing, blowing away half of his head. Not satisfied that he had sufficiently harmed the dead Duchess he went over to her prone figure, placed the rifle between her eyes and fired.

Having removed everything of value from their bodies and a few pesetas from the *mecánico,* the *milicianos* left them where they had fallen. They would be picked up by police vans that regularly cruised the streets looking for corpses to be brought to the morgue.

The Marquesa del Olivo forced herself to remain awake, hoping to hear the return of her daughter and son-in-law, but around five A.M. she fell into an exhausted, frightened sleep. At ten in the morning her personal maid awakened her. Calixto urgently wished to speak with her.

Admitted to her room the butler reported that the Duke and Duchess had not returned from the wedding and that he had gone to the palace of the Valdepeñas but was informed that all guests had left by five in the morning.

The Marquesa telephoned the Minister of the Interior under the previous government.

"Don't lose heart," he said. "Hopefully they were arrested by the militiamen and are safely locked up by the police." He said he would check with appropriate friends and report back.

The Marquesa despaired for the lives of her daughter and son-in-law. She had not left the palace grounds in a month. Nor had she permitted the children to go out. She had ordered sharp bronze tips welded onto each bar of the high iron gate that surrounded the palace and was kept locked day and night. And she armed four of the manservants to guard the gate around the clock.

The former Minister rang back with the ominous news that the Duques del Castillo de Tarifa were not in police custody.

The Marquesa thought of Calixto, but there were certain duties you did not call upon a servant to perform. She sent for her fourteen-year-old grandson. "*Querido,* sit down. I'm distressed to tell you that your parents did not return from the wedding last night, nor are they imprisoned." She paused and saw that he understood the implication. "I think you must look for them." She did not have to suggest where Alfonso should look. The police vans bringing corpses to the Madrid morgue were known by everyone.

The boy tore the sleeves off his shirt, ripped a hole in the knee of a leg of his trousers, then left on his mission. He stopped in the garden to muddy his shoes. He removed his lisle socks and rubbed dirt on his ankles.

Despite his now-common appearance he walked along back streets and when he saw militiamen, hid in doorways until they had passed. It was a hot day and three blocks from the morgue he smelled the stench of death. As he got closer it grew stronger, catching in his throat, gagging him.

The morgue, a granite municipal building, had been built for twenty corpses. There was no possibility of properly accommodating hundreds. Inside, Alfonso faced stacks of human bodies piled three and four high. Dizzied by fear, horror and smell he was aware of others moving among the rows of bodies, reaching beneath the corpses on top to pull at the hand of another, then dropping it and continuing on, searching.

He did not want to believe that he could find his parents among all those rigid, misshapen figures. He had never seen human death before. He did not want to see it anymore. He wanted to run out of there. But he continued searching.

Alfonso found his father. From a distance he recognized the blue and gold sash across his shirt. He was on a top layer. He had a large cavity above his nose obliterating his eyes and the upper part of his face. Beside him was his mother in the royal-blue taffeta ball gown she was wearing when she had kissed him goodnight. She too was missing part of her face and the top of her head.

Swarms of flies attracted by the dried blood landed on their exposed brains. Frantically, Alfonso chased them away. Using his mother's silk shawl he covered his parents' heads. He sat down with them. It was the only thing he could think to do. The flies continued attacking. Smelling the blood beneath the shawl they tried to creep under the edges. Futilely Alfonso swiped at them, gingerly, fearful of hitting his parents and hurting them. He knew they were dead but it did not fully penetrate his mind. How could he not have his mother and father anymore?

"*¿Que pasa?*" The man standing over him was an official who had been seated at a desk near the door where he could breathe.

"These are my parents."

The man looked at him. What was there to say?

"What should I do?" Alfonso asked.

"Have you the money to bury them?"

"My grandmother has."

The man gestured for the boy to follow him. Hating to leave them alone with the flies Alfonso followed on uncertain legs. At the desk the man opened a ledger. "Their names?"

Aware that this government employee was either sympathetic to or in fear of the Anarchists, Alfonso said, "My father's name is José Maria García."

Immediately he felt ashamed of his cowardice. They could kill him too if they wished but he wasn't going to deny his parents' names, his family's place in Spanish history. "My father's name is Don José Maria García de las Arenas y de Montalban. My mother is Doña Esperanza de Beltran El Bueno y de Sánchez del Castillo, Los Duques del Castillo de Tarifa."

The man looked up, actively seeing Alfonso for the first time, penetrating the muddied face, the torn clothes. Had he not been emotionally deadened by the recent months at his job he would have noticed the boy's diction. "I'm sorry for your great loss," he said, entering their names in his ledger.

When Alfonso saw his mother and father's names inscribed in a book of dead people, the tears began to fall. The official stood up. "We must move them close to the door." Alfonso followed him through the stacks of corpses. Reaching down he took hold of Alfonso's father. "Take the other arm."

Alfonso gripped his father's arm. It did not bend at the elbow.

"Now pull," the man instructed. "Hard!" and they dragged the body off the heap to the door. Alfonso sat on the floor beside it.

"Now we must get your mother."

Obeying, lifting her arm, Alfonso tried but couldn't bring himself to pull on her arm. He did not move her body at all. On the contrary it felt to him as if he were being pulled toward his mother and he crumpled to the floor beside her.

"All right, *hijo*, I can do this myself," said the man taking hold of her arms, pulling her toward the door. Her heels skidded along the stone floor and the golden pumps fell from her feet. Alfonso leaped up to retrieve them and put them back on her.

Then he collapsed. Not a faint. He remained conscious. The strength simply went out of his legs. Helping him up, the man gripped his arm until they were near the door, certain that if he did not support him the boy would topple over again. "You have to stop crying, *hijo*. You dare not even look sad. It's too dangerous. Go to the mortuary and have them send the hearse. But do not return here with it or you will betray yourself. There are *milicianos* hiding across the street, watching. If they think you found any family in here they will stop you and you do not want that. Not at all!"

"I'm grateful to you, Señor."

"Go before you're caught. *Y, que vaya con Dios.*" "May you go with God," this man had said. He was no Anarchist. Anarchists wouldn't even say *adiós* because it contained the word *Dios* and meant "to God."

A carefree expression invented onto his face, Alfonso prayed that he wouldn't be stopped and questioned because the anger he was feeling wasn't something he could contain. He wouldn't deny who he was. He would spit at them for killing his parents. And they would kill him. But that was impossible. He had to bury his mother and father and take care of his sisters and *abuela*.

At the funeral home Alfonso arranged for his parents' remains to be transported for burial at the *finca* in San Sebastian. Then he made his way along the streets toward home. He wondered what words he would use to tell his grandmother and sisters. And how would they be able to stand it?

Entering the front gates Alfonso climbed the staircase to his grandmother's apartment. Cayetana and Cristina were waiting with their grandmother, their small faces white, their bodies tremulous, frail. Alfonso's face spoke the words he had been trying to find, so he was left only to say, "I have made arrangements for the burial."

The Marquesa's body crumbled on the sofa. The girls stared as if they did not know him. Alfonso stood up straight. Taking his sisters in his arms forcefully he told his grandmother, "Abuela, we leave for San Sebastián today. We will bury Mamá and Papá and we will stay there with them for the rest of the summer. The sooner we are all out of Madrid, the better."

His grandmother nodded.

He telephoned Tio Guillermo to inform him of what had happened and of his plan.

He found Cayetana standing next to their parents' bed. He took the girls to the bathroom and washed both of their faces as well as his own. Then he sent for the *mayor domo*. "Calixto, my parents have been murdered by the *milicianos*. My grandmother, my sisters and I'll take them north to be buried. Notify the staff to pack their belongings, provide them with train tickets and tell them to meet us at *Los Escalones*, where we will all remain until this killing is brought to an end."

"Sr. Duque," he said, addressing the fourteen-year-old boy for the first time by the title he had just inherited, "with permission, I will remain in Madrid and protect the property of the Sr. Duque."

"Thank you dear Calixto but I'll understand if you would prefer not to remain in this perilous environment."

"Sr. Duque, I will defend this palace as I would every member of this family."

Traveling independently of their servants and governesses, attracting no attention, Alfonso, Cayetana, Cristina and the Marquesa arrived safely at *Los Escalones*. Immediately upon entering the grounds they saw signs of violence, sheep lying dead on the ground or hobbling around, crippled.

They went directly to Paco's *choza*. It was burned down to the dirt floor. Paco's dust covered face was tear-streaked. Two sacks covered the bodies of his mother and father. "A band of men from town came here yesterday. They demanded ten sheep. My father was unable to believe what they were saying and he ordered them to leave: 'This is the property of los Duques del Castillo de Tarifa, these animals belong to them. Go.'

"One of them took a knife from his pocket, 'Well, if we can't have them then the Duques won't have them either,' and he cut the Achilles tendons on the hind legs of a sheep he had by the ear."

Cristina whimpered, "But why would they do that to a poor animal?"

"So that he would be unable to walk, and if he cannot walk he cannot forage for grass and he'll die." He gestured around them, "And so it has passed. My father took a stick and tried to stop them so they killed him. And then they killed my mother."

The Marquesa wept, "If only your parents had just let them take the animals."

"Those men did not want sheep, Sra. Marquesa, they wanted revenge."

"Revenge?" Alfonso was mystified. "Revenge for what?"

"I don't know. That's the word I heard them use." He was too young to understand that the motive was rooted somewhere within the centuries of being abused and exploited. And the tragically useless attitude that if *they* couldn't have the sheep then their cause was served by preventing others from having them.

The Duke and Duchess of the Castle of Tarifa were buried at *Los Escalones*. Alfonso buried Paco's parents in the family cemetery and he brought Paco into the castle to live with them. In the morning Alfonso was awakened by his grandmother's maid, "Sr. Duque, please, come." No doubt unable to tolerate any more the Marquesa del Olivo had died in her sleep. Hers was the fifth body to be buried at Los Escalones in two days.

Tio Guillermo arrived from Madrid and told Alfonso, "All of Spain will soon be in flames. This violence won't end quickly. You are now the head of your family. It would be prudent to bring your sisters and yourself to safety in Biarritz." Taking Paco with them, Alfonso, the girls and the nannies crossed the Spanish-French border at Irún-Hendaye and were safely in Biarritz. They took an apartment in the Palace Hotel. Tio Guillermo arranged with a bank there to provide all they would need for the hotel and other expenses. He was a Spanish patriot who disdained breaking the law by removing pesetas from his country; however, he was also a realist and had long kept a comfortable account in Switzerland.

His prediction of no quick end to the violence was proven accurate. Spain was gripped in what came to be called the Red Terror. Even more than the aristocracy and the military, the clergy was the most despised and abused by the Anarchists. Within four months one hundred and sixty churches were burned, and as the priests, monks and nuns came running out fleeing the smoke and flames the Anarchists were waiting with machine guns to mow them down. In Málaga militiamen stripped nuns of their clothes, gang-raped them, lined them up naked on a concrete street and drove over them with steamrollers. A monk captured by a group of militiamen had his rosary beads forced into both ears until his eardrums burst. Another was dropped into an arena with eight fighting bulls. His hands and feet were not bound so that he could entertain the militiamen by trying to escape the horns of the animals, who quickly gored him to bits, repeatedly catching him on their horns and tossing him in the air until he had become only pieces. In all, some seven thousand priests, monks and nuns and twelve bishops perished in the savagery.

On June 16, 1936, Gil Robles, leader of the Spanish Catholic Party, stood up in Parliament and denounced the Popular Front government in a statement that was to become a part of Spanish history: ". . . A country can live under a Monarchy or a Republic, with a parliamentary or a presidential system, under Communism or Fascism. But it cannot live in anarchy. Now, alas, Spain is in anarchy and we are today present at the funeral service of democracy!"

In Biarritz, a month later, on July 18, 1936, listening to the radio, Alfonso, Paco, Cristina and Cayetana learned that the Spanish Army was rising against the government to restore order.

"At last," Alfonso shouted.

But it was not something to celebrate. All the blood that had already been shed was as nothing compared to what was to come.

The Spanish Civil War had begun.

Chapter Eight

For two years Cayetana, Cristina, Alfonso and Paco, closely united for all being orphans, remained in Biarritz. They went to Mass every day. Though mourning is normally observed for one year the girls continued to wear only black and the boys wore black neckties and armbands.

The four studied together with the governesses. In their free time Cayetana, Cristina and Alfonso worked further on Paco's education, making him read to them aloud, to write them notes, and they took pride in his progress.

To further his English, Alfonso taught him to sing American popular songs. "Once you learn the words of a song and you understand what they mean you never forget them. It's especially helpful with verbs."

But their interest was the war being fought just an hour away in their country. They were appalled to hear of massive foreign intervention: the red flags with hammer and sickle flying in Madrid, of Soviet Russia providing arms and tanks and of Russian Generals directing the war for the Popular Front government, known as "Republicans" or "Loyalists." Groups of idealists recruited worldwide by the Young Communist League, calling themselves the International Brigade, came "to fight Fascism," referring to the Spanish generals, the Nationalists, who had risen to restore order. And they suffered mixed emotions upon learning of Italy and Germany helping the Nationalist side with transport planes and with air force bombing missions against Spaniards and Spanish cities.

The blood continued hemorrhaging on both sides, the inhumanity of one provoking the inhumanity of the other. While the liberal writer García Lorca was gunned down by Nationalists, Loyalists "executed" the right-wing intellectual Ramiro de Maetzu.

In Ronda the "Reds" rounded up five hundred people guilty only of being members of a small middle class and hurled them from the Tajo gorge to their deaths on the rocks 450 feet below. On the other side General Franco ordered his own cousin shot as a Red. Nationalist killers accounted for fifty thousand deaths in the first months of the war, the majority hanged or shot, others beaten to death with iron crucifixes, an historic touch from the Carlist wars in the early nineteenth century. Peasants seeking agrarian reforms, demanding their own lands to work, were buried alive, the last words they heard being, "Here is your piece of ground, you son of a whore."

Fathers, sons and brothers killed each other. One was either a "Red" or a "Fascist," often depending merely upon what area of Spain he happened to live in and which side controlled it. There were no prisoner of war camps. When a captured Loyalist officer asked for an exchange of prisoners a Nationalist General was nauseated, "You expect us to exchange a Spanish gentleman for a Red dog?"

Alfonso's sole desire was to slip over the border into Spain and join the Nationalist forces to avenge the death of his parents and to save Spain from Communism. But, whenever he broached the subject to the governesses he was told, "You're all your sisters have in the world. You promised your uncle, Guillermo, to protect them. Besides, you're too young. It will be over soon."

Alfonso and Paco did not feel young. They were both sixteen and matured by tragedy. At nearly fifteen Cristina did not want to be protected, she wanted to return to her country and serve as a nurse. She urged Alfonso, "You and Paco should go back and fight the Reds who killed our parents. And I should help care for our wounded."

Alfonso listened to Cristina, agreeing, but also hearing Tio Guillermo telling him to take care of his sisters. Finally, he told her, "Paco and I have talked it over and early tomorrow we go over the border. But you must remain safely here until it's over."

In Spain, the poor and the wealthy alike had been brought up to understand their nation's history, its flag of gold and red. Cristina reminded Alfonso, ". . . the gold representing our wealth and our power during those centuries when we dominated the world, and the red for all the blood shed in all those wars against not only invaders but Spaniards against Spaniards. Alfonso, the blood is spilling again and it's my obligation to help my country-men. I'm no *cobarde*. I'm going with you."

"And Cayetana?"

"She's content to remain here. I go."

They confided in Cayetana what they were planning. Alfonso said, "When the war is over, wherever we are we will all return to our home in Madrid and wait for each other there." Though Paco had never been to their Madrid home, or even to Madrid, during these past two years they had spoken of it so much that he knew exactly where it was; he could envision the massive, bronze-studded olive-wood front doors; the music box with the dancing ballerinas.

"If by chance the palace has been destroyed, then we all go to the Ritz Hotel and wait for each other there. If the Ritz does not exist anymore . . ."

That night Cristina and Paco walked in the hotel garden. They sat on a bench and listened to the ocean's waves breaking. The sky was filled with stars and there was such an aura of peace that it was momentarily possible to forget the war. In a low voice Paco sang some of the American love songs he had learned. Cristina nestled into his shoulder.

"I'm in love with you," he said. "Do you mind?"

She took his hand, "I would be heartbroken if you were not. Haven't you noticed the way I look at you? And listen to you, and adore everything you say?"

He kissed her forehead shyly.

"I liked you as soon as I saw you that first summer," she admitted, "three years ago. When did you know you love me?"

"Since being together here. I wouldn't have said anything yet, but as we are going to war and might be killed, I wanted you to know."

"We won't be killed," she said. "God won't let anything more happen to us. But, Paco, promise to be careful."

"Being careful and going to war is a contradiction. But I won't be stupid. I won't make it any harder for Him to pull us through this. When the war is over, and if we're not . . . hurt . . . I'll ask you to become my *novia*."

"I'll accept."

"And then, after a suitable time, we can be married."

The three left the hotel at six in the morning, hoping to encounter the Nationalist forces that controlled that area, and enlist. In just a few hours they found a column of Nationalist infantry, and on July 2, 1938, Alfonso and Paco enlisted as privates and Cristina as a nurse's aide.

Alfonso and Paco were asked by their company sergeant. "Have you ever fired a gun?"

"Yes, *mi Sargento*," Alfonso replied. "Give me five practice shots with a rifle and I'll hit anything you point to."

Alfonso was so accurate with the cheap army rifle that he was separated from Paco and Cristina and sent to the front lines with an infantry division that was attacking Toledo, trying to bring aid to the *Alcázar*, the remaining fort held by General Moscardó and the Nationalists, which refused to surrender.

After watching him shoot, his new company commander ordered, "García de las Arenas, your job is to sit behind this rock and pick off every Red you see out there."

The image ever-present in his mind of his mother and father with the tops of their heads blown away, Alfonso sat behind the rock and slew his first enemy, then five more. With six cartridges he killed six *Rojos*. Each of them died instantly of a bullet between the eyes. Then boldly he crept forward until he was abreast of a machine-gun nest that had kept his company pinned down for two days. He fired four shots and killed the four machine gunners, two of them with bullets between the eyes, wiping out the nest, allowing his company to surge forward.

Destroying *Rojos* who had killed his parents brought him satisfaction. Doubly so when he could get a face-on target and hit between the eyes. It became a trademark with unexpected psychological value. In each battle whenever an enemy soldier was shot between the eyes the word went out that *"Entre Los Ojos,"* "Between the Eyes," was out there and they fell back, fighting defensively for fear of the deadly sharpshooter.

Between battles the men found time to have a beer and a laugh. A hero to his comrades at arms Alfonso always joined them in the beer. He felt affection for them but he never laughed with them. He couldn't find a reason to smile. Because of his extraordinary courage and skill he was well accepted, laughing or not, but due to his grim personality he became known as *"El que no sonrie, nunca!"* "He who never smiles."

Alfonso was shot in the left leg. The wound was dressed and it hurt, but it did not stop the work of *Entre Los Ojos*. He was decorated and given a field commission as Captain, but he wasn't given a command. He was more valuable at what he had been doing. He was an infantry company unto himself. In the next six months he killed seventy-three of the enemy.

Alfonso was bold but not reckless. Always on his mind was: *You have to survive this and take care of Cristina and Cayetana.*

On April 1, 1939, General Franco announced the end of the Spanish Civil War. The uprising to bring about law and order had become a three-year conflict twisting emotions throughout the world and killing nearly a million Spaniards, wiping out almost an entire generation of Spanish men.

It was May when Alfonso made his way back to Madrid. He walked along the again peaceful *Paseo de La Castellana* in the uniform of a Captain, wearing the medals he had won, greeted by all as a conquering hero but not feeling like one. As he walked he was reminded of his childhood, the starched nannies, the children playing, riding in the *tonneau* with "Miss." His mother and father.

The last sight of his parents was burned into his brain. He tried to remember them in the happy times, but those memories were always overwhelmed by images of the morgue and the flies trying to eat the dried blood from their shattered heads.

A year had passed since he had seen Cristina and Paco. As soon as he could he would call Cayetana in Biarritz. Perhaps they had contacted her.

And his home! How he looked forward to seeing it again! As he neared the palace he broke into a trot, then it was in sight and he began to run exuberantly through the front gates, up the long driveway.

The palace was in ruins. The garden was grown over. Every window was broken. The ancient front doors were gone.

Then he saw Calixto. The *mayor domo* was wearing his hunting-green livery but it was in tatters. His black hair was white. He walked bent over; his splendid posture deformed as if someone had taken a straight iron bar and forced it into a curve

Calixto studied the young man in the military uniform. Three years had passed in which a boy had become a man. He cried out, "*¿Sr. Duque?*"

They embraced as reunited members of the same family.

They walked through the house. There was no furniture, paintings, rugs. The wood paneling had been stripped away leaving bare stone walls. The house was a shell.

"I tried to protect the palace, Sr. Duque, and I managed until the war began. Then everything changed. With the government holding Madrid, the Anarchists requisitioned this palace, as they did other great palaces, as the headquarters for one of their leaders. A thug who called himself *El Macho* lived here with ten men. The winter of '37 was cold. In the salons with no fireplaces they made fires on the floors. When they used up all the firewood they took the wonderful furniture and, breaking the pieces apart, they burned them for heat."

He continued compulsively reliving the nightmare. "When the furniture was gone they pried the panels from the walls, sawed them into pieces and burned them. They ripped up the parquet floors. Finally they took down the great front doors for firewood.

"Anything that someone would buy they sold for whatever they could get, for nothing, the paintings, beds, sofas, rugs, grandfather clocks, flatware, everything."

Alfonso said, "They had no understanding of what they were doing, the value of those things."

"Yes, they did, Sr. Duque, because I told them. They scoffed. It gave them pleasure." He sobbed, "I'm sorry."

Alfonso put his arm around the old man's shoulder. "Please don't say that again, dear friend. I'm only grateful they didn't kill you."

"Oh, they would have," Calixto couldn't help smiling, "they would have, and with pleasure, except for one thing. *El Macho* discovered that he enjoyed having a servant. He would get drunk and order me to draw his bath, then sit in the bathtub of the Sr. Duque and command that I empty bottles of champagne over his head while he cackled, 'This is how el Duque del Castillo de Tarifa takes a bath.'

"They slaughtered the horses for food. They took the cars and used them as toys, crashing them into walls, fences. And rather than bothering to wind down the windows they smashed them with their rifle butts. They drove around Madrid until they ran out of fuel, and then abandoned those wonderful machines wherever they stopped. By spring, having looted and destroyed this palace *El Macho* moved to the palace of Los Marqueses de Santa Cruz and this became a barracks."

They walked together up the staircase, now devoid of carpet and the suits of armor that had adorned each landing. Every room was looted to the four walls. They looked into the playroom. The hand-carved wooden horses of the carousel were gone. "Burned for firewood," Calixto said.

The music box with the dancing ballerinas was gone. Sold. Calixto turned to Alfonso with grief-ridden eyes, "Sr. Duque, la Señorita Cayetana returned here when the war ended. She wept when she saw the condition of the house, the suites of los Sres. Duques, but when she saw this," he stretched out both arms pointing to the empty space where the music box had been, "she stood silently staring at it, then abruptly turned and ran from the house. I chased after her, begging, 'Señorita please come back.' 'No, Calixto,' she hugged me and fled into the streets. Still, I chased after her begging her to come back, but she told me, 'Never, Calixto, never.'"

Alfonso did not want to hear or see anymore. They went downstairs. Passing the ballroom where as children he and his sisters had watched their parents and family friends dance away so many beautiful evenings, Alfonso stopped walking. The paintings, the chandeliers and dance floor were gone. An entire wall was lined with urinals.

Chapter Nine

The Ritz Hotel had survived unscathed. At the reception desk Alfonso said, "I would like an apartment with four bedrooms. But I have little money at the moment." He handed over his papers that identified him as "Capitán Alfonso García de las Arenas y de Beltran El Bueno."

The reception manager bowed. "Permit me to say, Sr. Duque, that the heroism of *Entre Los Ojos* is engraved in the heart of every true Spaniard."

Excusing himself for a moment he returned with a stack of bank notes and began counting out thousands of pesetas. He was aware of the vast holdings of both of those eminent families, and the historical importance and *grandeza* of the García de las Arenas as well as the descendants of Beltran El Bueno, so if the Duke of the Castle of Tarifa was experiencing a temporary postwar cash shortage then certainly the Ritz was there to help. "Any amount the Sr. Duque wishes is at his disposal; the apartment and all hotel services. We can settle accounts this year, next year, whenever it may be convenient for the Sr. Duque."

From his apartment Alfonso placed a call to the Palace Hotel in Biarritz, praying that Cayetana had returned there. He waited by the phone for two hours before the operator rang and said she had the Palace Hotel on the line. Cayetana cried at hearing his voice. She, too, knew nothing of Cristina or Paco. He asked, "When are you coming home?"

"I was there. I'm never going back."

"But you dare not stay in France. The Germans will soon have the country entirely occupied."

"I'm a Spaniard. They won't bother me."

"That is much too dangerous. Come back, Cay. (rhymes with guy) Forget our home. Come to the Ritz. I have an apartment here for all of us."

"No, Fonso. Not for a long while. I saw Madrid. I will never let my heart be assaulted like that again."

Finally, "As you wish. But we'll keep closely in touch."

Then he set about trying to trace Cristina and Paco. He presented himself in uniform at the Ministry of War and asked for the officer in charge of soldiers missing in action. Because of his decorations and fame in battle he was escorted to the Minister of War, Lt. General José Varela, who quickly ascertained that at least their names did not appear on the lists of the known killed in action. But if they were alive and safe, or alive and wounded, and where, was another question. Despite all desire to help, the problem was that after three years of war Spain was decimated. Telephone lines that had been cut by one side or the other were under repair and it was almost impossible to communicate except by radio, but even that was difficult as many regiments were disbanding, and most of the officers and men were on their way to their homes. General Varela promised that he would make every effort to locate Cristina and Paco.

Alfonso went to the *Ministerio de Asuntos Exteriores,* the State Department, which kept watch over all noble titles. Unlike some European countries, in Spain only the person to whom it belongs by right of birth can use a title. It cannot be sold, nor can it be transferred, except within the same family, and false use is punishable by imprisonment. Alfonso filled out the papers necessary to take possession of his father's title.

That done he met with his father's lawyer, Ignacio Gomez-Arriba. Don Ignacio read the Last Wills and Testaments of los Duques del Castillo de Tarifa and the Marquesa del Olivo. The

Marquesa had no heirs except her daughter, the Duchess, so her fortune descended to Alfonso, Cayetana and Cristina. Everything was divided equally among them except that he, under the law of primogeniture, was the executor of the estates and sole heir to the family's titles. It took the lawyer thirty-five minutes to read the list of properties that Alfonso and his sisters had inherited. None of the wills made reference to any investments or assets other than the extensive lands.

"Would you have any idea how much income our properties produce?"

Don Ignacio shook his head, "Your father never divulged that sort of information."

"And the *escrituras?*" Alfonso asked, the deeds.

The lawyer gave him a key that had been taped to the Duke's will. "This is to your father's safe deposit box at the bank. A prudent man, such as he, would keep important papers in a bank vault. I'll accompany you there."

"Thank you, Don Ignacio. But before we leave please make a note to do what is required for me to give my sister Cristina the title of Marquesa del Olivo."

Apart from his own, of all the noble titles that had been left to them the best was the Marquesa del Olivo, which was only two years younger than the Duque del Castillo de Tarifa. Disappointed in Cayetana's unwillingness to help in their country's conflict he gave her the lesser title of Condesa de Santiago del Monte. Only a few hundred years old it was nevertheless an excellent title with *grandeza,* among the best that he owned. The twenty-two other titles left to him would remain unused until he gave them to his children.

The lawyer and Alfonso went together to the *Banco Español de Credito,* Spain's largest bank, in which the late Duke of the Castle of Tarifa had kept an account. Don Ignacio was a brother of the bank's president.

The account contained only three million pesetas, which in 1939 was the equivalent of ninety thousand dollars. It seemed paltry for one of the wealthiest men in Spain. However, it was prudent to have money invested rather than gaining no interest as cash. Surely the safe deposit box would reveal the nature of the Duke's investments. Showing the key Don Ignacio asked his brother to authorize Alfonso's access to the box.

"We won't require the key except for the number." Going downstairs to the vaults the banker spoke in a saddened voice, "During the last weeks of the war, as the Nationalists were about to take Madrid, the Reds, still being the legally elected government sent squads of men to all of Madrid's banks to break open and loot the safe deposit boxes of private citizens. They were armed and had court orders that legalized what they were doing. The government's concocted 'theory' was that anyone with wealth was a Fascist, and thus as an enemy of the state their worldly goods could be confiscated. Under that guise they stole all cash, gold, silver, jewels, everything of apparent value and sent two shiploads of their plunder to Mexico, where they are presently living on it as 'The Spanish Government in Exile.'"

Inside the vault room small steel doors hung on broken hinges from hundreds of safe deposit boxes. He looked at the number on the key. Removing the drawer and opening it he touched Alfonso on the shoulder. "I'm sorry, son. This is all that remains. I watched as they drilled and smashed open the boxes and I saw them reach into your father's. I couldn't see what they took, only this, which they threw to the floor. Their leader was annoyed: 'love letters,' he said and continued on to the next that might yield gold or silver."

It was a thin leather envelope sewn completely closed, with the same stitches Alfonso had been taught, covered with sealing wax and embossed with the *escudo* of the Dukedom of the Castle of Tarifa. On the flat surface, burned into the leather, were the words, "For my son, Alfonso, upon my death."

In his salon at the Ritz, using a straight razor Alfonso worked slowly to open the leather folder without damaging whatever its contents might be. He extracted a piece of parchment bearing an ancient script. There were seven signatures, the last of them his father's. He realized that the others were his ancestors, the six previous Dukes of the Castle of Tarifa, and that this note had been handed down from father to son for what was now eight generations.

GO TO MY WINE CELLAR. LOCK THE DOOR BEHIND YOU. REMOVE THE VELÁZQUEZ OF THE MEN DRINKING. IN THE STONE WALL BEHIND IT FIND TWO SMALL HOLES. INSERT A THIN BUT RIGID WIRE INTO ONE UNTIL IT WILL GO NO FURTHER. PRECISELY ONE METER. INSERT ANOTHER METER OF WIRE INTO THE OTHER HOLE. WHEN IT WILL ENTER NO FURTHER APPLY A BIT OF PRESSURE AND SEE WHAT OCCURS. ENJOY YOUR LIFE, MY SON, *Y QUE VA YA CON DIOS.*

PAPÁ

Alfonso phoned down to the *conserje* and asked to be provided with two lengths of stiff bailing wire, each a meter and twenty centimeters long. "I will pass your desk to fetch them on my way out." The lengths of wire were at the *conserjería*, wrapped in white tissue paper as if they were a long-stemmed rose. As Spanish gentlemen did not carry things, the *conserje* touched a bell on his desk and called out, *"Botones!"* literally meaning buttons, but used for "bellboy," deriving from the uniform having rows of brass buttons down the front. A *botones*, perhaps ten years old, picked up the package and followed Alfonso to a taxi. When Alfonso was seated, it was handed to him.

Calixto was supervising the unloading of a van containing furniture belonging to the palace, pieces that had been located in diverse parts of Madrid, some in the *rastro,* a flea market where every day well-known *Madrileños* searched the stalls hoping to buy back their family heirlooms. The Duke of the Castle of Tarifa's bed with his *escudo* inlaid in the headboard had been found by the police in the fifth-floor apartment of a leader of the militiamen.

"Sr. Duque, I can hardly bear to return these fine pieces to this house when it's in such a condition."

"Don't despair, Calixto, we will restore everything. One day we will all be able to forget that our home was ever different than before." He did not believe it for a moment.

Alfonso went down into the cellar to the *bodega*. The wine racks were empty. He had been too young to be interested in them before the war, but he remembered that there had been rows and rows of them, thousands of bottles.

He closed the cellar door and secured the bolt. The Velázquez was, of course, gone. The painting, a national art treasure, was catalogued, and the Franco government was making aggressive efforts toward the recovery of stolen, or "confiscated," property. If it had not been destroyed or taken to Mexico, it would be found eventually and returned along with the other missing masterworks.

Using a lantern Alfonso found the holes in the stone wall, inconspicuous pocks giving no impression of depth. He inserted a wire and it moved freely into the wall for one meter, then stopped. He inserted the second wire, also to the limit. He paused, then exerted pressure against it.

The stone wall began moving inward, opening as a door. The wall was a meter thick and consequently had to weigh several tons, yet it was so perfectly balanced that it opened as if on ball bearings until it was at a 90-degree angle.

Holding the lantern ahead of him, Alfonso stepped into the chamber. The first thing he saw was a marble plaque on the wall, its letters carved out as on a headstone.

THIS IS THE PRIVATE VAULT OF
THE DUKE OF THE CASTLE OF TARIFA
HE ALONE MAY KNOW IT EXISTS AND ENTER.
NOT THE DUCHESS, NOT THE CHILDREN OF THE DUKE.
A SECRET BETWEEN TWO PEOPLE IS NOT A SECRET.
1715

Covering one fully fifty-square-foot wall of the vault were framed collections of gold coins as old as the Spanish doubloon and Venetian ducats dated 1284, all in mint condition. Another wall enclosed in glass doors had velvet-covered shelves on which rested dozens of diadems of diamonds and emeralds, of sapphires and rubies. On another shelf there were golden, jeweled Fabergé pieces.

Hanging from a velvet-covered hook inside the breakfront was a heavy gold chain and jeweled cross that had been made in Imperial Russia by Fabergé, and given to one of Alfonso's ancestors by the King of Spain as a gesture of gratitude for some great deed. It was a bulky piece that could be worn in the 1800's on top of court attire as a necklace, a royal decoration. Sadness coursed through Alfonso as he realized that on the night his father was killed he had been wearing a miniature of the chain and cross that fit under modern evening clothes. Alfonso would have another replica made and wear it in memory of his father and as a reminder of his murderers. Not to hate them—his religion forbade that— but never to forget them, to be always wary.

Another wall held floor-to-ceiling shelves of heavy, solid gold goblets for white and red wine, champagne and water, gold serving plates and gold flatware for two hundred guests. Picking up one of the weighty forks Alfonso saw that it was of a different design than the family's everyday gold cutlery. He supposed they were more valuable. Then he knew it. The crest that appeared on each piece was the *escudo* of Felipe II.

Near the entrance to the vault was a breakfront with glass-paneled doors. Looking into it he felt grief in his heart at the sight of his mother's important jewelry, an emerald diadem with a large square cut emerald ring and emerald earrings. There was a bracelet of one-carat square-cut diamonds. He recognized at least fifty pieces that his mother had worn on important occasions. The only missing items were the sapphires she had on that last night. Judging by the plaque that admonished strict secrecy he assumed that his mother had not known of the vault and that his father had always removed what she wanted and later returned it. What good luck that his father had not trusted a conventional wall safe that could have been discovered, nor trusted a piece of furniture with a hidden compartment that could have been sold, or broken for firewood, in which case the Reds would have discovered and sold these jewels, which were more precious to him than anything else in the vault.

There were six large brass-strapped trunks. Alfonso opened one. It was stuffed with thousand peseta banknotes, as were the second, third, fourth, fifth and sixth. Taking up a handful, he counted a hundred bills. Then, it being too time consuming to count he began measuring it until he had a stack that would be approximately a million pesetas. It did not skim the top off of what only one trunk contained. He guessed that there were billions of pesetas in cash. And next to the trunks were dozens of canvas bags, round, like pumpkins, all of them burgeoning with money, mostly one-thousand peseta notes, but also bills of twenty-five, fifty, one hundred and five hundred, and silver coins of one, two and five pesetas.

Alfonso had never felt especially rich until this moment. He sat down at a desk that he supposed his father and his grandfather and their fathers before them had used to do their accounts. The drawers contained the *escrituras* to all of their properties. Tens of thousands of hectares. Side by side they would cover 5 percent of all Spain. In a separate folder was the deed to a sugar plantation in Cuba, the only foreign property. Unlike Tio Guillermo his father had not needed a Swiss account.

Alfonso remained in the vault for hours, discovering more and more wealth, one of the great fortunes of Europe that now belonged to him.

* * *

After two months of checking with the Ministry of War every day on Cristina and Paco, then returning to the Ritz, Alfonso still stopped at the *conserjería* each day, hoping for a letter or message from or about them. Always he was told sympathetically, "Nothing,

Sr. Duque." But this time the reply was, "A lady and a gentleman are waiting in the salon for the Sr. Duque."

Cristina and Paco were seated facing the mirrored double doors as he entered. They looked wonderful, she with her blue cape of the nursing corps and he wearing the uniform of a Captain of the Infantry. Alfonso caught his sister up in his arms, hugging her tight, tears falling from his eyes, actively aware that the hoping and praying was past. He let her go and hugged Paco, pounding his back with both hands as Paco pounded him. They sat down and Cristina said, "*Entre Los Ojos, eh, mi Capitán?* We heard so much about you."

Looking at his sister's beautiful face Alfonso saw a scar that pulled on the skin of her right jaw. It was three inches long and a quarter-inch deep. He stroked her face. "I'm sorry you were scarred."

"I was caught in a fire."

Paco said, "I see no scar, I see a medal. Cristina is more beautiful than ever." He told Alfonso, "The Reds made a mortar attack on the hospital where she was working, a clearly marked hospital."

Cristina said, "Paco caught one in his shoulder."

Alfonso nodded, "And I in the leg. But we are the lucky ones."

Then Cristina was bragging about Paco's heroism, for which his chest bore proof in the form of gold medals and colored ribbons; Paco informed Alfonso that Cristina was known as the "Angel of the Eighty-Ninth Infantry Regiment," having saved at least a hundred and thirty men from dying of wounds by extracting bullets and performing other minor surgery for lack of enough doctors.

Alfonso told them about Cayetana.

Cristina nodded sadly, "We went first to the house. *Pobre casa, pobre Calixto!* All those toilets."

His arms around their shoulders, Alfonso led them to the elevator and they ascended to the top floor. "I optimistically prepared for us all to live together as a family while we do what we can to get into a postwar life."

They got a call through to Cayetana. Then Alfonso showed them around the apartment.

In Paco's bedroom were suits and shirts and shoes. Alfonso explained, "I had them made on myself as the model. We always wore the same sizes and I thought that a year would be unlikely to change that." There were also neckties, pajamas, handkerchiefs and socks. All had been replaced as the *milicianos* had not left a single piece of clothing.

They went to Cristina's bedroom. Manufactured dresses did not exist in Madrid in 1939. Everything was made to order by oneself, by seamstresses, or *modistas,* designers at various levels. The best of them was Balenciaga, who had a shop of *alta moda* in Madrid under the name "Eisa," as well as his *atelier* in Paris. Alfonso said, "I went to Balenciaga but as I wasn't sure what you would like I ordered only two dresses for you to have as a start. We will go there tomorrow. But I was able to get you this."

Opening a blue leather folder Cristina found a government document stating that Doña Cristina del Mar García de las Arenas y Beltran El Bueno y Sánchez del Castillo had succeeded to the title of Marquesa del Olivo. She wrapped her arms around Alfonso and thanked him profusely. Then she turned to Paco, "This is extraordinarily generous. People do not give away titles, even to their sisters. If a man has many he'll keep them all for his children. And to give me the best he has . . ."

"The *second* best."

She smiled, *"Sí, Sr. Duque."*

At ten-thirty they descended to the dining room, Paco and Alfonso in black tie, Cristina in a blue, long-sleeved Balenciaga of thin wool that was dressy as silk. It was a design the up-and-coming *modista* had styled in Madrid out of the necessity for warmth at a time when there was little fuel for heating.

During the two months in which Alfonso had waited for them he had imagined them all together celebrating their reunion, and now that it was happening the enormity of their good fortune settled over him, momentarily masking the ever-present grief that the war had cost all of them their parents.

Despite the elegance of the service, the "Grand Hotel" dining room and string orchestra, the postwar food shortages were extreme and they dined on thin soup and then a *tortilla*. The oil in which it was fried was green as there were no refineries in Spain. But the food couldn't have mattered less to the three of them.

Alfonso observed how far Paco had come from the boy who had not known how to use a knife and fork. Having spent two years in the splendor of the Palace Hotel in Biarritz and then as an officer in the Nationalist Army he was completely at home at the equally imposing Ritz.

He had come to understand that Paco was his half brother. Alone in the field while waiting for the enemy to appear, he found that his thoughts remained in the past: he saw his father's and Paco's faces, and he remembered his mother asking Paco his birthday and then glaring at his father. He recalled his delight when at the end of that summer his father had given Paco the horse he had been riding, arranged for him to go to school in San Sebastian and gave his family permission to slaughter a baby lamb every month for their own table. He wished that his father had said something to him, confided their blood relationship, but he'd been only thirteen and then it was too late. The secret died unspoken. But Alfonso had not the slightest doubt that Castillo de Tarifa blood flowed through Paco's veins.

He studied his sister. At seventeen Cristina had all the sweetness of youth and also an attractive early maturity. Although she had had a pampered upbringing, attending to the dead and the dying had favorably affected her values. The war had matured all of them.

As the wonderful evening progressed Paco said, "Alfonso, I have something important to ask you as the head of Cristina's family. I'm sure you can see that Cristina and I are in love with each other. Before we left Biarritz we resolved that if we returned from the war we would become engaged and, in proper time, married. During this past year our feelings have strongly intensified. Therefore I have the privilege of asking for your consent."

The violins were playing Mozart and Alfonso saw Cristina smiling at Paco. How had he not seen it immediately? If not in Biarritz then here, from the first moment of seeing them together. Hearing their pride in each other. He felt a deep, physically painful sadness. Paco was startled to see something on Alfonso's face other than the pleasure he had expected from his best friend. Cristina was staring at Alfonso as though she did not recognize him. Paco became defensive, "I realize that I have nothing. Of course we have no thought of marrying until I can provide for us."

Alfonso shook his head, "It has nothing to do with that."

"Then, what is the problem? Blood . . . ancestry . . . the shepherd boy and the Marquesa?"

"No, dear Paco, I swear to you. Nothing like that."

Paco peered into Alfonso's eyes. As he studied the face he had thought he knew so well he suffered profound sorrow and disillusionment.

Alfonso looked from the sister he loved to the friend and brother he loved. It was his responsibility to come between them, to keep them from being together. His voice conveyed his stricken feelings. "You and Cristina cannot marry because you are her half brother. As you're mine. We all had the same father."

Paco was winded by the outlandish idea. After a moment he recovered and demanded, "How do you know that? Did your father tell you?"

"Nobody told me. But I know it. Look at you. How could you have been made by the man you believe was your father? You look nothing like him. Neither in stature nor face. You look like us. Isn't it obvious to you what happened?"

Paco had noticed the resemblance when he had seen them all together in photographs taken in Biarritz. He remembered the Duke of the Castle of Tarifa's face and he knew that his own looked very much the same. But he had attributed that to coincidence. It would never have occurred to him that he was sired by the Duke of the Castle of Tarifa. How would he even dream of having been born noble, or half noble?

Paco touched Cristina's hand. "Do you believe this, *Nena?*" meaning little girl, his pet name for her. She was looking from her brother to Paco . . . yes, he did look like he could be her brother. "But we can't be sure!" Paco protested. "Do we throw away everything we've dreamed about, just walk away from each other because maybe, just maybe we are related?"

Alfonso's voice was plaintive. "There's no one left to ask. But think about it: why else would he have given you that valuable horse, and spent the money to send you to school in San Sebastian, and given your family all those baby lambs? Just because you were a friend of mine? No. I could have lied to you just now and said, 'Yes, Papá told me.' But your genes are screaming it. You have nobility in everything you have done since the day we met." He looked at Cristina and she nodded, tears welling in her eyes. "Cristina believes it. And I think you do, too."

"I did not say that. I have no intention of giving up my life with Cristina just because you have some remote theory."

"Paco, *querido* Paco, you and Cristina are brother and sister. If you were to have children they could be subnormal, *mongólicos*, children who would probably never exceed the mental maturity of ten-year-olds even when they are physically aged twenty. And most often their lives are short because their hearts don't function properly, all part of the malformation."

"Then we forget children." It was said without conviction. He and Cristina had so eagerly anticipated the large family they wanted. Cristina was silent but Paco understood that her religious foundation would make a deliberately barren marriage almost impossible for her. He reasoned, "Supposing—just supposing—that we are related. Even if we had children it's not certain they would be retarded. There has been plenty of intermarriage in Spain."

"And, lamentably, there are plenty of *mongólicos*."

"But the majority are normal, healthy children."

"The Church forbids such a marriage."

151

"The Vatican could be induced to give approval. You could arrange it, Alfonso. It has been done before, many times."

He spoke gently, "Please, Paco, please believe that there's nothing I would like better than for you to be my brother-in-law. But you are already my brother. I cannot describe how overwhelmingly happy I would be for you to be the Marqués del Olivo, to look after Cristina's fortune. I could trust you to take care of her."

Paco couldn't feel titles, he couldn't feel lands or money, he could only feel the slipping away of his greatest desire. Weakly he said, "If you really meant that you would use your influence to make it possible."

"I cannot do that, Paco. It would be a sin."

Could he believe Alfonso? Would the aristocratic Alfonso really want him, the shepherd boy, to marry his sister? He had come to feel that there were no differences between them, neither in his nor Alfonso's hearts. But was it deeply rooted within him? Or was he in fact not a shepherd boy but a half brother of these people he loved?

Alfonso summoned the strength to say, "I believe that you and Cristina should stop seeing each other. Today. Do not drag on the impossible, making it even more painful. I think you should go away and study. Money will be provided."

"For the shepherd boy." Paco immediately wished he could retract the words.

"No. For my brother. From your father's fortune. To become a lawyer, as you always wanted."

"Yes, your brother will need to earn a living." He hated himself for trying to hurt Alfonso; he despised his own rancor, his attempt to extract some kind of pity.

"Paco, I understand the pain you feel, and I'm hurting, too. And Cristina. But you should be convinced that I'm sincere by the fact that I intend to legally recognize you as my brother and then give you one of our father's titles and estates. You can have *Los Escalones* if you wish. You can return to where you were born and live in the castle; it will be yours and all of its lands and you will be the Conde de Los Escalones."

Conde de Los Escalones was an old title that carried *grandeza*. And the property that went with it was worth billions of pesetas and generated immense income. For Alfonso to relinquish a major part of his heritage and his fortune, the family-resting place, not to save that historic title and estate for his eldest son, or even to have given it and the vast lands to his other sister, was, to Cristina, absolute proof of his sincerity. Paco understood it too, and there was a glaze across his eyes. Cristina's tears flowed freely. There is a time to cry.

Alfonso made the legal declaration acknowledging Paco to be his half brother, signed over to him the title of Conde de Los Escalones and transferred the *escritura* of the castle and estate to his name, thus with two strokes of a pen formalizing his nobility and making him wealthy.

Cristina and Paco agreed to stop seeing each other. Paco made arrangements to attend the University in Salamanca and he moved to another hotel. But neither one swore to try to forget the other.

* * *

Cayetana breezed into the apartment at the Ritz. Her visit wasn't the only surprise. Her dark hair was now a glossy, golden blonde and she wore a lime suit with a bright yellow flower. She was gorgeous.

"Cay! What happened to you?"

She sighed theatrically, "Fonso, you're supposed to exclaim, 'Cay, how utterly, utterly ravishing!'"

"Well, you would be if you were a Swede or a German."

"I wore black for three years. After you left Biarritz I wore black for the rest of the war. Spaniards do not leave Spain simply by being away from her. Even though I was in France, my brother and my sister, my country, were at war. I used to look in the mirror and see myself in black, my clothes nearly matching my dark hair. When the war ended I thought: *I'll never again wear black.* It's flattering and provocative, but I now have nothing in black. Though it will live with us forever I will never willingly be reminded of that misery."

She looked at Cristina's scar, touched it with her finger. She did not articulate what her eyes said she felt.

"Where is your luggage? I have a bedroom for you and we will all stay here until the restoration of our home is complete."

"Oh, Fonso, that does not faintly interest me. I'm having a wonderful time in France. I'm involved with a few young men whom I find diverting."

"But Cay, what are you saying? You cannot be 'involved with a *few* young men.' It's not done."

"In Spain." She made a face. "Nothing is done in Spain. At least not openly. There everything is done. Life is for living. Poof! In a second everything we had was gone. So as I no longer have anything, I'm ready for everything. As long as it's attractive and feels good. But relax. I certainly am not going to marry them. They are merely for amusement."

"Cay! I'm scandalized."

"That will pass, Fonso, dear."

Feeling all she had suffered, empathizing with her, he mimicked his sister, "You look utterly, utterly ravishing, Cay."

"That's so much better."

"In fact, you are so stunning that I want to show you off. Both of you. Let's go downstairs for lunch. I have something spectacular to say."

Seated at a corner table that afforded maximum privacy Alfonso ordered a bottle of the best champagne. When it was served he raised his glass, "There isn't enough champagne in the world, nor any good enough to adequately toast what I'm going to tell you."

"Fonso, you're driving me mad."

"I kept this to myself until I could share it with both of you." He lowered his voice so that it wouldn't carry past their table. "Cay, earlier you said 'everything we had was gone.' You were almost right. We lost our parents and that is irreplaceable. But we do have something: we are rich. Unimaginably, inconceivably, colossally rich! Wealthy, affluent, bountifully, copiously, embarrassingly rich! There isn't a big enough word for what we are. Papá left us so many enormous *fincas* and so many thousands of millions of pesetas in cash that we can all have anything we ever want and we can never spend it all. As the primogenitor it was left to me to administer. I'll open bank accounts for each of you and I will keep them overflowing. You need only write checks for anything you want."

Hours later, having digested that amazing news Alfonso urged, "Cay, reconsider and stay on with us in Madrid."

"One day, Fonso. But not yet. I still have a few outrageous things to do in France."

When they had taken her to the railroad station, Atocha, and watched her train pull away, he and Cristina stared at each other without a word they could think of to say. Nor was there anything he could do about Cayetana. He wasn't her father. He couldn't force her back to Spain.

"Life is miserably complicated," Cristina said. "Tomorrow Paco leaves for Salamanca to do the right thing. We live in the way we have been taught is proper and correct and none of us are happy. Cay lives in a scandalous way that I cannot even imagine and she's happy."

"Why would we believe she's happy?"

* * *

They lived each day as best they could, Cristina's thoughts always on Paco; Alfonso unable to pass a day without reliving the nightmare of the past. Always he drove out of his way to avoid passing the morgue.

They worked with architects to make plans for the restoration of their family home. Cristina had little appetite for returning there. "I'll always feel that those shits who took it over left a disease. I will always see them there. And their fucking urinals."

Startled by her language, yet understanding that a year in the army could affect anybody, he made no comment. He rather agreed with her.

"Alfonso, as long as we're so rich, why don't we build a new and modern home on the Castellana where there will be less memories, where there's more fresh air and sunshine?"

It was true that their palace in *Madrid de las Asturias,* the first neighborhood to have been built in the city, wasn't so pleasantly situated as the newer *Paseo de la Castellana.* And he wanted to please Cristina in any way she wished. But he couldn't stand the thought of being run out of his home. "For myself, I have to go back to my roots. We will fumigate, cleanse with fire if necessary. When it's ready to be lived in if you still feel this way, then we will build you a palace on the Castellana."

Alfonso did not mention to Cristina that he couldn't give up the vault in the basement that he could never duplicate. The last stonemason to share that secret had taken it to his grave. And who knew if an earlier Duke of the Castle of Tarifa had not prudently nudged the stonemason toward the "better life" a bit before his time? "A SECRET BETWEEN TWO PEOPLE IS NOT A SECRET." Whatever the case, those were different times and such an act wasn't one that Alfonso was prepared to perform.

He oiled the leather envelope that had led him to the vault. It and the parchment note were in his ancestors' desk where they would remain until the day he had a son. He would name his primogenitor to honor his father. He would change the name on the envelope to "José Maria," add his signature to those who had gone before him, sew the envelope closed, seal it with wax over the stitches and impress the *escudo* of the Castle of Tarifa into the wax.

In the autumn of 1942 the palace was restored, and Cristina chose to remain with her brother; they returned to their home, now protected by a fifteen-foot high wall.

Much of their art had been found in the *rastro* and in apartments inhabited by militiamen. Alfonso received back three El Grecos, six Tiepolos, a Van Gogh, three Velázquez, four Goyas, some Rubens, Raphael, Zurbarán, Sotomayor, Titian and a small drawing by Leonardo da Vinci, each of which Calixto hung where it had always been.

The *mayor domo*, also reasonably restored, had recruited a superb staff and again they lived in splendor. The twenty-year old Duke, wealthy, handsome and a war hero, and the nineteen-year old beautiful and rich Marquesa, also a heroine of the war, sparkled atop Madrid society. The food shortages meant that Alfonso could give only simple parties but he did so frequently, ostensibly to enjoy himself but in fact in the hope that his sister might meet an eligible man with whom she would fall in love. Cristina danced with the best-blooded, best-looking men of her country; she carried her scarred face with dignity and captured a bagful of eligible hearts.

During one of their supper dances she excused herself from her partner and, taking a glass of champagne from a passing waiter, she brought it to Alfonso, who was standing alone in a corner of the ballroom. Handing him the wine she said, *"El que no sonríe, nunca.'"*

"Sure I do," he forced a smile onto his face.

"When you see me watching."

Alfonso shrugged, unable to deny the undeniable. He had not regained his smile because he couldn't forget what had erased it, his grotesquely dead parents and the eighty human heads his rifle had destroyed in revenge with an ounce of lead between their eyes. And the others who had not given him frontal targets. In church he had confessed to killing more than a hundred of the enemy, and he was told that he was absolved of sin because it was a war, but he couldn't accept absolution. War or not, he knew that he had murdered over a hundred young men. How could anyone smile who understood that?

He wished he could remember his parents always as they had been on that night when they had come down the stairs so beautifully dressed. But without fail the image was obliterated by his last sight of them in the morgue, their heads blown away, flies trying to drink their blood. He longed for their company and their counsel about Cristina and Paco. How heavy his actions made him feel. What if he were wrong? She wasn't a madcap *Madrileña* who had quickly forgotten her first love. Clearly, none of the young men she had met had made her feel anything but indifference. And his own life? He had a lot of lovely dinner partners but he was a long way from being able to feel the emotion necessary to fall in love with anyone. He realized that he was young and that there was time, but he also understood that he had the responsibility to produce the next Duke of the Castle of Tarifa.

Cristina's dance partner came by and drew her away into the waltz. But each time she turned she looked for Alfonso and if there was a smile on his face she knew it was for her benefit, that it did not come from the heart. As her own did not.

For Paco, five monastic years passed before he returned to Madrid with scholastic honors and a job in a prestigious Madrid law firm.

On the night he returned, at their celebration dinner, Cristina announced to Alfonso, "Paco has his diploma, he has a wonderful job and we are going to be married. I have approval from the Vatican."

It was the last thing Alfonso had expected. She had given no indication. "Behind my back? You had no right."

"Alfonso, forgive me but you are wrong. Remember please, I'm twenty-three. My life is no longer your responsibility."

"I find it incredible that the Church would grant permission for a half brother and sister to marry. What did you tell them?"

"The truth. That there's no evidence, only your suspicion that Paco and I are related. But there's no support of any kind for your theory: not a single document or witness who can say 'I know this man is the son of the Duke of The Castle of Tarifa.' The Vatican said that under those conditions no permission is necessary."

"You have the will to disbelieve." Alfonso leaned close to Paco and implored Cristina, "Look at us, at our faces, our hair, the color of our eyes, the shapes of our bodies. We could be twins. Can you see us together and tell me that we are not of one father, who looked almost exactly like us?"

"Alfonso, we are a nation of many races. Thousands of Spaniards who are not related look similar. I do not believe that Paco and I are related. And I do know that we are more deeply in love. We have waited seven years. Alfonso, I want you to come to our wedding, to give me to Paco."

He remembered all the outstanding young men with whom she had danced and dined but who had not touched her heart. He looked into her dry yet crying eyes, at her scarred face. He heard her silently imploring, "Please let me be happy."

ALFONSO GARCÍA DE LAS ARENAS Y BELTRAN EL BUENO Y
MONTALBAN
DUQUE DEL CASTILLO DE TARIFA
REQUESTS THE PLEASURE OF YOUR COMPANY
AT THE WEDDING OF HIS SISTER
CRISTINA DEL MAR
MARQUESA DEL OLIVO
TO
FRANCISCO MORENO ORTEGA
CONDE DE LOS ESCALONES

The invitations were accepted by every *Grandee* of Spain. Cayetana, frolicking in Venice, came to Madrid a week early and was a "ravishing" maid of honor. With the prayer that he was wrong, Alfonso gave the bride away.

Cristina and Paco had bought a large house on *La Castellana* with a lawn where children could play in the sun. While Paco was at his law office Cristina passed happy hours furnishing their home. She prepared two nurseries, leaving space for more, anticipating the pleasure of their children occupying them, the joy of bringing them up with Paco.

Thus without his sister to help fill his life, six months later on January 15, 1947, Alfonso at the age of twenty-five married Magdalena de Soto y de Aragon, the Countess of Los Pyrenees, a member of a fine old Spanish family. Magdalena had the good luck to be noble, intelligent and beautiful, but the gods of money had turned away from her family because her paternal grandfather had too great a taste but too little talent for gambling. By the time Magdalena was born the family fortune had expired. Her father had followed a military career and had risen to Lieutenant General, the highest rank attainable in the Spanish Army. An aristocrat and a distinguished soldier, he wasn't a rich man. Magdalena and Alfonso admired and liked each other. It would be gossip to say that she married him for his money. That would discount his good looks, intelligence and charm. Further, she was an immensely desirable young woman pursued by several men considered to be as eligible as Alfonso. But tired of being "poor Magdalena" in a circle of friends who all were wealthy, and failing to have fallen in love with anyone, she chose to marry the man she liked most.

For his part, Alfonso did not value being in love as it wasn't something he had ever experienced. He saw Magdalena as the ideal mother for the next Duke of the Castle of Tarifa. In their own ways they needed each other just as much as people who are deeply in love.

Alfonso cautioned, "I cannot pretend that I'm wildly, mindlessly in love as the popular songs say some people are, and as I would like to be. Perhaps it's because of my childhood, the war . . . I don't know, but I do not have those feelings. Maybe the children we both want will change that. Honestly, I doubt it. I think I have been twisted into someone without the ability for certain emotions. But I promise that I'll always respect you and take care of you and love you in the way I love you now."

Magdalena accepted that condition. "I will be happy to be your wife, to bear your children, to be your friend, to respect you and care for you. If someday something happens that changes us into figures from a romantic novel, so much the better. If not, I believe we can make a good life together."

They returned from their honeymoon and began their married life in Madrid. While Alfonso looked after financial matters Magdalena involved herself in good works. She also acquired the most provocative lingerie she could find in the conservative Spain of the forties. She was an excellent horsewoman and she learned to play *Mus* and golf and to improve her shooting, hoping to become the companion with whom her husband would fall in love.

Then they fell out of public life because Magdalena was *embarazada*. On exactly the expected day she gave birth to a healthy boy they named José Maria to honor Alfonso's father. Alfonso went to his vault and prepared the leather envelope that the boy would one day inherit. Then he studied a wall of treasures, looking for a special gift for Magdalena. He selected an emerald diadem.

Touched, but unaccustomed to owning anything of such value she protested.

"Magda, allow me the pleasure of giving my wife a present. Look what you have given me. A son."

They hired an English nanny who took up residence with José Maria in the section of the palace in which Alfonso, Cayetana and Cristina had spent their happy childhoods.

* * *

From the day Alfonso learned that Cristina was expecting a baby, he went to his chapel every morning and prayed for her child to be healthy. He willed himself to believe that he was a meddler with an over imaginative mind; that Cristina and Paco were right, that Spain was a nation of many races and many Spaniards looked alike without being brother and sister.

At the hospital *San Francisco de Asis*, Alfonso kept Paco company during the hours of waiting and was in the room when the nurse brought the baby to be seen by her mother. The infant had oval shaped eyes, oriental in appearance. Cristina hugged her child to her breast, her face ecstatic as if she were seeing and thanking God. But Alfonso knew what those eyes indicated. Eventually the doctor would tell Cristina that she had given birth to a subnormal daughter, a *mongólica*.

Paco was seated by the side of his wife's bed, holding her hand. Alfonso thought, *They were foolish but not evil. They are in love. People in love do foolish, sometimes tragic things. It's their child not yours, they will love her; retarded or not, they will love their child.*

He touched her little hand. "She's beautiful."

Paco said, "We would be honored for you to be her godfather."

"The honor is mine. Have you decided on her name?"

"Yes," his sister said, "Esperanza. After Mamá ."

Alfonso thought of the irony in a child named Hope, when there was none.

* * *

"Paco, we have sinned."

"No, *Nena,* we made a bad mistake, not a sin. Alfonso was right all along. We had the will to disbelieve."

Weeks later, their child was asleep in her bassinet in their bedroom, Paco and Cristina were in their nightclothes. Since the baby's birth enough time had passed for them to resume lovemaking but though both of them yearned for it neither suggested it. Night after night they put the baby to sleep, kissed each other on the cheeks, put out the light and prayed for the painkiller of sleep.

Paco did not allow his wife to see the lust he felt for her.

Cristina did not mention her suffocating desire to put her arms around her husband, to draw him to her and make love to him and with him.

He looked toward her beside him in bed. It was easier to say some things in the dark. "I went to confession today and admitted that I still long for you."

"It isn't a sin to want each other as long as we don't . . ." Cristina looked miserably toward her husband. "What did the priest say?"

"What we both know: that we can not have intercourse except for the purpose of conceiving. But that now believing that we are brother and sister it would be a sin to have sex in the first place let alone run the risk of another subnormal child. Nor could we have an annulment because there are no legal grounds, no document or witness to prove that we are brother and sister."

"Annulment?" Cristina was alarmed. "Darling, the last thing I want is to be separated from you. I would never ever think of leaving you." She put on the light and looked at him searchingly. "Unless, of course, you want your freedom to have a complete life."

"Never. I only asked because you deserve that choice."

"Did the priest offer any suggestion?"

Paco shook his head. "He said the only road we have open is to continue to love each other and live together celibately. Nothing more."

Cristina said, "That will be enough for me."

"Me, too," Paco said hoarsely.

They hugged and put out the light, each praying to find peace in their private prisons.

* * *

After giving birth to José Maria, Magdalena did everything necessary to regain her figure and was quickly able to wear the clothes she had taken on their honeymoon. In less than a year she told Alfonso that she was again pregnant. Delighted, he said, "Luis. If it's a boy then this time we will honor your father."

Tio Guillermo died, and as he was a bachelor all of his properties and titles were inherited by Alfonso. Especially attractive to him and to Magdalena was the *finca* just outside of Madrid on the road to Toledo, where he and his sisters had ridden horses and shot clay pigeons during so many weekends. "Let's redecorate the house," she suggested, "and make it into our weekend home."

"Of course. Anything you wish. Anything." And he meant it because he loved her, but not as she and he had hoped might happen. Sadly he had been right, he wasn't capable of falling in love.

When their second son was born Alfonso gave Magdalena a diamond necklace and earrings that had belonged to his mother. Putting them on, looking at herself in a mirror, she was deeply grateful for the valuable gift but joked, "I feel that I'm being paid a fee as a brood mare."

"You must have objects of value in case you ever need to have money anywhere else in the world."

"But, Alfonso, everything is under control. Spain is at peace."

He looked at the woman for whom he felt strong affection and the need to protect, as he would a sister. "What's wrong with having something you may never need? Besides, you look beautiful in them."

Chapter Ten

It was 1952. Alfonso smelled the sweetness in the air as he rode on horseback across his Cuban sugar plantation. He had been eager to see it since he had inherited that distant property, but the Second World War caused him to wait until late 1952, when travel to Cuba was again possible and reasonably comfortable.

The plantation had been in his family since 1539, when Hernando de Soto, no relation to Magdalena, was Governor of Cuba, and his family had since intermarried with the descendants of Beltran El Bueno. Alfonso rode for several hours through the rich fields and then returned to the house in which the caretaker, Juan Campos, lived with his family. It was apparent that the caretakers had been taking care of themselves.

The house was a mansion. It was the first visit by a Duke of the Castle of Tarifa in four centuries, and Juan Campos was ill at ease due to the surprise arrival of the descendant of the family he and his ancestors had been bilking without remorse for hundreds of years. Showing Alfonso through "your house, Sr. Duque" was embarrassing because the house was filled with photos and memorabilia pertaining to the Campos families, past and present, with not a hint of the existence of the true owners. In fact, not for generations had any of the Campos family of caretakers consciously remembered that there was an owner who lived across the ocean.

Further, everything about Campos called out "money," from his heavy gold Patek Philippe, obviously expensive clothes, the number and quality of his servants, and a matching pair of 1952 Cadillacs in the garage. The man was clearly a multimillionaire plantation owner lacking nothing except the deed to the property.

Having had ten years experience with the family *fincas* in Spain, a dry and barren land compared to the fertile Cuban soil and humid climate, as well as seeing the quantity and quality of the sugar cane growing, Alfonso was certain that the plantation was extremely valuable. He just did not know how to calculate what that value might be. He was confident that he would never see honest books, nor would he get an honest accounting and there seemed little he could do about it. At age twenty-eight he had the wisdom to understand that he was a foreigner in a corrupt country, whereas surely Campos was politically entrenched with Batista's government and with everyone he would need to win a lawsuit and perhaps legally gain something he had never owned.

For sure, absentee ownership was unworkable, and Alfonso had nobody he could put in charge of this property. No Spaniard from Madrid could outwit a Cuban in Havana. It would take years to catch on to the game. Further, though legally Alfonso was the property owner, this man genuinely felt as if it were his own, his land, his home, as had his father and grandfather. It would be unfair, at least unkind, to wrench his lifestyle away from him. The logical solution was to sell Campos the property.

Seated in "his library" Alfonso maintained a stern facial expression for the purpose of negotiating. Dourly he asked, "How much would you say you have been forgetting to pay me each year?"

"Sr. Duque, I could say that I have been looking after your property as if it were my own. The double meaning is intended. I could tell you that the harvests were bad, but the fact is I have done well here, and my father before me."

Impressed by the candor, even while understanding that Campos' prosperity was too obvious to deny, Alfonso asked, "How do you explain never sending an accounting to my father, or to me?"

"I was never asked. And, honestly, it never occurred to me. However, I'm prepared to make amends by means of a generous offer to buy this property. One million American dollars."

"I have no interest in selling my heritage."

"Two million American dollars."

So, a 100 percent increase so easily! "Nor selling it to someone who is trying to steal it from me. I'm thinking of burning it down."

The negotiating ended when Alfonso accepted five million dollars in the form of a cashier's check on a branch of an American bank.

Before leaving Havana he shopped for souvenirs for his sons José Maria and Luis. God had been generous: the boys were handsome and bright. Only on a fluke could the issue of Alfonso and Magdalena fail to be healthy, intelligent and good looking. And another child was on the way.

He bought his children and his niece, Esperanza, coconuts that the Cubans carved into amusing savage heads, using seashells for eyes and ears, noses and teeth, also some South American musical instruments, rattles called *maracas*.

Alfonso stopped in Miami Beach before going on to New York to sail for Spain. As he checked into a hotel he was told that his room rate was fifty dollars a night. Compared to Spanish prices it was a fortune. "Why so expensive?"

"It faces the ocean, sir."

Walking along the beach he noted other hotels under construction, large ones. *Interesting.* Spain had nearly nothing developed on its thousand miles of Mediterranean coastline. Only in San Sebastian was there a seaside resort, but the season was only the month of August so there was nothing like these large and opulent hotels in the south of the United States, providing warmth and sunshine almost all year long. He knew of nothing like them in the sunny and warm south of Spain.

He wrote to Cristina, Paco and Cayetana about the five million dollar sale of their property.

... KNOWING OUR COUNTRY'S HISTORY IT'S TEMPTING TO HAVE A NEST EGG INVESTED IN SOME POLITICALLY STABLE PLACE SUCH AS THE UNITED STATES OR SWITZERLAND. YOU AND I AWAIT THE DAY WHEN FRANCO WILL RE-ESTABLISH THE MONARCHY AND WE WILL HAVE A KING. SOCIALLY, A KING IS PRETTIER THAN A DICTATOR. BUT, FOR PRACTICAL REASONS I'M HAPPY TO HAVE FRANCO. HE'S STRONG, AND THOUGH STRONG MEN ARE NOT IN STYLE TODAY HE'S UNIT-ING THE COUNTRY, WE HAVE LAW AND ORDER AS IT HASN'T EXISTED IN SPAIN SINCE FERDINAND AND ISABELLA. I THINK WE CAN INVEST SAFELY WITH HIM IN POWER.

ON AN EMOTIONAL LEVEL, IT WILL PLEASE ME TO BRING FOR-EIGN MONEY INTO OUR COUNTRY, WHERE IT'S SO SORELY NEEDED ...

Upon his return to Spain Alfonso changed the five million dol-lars into pesetas and invested it where he saw growth probability: the national telephone company and Madrid's and Barcelona's electric companies. As there was no income tax under the Franco government he also began removing the millions of pesetas in cash from his vault, investing it in utilities to grow and bear income, but leaving more than enough to continue providing the good living that he and his sisters and Paco enjoyed.

Alfonso had Christmas and New Year's with his family. Then, on January 6, he and Magdalena took their children to visit Cristina, Paco and Esperanza in their house on *La Castellana* to celebrate *La Fiesta de Los Tres Reyes Magos,* the festival of the Three Wise Kings, Epiphany, the day when Spanish children are given their Christmas presents.

Esperanza was an especially sweet child, adored by her cousins José Maria and Luis. Though they had never been told of her ill-ness Alfonso wondered if they sensed that she was different and instinctively felt protective of her. The children tore the ribbons and paper from their packages. At nearly four, Esperanza was less able with her hands than José Maria, who was a year her junior. And whereas José Maria and Luis were amused by the simple souvenirs from Cuba, Esperanza was ecstatic.

It was painful to understand that his own children would mature naturally and begin receiving their gifts on Christmas Day with the adults, but Esperanza would always be celebrating *Los Tres Reyes*. Alfonso grieved for what Cristina and Paco were suffering and would suffer all their lives. Four years had passed without Cristina becoming pregnant again. He assumed they had successfully traversed that time practicing the rhythm method of contraception. He couldn't know that they wouldn't sin, nor dare take that risk, that they suffered the agony of celibacy and anticipated nothing else ". . . until death do us part."

* * *

Impressed by what he had seen in Miami, in late January of 1951 Alfonso traveled by train from Madrid to Málaga, a major port city on Spain's southern coast. From there, dressed in simple clothes he rode on horseback along the coast road, westward in the direction of Cádiz, studying the land. Some fifteen kilometers from the railroad station he came to a sign indicating the Málaga airport that called itself, rather grandly, *Aeropuerto Internacional de Málaga*. Though it was little more than a landing strip and a garage it was indeed receiving flights from the colder countries of Europe.

In Torremolinos, the first town after Málaga, Alfonso was interested to see a few small hotels. Stopping at one for the night he went into the dining room and listened to the languages being spoken, English, German and Scandinavian. When the waiter came to take his order, Alfonso uncharacteristically encouraged conversation, "These people are all foreigners?"

"Yes. And rich ones."

"How do you know that?"

"*Hombre*, in the first place they are always laughing. They are here taking the sun, not working, as I am. Second, they have

169

come here on the airplane. Third, every time we raise the prices they complain to us, but they whisper to each other 'It's still dirt cheap.'"

"You understand their languages?"

"I worked in Gibraltar for ten years so I speak English. And I study German and Swedish."

Alfonso noted that indeed they were always laughing. Why not? They were tanned, away from their problems, the food and wine were good, far less expensive than in their own countries, and they were in a warm climate instead of freezing in the north of Europe.

In the morning continuing on horseback Alfonso understood that what he had seen was the beginning of tourism on Spain's southern coast and he recognized the opportunity to develop a small investment into something important. Once past Torremolinos he encountered only an occasional farmhouse, olive groves and goatherders, the landowners who lived off their trees or their goats, bartering for their needs.

As Spain did not begin manufacturing automobiles until 1954, there were few cars, mostly expensive imports, and as he distinctly did not want to appear prosperous, traveling on horseback enabled Alfonso to blend in and to stop and chat with these simple people, who were glad for a few minutes with a human being, but not much more because they were more comfortable with their goats than with strangers.

A few kilometers before Marbella, a combination fishing village and mining town, he spoke with a sun-wizened old man who wore a black beret, homemade *alpargatas* and a rope through his belt loops. Alfonso introduced himself by his abbreviated family name, Alfonso García. After discussing the weather and the goats the man acknowledged that the land reaching from the sea to six kilometers back into the mountains and three kilometers broad was his. Alfonso made admiring sounds and inquired if he would be willing to sell some of it. "For *metálico*," he emphasized, suspecting that the man had probably not held any money in his hands since before the war. *Metálico,* a term for "cash," dates back to before paper money, when there were only coins.

To the goat herder, who had never been elsewhere and had no knowledge of the existence of a seaside resort, the land at the seashore was useless. It was merely sand and could grow only cactus, nothing that his goats would eat. Nor could one plant fruit or olive trees so close to the sea because the strong coastal winds carried the salt air, *la marisma,* like a flame to burn anything green. The only land he valued was in the hills where they were standing and watching his goats feed on the greenery.

The goat herder gestured to the oceanfront property and said he might be willing to sell some of that land, and graciously added, "Though I think you would be crazy, for what can you do with it?"

Reluctant to rape this decent man's ignorance Alfonso allowed, "Perhaps build a hotel."

Now the goat herder knew this *tio,* guy was crazy and hurried to separate the fool from his money before he changed his mind. Alfonso bought three kilometers of "worthless" oceanfront property, half a kilometer deep, for one peseta—approximately a penny and a half—per square meter. Roughly, fifteen thousand dollars for fifty acres of oceanfront property in an area with a year-round warm climate. And, in so doing, he made the goat herder a relatively rich man. In three months Alfonso acquired extensive tracts of oceanfront property as well as connecting land into the hills of Fuengirola, Marbella, San Pedro de Alcántara and Estepona, and he had barely spent the equivalent of two hundred thousand dollars.

Cristina and Cayetana, who had returned from France and taken residence in Madrid, were flabbergasted. Cayetana was the more vocal, "With all the *fincas* we own you take good cash and buy us still more?"

He thought that Cay had not learned much from her long stay at the oceanfront Palace Hotel in Biarritz. Though in her defense, the French resort had a poor climate and a short season.

"Fonso, you bought land that can grow nothing?"

"It will grow money. With air travel developing, the English, Germans and Scandinavians will go where they can be warm. At the right time we will sell them the land they will want for their golf courses and resort homes. I wouldn't be surprised if in twenty years we got back twenty, even thirty pesetas for every one invested. Maybe fifty."

PART THREE

"**D**o you feel you understand my life now?" Alfonso asked America. "My ancestors, my sisters and Paco, that I spent the last twenty-five years of my life building a family and my business until fate put me in Marbella to find you and happiness? Do you see now that you have never been the 'other woman'? You're *the* woman."

They were lunching at a *chiringuito* and several flies settled on the table looking for crumbs. Fiercely Alfonso swiped at them. Now, understanding his aversion, America put her hand on his.

Marisa and Carlos were in Madrid for the winter. They would return for Christmas and Easter week and were delighted to have America using their house for as long as she wished. For appearances Alfonso lived in his own small beach house a few hundred meters away, but in fact he and America took the sun and the moon at Marisa and Carlos' house. As they walked together on the beach a lady smiled and said, "*Adiós*." America asked, "Why would she say goodbye when she didn't stop to say hello?"

"*Adiós* does mean goodbye, but it's a short way of saying '*Vaya con Dios,*' go with God, a pleasant greeting."

In Sevilla, passing a shoe shop Alfonso saw a pair of gold pumps in the window. Involuntarily he envisioned his mother walking down the stairs of their home, then the next day in the morgue. He trembled and to cover it he faked a laugh, "I'm reminded of Juan March, Spain's richest man, who began his business life by

smuggling cigarettes. He was ingenious. After the war this decimated country had no leather shoes. Nor the animals from which
to make them. March went to Italy and bought 100,000 pairs and
had them shipped to him, half to Barcelona and half to Málaga.
However, the half that went to Barcelona were all for the left foot
while the half to Málaga were all for the right. His Customs agent
in Barcelona went through the act of discovering that 'an error'
had been made and as 100,000 left shoes were worthless he certainly wasn't going to pay a Customs duty on them nor would he
pay the cost of shipping them back. The officials agreed and were
glad to let them pass and be rid of the problem. The same thing
happened in Málaga. The result was he imported a hundred thousand pairs of shoes without paying *ní una peseta* in duty and sold
them at a large profit."

America touched Alfonso's face and felt the dampness. "That's
a good story," she said. "But you told it to me because those gold
pumps made you think of your mother." He looked into her eyes,
put his arm around her shoulder and they continued walking.

One morning, when he was away, she awoke knowing it was
Angel's birthday and she lay in bed crying, imagining the happy
day it would have been, the presents from Grandma and Grandpa
and Uncle Gat, the party and everyone cheering as Angel blew out
the seven candles on the cake. She forced herself out of bed and
into her riding clothes and galloped along the beach. Returning
to the house she received a message that Alfonso would arrive that
afternoon. Thursday? She phoned him at the bank, as Sunday
nights she drove him to the airport in Málaga and returned to
meet him there on Fridays, so this would mean he would arrive a
day early.

"I'm just leaving for the airport. I'm desperate for an extra day
with you. The bank will survive without my direction."

"Can it?"

"If I say so, it must. I'm the chief."

She laughed at his literal translation of *jefe*, chief, boss.

She was waiting for him at the airport. "I know why you are here today. Thank you."

Though Angel kept returning to her thoughts the ache was softened by knowing that he had come to her a day early specifically to comfort her, to divert her when possible, and she had the strange feeling that the three of them were together.

The following Friday, driving with him toward Marbella there was only the sound of passing cars and the Mediterranean being splashed apart by the rocks on shore. Alfonso wasn't his usually animated self.

America observed, "It's awfully glum in this car."

"Of course I'm glum. The two months will end and I encounter it difficult to let you go again. There's a limit to gallantry. I'm now thinking of my own happiness."

"Excellent. So am I. Therefore, I'm not returning home."

"Say that clearly, please."

"I'm saying that I missed yesterday's flight to New York, and I'm going to miss today's, tomorrow's and the next day and the next day and the day after that."

"That's not realistic. You have no future with me."

"Well, *mi amor,* I recognize the need for a good future. But I'm certainly not going to buy it with what I've got going for me right now in the present."

He turned in his seat to face her. "You must understand that I won't be able to be with you on any important holidays. You will be alone on Christmas, New Year's Eve, Easter Sunday, on my children's birthdays when they fall on weekends. Children require occasions to maintain a sense of family. At best I can only be with you on weekends."

"I was alone for three years until I was given you. Don't worry. I'll use my time well. For one thing I'll go to France and England and get temporary work as a pilot to log flying time and maintain my certifications. I worked too hard to get them to let them expire. I may want them some day. Also, I enjoy flying."

He spoke hard and fast, afraid he might not get the words out if he did not. "You should find a man with whom you won't always be second to his family."

"I don't want him. The happiness that I've got now . . ." she clasped his arm, ". . . in my hand, is irreplaceable. I'm not returning to Texas. I'm staying here."

She wrote to her family. And to Jerry Gottlieb:

CONGRATULATIONS ON BECOMING THE NEW PRESIDENT OF JETWAYS, WITH A 50 PERCENT INCREASE IN SALARY, A NEW COMPANY CADILLAC, AND WE'LL DISCUSS STOCK OPTIONS VS. PARTICIPATION IN PROFITS.

I'M NOT COMING HOME, JERRY, NOT IN THE FORESEEABLE FUTURE. I'M TAKING A LEAVE OF ABSENCE FROM JETWAYS. YOU WILL PROBABLY HAVE TO COME OVER HERE ONCE OR TWICE A YEAR WITH YOUR FAMILY AT COMPANY EXPENSE AND MAKE A REPORT TO THE STOCKHOLDER. LOOK AFTER JETWAYS AND MAKE A LOT OF MONEY FOR US BOTH . . .

When she had mailed the letter she thought, *that was a big move*, but she didn't feel it. Separating herself from her family and her country was theoretically difficult, but leaving Alfonso was unthinkable. So there was no decision: it was thoroughly untraumatic.

Gat called. "I did not realize that insanity ran in our family."

"Don't you think that's a bit exaggerated?"

"I think you're a whole lot exaggerated. Holy Toledo, Ame, when the folks and I gave you the nod on an extended vacation we did not expect you to make it permanent. You promised you'd be home for Christmas. They've been missing you, badly, just this long. So have I. Now we're *never* going to see you?"

"Gat, when I was next-door in Oklahoma City how often did I see you or Mom and Dad?"

"But we knew where you were, that you were okay."

"You know that now, too. If you'll accept my word, and be honest with yourself, you'll know that I'm a lot—a great, great, great lot more okay now than I was when I was at home building Jetways and praying that God would call me to join my daughter. Plus, I have been talking to you on the phone once or twice a week since I've been here. And do you mind if I ask what's wrong with you coming over here and seeing me? You'll love it."

"Sure we'll come over. But it's not the same."

"Gat, please try to believe that I've found a man I love, with whom I belong, and I'm enjoying a kind of happiness I never knew existed."

"I want to believe it, Ame, but you're going down a one-way street the wrong way giving your life to a married man."

"I'm not giving my life to anyone but me. After thinking my life was over I have found a way to feel complete again, to enjoy most of every day instead of only suffering through them."

America walked onto the terrace of Marisa's house and looked out at December on the Mediterranean: sunshine, cloudless blue sky, an armada of small fishing boats fifty yards from the shore, moving back and forth, scraping the sand for cockleshells and mussels, their small motors making a peaceful putt-putt-putting sound. A flock of seagulls followed the more distant fishing boats, hoping to swoop down and catch something dropped from their nets.

Two *Guardias Civiles* walked across the lawn, dramatic in forest-green uniforms with black patent-leather belting, holsters and *tricornios*. On chilly nights they wore long, forest-green capes. The policemen walked casually but looked carefully. Noting America standing on the terrace they saluted and continued on. It occurred to her that at home policemen did not walk across one's lawn, yet she did not sense any invasion of privacy. She enjoyed seeing them.

Juan appeared and said that Sister Maria Josefa, the nun from *Hogar San Carlos*, was outside. "Would the Señora be so kind as to receive her?"

"Of course. Bring her right in."

She made another contribution of a hundred thousand pesetas, and through Juan she asked about the children and promised always to be available to help. Then she said, "Wait a minute. Juan, ask sister if the little girls have time to come to a picnic, a party on the beach?"

On the following Saturday, a bus America rented picked up the twenty orphaned children at *Hogar San Carlos* and Sister Maria Josefa and two other nuns and brought them to Marisa's house for a day on the beach. America had learned that hot dogs, *salchichas,* were as popular with Spanish children as with Americans. She hired a man to keep them constantly grilling, along with hamburgers and French-fried potatoes, and also an ice-cream man who brought his entire stand and handed out pops, cups and ice-cream sandwiches as the children wanted.

America and the nuns sat on the terrace, watching the children delighting in the sea with a lifeguard she had hired, and playing games on the beach. Children's tastes in food and entertainments was fairly universal. She told the nuns that she would like to give a similar party on the last Saturday of every month. America had asked Juan to sit with her and the nuns and translate. When the day was done, when it was time for the children to return to Málaga, the children all rushed up to America and hugged her and kissed her, thanking her for their beautiful day. They spoke in Spanish and she in English. When they were gone America understood that they had communicated loving emotions, but she disliked being unable to have even short conversations without an interpreter.

Though she and Alfonso communicated fluently with their bodies, and his English, America understood that if she could speak Spanish really well, though he wouldn't love her more, it would be easier and more fun for him. She went to the home of Casilda Belmonte, a woman who gave Spanish lessons. "When would you like to begin?" Casilda asked.

"How about now? Can you work all day, Monday through Friday, having lunch with me, shopping, teaching me, correcting me? Not just grammar and vocabulary. I want the 'music,' too, so that I don't have a foreign accent."

"To eliminate your native accent is almost impossible. Besides, if your grammar is flawless, if you have a good vocabulary and a grasp of jargon, a trace of foreign accent will make your Spanish all the more appreciated."

Casilda said, "I have other students but my sister also teaches, I'll ask her to take over for me. Yes, I can do it. From ten in the morning until six?"

"And could your sister then work with me from six until ten or eleven at night?"

Thus, they were almost live-in teachers.

* * *

At the controls of a twin-engine Beechcraft, America flew over Andalucía with Alfonso at her side scanning the countryside through binoculars. She had asked him to show her some of his properties. "Only an American would think of this," he said admiringly, "to fly around the country and see your *fincas*."

"I regret to agree with you," she sighed, referring to a thought she had had of opening a business similar to Jetways. Alfonso had told her it wasn't a feasible idea and with very little research she found that he was right. Though Spain had become the tenth industrial power of the world, there were few Spaniards who would think of hiring a private plane to take them where a commercial airliner could at a fraction of the cost. They did not evaluate the convenience or their executive time in the same way that Americans and some Europeans do.

"Why would you want to work when you don't have to?" Alfonso asked, as he had the first time she had spoken about finding a business. "Why? I will take care of you, buy you a house in Marbella . . ."

"Look, my dear Latin lover, it's not that I'm against being a kept woman, in fact it's kind of sexy, but the fact is I'm financially able to take care of myself."

"If you insist. But why work when you have no need to?"

"*You* do."

"I should be declared insane. Then I could see you Monday through Friday as well." But it was just banter. He knew he wouldn't abandon his family. Also, he understood her American work ethic and recognized that it would be a waste of her mentality and energy to remain without something vital to occupy her while he was away during the week.

Alfonso pointed to areas where values were increasing so quickly with no end in sight, as America flew them over Torremolinos, then Fuengirola,

"You sure knew how to speculate."

"I was more lucky than clever. I foresaw tourism, but never imagined there would be such a boom and that it would return five *thousand* times my investment. By 1980 it will rise to ten thousand pesetas per square meter, or more. Unless there's a break in the boom. That could happen."

"Not unless they turn off the sun. Or if the world goes broke. What did you do with your profits?"

"I founded *Banco Castillo de Tarifa*."

"How did you know how to run a bank?"

"I knew nothing. I hired the smartest bank executive I could find. And two accounting firms that did not know of each other doing the same job. After three years, when the numbers kept coming up the same, and my manager and his family's lifestyle had not improved suspiciously, I made him a partner. He's still with me but by now I have learned enough to be able to operate the bank myself. And José Maria shows great promise as my successor. He's a born financier." His face reflecting love and pride he added, "He's one of the great joys of my life."

Passing central Marbella, Alfonso peered through the binoculars. "That land just below is mine but I did not buy it. That *finca* has belonged to my family since 1578."

It made her smile. "In America when someone wants to impress you they'll brag, 'This house has been in the family for eighty years.'"

"We have a shoot there every October. You were in Texas when it took place this year. There are no housing facilities so we stay at the Marbella Club."

"But there's a large house down there."

"It hasn't been lived in for two hundred years. It has no bathrooms, no furniture."

America descended to fifteen hundred feet and circled the terrain.

"It was a good *finca* before the war. Five thousand hectares that grew almonds, olives, lemons, oranges, garlic, onions, almost every kind of vegetable. But it was destroyed. Those two small houses are used by the families who work it. The tenant farmers in one, and two gamekeepers in the other."

"I can't imagine all that land not producing. This climate should be able to grow nearly anything."

"In theory, yes. But, it barely supports the tenants. They would do themselves a favor to go to work in a hotel or a restaurant."

America circled several times. She had a strong desire to see it from the ground. To walk on it. There was a dirt road along the side of the property, and not a car in sight. "Do you mind if we go down and have a look?"

"Are you suggesting landing the plane? Without an airport?"

"Sure. Right there."

"Can we land on that?"

"As the old joke goes, 'I could land this baby on a dime and give you three cents change,'" and as he laughed, enjoying what was, to him, new, she sighed, "I sure hope I'll be as big a hit with you when I become fluent in Spanish," and she set the plane down easily.

Something about this *finca* reached out to America. Her father's ranch looked completely different, cultivated, modern. This land was so rough and natural. The fences were constructed of dead branches of trees and small rocks. As they walked through a stone arch at the entrance to the property America knew that she wanted to live there, to get her hands, her heart into that land. It seemed to call out for help. All those years of hearing her father talk farming now rose up within her, and she yearned to use her background and resources to bring that unhappy land back to health and prosperity.

The farmhouse enchanted her. It was handsome in its design. And the stone from which it was made had been quarried nearby, giving it the appearance of belonging to the terrain. Standing on the porch that she envisioned as a comfortable terrace the view was spectacular. It was virgin land all the way to the Mediterranean, then the Rock of Gibraltar slightly to the right and the two humps of Ceuta, the Spanish enclave across the water in Morocco. She stood there gripped, as always, by the sight of the sea, all that water, all that peace and quiet, the way God had made the world.

She looked behind them and up at the mountain range, so beautiful as to appear unreal, like a movie set. "Would you sell me this farm?"

"Absurd."

"Are you holding it as an investment?"

"No, it's too high up. Even those few acres along the beach are outside the center of the boom. It won't be touristically valuable for a long time. This would be a terrible investment for you. There's no water supply for farming; it was destroyed in the war. Look at how poor those trees are, the worms starve to death on the lettuce. Truly it produces next to nothing."

America scooped up a handful of dirt and sifted it through her fingers. It was sandy but that did not discourage her. "I could make it produce."

"I do not want you to lose your money on my land. I want you to understand that this is a hopeless proposition. The only thing of value here are the partridge and pheasant we sell every October after the shoot."

"You can keep the birds. Have the shoot every year. I just want to farm this land. If you won't sell it, then lease it to me until I prove that I can make it pay. Then sell it to me at a prearranged price."

"Very well, one peseta a month."

America took his hand in hers. "This is a business matter. I would appreciate a formal piece of paper naming an appropriate price, signed by you and by me. In addition, I would like an option to buy the land in front of me to the beach to guarantee nothing will be built there."

"You are serious. All right, then, your rent will be five thousand pesetas a month with an option to buy at one peseta per meter. And the waterfront property at one thousand per meter."

"You're getting five thousand down the coast."

"A fair price for here is one thousand per meter."

"It's better than fair. It's generous."

"My darling, forgetting the strip of waterfront that I'll never sell in order to protect your property, purchase of the principal *finca* represents a large sum. One peseta sounds cheap but the property contains some fifty million meters. That's fifty million pesetas, approximately seven hundred and fifty thousand dollars."

She had paid more for just one airplane.

Alfonso felt guilty allowing her to invest in something in which he did not believe. Yet, he loved the idea of her planting her roots more deeply in Spain, and with him.

America consulted with her father out of courtesy as well as respect for his wisdom and business acumen. His comment wasn't what she had hoped for. "I cannot tell you that I consider it sound to sell a thriving, modern business in the United States and put your money into a farm in what is considered a poor country."

"But shouldn't money serve to make us happy?"

"In a measure, yes. But you have a responsibility to your money. You mustn't dissipate it just to amuse yourself. You should make it grow. I don't know anything about Spain or its agricultural needs, the competition, the export possibilities. Again I leave it to you to make the final decision, so, as I said when you were thinking about starting up an air courier service, study it well and give very serious thought about selling a sure thing and investing in a maybe."

She hated giving up all or even part of the company on which she had risked everything she had, on which she had worked so hard.

But there was another life that she craved and she felt confident that despite substantial risk, with hard work she could make it successful.

> DEAR JERRY,
> I'M PLANNING TO SELL ALL OR PART OF JETWAYS AS I AM INTER-
> ESTED IN A DIFFERENT INVESTMENT. I AUTHORIZE YOU TO
> HAVE OUR LAWYERS DRAW UP A NEW CONTRACT FOR YOU TO
> INCLUDE A ONE MILLION DOLLAR GOLDEN PARACHUTE AND
> CONSULTING FEES. YOU HAVE BEEN A BLESSING TO THE COM-
> PANY AND I DON'T WANT THE SALE TO PREJUDICE THE FUTURE
> THAT YOU HAVE SO WELL EARNED.
>
> WHEN YOUR CONTRACT IS DONE AND BINDING, PLEASE CON-
> SULT WITH AN INVESTMENT-BANKING HOUSE REGARDING THE
> ADVISABILITY OF AN OUTRIGHT SALE OF JETWAYS, MOST LIKELY
> TO A SIMILAR ENTITY, VERSUS TAKING THE COMPANY PUBLIC AND
> SELLING ENOUGH OF MY SHARES TO GIVE ME TWO MILLION DOL-
> LARS IN WORKING CAPITAL FOR MY PROPOSED VENTURE HERE.
> FONDLY,
> AMERICA

Jerry followed her instructions and America received his new employment contract with the million dollar golden parachute if anyone should discharge him and a fifty thousand dollar per year consultant's fee for ten years. She signed it with pleasure.

A week later she received the following telegram:

> GOLDMAN SACHS AND SMITH BARNEY SHEARSON RECOMMEND
> THAT JETWAYS GOES PUBLIC AND THAT YOU SELL OFF ONLY
> THE SHARES YOU NEED TO ACCUMULATE THE CAPITAL YOU
> WANT FOR NEW VENTURE. IF YOU WERE TO SELL OUTRIGHT
> TO OTHER COURIER COMPANY YOU WOULD BE EXPOSED
> TO TAX ON THE ENTIRE VALUE OF THE SALE BEYOND YOUR
> INITIAL INVESTMENT. MANY THANKS FOR YOUR CONCERN FOR
> ME. FONDLY. JERRY

Chapter Eleven

Alfonso called her from Madrid, "*Mi amor,* would you like a guest for lunch tomorrow? Somebody tall, dark, not bad looking, titled, and who wants to sing to you?"

"Tomorrow? On Wednesday?"

"It isn't merely Wednesday. It's the first day of *La Primavera,* my favorite time of year. It's the beginning of everything, when the days are the longest and I can spend the most time with you. I do not think that the Bible mentions it but I'm confident that spring is when God began creating the world, and I yearn to spend the first day of spring with you."

"Oh, how I'd love it. But what about the bank?"

"Haven't I told you I'm the chief?" He was happy to hear her giggle. He was now aware that it amused her and had used it deliberately. "It can run for a few days without me. José Maria, at only twenty-four, is the most responsible man in the bank and making himself indispensable."

"Darling, I've already started the *cocido* cooking."

"And will your guest be imposing if he stays for dinner? And then for Thursday, Friday, Saturday and Sunday?"

That evening, at dinner with his family, Trini the youngest, asked, "Papá, will you take me horseback riding on my birthday?"

It stunned him. How could he have forgotten? Trini's birthday was March 22, Thursday. This would be her twelfth. When he didn't say yes immediately the dining room became silent. He felt

José Maria staring at him. Magdalena also was looking at him with surprise.

Trini whimpered, "But you always take us someplace on our birthdays, *Pápi*."

"My darling, of course I do. But this year has to be different. Tomorrow morning, early, I must leave town on business and I won't be here for your birthday. I can't come back until Sunday night. But I'll make it up to you. Next week we'll go horseback riding every afternoon."

Trini did not react with the pleasure he had hoped for. On the edge of tears she turned to Magdalena, "Mamá, will you take me somewhere?"

"Of course I will, darling. Anywhere you like. And we'll have a wonderful birthday dinner and a delicious cake."

José Maria added, "And I'll take you riding on your birthday, and we'll jump fences."

Alfonso stood up and went over to Trini and kissed her on the forehead. He hugged her. "My sweet, precious one, we will all take you riding. You're more important to me than my business. So I'll change my business. I'll be gone tomorrow but I'll be back Thursday morning to celebrate your birthday." He was rewarded by her radiant face. He looked at José Maria, who was clearly relieved and he spoke to his children as one, "You are all the most important things in my life. And you always will be."

He recognized that he wasn't giving them the time and attention to support such a statement. José Maria was twenty-four, Luis twenty-three and Rafael twenty. Throughout their childhoods he had been father and companion, treating them as his father had treated him, teaching them to shoot, taking them to *cacerias*, being present as they graduated various levels of school. Wanting to be present. And they had felt that support. Now they had their friends and girlfriends and boyfriends, they didn't need or miss his attention. Even the twins, Carmen and Maria del Mar, at nineteen were thoroughly occupied with their young men, coincidentally brothers, though not twins. They were the eldest sons of good friends, a fine Spanish family. The father, Rafael Lopez-Sáez, was Captain General of Aviation in Madrid, which meant that he commanded the Spanish Air Force and Combat Group as well as the American air base at Torrejón. Alfonso knew the boys and liked them and he expected that soon he would be visited by one or both of them for his consent to marriage.

However, Alfonso, now seventeen, could certainly use a more active father. Elena and Trini, fifteen and twelve, had their mother but they should have had a father, too, a traditional family, not a superficial father. Yet he did not know how to give himself sufficiently to them and also enjoy the only love of his lifetime. For twenty-five years of marriage he had been without joy except for pleasure derived from his children. And that was a far cry from what a man feels when he is deeply in love with a woman. When he had met America it was as if he were a youth. He hungered for every minute he could have with her. With America he cared about everything again, his taste buds, physically and emotionally had sprung to life. He was eager for every minute, every meal, every experience. He couldn't give that up. Yet he would have to find ways to give more to the three youngest children. Stay home for occasional Friday dinners and then leave while they watch television. It would be unfair to America. She had little enough of him. Yet his family obligations were his agreement with her. He looked at Magdalena, he thought of America. He had two wives and he wasn't giving enough to either of them.

* * *

Alfonso stepped off the plane carrying two Belgian Pointer puppies, white with black spots. As America drove them along the coastline he said, "I wanted to give them to you ever since that day we were reading *¡HOLA!* and you saw the picture of Julio Iglesias with his dog and you said, 'That is the most beautiful animal I've ever seen.' But I couldn't until you had decided to stay. They are also for me. To know that you will have extra protection and company when I'm away." As they drove he said, "The bad news is that I can only stay tonight . . . ," and he explained why.

"Well, we have all day. The first day of spring together."

"I'll take the last flight back."

"The *golfo*. We call it the red-eye in America."

He was amused. "How do you know it's called the *golfo*?"

"Casilda told me that stay-ups are called *golfos*," she said, pleased that she was beginning to make a breakthrough in his language.

"Be careful, my love, a slight change of gender to *golfa* would mean prostitute."

On the terrace at Marisa's house the puppies were jumping all over America as she was kissing them and they were licking her face and arms. He said, "Obviously, I had no time to train them to act like gentlemen."

"Oh, Alfonso, are they ever gorgeous! I'll never train them not to be affectionate with me."

Alfonso was stroking the head of the smaller one, "I thought we could name him *Primavera,* springtime. Though a word ending in 'a' is usually feminine there are exceptions so we can take poetic license." He looked at the slightly larger dog that America was scratching behind the ears and whose tail was wagging like a metronome at high speed. "How about Happiness?" she asked.

"*Alegría,*" he said. More poetic license, but why not? Alegría he is."

"I'll call him Al. That'll fix the gender problem."

That night, kissing her goodbye in the car before catching the *golfo,* Alfonso sighed, "How I hate leaving you alone."

"I'm never alone anymore. You're always with me. And now I have Primavera and Al."

* * *

Alfonso set the alarm clock to wake him early. He knocked on Trini's bedroom door. She was still blinking the sleep away when he kissed her, "Happy birthday, darling. No school for you today.

Get into your riding clothes and let's make a full and wonderful day out of it." She leaped out of bed and rushed to get dressed.

At breakfast, with all the family in boots and breeches or jodhpurs he said, "After we've ridden at the Hippodrome for a few hours we'll go to Tio Guillermo's and steeplechase, shoot clay pigeons and have a picnic lunch. I won't go to work today. Your birthday is a National Holiday." Trini giggled. "It's a holiday for us. But not for José Maria, who'll have to go to the bank in the morning to make sure the money is still there. If it is, then he can join us for lunch and then we'll all go to the Ritz for tea." The day went off like a charm, and seeing the joy he had created for them all Alfonso couldn't help thinking how simple it was to make his loved ones happy. Yet how difficult.

At dinner that night Elena asked, "Papá, are you going away again this weekend?"

"Yes, sweetheart."

"Can we come with you to the *finca?*"

Cautiously Alfonso asked, "Why do you think I'm going to a *finca*, darling?"

"José Maria said that you can't leave the bank during the week so you have to look after our *fincas* on weekends. Can we come with you, Papá?"

"I'm sorry, my darling. It's a difficult trip and I'm so busy that you'd never see me and there's nobody there to cook a decent meal for you; the bedrooms of the old house are cold . . . it's not for you."

Continuing to eat his dinner Alfonso looked casually from Magdalena to each of the children, trying to see if they knew he was lying. Magdalena knew, and of course so must José Maria, though he couldn't imagine how. He couldn't tell about the others.

* * *

The donkeys and manual plow had been replaced by a John Deere caterpillar tractor; a procession of trucks continued arriving

191

with rich soil from Coin, (co-een) a *pueblo* up the mountain; large reserves of water had been discovered after drilling only 1,500 feet below her land; plumbers and masons were putting in an irrigation system; others were installing electricity.

America was surrounded by workmen, speaking to them in Spanish, her two dogs prancing at her side. The roof of the main house was being repaired and running water was being installed in the kitchen and bathrooms. Where two months before there had been six small bedrooms now two of them were comfortable bathrooms and one was a library/sitting room that combined into a suite with the master bedroom and a spacious guest room. She had obtained a telephone line and was putting plumbing and electricity into the farmers' and gamekeepers' houses, as well as tile floors, refrigerators, ovens and electric heaters. Higher up on the mountain next to a stream a bulldozer was scooping out a two-acre bowl for a lake she was going to stock with fish.

She had kept Alfonso away from the *finca* until it had begun to take shape. He said, "I'm astounded. Never have I seen anything so dramatically improved. Being in love with you caused me to forget your brilliance in business, what you accomplished in aviation. Really, what you have done here—it's impressive."

Her face radiated her pleasure. "I maintained the basic structure of the house, but I've got to admit that putting plumbing into these one-meter thick walls was a killer."

"There's a Spanish saying that 'cement likes the first hundred years to harden.'"

Closets had not existed when the house was built and as America did not want to change the proportions of the rooms she intended to use armoires. "Where would you suggest I buy the nicest, typically Spanish furniture?"

"Furniture?" He looked bewildered.

"You know, those things you sleep on, sit on, put your shirts and sweaters in?"

"It just struck me as odd to buy furniture. I have quite a few homes yet I've never bought a single chair, table, bed, lamp, nothing. Almost every year some maiden aunt or childless cousin dies and leaves me more furniture, more china and silver. Buy nothing. I have a warehouse full. I'll send everything you need."

* * *

At the dinner table in Madrid, Maria del Mar asked, "Papá, may we bring Rafa and Cristóbal to the *cacería* in Marbella next month?" She was referring to her and her twin sister's *novios*.

"Of course. Wonderful. I'll have Mari Sol reserve another double room at the Marbella Club. Do they shoot?" he asked, understanding that the *cacería* is a rich man's sport, requiring expensive equipment and shells and above all the free time to participate in the shoots that take place during the week as well as weekends. Though the boys' father was a distinguished *militar,* and economically comfortable, he wasn't a rich man and Rafa and Cristóbal were boys who had to work for their livings.

Magdalena said, "I think the boys will be more interested in talking to you than in the shoot."

Alfonso remembered anticipating that this wasn't far off and he had a pleasant feeling about it. "I look forward to speaking with them." He changed the subject. "You will all be amazed at what the new owner has done with that once useless *finca*. It's going to become a highly profitable agricultural property."

José Maria asked, "But how can we have a *cacería* on someone else's property?"

"It was a stipulation in the sale. We retained all rights to the game."

José Maria was impressed. "And fifty million for a property we don't need." He looked at his father. "Strong."

* * *

Still living in Marisa's house, America rose daily at eight A.M. Primavera and Alegría slept in baskets by the side of her bed. She let them out of the house, dressed and went eagerly to her *finca* to enjoy breakfast on the terrace. It was a cool day and with no haze the texture of the Rock of Gibraltar could be seen so clearly that she had the feeling she could reach out and touch it. The beauty of nature awakened her as surely as the caffeine in her coffee. She read the Spanish newspapers she had bought on the way there, *SUR*, published in Málaga, and *ABC*, from Madrid, and listened to the morning news in Spanish on *Radio Nacionál Españól.* Alfonso called every morning at nine-thirty from the bank, just a "good morning" call. They spoke at greater length in the afternoons after banking hours.

Casilda arrived at ten A.M. and accompanied America while she and her foreman inspected the projects under way. When they were alone Casilda corrected language and usage mistakes, and they studied together for several hours.

After lunch, at three P.M. she watched *Telediario,* the first news telecast of the day. She could have installed an antenna to pick up the BBC from Gibraltar, but she wanted to learn Spanish more than to hear the news unerringly. For that she read the *International Herald Tribune* and *Time* magazine. In the evenings she read Spanish novels and nonfiction and also the celebrity magazines *¡HOLA!* and *Semana.* Often she was jolted upon seeing photos of Alfonso and his wife at a wedding or a charity ball. Magdalena was undeniably a very beautiful, elegant woman.

She was observing work on her lake when two moving vans arrived from Sevilla, the city from which Alfonso's Tia Pilar, the Condesa de Villagoya, had recently departed for the anticipated better life. The vans brought beds, end tables, armoires, a long dining table ideal for the oblong dining room. There was a wonderful desk with a note Alfonso had attached to it, explaining how to open two concealed drawers, and several excellent iron sculptures, Bidasoa porcelains, and decorative communal eating bowls from Menorca. One of her favorites in the shipment was a small desk with a fall front and forty small drawers. In a note hanging from a knob Alfonso explained that it was a *vargueño,* one of the most distinguished types of furniture in Spain in the 16th, 17th and 18th centuries and that in those days these desks traveled with their owners somewhat as we use brief cases today. When in the house they were placed on a base.

Everything Alfonso had sent was an antique because that was all the family had. Presumably Aunt Pilar had also never bought furniture. The headboard of the bed America chose for herself was dark mahogany, inlaid with a lighter color wood forming a countess' crown and the initial V.

She had hired a young couple, Encarna and Rafael, the girl as cook and housekeeper and the young man as gardener to develop a cutting garden and do whatever heavy work was needed. America separated her home from her business and did not want to be borrowing time from the farm staff. Each of them had his full day's work. For Encarna and Rafael she built a connecting cottage of one bedroom, a kitchen and sitting room, designed so that she could add on if they had children. She furnished it with television, pretty towels, linens and comfortable furniture.

At the time of the *cacería* America understood that her absence from Marbella would be appropriate and she took the opportunity to visit her parents and Gat. Rafael brought her car to the front door to drive her to the airport and America kissed Encarna goodbye. They both, particularly Rafael, had come to love Primavera and Alegría . The dogs, sensing that something unpleasant was happening, were quiet. She knelt down and kissed both of them and stroked their heads. "I hate leaving all of you."

* * *

As it's the host of the *cacería* who assigns the posts Alfonso had put the twins at blinds at his side. Cristóbal sat with Maria del Mar and Rafa with Carmen. He had guessed right, the boys did not shoot. But they certainly were in love with his daughters. They loaded their guns, collected the birds they downed and spent few seconds with their eyes on anything except their *novias*. As they moved from post to post in a Jeep he observed them feeding each other *tapas* and having an extraordinarily good time together. How charming he thought that two brothers had fallen in love with two sisters. They had been going together for over a year. Alfonso had made some discreet inquiries. Cristóbal was in the Diplomatic Service and was highly regarded at the Ministry of Foreign Affairs, no small or easy matter. Rafa worked at the Madrid headquarters of *Banco Coca* and according to Ignacio Coca he was industrious and talented. Surely they would be successful in their respective careers. Especially with economic aid at the appropriate time.

When they returned to the Marbella Club the boys approached him. Cristóbal said, "Sir, thank you so much for inviting us. It was a fabulous day."

Rafa added, "Yes, thank you so much. Sir, may we have a few words with you on another subject?"

"With pleasure. Let's go into the bar."

They sat down on two facing couches with a cocktail table between them. Alfonso ordered a bottle of *cava* and wishing to make it easy for them said, "I think we'll enjoy our drinks more if I tell you that if I'm correct, you want to discuss marriage to my daughters, and my answer is an enthusiastic yes."

Rafa and Cristóbal's faces were alight like thousand-candle power lamps. They hadn't dreamed it would be so easy. Cristóbal said, "We don't have much money but we both have good educations and good jobs. As Mari may have told you there's talk around the Ministry that I'm going to be posted in London under the Ambassador to the Court of St. James. That means we'll be away quite a lot. Of course I would like to eventually become an Ambassador or ultimately Minister of Foreign Affairs."

Alfonso replied, "We will miss Maria del Mar but living abroad will be a good experience for her. Our Foreign Service is very important. Hopefully she'll be of help to you."

Rafa said, "I don't make a fortune working at *Banco Coca* so Carmen won't be able to live as she does with you, of course, but I can provide for her reasonably well."

Alfonso joked, "And you can always come home for a sandwich." Then he smiled warmly, "I'm sure you will both do well in your careers. What my wife and I care most about is that you love Carmen and Maria del Mar. The rest, with some hard work, will take care of itself. And as we are going to be family, please call me Alfonso."

The boys went virtually dancing to their room and Alfonso returned to the bungalow he and his family were sharing. The twins, Magdalena, the older brothers, all were waiting for him with "Well?" stamped on their faces. Alfonso kissed each of the girls, "Congratulations. They are splendid young men. I'm proud of you."

Magdalena said, "Pending your approval we've been thinking about a double wedding in the spring and of course the reception will be at home . . ."

"Wonderful."

"A double wedding!" José Maria exclaimed. "We could sell exclusive rights to *¡HOLA!* for a couple of million and finance the honeymoons. The marriage of our family's twin daughters with two sons of the Captain General of Aviation in Madrid is news."

"José Maria!" Carmen gasped, "You are really gross!"

Maria del Mar rolled her eyes, "Blechhh!"

Alfonso enjoyed José Maria's business orientation. He was right: the magazine would pay a lot for the exclusive story and photos. Carmen was also right: the idea was gross, grotesque. Neither family wanted to see a lovely double wedding turned into a circus. He said, "We are not public figures. The press will be invited to take a few pictures but it will be a private celebration with only our families and friends present."

* * *

Across the ocean America walked with her brother to the burial grounds. She carried a bunch of wildflowers and placed them on the stone that said "Angel," alongside flowers someone else had brought. She looked at Gat.

"I come by every day or so."

She kissed him. "Thank you. I'll think of that every day and feel good about it."

"Now that you're here, Ame, won't you stay home for Christmas?"

"Gat, I've got a huge farm I'm running. I truly can't leave it for almost two months."

"In other words, being around before Mom and Dad die isn't really important."

"That's cheap, Gat."

"You're right. I'm sorry. But what is this expatriate deal, anyway? I really don't get it. How can you give up your own country, the greatest country in the world, for another?"

"Emotionally and mentally I now belong to another life, another world. But I haven't given up my country. I still love the United States as much as you do—it will always be my homeland, my motherland, but I'm *in* love with Spain."

"But it's really that you love that guy even more." He smacked himself on his forehead and made a self-recriminating look. He held her face in his hands. "Forget I mentioned it, please. You're a lot better off than when you were working yourself to death at Jetways but still unable to forget. I'm glad you found yourself some happiness. I guess that what I was getting at is that I just wish he wasn't married."

"We wish a lot of things," she said softly.

"Speaking of that, don't ever again question your judgment on leaving J.J. He's serving a six-year prison term for insider trading. He was fined twenty million dollars and the SEC has barred him for life from working in or around securities. I don't think Angel would have been proud of her father."

She found that she did not feel pleased or sorry for J.J. The news could be about a stranger named Smith.

* * *

America would be able to move into her own house a few days before Christmas of 1973. As they sat on Marisa's terrace Alfonso said bleakly, "How I long to be with you on your first Christmas in your new home! But this year our traditional Christmas lunch will also include my two future *yernos* and *consuegros*."

"I don't know that last word."

"It doesn't exist in English. *Suegros* means father and mother in-law. *Consuegros* is a warm word describing our relationships as fathers- and mothers-in-law of the same two children." He fell silent, aware of how strongly his family Christmas would contrast with hers. "I won't even be able to call you. But I can be here with you on the 26th, leave on the 31st for *Noche Vieja,* and return on the 1st. I can stay for almost a week then, through the *Tres Reyes* because Magdalena is taking Elena and Trini to St. Moritz so they can ski, José Maria and Luis will be working, banks don't close when the schools do, and Rafael and Alfonso have their own plans with friends. The twins, of course, will be thoroughly occupied with their *novios*." He took her in his arms. "I apologize for letting you get into this impossible situation."

"Don't. I haven't had a Christmas feeling since Angel. And it's not 'impossible.' I love you. I can't imagine any woman who's happier than I am."

When he had left, she prepared to move from Marisa's house. She asked Juan, "Give Sister Maria Josefa my new address, and tell her she'll always be welcomed and that the picnics will continue every month. But tell her also that she doesn't have to come see me if she needs her time for other things. I'll send a check to the *Hogar* every June and every December."

Marisa and Carlos and their children came to spend the holidays in Marbella, and they all went to Midnight Mass together on Christmas Eve at Marbella's principal church, *Santa Maria de la Encarnación,* on which construction had begun in 1618. America stayed overnight with them. She did not want to awaken in her new house alone on Christmas morning.

Alfonso arrived the next day. America met him at the airport in a Range Rover she had bought for the *finca*. It was a useful coincidence because he had brought a long and heavy package. In her living room, they opened it together. It was a ceramic plaque made in Talavera de la Reina, a town an hour from Madrid. The plaque was five feet long and two feet wide and the letters baked onto it said: FINCA DE LA TEJANA, Farm of the Texan. "For the arch at your front entrance."

"There couldn't be a nicer Christmas present."

"It's only a housewarming gift. So are these," and he gave her boxes of letterhead, notepaper and envelopes engraved *finca de la tejana*. "This is your Christmas present," and he put a bracelet of 25 one-carat square-cut diamonds around her wrist. Despite her family's wealth she had never had any serious jewelry. As happy as a child she kissed him then held out her arm, twisting it to see the gems sparkle.

"It's absolutely super, super, gorgeous. Thank you."

"It belonged to my mother."

"Then shouldn't you give it to your wife?"

"My parents left many things that I have given to my wife. And Magdalena deserves them. But if Mamá knew the happiness you bring me she would approve of what little gestures I make to you. I used to try so hard to be happy. Unsuccessfully. But, as you've observed, since meeting you I'm no longer '*El que no sonrie, nunca.*' You're my smile."

"As you surely are mine."

He gave her a small jewelry box. "I had this made for you."

Opening it she held up a necklace from which hung three gold and enamel flags: of the U.S.A., Texas and Spain. She kissed the flags and she kissed Alfonso. "It's the most thoughtful gift I've ever received."

He stood up. "Do you have any chilled *cava* in this lovely establishment?"

"Yes, but wouldn't you prefer a whiskey?"

"No. I would like to celebrate our first night together in your new house." He paused, "Would you think me corny if I wanted to carry you over the threshold?"

"Only if you won't laugh when I want to bring you breakfast in bed."

In the morning she served him ham and fried eggs *con encaje* and, with a little help from Encarna, some award-winning *migas*. As they devoured the meal she felt that not since Angel had she enjoyed anything so much as taking care of him in her own home.

At the stable she showed him a matching pair of sixteen-hand chestnut-colored hunters, a mare and a gelding she had bought for them in Jeréz de la Frontera.

Alfonso studied the animals. "They have *grandeza*."

"Then let's name them Marqués and Marquesa."

They passed hours on the horses, traversing the born-again land. At the beginning Alfonso was quiet. America asked, "I sense that something's bothering you. Was Christmas lunch unsuccessful?"

"No, it was perfect. Rafa and Cristóbal are charming, bright, lovable, and their parents, Rafael and Carmela, have been friends of ours since just after the war. The problem was Christmas evening, when Elena's date came to escort her to a party. I did not realize until then that I'm prejudiced and a snob. The kid wears his hair in a long ponytail. And he wears an earring. He's a thirty-year-old bohemian painter. And, God forbid, a leftist. We know nothing of his family. His name is Francisco Gómez but his friends seem to call him 'Van Gogh.' He comes from Cádiz. Nobody is pleased with him except Elena."

"Hold it! She's only seventeen. She'll get over him."

"I'm not sure. She doesn't want to go to St. Moritz. She wants to stay in Madrid with him."

"At seventeen! Unchaperoned for a week with a thirty-year-old hippy?"

"Don't worry. She's going to St. Moritz with Magda and Trini. But what a shock! Elena has always been a serious girl. How can she be attracted to a type like that?"

"Maybe he reads poetry to her."

"Please."

"Is he good-looking?"

"Technically, yes, very. But how can I find any man good-looking who wears an earring and a ponytail?"

"Look what *I* married."

"Yours wasn't so illogical. But this won't end in marriage. I will never consent or permit that. I'll send her to university in Alaska if necessary. Let's change the subject."

And then the five days were over and she was driving him to the airport, wishing him "Happy New Year" and waiting until she saw his plane in the air before she turned and went back to her car, her *finca* and a different existence until he returned and she could feel complete again.

Driving from the airport on New Year's Day, Alfonso told her, "Cristina, Paco and Esperanza arrive tomorrow to spend a week with Carlos and Marisa."

She tried not to show disappointment. "I guess we won't get much time together."

"*Mi amor*, I wouldn't lose a second of our time together. I've told Cristina all about you."

"But she's close to Magdalena!"

"Trust me. Cristina and Paco shared my youth with me, as I did theirs. They will be ecstatic when they see how happy I am with you. That's all they'll care about. Further, I have told Magdalena about you. She and I are too close to go on living a life of hypocrisy."

"Good heavens! What did she say?"

"She was hardly surprised. All those long silences as my mind wandered to you. Every weekend in a little house I've owned in Marbella for years but rarely used. She disliked it but I promised that I would continue to celebrate the traditional holidays with her and the children."

They had dinner on the terrace. Looking down the hill they could see the full moon reflecting on the water of the Mediterranean, casting a silver boulevard to Gibraltar. America asked, "Is there anything more beautiful?" Cuddled up next to Alfonso on a sofa she said, "I'm happy for me but I can't help feeling sad for Magdalena."

"I, too. She's been a good wife. Perfect. Except that we have never been in love. And though I could go through the motions for many years, now my love for you, the joy I feel in being with you, eclipses everything else." He was pensive. "How strange fate can be: to meet your first, your great love when more than half your life is gone."

Driving toward Carlos and Marisa's house Alfonso touched America's hand and was startled to find it so cold.

"I'm shivering in my boots."

He squeezed her hand gently. "For no reason. You'll see."

America recognized Paco and Cristina from that first day at the Marbella Club. And, it occurred to her that though it was barely two years ago it was another life. She was reborn. She had arrived in Spain an emotional disaster. Now, loving Alfonso, and being loved by him, having her *finca,* she felt strong, secure. There was still a hole in her heart, it would always be there, but it hurt less and more time passed between the moments when she felt the pain.

To her immense delight Paco and Cristina each kissed her hello and hugged her. After dinner they had coffee on the terrace. Though it was winter the air was mild, the roof kept the humidity off them and Marisa's outdoor fireplace burned roots of olive trees, providing the final drying of the air.

America sat on a couch and played with Esperanza. The average adult is afraid of, or does not know how to speak to a person who, though in her mid-twenties, has the body of a twelve year old and the mind and spirit of an eight year old. But it came easily to America, and they chattered and laughed together like old friends. When Cristina said that it was bedtime, Esperanza would only go to her room if America would come and tell her a story. Watching them leave, America and Esperanza holding hands, and having observed her many times with Carlos and Marisa's twins, Alfonso understood the sacrifice she was making to be with him instead of a man with whom she could have another child.

America sat on the edge of Esperanza's bed and told her the story of Alice in Wonderland. It made her remember happy moments with Angel and it felt good. When she saw the child struggling to keep her eyes open she kissed her forehead and said, "I'll tell you more about Alice every time I see you."

When Esperanza dozed off and the two women had slipped out Cristina said, "Alfonso mentioned that he has told you everything about our family, and he has told us about your child. It makes it easier for us to talk. I hope that Esperanza doesn't cause sad memories."

"On the contrary, she has the same sweetness Angel had. Being with her makes me happy."

Paco and Alfonso were in a semi-heated conversation. Paco was on his feet, "In the sixties Franco said he wouldn't make the classic mistake of the *torero* that stays on too long in the ring though he's not as strong as he was, not as agile. Well, here we are in the seventies. Franco is still in the ring. He's not as strong, not as agile, but he'll never let go of the power until he dies."

Alfonso demanded, "Think of '36. Tell me what you find wrong with law and order? With peace, prosperity?"

"Nothing, obviously. I revere Franco. He gave us our best years in the last four hundred. And I recognize that certain circumstances call for an all-powerful leader. But as a permanent form of government I'm categorically opposed to a *dictadura*, dictatorship."

"It has been a *dictablanda*," Alfonso corrected, using the *Franquista* play on the words *dura*, hard, and *blanda*, soft.

Irritated, Paco agreed. "Of course he's been benevolent. But he educated Prince Juan Carlos to take over, and the time has come!"

"With Franco we know what we have. How do you know what it'll be like under Juan Carlos?"

"Franco is seventy-nine. We will soon find out. But how much more prudent if he would step back and let Juan Carlos become King with the advantage of having Franco and his prestige in the background to stabilize the new government!"

"Yes. 'The role of Queen Mother was played by Francisco Franco.'" Not wishing to continue the oft-discussed subject, Alfonso was pleased when Cristina said to America, "My brother says you've done wonders with the *finca*."

Also eager to swing the conversation away from politics, and grateful for the compliment, America volunteered, "We're hoping to increase production by 50 percent per year for the next four years. This climate is fantastic. In five years I'm looking for our produce to be as good as the best of its kind in the world, which means we'll be able to export at premium prices in 1978."

Alfonso asked, "Has anyone noticed that we're speaking entirely in Spanish? With an American woman who has been in Spain only two years!"

Paco said, "Frankly, I did *not* notice. America, you're so comfortable in Spanish, your vocabulary, verbs, even slang. I know how difficult that is. In my case, with English, the words went in one ear and out the other a hundred times before they finally came out of my mouth. And you have only a trace of an accent. How did you accomplish that?"

Delighted, America shrugged elaborately, "It was nothing. I merely took lessons ten hours a day, every day."

"Impresionante!"

Cristina agreed, "And your knowledge of agriculture? You learned all this from your father?"

"I inherited my love for farming from Daddy, and I majored in Agricultural Science at Texas A&M. I'd be delighted to show you around the *finca* if you're interested."

In the morning, mounted on Marqués and Marquesa, America and Cristina rode leisurely over the grounds. "I appreciate your invitation."

"I appreciate that you've come. It would have been more likely for you to want to have nothing to do with me."

"My brother has waited a long time to be happy. We all love Magda. She's a fine and remarkable woman. She and Alfonso are dear friends who live in harmony. But there are no sparks. There never have been. He loves her, of course. But you have made him come alive in a way that he hasn't since we were children, before our parents were killed. He was only fourteen when he had to suffer the experience of searching for them among hundreds of corpses in the Madrid morgue. I'm sure he couldn't have described strongly enough the ghastliness of that experience. Or of killing over a hundred of his own, young countrymen in battle. After the war I thought that he would never be able to be happy. I watched him pass some thirty-five years like that. Now, it's as though a miracle occurred so I'm profoundly grateful for your presence in his life."

"We were blessed to be given each other. Alfonso has done the same for me. After the loss of my child I believed I would never be able to be happy again, nor want to be."

"I'm also deeply appreciative of the wonderful way you have with Esperanza. The first thing she asked me this morning was are you going to come over and see her."

"Every day. Does she feel that she's different from other children?"

"It's so hard to know if, or when, she'll begin to sense it. She's led a sheltered life because we didn't want to send her to a school for subnormal children. So we've had private teachers for her. We haven't adopted children so that she could have brothers and sisters because we worry that she might feel threatened by them. Also, as she would see them mature she might begin to understand that she *is* different. We try to think of every way possible to protect her, but the world that will have to touch her one day can be very cruel . . ."

* * *

Cayetana called a family meeting in a private dining room upstairs at Jockey, Madrid's best restaurant; she, Paco, Cristina and Alfonso. "I felt ashamed when I listened to Cristina telling me what that American woman has accomplished with that land that we've let rot all these years. It reminded me of the Israelis growing oranges in the desert and I thought, 'Maybe we're *too* rich.' We own millions of hectares of land all over Spain with which we do nothing except extract an annual pound of flesh from the tenants who struggle to eke out a living on those *fincas*. That explains why they do so poorly. Why should they break their backs with a shovel and a hoe to make us richer while they barely survive in *chozas*? We all know that the reason Spain has had problems for so many centuries is because there have been rather too many very rich and far too many very poor. Thank God we are among the rich. But why don't we create some incentive for the poor, give them a chance to prosper? And do something for our country? Take our properties in Guadalajara as a starting point: none of us needs that land or its income. We have so much more—it's embarrassing. Why don't we give those farmers a reason to bring those lands to life? Let's make them gifts of the hectares they are working, as much as they can handle at no cost, no rental."

Alfonso was impressed by this coming from Cayetana, who until then had never shown a love of country or of anything but her own pleasures. Paco said, "It's a wonderful idea. But bear in mind that Tolstoy did something similar and his wife and children claimed he'd gone mad and wanted to have him committed."

"Magdalena and our children are not going to turn on us." He felt excited by the plan. "But our people have neither the money for proper machinery nor the knowledge of how to apply modern methods. America had capital and she'd studied."

Cayetana said, "We'll make it possible for them to buy the necessary machinery."

"The bank will offer low-interest loans."

"No, that would smell like a money-lending scheme. The loans must be interest-free. The four of us will share the costs."

Ten days later the newspapers and the radio in the Province of Guadalajara carried the following announcement:

THE DUKE OF THE CASTLE OF TARIFA OFFERS, FREE OF CHARGE, TO ANY FARMER WHO WISHES, ALL THE LAND THAT HE CAN WORK. THIS LAND CANNOT BE SOLD BUT WILL REMAIN IN THE POSSESSION OF THE FARMER AND HIS HEIRS FOR AS LONG AS THEY KEEP IT PRODUCTIVE. EXPERT AGRICULTURISTS WILL BE AVAILABLE TO INSTRUCT IN MODERN FARMING METHODS AT NO COST.

THE BANK OF THE CASTLE OF TARIFA WILL MAKE INTEREST-FREE LOANS FOR MODERN FARM MACHINERY REQUIRED TO MAKE THE LAND MOST PRODUCTIVE. THOSE INTERESTED, PLEASE APPLY AT ANY BRANCH OFFICE OF THE BANK OF TARIFA.

Within one month 1.5 million hectares of land were signed over to 253 farmers. 26 million dollars' worth of tractors, seeders, reapers and other tools was on order, paid for in advance by the Bank of Tarifa, and with America's help a team of Spanish-speaking American agriculturalists were on their way to Guadalajara.

Alfonso was dressing to go to the bank when José Maria knocked on the door and let himself into the dressing room. "Papá?"

"Come in, son, come in."

"Have you seen this morning's *ABC*?"

"Not yet."

"Listen to this editorial:

WITH THE AGRARIAN REFORM SET INTO MOTION BY THE DUKE OF THE CASTLE OF TARIFA, SPAIN MAY NOW FINALLY FIND HER-SELF AGRICULTURALLY INDEPENDENT. THIS NATION HAS FOR CENTURIES LIVED ON IMPORTED WHEAT. HOWEVER, SOON, THANKS TO THE EXTRAORDINARY GENEROSITY AND PATRIOT-

ISM OF THE DUKE OF THE CASTLE OF TARIFA, WE MAY NO LONGER NEED TO IMPORT WHEAT FROM ARGENTINA AND ELSEWHERE. HISTORICALLY, AGRARIAN REFORM HAS ALWAYS BEEN PROMISED, SOMETIMES EVEN DELIVERED IN SMALL MEASURE BY POLITICIANS SEEKING VOTES FROM THE POOR. NEVER BEFORE IN RECORDED HISTORY HAS IT BEEN PROVIDED, AND IN GRAND MEASURE, BY A SINGLE CITIZEN WITH NOTHING TO GAIN OTHER THAN BEING OF HELP TO HIS COUNTRY AND HIS COUNTRYMEN. *¡CHAPO! Y UN FORTÍSIMO ABRAZO PARA EL SR. DUQUE.*

José Maria said, "I would like to shake my father's hand." Alfonso hugged his primogenitor to him in a strong *abrazo*. "They should build a statue to you, Papá ."

"It was Aunt Cay's idea. And Aunt Cristina and Uncle Paco had as much to do with it as I."

"No, Papá. It couldn't have happened without you. You control all of the family's lands. You own the bank that made the loans. I know that in theory you and Aunt Cay and Aunt Cristina and Uncle Paco are splitting the costs, but I also know who, in reality, will absorb the loss if the loans don't get paid. You did something historic. One day it will be included in books written about the history of our country."

That afternoon José Maria returned home from the bank at six-fifteen and went into the library for a book on economics. The room was filled with women. "Oh! Excuse me." He quickly withdrew. His mother called out, "We've finished our meeting. Have tea with us."

He recognized a number of his mother's friends and understood it had been a meeting of the Red Cross. He kissed the ladies he knew, then stopped in front of a girl about his age, with below-the-shoulder, black silky hair and intense violet eyes. His own were frozen onto hers. He had never seen such beautiful eyes, or such a stunning girl. She was slender and though seated, obviously quite tall. She was wearing a Black Watch plaid skirt; a black velvet jacket piped in the same plaid, and low-heeled black patent-leather shoes with silver buckles.

Studying him she thought that he was just the right amount taller than she; slim, hair the color of her own, dark eyes, good nose, inviting mouth and well dressed in a double-breasted dark gray suit.

Magdalena broke into the moment, "Puri, I would like to present my eldest son, José Maria. José Maria this is Purificación Notario Jiménez, the newest member of the Executive Committee."

She smelled delicious when he kissed her lightly on both cheeks as he had the older ladies, but with a great deal more pleasure. In fact this stunning girl had indeed stunned him. He felt short of breath. Then he raised her hand as if to kiss it but not quite, as was correct. *"Encantado,"* delighted, he said.

"Encantada," she replied, smiling, her eyes locked onto his.

Magdalena brought a cup of tea for him. "Sit down, José Maria." He looked at the empty seat on the couch next to Purificación, "May I?"

"I would like that."

Magdalena prudently waited until he was safely seated before handing him the cup and saucer: he took them, unaware of having anything in his hand. She said, "Puri is the driving force behind the collections we make at tables next month."

"How wonderful. Where will your table be located?" he asked, hoping it would be in front of his bank.

"I don't have one. I assign the ladies to all the tables and I spend the day going from one to another, with a policeman, removing the cash so there's no danger of robberies. There are people who will steal, even from the Red Cross."

The others were leaving. "Do you have a car?" he asked praying that she did not.

"No, I came with Mariola Calleja."

"Great. She just left without you. She must be a friend of mine. May I drive you home?"

"Thank you. You're very kind," and, she thought, super attractive.

He hoped she lived a hundred kilometers away.

"Our house is just behind Plaza Colón."

Damn. "I know it's short notice but would you possibly be free for dinner tonight?"

"I'm completely free," and her gorgeous eyes sparkled bewitchingly.

At dinner that evening Alfonso asked Magdalena, "Where is José Maria?"

"I may be something of a matchmaker. He's taking Puri Notario to dinner."

"Oh?"

"Yes. They met this afternoon. I would call it an encounter."

"Is she the daughter of Mario and Marta?"

"Their eldest."

"Beautiful girl."

"And lovely. She works tremendously hard and well for us."

"I hope it takes. Frankly, I've been wondering if he was planning to marry the bank."

"Yesterday I might have agreed with you."

A ski resort was being developed in the Sierra Nevada, the mountains above Granada. The promoters and the Granada Tourist Bureau had invited the most-celebrated Spaniards for a weekend of "Ski and Surf," the surf being the beaches of Granada at the foot of the mountain. These notables were to allow photographs by the press in order to glamorize and publicize the resort.

Though she brought her daughters to Switzerland for them to ski, Magdalena herself had no interest in it. Further, that weekend she was committed to a Cancer Society meeting in Madrid so Alfonso was able to bring America.

"Paparazzi have come from all over Spain for this promotion," Alfonso told her, "so we must be discreet, alert not to be seen by ourselves."

America had never mentioned that she had been a finalist in tryouts for the U.S. Olympic ski team so he was astonished to see her zipping along the snow as sure-footed as a penguin and a lot more graceful and attractive in her new skin-tight green ski suit.

While Alfonso allowed photographers to take pictures of "The Duke of the Castle of Tarifa enjoying the snow sport in the Sierra Nevada," that turned out to be journalistic jiu jitsu. Yes, he enjoyed watching the good skiers gliding downhill, and he admired the speed. But when he tried it, as he fell down every yard or two, he found that he was neither gliding downhill, nor gathering speed, nor enjoying it at all. And he wondered where he had gotten the idea that snow was soft. Though he hated being awkward at anything, seeing America happy, he kept at it. Being naturally athletic he hoped he could improve quickly, and dominate, if not master it. He was aware that she was always the learner in a foreign country. The effort and devotion to him which that took rarely escaped him. Nor that she had given up her family, her roots, and an easier way of life, for a childless weekend marriage. The least he could do was make a fool of himself on the slopes until he was able to accompany her at something in which she excelled.

America admired his tenacity and wanted to help him but Alfonso declined. "Go ahead and have fun with the good skiers until I learn how to do this."

"I'm not here to be with the other skiers. Besides, you need a coach. I can help you catch on to it faster."

"How long do you think this will take me?"

"About five hundred more falls, a few tendons, ligaments, maybe a knee and an ankle."

Yet, that weekend, through force of will he made enormous strides for a nearly fifty-year-old beginner. And seeing America so at home and happy in the snow Alfonso decided to buy an apartment in the Sierra Nevada, and the adjoining flat for his servants. At his suggestion Cristina and Paco and Marisa and Carlos also bought apartments, as did other of his friends.

His only rejection was from Cayetana. "Fonso, you must be completely mad. Fall on my ass in that cold? When I can be here in Marbella in my spectacular new home, in the sun, with everything I want?"

Her house was just being finished so Alfonso had not seen it, but Cayetana assured him, "You'll be mad for it. I can't wait for you to see my bullring."

"When did you become interested in *la corrida?*"

"Never. I loathe bullfights. No matter, Fonso, you will understand when you see it."

* * *

People who follow other people followed Alfonso and bought apartments; soon the Sierra Nevada became the place to be, and in recognition of his valuable help Alfonso was presented with a lifetime pass on the ski lift. The guard at the bottom of the lift bowed and gestured for him and his party to go ahead, *"Adelante, Sr. Duque."*

America had never attended dinners or other Alfonso-related social occasions in Madrid. That was Magdalena's territory and it would have been an indiscretion to appear there. But the Sierra Nevada was another Marbella in the sense that Magdalena did not go there and Alfonso did not hesitate to be seen with America in groups of four or six. However, though she stayed with him at his apartment, she also booked a room at the hotel, in the same way in which he stayed with America in her home but made appearances at his own house in Marbella.

Having dinner in a restaurant with her, Marisa and Carlos, Alfonso was startled to see his son José Maria arrive with Puri and a group of young friends. The young man and pretty girl walked over to the table to greet Alfonso, kissing him and Marisa and

Carlos and then found themselves facing America. Alfonso said, "I would like you to meet my eldest son José Maria and Puri Notario. This is America Harvey, a good friend of ours."

She offered her hand, which the unnerved young couple each took in turn.

"What are you doing up here?" Alfonso asked awkwardly.

"We were in Granada with Puri's parents and some friends and thought it would be fun to come up and have a look at the skiing."

"Where are you staying?"

"We have rooms at the hotel."

"But I have an apartment here."

"Thanks, but it was a spur-of-the-moment idea, and there are too many of us. We're leaving in the morning. Well . . . nice meeting you, Miss Harvey," and he and Puri backed away, forgetting to say goodbye to his father and Marisa and Carlos.

America blanched. Alfonso reassured her, "There's absolutely nothing improper for a man to be out with friends and a dinner companion. Let's continue as we were, talking, laughing as if nothing happened, because nothing did."

But that night America returned to the hotel and hoped to be seen going to her room to sleep. And Alfonso did not sleep at all.

The photograph that appeared in *¡HOLA!* to publicize the new ski resort could be considered innocent or scandalous, depending on the eye of the beholder. It was a photo of Alfonso and America with Carlos and Marisa on the slopes. But, as too many *Madrileños* were happy to ask, "What was Alfonso doing with one arm around the beautiful young woman's waist and his other hand brushing something from her face?"

Magdalena, waiting in a dentist office with the twins on the day after the magazine was published, idly picked up that issue of *¡HOLA!* The girls, who always read the magazine on the day it came out, panicked. Maria del Mar grabbed another magazine. "Mamá, this one has a fabulous story on Julio Iglesias . . ." and she tried to take away the *¡HOLA!* Magdalena was amused, "Mári, when did you ever hear that I'm a fan of Julio Iglesias?" and she continued turning pages until she stopped. Her face became white and the girls thought she would faint.

America called Alfonso at the office. "Have you seen it?"

"Yes."

"How did Magdalena react?"

"She had not seen it as of yesterday. But by today surely someone will show it to her. She'll be embarrassed, and rightfully angry at my lack of discretion."

"And the children?"

"How can they feel about seeing their father acting affectionately with another woman? We tried to avoid something like this. I can't imagine how that picture got taken."

"Zoom lens. Paparazzi."

On the following Monday morning in Madrid, as Alfonso was occupied with making a double Windsor on a necktie Magdalena came into his dressing room and sat down on the chair behind him. Seeing her in the mirror, sensing her discomfort, he turned and asked if she was feeling ill.

"No, I feel fine, thank you. It's just . . . there's something I must ask of you. A favor."

She seemed so reticent. "Magda. Tell me what you want. Anything."

"Well, it won't be pleasant for you. Unfortunately the Red Cross Ball has to be held on a Saturday night this year. As President, mine will be the most prominent table. I have invited eight of our friends . . ." she glanced away, ". . . but I need a . . . .husband to escort me."

He looked at her saddened face, understanding how unjust it was for her to have to plead for what was her right. And such sterling character not to remind him of the magazine photograph and the need to counter it. On the other hand he also had a commitment to America. The weekends were hers. And this wasn't a "family" holiday. It was one of his and America's weekends, for which she waited five days.

"I'll feel honored to escort you."

Magdalena added, timidly, "And then there's the Patrons' Lunch on Sunday."

He told America by phone that afternoon, "It would humiliate her if I were not there, especially after the picture. People love to gossip. Even though we've been discreet your existence in my life is now thoroughly known. Magdalena has worked diligently and she should be able to enjoy being President of the Red Cross rather than wanting to shrink from smirks and gossip like '. . . but is her husband with that American woman?'"

When they had hung up America put away the small American flags and other decorations she had sent for to celebrate the Fourth of July on Saturday with Alfonso. As she put them into a closet for another year she mentally replayed the many Fourth of July parties on the ranch: the barbecue oven sunk into the ground, cooking the succulent ribs; her parents hosting the friends from San Antonio and those from Dallas and Houston who flew their planes in; being together with Gat at the all-day party every year since childhood, and finally the fireworks that ended the celebration. She was conscious of cropping J.J. out of the picture. After she moved to Oklahoma City she couldn't attend her family's Fourth of July celebrations. And when Angel died they stopped having them, so her child had never been a part of those images. America's thoughts lingered on the ranch. And her trees. Her flag. It would seem you'd need a bulldozer to pull up roots that deep.

She walked out onto the terrace and looked at her land. It made her feel better. She looked down at the Mediterranean and told herself to stop being a child. What, in fact, was the Fourth of July weekend? A tradition, a habit. Her love for Alfonso was irreplaceable. And his for her. From the beginning he had made it clear that he wouldn't mistreat his wife. She could only love him more for his fairness to Magdalena.

Fortunately, the children from *Hogar San Carlos* would be with her on Saturday. America had continued her monthly picnics for the *Hogar,* developing them into more elaborate outings for the children by renting ponies for them to ride and other amusements to make these days the happiest possible for them. Even when Alfonso was there she took these few hours for the girls. And as she had watched them maturing, from year to year, she realized that soon they would outgrow the *Hogar* and need to go to work. She had come to feel they were her own children and she aspired for them to have better opportunities than unskilled labor: she wanted them to have the higher education that would qualify them to enter the country's upper workforce. She formed the *Fundación Universitario* with a substantial endowment, and called on Alfonso to help her invest it so that there would be funds for each of the girls to have college educations.

After the children had left she got through the rest of the weekend by looking for all the meaningless tasks she had put aside for "later, when there's time," like letters she needed to answer that were fewer and fewer as the years passed and she lost contact with her San Antonio friends, and organizing her clothes closet. As the hours dragged by she felt that she couldn't endure the days that would have to pass before they were together. On Sunday evening, dining alone, then getting into bed by herself America couldn't find comfort in the company of the dogs, or even in matters of the *finca.* She longed to be touching Alfonso. Even just to be looking at him. Anything but being so alone.

When he called from his office on Monday morning she said, "I have a wonderful idea. Why don't I come to Madrid to do some shopping and we can slip off and have lunch together?"

"*Mi amor,* I would like nothing better. Nothing in this world. But it's impossible. My face is too well known. It would cause still more talk."

"Then I'll check into a small hotel and you can visit me."

"My darling, it's just not possible unless we want to risk a scandal. And hurt people again."

"But when we first met, you took me everywhere, even to a *cacería* with all of your friends."

"You were seen as a companion then, at most a brief indiscretion, an American on holiday in Spain. But today we are a seriously talked-about love affair."

She busied herself with her work during the day but night fell like a stone. As she half slept she reached across the bed, knowing she couldn't touch him, but still she tried, imagining what his skin would feel like.

The new issue of *¡HOLA!* carried seven full-color pages covering the Red Cross Ball. Magdalena, wearing an emerald-green satin Grecian gown and an emerald diadem with emerald necklace and earrings, was pictured with the-Duke-of-this and the-President-of-that, and in photos with Alfonso. In one they were dancing together. In another they were at the dinner table and Magdalena was laughing, looking across the table at Alfonso, who apparently had said something amusing. In another photo Alfonso was dancing with a ravishing blonde woman. She scrutinized the caption. It was Cayetana.

There was a large table of all of Alfonso and Magdalena's children. Among them were a young girl and a man with a ponytail. The twins were with Rafa and Cristóbal. José Maria's girl friend, Puri, was even prettier when not in shock. Everyone she had met or heard about was there, Cristina and Paco, Marisa and Carlos . . . and she was in Marbella, understanding what a small part of a week two days are, what a small part of his life she occupied.

PART FOUR

In September of 1975 General Francisco Franco Bahamonde became seriously ill, and, it was said, "thirty million hearts stopped beating." Life without Franco had often been spoken of but never really imagined. Half of Spain's population, all people under the age of thirty-five, had never known a Chief of State other than *El Caudillo,* had never seen a Spanish postage stamp or a coin that wasn't adorned with Franco's left profile, had never been in a public building or important plaza that did not display his portrait or sculpture.

Attended by a team of fifteen doctors, including his son-in-law, the prominent heart surgeon Dr. Cristóbal Martinez Bordiú, the Marqués de Villaverde, the eighty-four-year-old Chief of State clung to life through September, into October, and through October into November.

On November 20, 1975, the man who had governed his country for thirty-six years died in his sleep.

In his farewell to Spain and to all Spaniards, written by hand on two pages of the pads he always used, read on radio and television by Prime Minister Carlos Arias Navarro, Franco asked:

"FOR THE LOVE I FEEL FOR OUR LAND I ASK YOU TO PERSE-
VERE IN UNITY AND PEACE AND TO GATHER AROUND THE
FUTURE KING OF SPAIN, DON JUAN CARLOS DE BORBÓN, WITH

THE SAME SUPPORT AND COOPERATION THAT I HAVE ALWAYS
HAD FROM YOU . . .
. . . IN MY LAST MOMENT I WOULD LIKE TO UNITE THE NAME
OF GOD AND OF SPAIN AND IN THE SHADOW OF MY DEATH,
WITH ARMS AROUND YOU ALL, TO CRY OUT TOGETHER FOR
THE LAST TIME, ¡ARRIBA ESPAÑA! VIVA ESPAÑA!"

Under King Juan Carlos, Spain began her transition from
dictatorship to democracy. The King dismissed Arias Navarro
because he was too closely associated with the Franco regime and
in his place he appointed a young, handsome and able politician,
Adolfo Suarez, who announced that there would be a national referendum in which the people would vote for or against democracy. If they voted in favor then a date would be set for the first
national election in Spain in almost forty years. He also legalized
the Socialist and Communist parties.

Alfonso sat in America's living room clutching a newspaper,
disbelieving the words as he read them. He looked at America, at
Cristina and at Paco, stared from face to face, aghast. "To legalize
the Communist and Socialist parties? After *El Generalísimo* kept them
out of Spain for thirty-six years. Now to let *La Pasionaria* come back
from Moscow, to give Santiago Carrillo political importance . . ."

"They will have *no* importance," Paco said. "Franco kept them
out, you say, but as he grew older they'd begun returning here,
underground. Martyrs. They'll look a lot less glamorous in the
light. *La Pasionaria* will be just an old lady, home from decades of
exile in Soviet Russia, a pathetic symbol of failure. Few people will
vote for her or for Carrillo."

Alfonso looked thoughtfully at Paco. "Do you believe that goat
herders and olive pickers who read no newspapers, have no education, no experience or view of the country or of the world beyond
the few hectares they live on should decide upon the merits of a
man based entirely upon what he tells them—and have the same
weight as you, an educated, politically sophisticated man, to vote
for him as our President?"

JANE AND BURT BOYAR

"I do," Paco said without hesitation. "I do not say it's ideal, but it's democracy."

Alfonso waved his arms in the air as if trying to wave away Paco's words. "Democracy isn't for Spain. It has never worked here. Spaniards need a strong hand. Isabella knew that and under her Spain attained law and order and gained most of the world. In 1936 we were a hair's-breadth from becoming a Communist satellite of Russia. Only Franco saved us. His strength ended four centuries of an invertebrate Spain, of countless civil wars, chronic famine, military coups beyond number—all failures, as were the Republics. He alone stopped Spaniards from killing Spaniards. Now we are going back to a proven losing game and you shrug 'It's not ideal.'"

"I said that in a free society people have the right to choose their leader."

"Even if leads to another war, more killing?"

"That, I think, is overly pessimistic."

"Franco's plan for an Organic Democracy has all the good of democracy, while avoiding the fatal flaw of uneducated voting. The man kept Spain out of Russia's hands, out of World War II, and brought her back from being a starving tragedy to where she's now the tenth industrial power of the world. Don't we owe it to him to try his plan, give it at least two years?"

"Alfonso, 'organic democracy' is double-talk. It calls for an appointed government. The only voting is among the appointees. Democracy without a popular vote isn't democracy. It's Francoism. But you cannot have Francoism without Franco. If you try, the odds are that you'll get another Hitler or Stalin, Perón, Batista or Castro. Take note that Franco, a truly benign dictator, had the wisdom not to risk leaving another dictator in power." Paco's voice softened, "He's gone, Alfonso. Be grateful that we had him. But now Spain must find her way without him."

Cristina asked America, "Your country is the prototype for democracy, what do *you* think?"

"Well, there's a saying that 'Democracy is the worst form of government except for the alternatives.' And there are many Americans who will tell you that democracy doesn't work even in America, that we survive despite one-man-one-vote rather than because of it."

Alfonso seized on that. "Then you agree democracy has no place in Spain."

"I did not mean or say that. I know little about politics and even less about Spanish politics, which hasn't been visible since I've been here."

"Of course not, "Alfonso explained, "Franco wasn't a politician, he was a leader who governed."

Paco said, "The referendum will be overwhelmingly in favor of a vote for democracy. The people want their rights."

"Their 'rights.'" Alfonso asked America, "Do you know what it means in Spain when the people want their 'rights'? Demands for more money and fewer hours of work, crippling strikes to extract them, and consequently less production. With reduced production the economy falters, the people become dissatisfied and we're threatened with a return to anarchy. Spain is the only country in the world, in all history, in which anarchism became a major political force. If we have democracy in Spain it could again turn into anarchy and we could go back to the chaos of '36." He stared plaintively at Cristina and Paco, "Could you stand that again? 1936! I can still smell the death."

"Don't worry about it," Paco said dismissively, "this is 1975. Forty years have passed. Thanks to Franco we have a large middle class that did not exist in '36. All these doctors and small businessmen who used to go to work on bicycles are delighted with their two cars and their TV sets and telephones. They are not going to fight another Civil War."

"Paco, can you tell me who wrote: 'Let Spaniards remember that each nation is a prey to its particular furies, and they are different in each case. Spain's furies are the anarchical spirit, negative criticism, lack of solidarity between men, mutual enmity. Any political system that nurtures in its bosom the fostering of those defects, the setting loose of these familiar Spanish furies, will sooner or later wreak havoc on all material progress and improvements in our citizens' lives'?"

"Francisco Franco."

"And who said: 'Those who cannot remember the past are condemned to repeat it'?"

"Santayana."

"If you can remember their words, then why won't you listen to what they are telling you?"

Alfonso hoped that perhaps the referendum would result in a "No" vote. But he knew better. History had proven that when you go to the people and ask if they want a change, any change, they usually vote in favor. The referendum in 1976 was no different and with the way open to elections Spain fell into her characteristic "every man is a political party unto himself." None of the potentially winning candidates wanted to combine with others. Each wanted to be the leader. There were more than three hundred registered political parties.

The election was won in 1978 by the party of the center-right, and the party leader, Adolfo Suarez, was sworn in by the King of Spain as Prime Minister.

Forming his cabinet Suarez called upon the senior partner in Paco's law firm to be *Ministro del Interior,* a ministry that supervises the national police. "Come with me," he urged Paco. "If Spain is to be a democracy let us put ourselves to work toward her success."

America phoned to congratulate Cristina on Paco's becoming Undersecretary of the Interior. "Thank you," Cristina said, "and for the charming birthday drawing you sent to Esperanza. She kept asking 'Is 'Merica coming?' She's lucky to be spared the sadness of understanding that there are things beyond control, that I couldn't invite you and Magdalena to the same party. Her aunt isn't so lucky, as she heard constantly, Mamá, when 'Merica coming? Papá, when 'Merica coming?' I'm afraid that for Magda the party wasn't very successful." America was dismayed for Magdalena and mortified for Alfonso, but there was nothing she could do to remove that pain and embarrassment without dropping from the scene.

* * *

Finca de la Tejana was dressed in balloons; music was playing from loudspeakers installed on trees and all over the grounds around the house. A large papier mâché figure of Alice in Wonderland was at the front door to greet the guests, principally Esperanza.

A car drew up and Esperanza was running to the house. The twenty-four-year-old child was dressed in a party dress and a picture hat with ribbons down the back. She leaped into America's arms. Alfonso came out the front door and lifted Esperanza off the floor, swinging her around, putting her on her feet, bowing and kissing her hand, greeting her as if she were royalty: "*Reina de Inglaterra! Princesa de las Austriacas! Reina de España!*"

There was an outdoor party lunch on a whimsically decorated table. On the chair to Esperanza's left was a four-foot-high plush teddy bear and to her right a slightly larger panda. The birthday cake was a chocolate house mounted in the center of a forest of chocolate trees, gumdrop stones, chocolate twigs on the ground and chocolate meringue as logs. Alfonso leaned over to America, "You never cease to amaze and enchant me." Everyone sang "Feliz Cumpleaños" ("Happy Birthday") and Esperanza was dancing a solo, pirouetting.

Paco observed, "She's so graceful." Then she was pulling America onto the dance floor and they did the frug, which America had taught her.

"Today is really my birthday, isn't it, Merica?"

"Darling, you will always have two birthdays every year because you're so special."

When it was time for Esperanza to sleep she went contentedly with her teddy bear, her panda and America to the guest room that contained her birthday presents and was filled with flowers and balloons and confetti.

Cristina, Paco, Alfonso and America sat by the fire. Cristina took America's hand in her own. "We have been blessed that God put you in our lives."

Unfortunately, her nephew, José Maria, did not share that sentiment. At Cristina's party for Esperanza he had been infuriated at hearing his cousin constantly asking for "Merica," and wounded by his mother's obvious pain over it. When he was alone with her at home he asked, "Do you know who this 'Merica' is?"

"It's not important. Let's not discuss it."

"Obviously it's *very* important. My father is hurting my mother. What's wrong with Aunt Cristina and Uncle Paco? Are they crazy? How do they let Esperanza even come to know this woman?"

"Darling, clearly she brings your father great happiness, something I'm unable to do, and Cristina and Paco appreciate that."

"Well, I don't appreciate it and I'm not going to tolerate it. I intend to tell him that I'm not going to work in his bank nor live under his roof while he leaves you alone every weekend for this floozy."

Magdalena was distraught. To have her eldest son move out in anger would be too much to bear. "José Maria, I ask you as a favor to me to say nothing, do nothing, show nothing. The lady in question is no floozy. I rather wish she were. She's a young American of quality whose name happens to be America, not Merica, as Esperanza says it."

"I'm aware of that. Puri and I were introduced to her in the Sierra Nevada. She's the one who was with him in *¡HOLA!*"

"The photograph is long forgotten. What is important for you and your brothers and sisters to understand is that your father's actions are not reprehensible. Not in the least. He and I have an unusual relationship that we both accepted before we married. Though I appreciate and love you for your defense of me, if you should make an issue of this and disrupt the family you would be treating your father unjustly and doing no service on my behalf."

Chapter Twelve

America heard a shotgun burst in the distance. Then the second barrel. She was in the kitchen preparing Sunday breakfast for Alfonso. Then there was a barrage of guns exploding. Primavera and Alegría, who had been sniffing around for a second breakfast, both lay down on the kitchen floor, frightened.

Alfonso rushed in. Have you given anyone permission to shoot on your grounds?"

"No."

"Poachers," he said. They saddled their horses and rode toward the sound of shotgun fire coming from a wooded area near the lake America had built and stocked.

They encountered the two gamekeepers rushing toward the house. "Sr. Duque, there are men from San Pedro, Ojen . . ." His right eye was cut and his lip was bleeding. The other gamekeeper had a gash on his forehead. "We told them this was private land of the Sr. Duque, which, of course, they have known all of their lives, but there are at least fifty of them."

"Call the *Comisaría de Policía*. Advise them that armed trespassers have attacked you." He turned to America, "Go back with Gabriel and Juan."

"No way. This is my farm they're on."

They galloped off toward the sound of gunfire.

The men were shooting in all directions at anything that moved. Alfonso thought ruefully that the best thing to do would be to leave them alone and they would end up shooting each other, but he called out to them so that they might not fire in America's and his direction.

There were easily fifty men. Among them was Santiago, a man Alfonso paid to organize the beaters at his annual *cacería*.

"*Buenos días, Sr. Duque,*" Santiago called out, as if he were not at that moment trespassing and poaching pheasant and partridges on the man's property.

"*Buenos días,* Santiago."

A rough voice from within the crowd called out, "Don Santiago to you, *Señorito,*" emphasizing the word, offensive when used for an adult, inferring "little master" or "playboy."

There was the kind of laughter when men outnumber another by fifty to one.

Santiago shouted, "*Callados!*" ordering them to be quiet.

America noticed one of the men, a redhead, staring boldly at her breasts.

Alfonso judged that though Santiago had been happy to come there and shoot, he was now uncomfortable and would leave, given a way to save face in front of the others.

"Santiago, I would invite you and your friends for a shoot but though I used to own this *finca* it has been sold to Señorita Harvey."

The redhead smirked, "Wouldn't we like to watch her paying for it!"

Santiago backhanded him across the face, "Get out of here, you cheap garbage. Go!"

When the moment had passed Alfonso continued, "Santiago, please ask your friends to withdraw."

Before Santiago could reply, a brute Alfonso did not know, stepped out of the crowd. "Listen, *Señorito,* this land belongs to Spain and Spain belongs to the Spaniards. And if we want to shoot birds then nobody had better try to stop us. You have had all this to yourself for long enough, *Señorito.* Besides, we don't need foreigners buying up Spain."

Realizing that the man assumed that an American woman wouldn't understand what he had said, Alfonso tried reason, "Aside from ownership, and for the tourism that is Spain's most important industry, there are too many guns. I have never had more than a dozen guns here, and only once a year. If you continue like this you will destroy all bird life and there will be none left to reproduce for next year."

The brute shrugged, "As we do not expect you to invite us to your *cacería* next year it doesn't worry us."

"Shit on all this talking," shouted another, "I've come here to shoot." He fired his shotgun in the air.

America was staring at a large fishing net that two men were dragging up a hill. "What are you doing?" she shouted, dreading the obvious answer.

"Going fishing," replied a stocky man she recognized.

"In my lake?"

"In the people's lake. It's especially my lake. I sweated for a month on the construction."

"And I paid you for every minute of your labor. And I voluntarily gave you a 50 percent bonus for finishing on time."

"And I said, 'Thank you.' Now we're going fishing."

"What you're doing is a crime."

"Where there's an empty stomach there's no crime."

America stared at him and at the others, the local electricians, plumbers, carpenters, masons, shopkeepers, all of whom were prospering on tourism. None among them was hungry. They all owned cars and TV sets and most of them had ample stomachs developed by three square meals a day. She said, "Not one of you is fishing or shooting pheasant out of need to feed yourselves or your families." It did not matter that no one replied, she just wanted to have said it.

These are "the people," Alfonso was thinking, looking from one to another of their belligerent, even malignant faces. *They invest nothing, they create nothing, preserve nothing. They use what exists until they use it out of existence. "If I can't have it then you won't have it either." Like the sheep at Los Escalones.*

America and Alfonso sat on their horses, helpless to do more than watch them kill his birds and vandalize her lake. After a while their presence made the men uncomfortable and they began straggling away. But they would be back. Respect for private property, for law and order, was ebbing.

Walking their horses toward the house Alfonso was silent. America observed, "You're not feeling very macho. But my darling, there were fifty of them, all with shotguns. It took a strong man not to have done something stupid to prove masculinity."

"Thank you, but I truly am not concerned with masculinity. We have been observing the beginning of lawlessness that historically becomes epidemic in Spain and has always led to bloodshed. For centuries each time Spain falls into disorder it leads to civil war."

At the house the guard reported having spoken to the police. "They won't respond, Sr. Duque."

Alfonso telephoned the headquarters of the National Police and reported the beating of his two guards, the trespassing, the looting of his and America's property. He listened to the policeman on the other end of the line. Then he hung up and sat down next to America. "The police won't move to stop this. They won't make waves."

"Did they say that?"

"No, but obviously the government is interested in the coming election. The property and rights of one landowner are not as important to them as the votes of fifty men who wish to shoot partridges."

"But Paco is the *Sub Ministro del Interior*. The police fall under his jurisdiction. Couldn't he do something?"

"He doesn't make government policy. Nor would I ask him to intervene. This is an example of his 'democracy.'"

* * *

"Elena, darling, I beg you to give up this relationship. You haven't been brought up to live the life you're leading and will continue to lead with this man."

"I cannot give him up, Papá, I love him, he loves me and I plan to marry him."

They were seated in Alfonso's library before dinner. He had feared this because neither he nor Magdalena, nor peer pressure from her brothers and sisters, had altered Elena's determination to continue her romance with, he sighed silently, Van Gogh.

"My darling, I plead with you to reconsider. I'm your father and I love you and I want you to be happy. But, try as I may, and I have thought of this and talked of this for hours with your mother, who agrees with me, I cannot believe that your life will be happy with this man. First of all he's nearly old enough to be your father . . ."

She glared, bitterly. "Maybe that's what I'm looking for."

* * *

"I can't think of anything stronger to have said," Alfonso told America. "I acknowledged that I had not been a great father but pointed out that this man would make a worse father—or husband—even than I. At least I've protected her. I'm a responsible and serious person in many of my ways. But according to everyone who knows this man, he's totally irresponsible. I told her I couldn't in conscience give my consent or be a party in any way to this grave error. Nor could her mother.

"Nor am I influenced by my inability to understand a man who wears an earring and a ponytail. My other children have gone out of their way to spend time with him, double and triple dating. José Maria and Puri and Luis have spent as much time as they could endure with this man and they say he does not have it in him to take care of a wife. He's never punctual; he forgets appointments; as a painter he often doesn't work because he says he doesn't feel inspired. Pablo Picasso, who was also a painter, said, 'the work is the thing. To do it and do it and do it . . .' But this man needs 'inspiration' or he takes the day off. They say he's fun, bright, good sense of humor but totally incapable of assuming the care of another person. He can't even take care of himself."

"Does he use drugs?"

"I asked José Maria. He said they never saw any suggestion of it."

"Do you think he's after her money?"

"Who can know these things? That's one of the prices a child pays for being wealthy. In fairness, he may not know if he is attracted by the glamor of wealth, the good living, clothes, fame, titles, the palace she lives in, servants—it's hypnotic. Or maybe he really loves her for herself alone. But from what her brothers say he's a hopeless candidate for a husband."

"What are you going to do?"

"What more can I do except wait and pray?"

He called America in the morning. "When I got home last night Magdalena told me Elena had moved out of our home. She's living with that man. She's pregnant."

He told Mari Sol, "No calls," and sat at his desk. *It's my fault. I wasn't there for her as I was for the others. I didn't take her to Mass since she was fourteen. Yes, I saw her at dinner four times a week and then she went to her room to study, or to watch television.*

That night he spoke with Magdalena, "They have nothing to live on. And she's expecting. She needs proper nourishment and care. We should provide an income so that she doesn't suffer."

"But that's all," Magdalena said firmly. "She has made a mistake and certainly we'll care for her. But we must not make a bed of roses for that man. We have to learn, first, what he'll do for her."

In the morning Magdalena got Van Gogh's address from José Maria, who had been there, and was driven by her *mecánico* to see Elena. The neighborhood was what one would expect of a man who has no money.

Elena kissed and hugged her mother. Van Gogh, who had been working, put down his brush but not his palette to greet

Magdalena, then excused himself, "I've gotten motivation and I don't want to break my rhythm."

"Please do go back to work. I apologize for barging in without notice . . ." She stopped, not wishing to mention that she had not called because they had no telephone.

The apartment, in the basement of the old tenement building, was a single room with a tiny bathroom and a hot plate on which to prepare meals. It had one small window near the ceiling that looked out on a garbage container and pedestrians' legs up to the knee. There was a single bed, one chair and cardboard boxes that contained his clothes and now Elena's. The floor was concrete and there wasn't even a rug by the bed. The only "carpet" was a mass of cockroaches. There was a small TV set. The walls were covered with unframed pictures, obviously all by the same artist. One was a white background with a large number 2 in black as the subject of the painting, another in red with an orange number 3, and another in green with a blue number 4. Another was a Coca-Cola can that Magdalena imagined had been "inspired" by Andy Warhol's Campbell's Soup can. Magdalena looked at the canvas for which he couldn't break his rhythm. A STOP sign. She thought that the graffiti on the walls of the building had been done by someone more creative.

"Let's not be distracting," she whispered. "We'll go out and have coffee." Seated at a table in a bar of the poor neighborhood, certain that the cup and saucer had been merely rinsed out in cold water, she was unwilling to put the cup to her lips.

"It's not what I've been accustomed to, but I don't mind. Van insists I sleep on the bed. He uses the floor. We'll buy a larger bed when he sells a picture."

"Then you're happy?"

"Very. Material things are not what count in life. True living is to express oneself. Having money is a convenience but irrelevant to happiness. One's mission is to leave something behind, something of oneself. I can do it with our baby. Van with his art."

Magdalena thought that those statements should have been in quotes. This certainly wasn't her daughter speaking. Fearful of alienating her she did not ask if Van had ever sold a picture. Her educated opinion of his work was that anyone who paid money for what he painted needed to cover a large hole in a wall.

"Elena, you've made a very strong statement by leaving the comfort of your home and family for the man you love. Your father asked me to tell you that though he hasn't changed his position, he hopes that you and Van come home for meals as often as you like." She put an envelope in Elena's hand. It contained twenty-five thousand pesetas. "Do not be proud. You must eat well for your baby. I, or one of your brothers, will come here every Tuesday at this time with the same envelope. Please call us every day. I can't bear the thought of not hearing your voice and knowing that you're well. And I'm sure that Papá would welcome a call at his office."

Elena shuddered. "I couldn't. I'm so humiliated. I said something so terrible to him."

"He did not confide that in me. But when you are a parent you will find that there's nothing you won't forgive in your child. I'm sure he'd be grateful to hear from you."

"No. I was too awful. *I* can't forgive me, let alone hope that *he* will."

"He will. However, if it was that bad I won't suggest to Papá that he visit here." She didn't say that she couldn't imagine Alfonso allowing his daughter to remain there. "Let time take care of how you feel. Meanwhile, be sure to go to Dr. García del Pozo regularly. I spoke with him this morning. You have an appointment with him tomorrow at noon. Do not worry about his fees. He'll send the bills to me. And when the time comes for you to give birth you should be at *La Luz*, with which he's associated. Again, the costs will be your father's."

"Mamá, when I took the decision to leave home I did not expect to be subsidized. I understood exactly what I was leaving behind and going to and I made the choice. After what I said to Papá I have no right to take his money."

"Elena, he'll never stop being your father. Further, I'm not telling you to go to Loewe and buy a new fall wardrobe and a fur coat. I'm only trying to protect your health."

"Okay, thank you. Do you think Van's work will sell one day?"

"I'm not qualified to answer that."

"You're on the Executive Board of El Prado."

"That isn't modern art such as Van is trying to produce."

Magdalena couldn't bear to tell her daughter what she thought of his future so she stood up. "Let me go and say *hasta luego.*"

He had finished the STOP sign. "What may I call you?" he asked.

At least he had manners. "Please call me Mamá, as Elena does."

Elena called home and spoke with her mother and brothers and sisters every day, but she did not have the courage to call her father. And when she brought Van Gogh home for dinner it was always on a weekend when she was sure she wouldn't have to face him.

* * *

The people of the Basque region, wanting independence, their own police force, their own language and the right to collect taxes, but suppressed under Franco's rule, now, under a more lenient government, began a campaign of terror. Through the militant arm of ETA, a Basque language acronym for "Basque Homeland and Liberty," they randomly murdered *Guardias Civiles.* They struck without warning. Policemen standing on a street corner in Madrid were mowed down from a car that suddenly stopped and annihilated them by submachine gun fire. Even retired policemen were riddled to death while having a cup of coffee or coming out of their homes.

On the Costa del Sol, the area most valuable to Spanish tourism, ETA warned the police that the beaches were mined with bombs. The warnings were received during the night, leaving time for the bombs to be found and defused. But ETA planted the news with the British, German and other European press agencies, and it was published all over the world:

"BOMBS ON BEACH ON COSTA DEL SOL"
"SUN & DEATH IN SPAIN"

ETA's point had not been to kill tourists but to hurt the Spanish economy by frightening away the spenders of all that foreign currency so that the Spanish government would sit down and negotiate the Basque desires. The country was caught in a spasm of fear as the daily papers reported the bombing of banks, airports and the telephone company's technical center in Madrid, throwing the city into a telephonic silence that lasted a week before the damage could be repaired. The press unrestrainedly portrayed the anguish, the bloodshed; the nation's helplessness against large-scale terrorism.

To pay for the guns and bombs and the killers who used them, ETA worked the protection racket, imposing a "Revolutionary Tax" on industrialists who either paid up or lived the nightmare of waiting to be murdered. The President of *Banco de Bilbao* refused to be blackmailed, but then for fear of his life he had to leave his home and sleep in a different place every night, entering and leaving his office at odd hours.

Lunching with Alfonso at Jockey, Paco said, "I hate to alarm you but we've arrested ETA members and found lists of people to be killed or kidnapped, with meticulous dossiers on the targets' habits. You're high on their list. In fact so is your *consuegro*. But the military police are in charge of protecting him. My concern is you. Your dossier records the hour you leave for work, your route, the hour you return home for lunch, the flight you take every Friday to Málaga and the Sunday flight back, all of the children's routines and Magdalena's. Change all of those routines. And hire around-the-clock bodyguards, and for each of the children, and Magdalena as well, install alarm systems all over your home . . ."

Carmelo, the maitre d', approached the table. "There's a telephone call for el Sr. Duque." His face reflected Alfonso's own surprise, for he never received telephone calls while lunching. That was Hollywood, not Madrid.

"I asked the gentleman to identify himself but he would not, saying only to advise the Sr. Duque that it was life and death."

The voice on the telephone had the unmistakable Basque accent. "I do hope I did not disturb your meal with your brother, the *Sub Ministro del Interior,* Sr. Duque, but we are giving you the courtesy of suggesting that you arrange your affairs, because soon we are going to kidnap you. Begin collecting cash in old bills, two hundred million pesetas . . ."

Returning to the table Alfonso told Paco, "You certainly were right that they know all about us. Even with whom I'm lunching."

"We are in a war in which the enemy knows us but we don't know the enemy. That person probably saw me pick you up at the bank and followed us here."

They went together to the Ministry of the Interior and reported the conversation to the recently formed Anti-Terrorist Division. The police put little credibility in the warning on the theory that if there were a genuine kidnap plot then it would be unlikely for them to have made it more difficult to pull off by tipping their hand. It was treated as psychological terrorism, undoubtedly preparation to extort a revolutionary tax.

It had its effect. Like all wealthy men in Spain, and ranking military, Alfonso was impelled to follow Paco's advice. He hired bodyguards, varied his movements and installed closed-circuit television surveillance of all exterior doors and the garden. The wall around the house was topped with razor wire. The doors were reinforced with steel and had new locks that bolted them closed at six points. They were hideous reminders of 1936 and his grandmother futilely ordering sharp tips on the iron gate surrounding the palace.

Alfonso sent security men to *Finca de la Tejana* to install jimmy-proof locks, peepholes on all outside doors, and an alarm system, as well as a "panic button" beside America's bed that rang in Encarna and Rafael's quarters. Watching them being installed she couldn't help but contrast the Spain of the moment with the Spain of 1970, when she had slept at Marisa's house with the doors open, left the keys in the car's ignition, when there was a complete sense of safety and tranquility. She was desperately afraid for Alfonso.

Kidnapping was ETA's most lucrative manner of financing itself. The family of a Valencia meatpacker had just paid one hundred million pesetas for his safe return. Another industrialist brought two hundred million. It was happening with such frequency and rich results that the government passed a law against the payment of ransom to kidnappers.

Bitterly Alfonso observed, "Under democracy we need a law making it illegal to pay ransom. Under our less idyllic—onerous to some—dictatorship, we required only a law against kidnapping. *Pobre España*. Today we have the fruits of democracy: freedom of speech and press that too often is totally irresponsible, included in a package with terrorism, drugs and shameless scandal magazines."

Franquistas appalled by the abrupt lawlessness were quick to claim, "This could never have happened under Franco," and they hinted darkly that the day was near when there would again be *Franquismo* even without Franco, i.e., a military overthrow of the government. Others who had welcomed the "change" rather wished that it had not happened, or at least they admitted they had not anticipated the other edge of the sword. And the best-selling book in Spain was *Franco, Al Tercer Año Resucito*, a humorous account of Franco returning from his grave after three years and the run-for-their-lives reactions of the leftist Spanish politicians who had brought the country to this disorder, so distant from where he had left it.

Alfonso and America went to a dinner in Marbella at Gianni De Lorenzo's *finca*. Gianni was known for having elegant dinners in his home, an artfully reconstructed convent. The guitars were there, the night-blooming jasmine perfumed the grounds, the food and wines were as Alfonso had said they would be, but there was a distinct change in the mood of the people. Now violence, bloodshed and fear of tomorrow were the topics, as they had become everywhere in Spain whenever Spaniards gathered.

"Flight money is the thing today," a long-time resident said. "I know of three beachfront villas around the Marbella club for sale at sacrifice prices, to foreigners only, who can pay the appraised value in pesetas and the bulk of the money in dollars or Swiss francs outside the country."

Another guest asked, "And have you noticed how many of our friends have stopped using their titles?"

An Italian noblewoman shrugged, "We stopped using our titles years ago. It became too dangerous. We all have friends who were killed or attacked simply because they were titled."

1936, we are returning to 1936.

As coffee was being served Alfonso felt warm, excused himself from America and went outside. He did not want her to see him in this state of despair. He went to the parking lot to sit in his car. Approaching it, he looked with distaste at the scratches and dents on the fenders and doors that he deliberately had not had fixed. He detested camouflaging himself with the uncared-for automobile as he had done as a child, with the torn and dirtied clothes he had worn when he had gone in search of his parents. The image of the morgue, of the mounds of arms and legs and heads, hurtled irrepressibly out of the past.

As he inserted his key to unlock the car door Alfonso felt an arm around his neck and a sharp blade against the side of his throat. A voice behind him threatened, "If you move, you die," and Alfonso felt the pain of the knife's tip cutting the skin. "You can be certain that one *Señorito* less won't sadden me. So, slowly now, very slowly, put your hands in your pockets and remove everything in them. Now remove your chain and cross, cuff-links . . ."

Alfonso awoke on the ground with a terrible ache in his head. His car was gone. He brushed the dust off his black trousers and, shirt and cuffs open, weakened, yet grateful that he was alive, returned to the house.

Gianni saw him first. "My God, even here." He was referring to the fact that his house was removed from mainstream Marbella. But obviously someone had learned of the party and correctly concluded that where the rich and glamorous gather there was going to be money and jewelry. Gianni brought him a hooker of scotch and a set of cufflinks and studs. With the other guests gathered around him Alfonso politely answered questions.

"Fonso," he heard, and he welcomed Cayetana's voice, confident that she would bring the disagreeable subject to a close. Cayetana never attended dinner parties until after the meal had been served. She wanted control over what she ate.

Standing before him, tall, slim, with shining golden hair she was "ravishing" in a white leather jumpsuit. Her legs were long and strong, yet slender. One could see the cultivated muscles beneath the tight leather. Cayetana was fifty-five, she looked thirty and her two escorts no more than twenty, both blonde, tanned, wearing black trousers and white silk shirts as if they were in uniform. Superbly built they stood at her side as if in attendance. "These are Alex and Bill," she said gesturing toward them.

Alfonso began to stand up but Cayetana eased him back against the sofa. She leaned down and let him kiss her.

He said, "May I present my sister Cayetana, la Condesa de Santiago del Monte. My very dear friend America Harvey."

Cayetana offered her hand. "Cristina has spoken of you. I appreciate you."

She took a handkerchief from her purse, dipped it into his whiskey and applied it against the side of Alfonso's neck. It stung. "Sorry, but we must clean this." She re-dipped the handkerchief in his scotch and dabbed it on the wound.

Alfonso held the wet linen to his neck. "Smells good, doctor. A lot better than the alcohol your colleagues use."

"You are coming to my house tonight. You have never been and it's about time that you know what sister dear is up to. I've invited Gianni and a few others for some light entertainment. You two will make ten. Exactly as many as I can handle."

"I thought you'd built a large house."

"The house is large. But the bullring seats ten, comfortably."

"Bulls? At this hour?"

Cayetana was amused, "It's indoors, Fonso, with lights. The house is difficult to find and impossible to enter without me so we must go in caravan. I'll be parked out front in twenty minutes."

Gianni offered, "As your car is gone, you and America come with me." He added, "If you want to go." He glanced meaningfully at America, whose attention was on the departing Cayetana.

"Why would I *not* want to go to my sister's home?"

"You've never been there? Nobody's told you?"

"Told me what? I know it's large, that it has a small bullring and stables and I'm sure it's beautiful." He was piqued by the innuendo. Then he realized that he was greatly overwrought and touched his friend on the shoulder, "Forgive me, Gianni."

Cayetana's car was a white Rolls-Royce convertible. She sat at the wheel, her escorts in the back seat. Two other cars were waiting behind her when Alfonso, America and Gianni drove up in his less spectacular Bentley. For fifteen minutes they followed her, winding higher into the hills over Marbella, finally coming to a twelve-foot-tall stone wall topped with razor wiring that enclosed a large property. There were equally high, well-lighted bronze portals in front of which Cayetana stopped.

A small door within one of the portals opened and a uniformed armed guard stepped out. He approached the driver's side, spoke with Cayetana, looked into the back seat to assure himself that his employer wasn't speaking under intimidation, then stepped back and saluted Cayetana. He returned through the small door and in a moment both portals began opening to admit the caravan. On either side of the entrance were uniformed guards, also armed.

"Your sister runs a tight ship," America observed.

"One can only admire strict security, but it rather conflicts with driving around in a white Rolls."

They were in a spacious courtyard with a lighted fountain in the center. Cayetana circled and stopped at the front entrance of the main house.

Leaving her car she told Gianni, "I want to show the house to Alfonso and America. You go ahead to the bullring with the others." She also dismissed her escorts.

The front door was opened by a well-built, handsome young butler who wore white tie and tails. He bowed his head to Cayetana in the precise *reverencia* that men in Spain do for the royal family, the male equivalent of a curtsey, but it's a sign of respect only for the royal family: the King, Queen, their parents, brothers and sisters, the Prince, *Infantas,* the name by which daughters of the Spanish King and Queen are called; never for merely titled people no matter how noble the title. Cayetana accepted it as her due.

Alfonso asked, "Who's his tailor?"

"The same as yours, Fonso dear."

"An expensive way to dress a servant."

"Quite. But I have no husband to support, no children, and I want the servants to be splendid. After all, I have to look at them. I send them all to Madrid to be dressed by a top couturier and your tailor. In fact, didn't Mamá and Papá dress them all beautifully? And don't you?"

"At a uniform maker, not my tailor."

Cayetana led them into the living room. The furniture and the art that covered the walls was the best of the modern designers and artists. Bronze Giacometti lamps and tables, Mies van der Rohe chairs and sofa, Eero Saarinen. Sculpture to utilize.

America gazed about the room. "It's powerful."

"Though not exactly what we were brought up on."

"That no longer exists for me, Fonso. You recreated it. I make an effort to forget it."

At the end of the room was a swimming pool that extended to the outside so that it was indoor—outdoor. Alfonso saw the blood drain from America's face and he led her to a chair. It was the first such pool she had seen since that last day at J.J.'s house.

Cayetana was alarmed. "Are you all right? Can I get you a smelling salt or a whiskey?"

America stood up, "No, thank you so much. I'm fine. I'd love to see the rest of your beautiful house."

Cay led them through the dining room and into the kitchen, stainless steel with industrial refrigerators and ovens to prepare a major banquet. A chef inclined his head forward and a pretty, young sous-chef curtsied.

Alfonso said, "I feel like I'm visiting some potentate, not my eccentric sister."

Cayetana opened a thick, soundproof door and showed them a two-lane shooting gallery. Her brother said, "I had no idea you enjoyed shooting this much."

I don't. This is for when I have a *cacería* and I invite a gun I'm not certain about. Before I expose myself, and my friends, to an unknown quantity I ask them to have some practice rounds in here. One can quickly see what they know or do not."

One of several guest suites upstairs had a barber's chair in the bathroom. "For my lovers." Next door to it was a well-equipped gym with a large massage table. "For me. Two hours a day. Religiously."

When they reached Cayetana's own bedroom a chambermaid was turning down the bed. The girl was gorgeous. Almost six feet tall and slender with a sculpted bosom, she was dressed in a short-skirted silk taffeta maid's uniform. Her traffic-stopping legs were enhanced by glimmering black stockings and she wore black patent-leather high heels. She curtsied to Cayetana and backed away.

America marveled, "Do you get your servants from central casting?"

Cayetana smiled.

"Cay. Where do you get such people?"

"Oh, Fonso, you have always been so impatient and serious. Everything will be answered. When I'm ready."

Passing again through the large entrance hall America exclaimed, "I love your sculpture."

"I'm so pleased. Let me show you one more at the outdoor end of the pool." The swimming pool was illuminated, made of blue tiles so the water looked like the Mediterranean. America did not allow her eyes to see it. At the far end was a lighted alcove in which stood a Greek statue of a young man and woman in an embrace.

Alfonso thought it was extraordinarily attractive, provocative. Then he sighed, "I'm tired. I could swear I saw the sculpture move."

Cayetana muttered, "They are not *supposed* to move!" She called out, "You may rest," and the two figures stepped out of their pose. They were completely nude, wearing body paint that made them look like antique white marble. A *tableau vivant.* Cayetana called to them bitingly, "Report to the bullring. Now."

Alfonso was laughing, "Wait a minute. Do you hire those models to decorate your garden like other people put out Henry Moores?"

"Mine are prettier. And a lot cheaper. *Vámanos!* We'll join the others."

Cayetana opened a door to the bullring. It was a round building approximately twenty yards in diameter. She gestured for the others to precede her and they entered a salon that was curved to fit the contour of the building. Comfortable sofas with coffee tables faced a wall curtained in the same velvet print as the upholstery. Three waitresses, all supermodel pretty, in mini-skirted black taffeta uniforms with white lace trim, white lace caps and white gloves, were passing trays of glasses bubbling with *cava.*

Observing the curtain in front of them America could imagine it opening on a large movie screen. Something told her it wouldn't be showing "Snow White and the Seven Dwarfs."

After everyone had had a few glasses of *Cava and Petits Fours* Cayetana pressed a button, the lights began dimming, the curtains drew apart and instead of a movie screen they were looking through a twenty-foot-wide one-way picture window into a bedroom containing a king-sized bed. Cayetana's escort, Bill, was naked and shackled to the back wall. Alex, her other escort, also naked was suspended by his wrists from chains that hung from the ceiling, his toes just touching the floor.

Alfonso looked at America, asking if she wanted to leave. She shook her head. It would be discourteous and she was fascinated.

A door to the bedroom opened and two blonde, Amazonian young women entered, tall, slender and strong like Cayetana herself. Again, it was obvious that their erotic costumes were couture quality. They held chains, leashes, actually, attached to the collars around the necks of Cayetana's "statues." Their body makeup had been washed off but they were still naked. Their captors moved efficiently, shackling the man to the wall, the woman to another pair of hanging chains, suspending her slightly until she, too, stood barely on tiptoe. Then the two Amazons detached short whips that hung from their waists.

Cayetana sat next to Alfonso who was stunned. "Who are they? What *is* all this?"

"They are my slaves. All of the people you see working here, the waitresses, the staff in my house, Alex and Bill and the Greek statues who are about to be punished for infractions, they are my slaves. They all are, except the uniformed security guards at the gate. They are professionals."

"What are you talking about? Nobody has slaves."

"Fonso, don't be naive. First of all, as you can see, *I* have. Secondly, many people have slaves. The difference is merely in what one calls them and demands of them. The Golden Rule is: we who are golden, rule. That isn't pretty, but it's incontrovertible truth. At your bank, for example, is there an employee who doesn't fear your power to dismiss him? Would he not do anything you demand to keep his job? Does he like that situation? Of course not. Whereas, here, everybody enjoys themselves."

"Cayetana, this isn't a bank! This erotica is perverted. You need a psychiatrist."

"That's the *last* thing I want! Fonso, a psychiatrist might straighten me out. I'm kinky. And I like it."

"But this must be against the law!"

"Not at all. No one is here against his or her will. They are all consenting adults in a private home."

"How could you have gotten involved in this?

"When I discovered how much I enjoyed sex I realized that to get the most out of it I should learn everything I possibly could. So I went to the best. I studied under Madame Claude."

"You cannot mean *the* Madame Claude? In Paris?"

"Exactly. She had no idea I was studying. I worked as one of her girls. We used each other."

"I don't believe that my sister is telling me that she worked as a prostitute in Paris."

"Not only in Paris. I was sent all over the world: Monte Carlo for potentates, Las Vegas for high rollers. And always first class in every way. I was a weekend birthday gift for a chief of state. Paid for by his wife. Her thing was to tell me what to do to him and then watch. They brought me there and sent me back in their 747, just me and the crew. It was the only time I've ever flown in a sauna and had myself seat-belted into bed. I learned a lot. And, Fonso, I made a mountain of money! Madame Claude rented out my bones for two thousand American dollars a night and even though she kept a quarter of it I did enormously well. I worked for one hundred and eighty days. Multiply that by fifteen hundred dollars. Two hundred and seventy thousand dollars in six months isn't just fucking around."

"What name did you use?" he asked with trepidation.

"Don't be silly. Not my real name, not my title. Though I really should have. That was a mistake. A Spanish Countess could have drawn *five* thousand a night." She shrugged, "But I wasn't in it for the money."

Alfonso was piqued by the S/M scene going on before them. "Couldn't you at least keep your personal tastes to yourself? Not make a public entertainment of them?"

"First of all the bullring isn't open to the 'public' and discretion is mandatory of those friends who are invited. But keep it to myself? Why? Everyone likes sex, and lots of people are kinky. And anyone here who objects need not come back. But nearly everyone does. It's the hottest invitation in town."

"Where do these," he grimaced, "'slaves' come from?"

"They are kids who come to Marbella from Scandinavia, from Germany, from all over Europe, either to marry well or to take the sun, for whatever reason, and they run out of money. You can see them at *Puerto Banus* at the corner bar; nursing the cheapest drink they can buy, trying to think of a way out, or a way home. They see my Rolls and me, and they sit up, trying to look attractive. If I think they are I beckon to them to come over. I listen to what they have to say, which of course I know in advance. There are five or six versions of the same story as to why potentially good-looking, healthy young people are here looking like shit, desolate, seedy, without a peseta.

"I offer them a solution they never imagined: I tell them they can come to a luxurious home in the mountains for a period of not less than one month, unless they displease me. I tell them that there will be no tobacco, no alcohol, no drugs, that I will feed them health-giving, deliciously prepared meals, clothe them richly, and that when they leave I'll give them twice the amount of their air fare home. My requirements are that they develop deep tans and exercise under the supervision of my trainer so that they will have beautiful bodies, and that they will have sex with me whenever and in whatever manner I say, or with each other if I allow it." She rolled her eyes, "Which, of course, I do. Even *I* can't handle *all* of them. They must submit to a medical examination. I tell them clearly that they are entering a "Private Kingdom of Female Supremacy," in which I am the "Monarch." They will obey my every whim or be punished at my whim. Only by women. No man ever strikes a woman here.

"The only problem I have is that it can be awkward with friends. For example, Gianni always wants to play. But the girls don't care for him, he's too fat. Other than with me they are not obliged to have anything to do with anyone they don't want."

"Aside from everything else, how can you take strangers into your car these days? A Rolls of all things. Don't you realize they could mug you, steal the car? Maybe kill you."

"Fonso! Killing me is the last thing they want. By the time I invite them into my car they are convinced that they are on the way to something far better than they could have by mugging me, or stealing my car and probably being arrested. Still, I'm not imprudent. I have them sit in the back seat; beneath the carpet, bolted to the floor, are two stainless-steel chains attached to hand-cuffs. When I snap the cuffs closed they can raise their hands only to their laps. It's a 'moment of truth' when they hear the cuffs click closed. If they resist and change their minds, I release them. If not, we come home."

Cayetana continued, "My slaves sleep in what the architect's plans call the stables but the 'stalls' are in fact comfortable private bed-rooms with private baths. If they are impatient about taking the sun and developing the color I like, I have them chained to sun beds. They submit to wearing chains, at my whim, anything, at my whim."

"And they don't try to escape?"

Cayetana was exasperated. "Fonso, why would they want to escape from paradise? I do ask them after the first week if they wish to leave. I don't want any unhappy people around me. But no one ever has. Bill's been here three months. Today he begged me to let him stay until next year. We're a happy group. They eat well, they get in great shape, they have a lot of sex and nothing to worry about, just do as they're told, which is never distasteful to them. By the time they leave here they're far better off than on arrival. They haven't smoked, taken alcohol or touched drugs. They are cleansed, fit and in condition to go back into the real world—from which they had dropped out—and go on to better things than being hustlers or beach bums."

She studied his face. "I gather that you see this as bad," Cayetana sighed. "Fonso, I have been trying to tell you for years: all that I consider important is health, money and sex. I work at one, I'm lucky to have been born with the other, and I indulge myself in all I want of the latter."

"I wonder why you've never been interested in finding 'the right man,' as they say."

"There are a lot of right men, Fonso. It's just that I want them all."

"And it's strange that children never interested you."

"Oh, wouldn't I have made the perfect mother?" She shook her head, "No, my dear, neither husband nor children. Never. I don't want to need anyone. I don't want to suffer if they leave me or die. At first, when our parents were dead, and then you and Cristina and Paco went to war, I thought, 'I have nothing.' And it nearly destroyed me. But finally I came around to thinking that if you have nothing you have no obligation to anything. You can enjoy freedom, do anything that pleases you. *Et voilà!* I do anything that pleases me. And I am very happy."

After the guests had watched the performance Cayetana pressed the button and the curtain closed. Alfonso felt that he would be irresponsible if he did not make an effort to say something to Cayetana. Something! "I need to speak with you. Privately."

"We can take a walk outside." When they were a short distance from the bullring he said, "We have too much, materially, to feel sorry for ourselves, but in fact we had horrendous beginnings that affected our values. I'm aware that you do not want advice but you're dear to me and I'm troubled by the lifestyle you've chosen. Understand that I'm not speaking as the supposed 'head of the family' but as one who loves you."

"I do understand and I'm grateful, Fonso, darling. I agree with you and have been weighing some ideas."

"Tell me."

"Real estate in Marbella is going through the sky and I have all this land around me that I neither need nor use except for an annual shoot that I could happily live without. I should break it into parcels and build a few houses on speculation."

"That sounds wonderful."

"With a golf course."

"Great idea! Golfers will pay fortunes to live on a beautiful fairway."

"I will also build a small, first-class hospital."

"Clever. People buying luxury houses are logically going to be near middle age or beyond, and with the seclusion of this land an on-site health facility would be an invaluable attraction."

"I have the land and I have the money. The difficult part will be to find the eighteen most beautiful girls in the world."

Alfonso smiled. Cayetana was running to form. "As the caddies?"

"Of course not, Fonso. As the holes."

She had completely taken him in. Anything to avoid being serious. Cayetana enjoyed pursuing her joke. "Fonso, can you just imagine how men would flock to buy houses around my golf course?"

"And the hospital is in case one of the 'golfers' tries to play the full eighteen . . . ?"

"*¡Exactamnte!* I would also commission a sculptor to make a statue of anyone who finishes the course."

"Cay, maybe you understand life better than I. He sighed, shaking his head, "Perhaps one shouldn't take life seriously."

"That's what I've been telling you for years, Fonso, dear. My life's work is living."

When they returned to the others the waitresses were serving *churros* and hot chocolate. Alfonso and his sister sat down with America.

Cayetana asked, "Did you enjoy yourself?"

"It certainly was a change from *sevillanas* after dinner."

"Evasive!" She smiled. "But perhaps you'll come back." She anticipated Alfonso, "Only to spectate." Then to America, "We have many variations. I'll call you and describe what's on for the night. You can't possibly enjoy being alone all week. I'll send my car for you. Come for what would amuse you. We have ladies' singles, men's singles, mixed doubles, S&M, bondage, round robins. And, I assure you, no veterans' events. Good night, my darlings." She kissed her brother on both cheeks, "Don't judge me, Fonso. Try to enjoy the fact that I have made a very happy middle or ending from a most unhappy beginning."

One of Cayetana's security men drove them to *Finca de la Tejana*. When they were alone, seated in the salon, Alfonso said, "I'd like . . . No! I need a drink!"

Thoroughly confounded he asked, "What do you think of my crazy sister?"

"I like her. I'm not going to pass judgment on her way of finding happiness. It's straightforward, no less immoral than my own, and it hurts no one. But that's not what you're asking, not what you're talking about. You're still hearing your Tio Guillermo: 'You are the head of the family now.' But Alfonso, Cayetana isn't able to do what you advise. I couldn't do what *my* brother begged me to do. And I will never regret that. If I were you I would love Cayetana as she is. You cannot change her. You can only lose her."

"The war," Alfonso mused, "the early loss of our parents, our home. It scarred us all. Cristina's scar is visible. Mine and Paco's and Cay's are not. Yet they all itch. I suppose that we each scratch at the scars in our own way. But scars don't go away." He looked up, "I don't mean to feel sorry for us alone. Everyone in Spain who lived through those times, on both sides of the war, and who lost family, or the respect and love for his countrymen, we all have scars."

Then the grotesque images of the past swarmed over him. "Cayetana's compulsion to amuse herself isn't so much to find pleasure as to escape pain, to wipe away images from her mind. She tries to obscure the ugly and unacceptable with what she sees as beautiful substitutes, to outrun the past. But no one can run fast enough. That blackness, that black hole of death, the stench, the loss. It's always with you."

Chapter Thirteen

America looked out the window of the apartment in the Sierra Nevada at the fresh snow on the mountain. Good skiing would distract Alfonso. After only a few seasons he had become proficient. Not a classic skier but secure on his skis, and fearless.

Coming out of the bedroom, still sleepy, wearing a paisley silk robe he kissed America good morning and then enjoyed the coffee she had prepared. Awake and alert he said, "Let's make the bed."

The second apartment that he had bought to house his servants wasn't occupied. Whereas until recently in Spain having a steady job in a good house was something to be proud of, with the advent of democracy domestic service had plummeted out of fashion. Though his Madrid staff still functioned as before, Alfonso's personal manservant, Felipe, had let it be known that he would prefer not to go to the Sierra Nevada every weekend. He wanted the time to himself. Alfonso liked Felipe and rather than have service without a smile he adapted to the times.

He found that he loved independence and privacy. When he and America had made the bed he went to a closet and removed a vacuum cleaner. Plugging it into the wall socket he methodically began running it across the carpeting. And he loved the supermarket. He had never been in one before and it amazed him to be able to buy ". . . *cocido* in a can! And delicious!" Putting the vacuum cleaner away he said, "*Mi amor,* call Carlos and Marisa and tell them to meet us at noon at the lift."

She reached for the telephone, but stopped. Not that she minded serving him in any way that would make him happy. But he had not asked her, he had given her an assignment, as if she were Felipe or Mari Sol. "What would you think of calling them yourself?"

"Of course. How do you do it?"

"You don't know?" He shook his head. "Have you really never dialed a telephone?"

"Never. In the office there's Mari Sol. And there's always Felipe or someone else at home."

Amazing. "Okay. Pick up the receiver. Do you hear anything?"

"A buzzing sound."

"That is a dial tone. You always wait for that before you dial. Now dial the numbers 33 26 95."

Tentatively he reached an index finger toward the telephone and dialed 3. When that was successfully done, he dialed the other 3 then 26 95."

"Now you will hear it ringing. Wait for them to answer."

He heard a voice and with a touch of pride announced, "Carlos. I am Alfonso. Good morning. I have just telephoned you to suggest that we meet at the lift at noon. Does that suit you both? *Muy bien, hasta luego.*" He replaced the receiver on the telephone, delighted by the adventure.

As America had anticipated, Alfonso was happy hurrying across the good new snow toward the ski lift, she beside him, Marisa and Carlos and other friends all around, joking. He was able, for a while at least, to forget his fear of the return of '36, the kidnap threat, the mugging, his confusion over his sister, the poachers. And the infinite sadness over Elena, for which he couldn't stop blaming himself.

The ski-lift attendant smiled broadly, "Does the Sr. Duque have a ticket for the lift?"

The question startled Alfonso and caused a nervous silence around him. He looked at the attendant, who had worked there for the three years Alfonso had been skiing. The attendant was blocking his way. "I have a lifetime pass. But I haven't carried it since the first day you saw it."

"I'm so sorry, Sr. Duque, but my orders are that everyone must present a ticket or a pass."

"Are you telling me that I must return to my apartment and get the pass that you know very well I have?"

"The Sr. Duque will please forgive me but I do not remember. Perhaps the Sr. Duque would prefer to buy a ticket like everyone else instead of walking back to his apartment?"

To do that Alfonso would have to leave the head of the line, buy the ticket and then get in the back of the line. There was a large crowd and it could take him an hour to get onto the lift. His ski pass, however, in the same way as being with a ski instructor, gave him and his party the privilege of going to the front of the line without waiting.

"What is the Sr. Duque's decision? I respectfully point out that there are people other than the Sr. Duque who are waiting to ride on the lift."

Alfonso snapped, "The Sr. Duque will go for his pass."

Never before had America known Alfonso to be rude, even curt with anyone, let alone to speak of himself in the third person. Leaving his equipment with her he trudged the half mile back to the apartment and returned with the pass.

The lift took them all to the top and the exhilarating downhill flight obliterated the weird performance of the ticket taker. Looking forward to again hurtling down the side of the mountain Alfonso heard: "Does the Sr. Duque have a ticket for the lift?" It was the same man who had seen it only fifteen minutes before, the same implacable expression on his face.

Alfonso had secured the pass in an inside zip pocket. He put down his skis, helmet and visor, opened his jacket, and produced the pass.

Studying it as if deliberating its validity, finally the attendant nodded, "Ahhhh, thank you Sr. Duque."

When they were seated on the lift Marisa asked, "What *is* this?"

Alfonso waved his hand in the air as if dissolving a cloud of smoke that had hovered but that he was able to dismiss and make disappear. The descent was his best ever. He set out to get back up to the top and repeat it.

"Does the Sr. Duque have a ticket for the ski lift?"

America glared, "You saw his pass twice in half an hour."

Ignoring her, holding out his hand, the attendant repeated, "Does the Sr. Duque have a ticket for the ski-lift?"

Alfonso dropped his gear to the ground and unzipped the suit.

"Ahhhh, a lifetime pass. Thank you, Sr. Duque."

Halfway down the slope Alfonso's right ski touched a rock beneath the surface and it jostled him off-balance. Unnerved by the harassment of the ticket taker, his reflexes were slowed and he took a terrific fall, banging his forehead into one of his skis, lacerating the skin, his blood staining the snow.

Carlos, America and Marisa agreed that the appropriate move was a slow descent and then a visit to the clinic. Alfonso was embarrassed by all the concern but he followed their lead. The doctor sterilized the wound, used some adhesive stitches, and wrapped a few yards of bandage around Alfonso's head.

Back in his apartment, Marisa was trembling, looking at his bandaged head, still hearing the insolent ticket taker, seeing the scab from the cut on Alfonso's neck when he had been mugged at Gianni's party. Carlos took her in his arms, but her body continued trembling. "The peace is over," she sobbed.

"*Tranquila,*" Carlos soothed, "nothing is over. Spain is simply going to be like everywhere else."

"You should know better."

"Darling, we have had it very good here, to the point of being unreal. You have lived in the States, these things have been happening there for years. Does a New York City taxi driver open your door? Treat you with respect? Never. Yet life goes on. It will be the same here. Not so good as it was, but no worse than anywhere else."

Again Marisa shook her head. "No. History is repeating itself. It's always worse in Spain. Here they are *revanchistas*. They will want revenge...blood."

At a bar frequented by the working people of the Sierra Nevada the lift attendant bragged, "I fucked him three times. 'Does the Sr. Duque have a ticket?'" He parroted his saccharin, falsely respectful tone of voice. Noticing that few of the workers were amused by it, he said, "Listen, these *Señoritos* have had it their way for all these years. Now it's our turn. And I'll shit on them every chance I get."

The mechanic who maintained the lift asked, "Was he ever unpleasant or unkind to you?"

No reply.

"And who helped make this resort successful so we are able to earn good livings here? You have a big stomach but a short memory. Where were we before we had these jobs? You had no fat stomach then."

The bartender agreed. "What did it get you? Did you put a hundred pesetas more in your pocket for annoying that man?"

"No, but it gets me back at him."

"For what?"

"For all the years I had nothing."

If Alfonso had been able to hear that he would have re-heard the boy Paco in front of his burned *choza* telling him and his sisters and *abuela* that those men had wanted revenge. Not food, but revenge.

And then there had been a civil war.

The girls were still dressing for dinner when Carlos arrived at Alfonso's apartment, poured himself a scotch and soda and joined him staring into the fireplace.

Alfonso said, "Marisa is right. But, why the hatred? Everyone wants to be rich. Why hate us for being what they would like to be?"

"Does it matter? Fuck the peasants."

"It does matter, Carlos. Because after the hatred comes the violence. How can they have forgotten that? Can't they remember that both sides die?"

The passport clerk had never had such a request. On the contrary, people who did not qualify for a diplomatic passport often tried to bribe him into issuing one. A diplomatic passport was a convenience, whisking one through Customs and Immigration and making travel more comfortable in general. "Excuse me Sra. Condesa, I'm confused. The Sra. Condesa wishes to exchange her diplomatic passport for a normal passport, omitting the title of the Sra. Condesa and the statement that she is a Grandee of Spain?"

"Exactly," Marisa answered. "Only my name. Maria Tarancón y Domecq. Nothing more."

She had *grandeza* with her husband's title, the Count of Avila, whose father, like Alfonso's, had been stopped on the streets by a band of militiamen and "executed." And she had inherited *grandeza* from her father's title, derived from the name of a city that his ancestor had defended against invading Moors.

Though she took pride in her ancestors she did not wish to hasten meeting them. If the violence erupted again and if the policeman at Passport Control in the airport happened to be anti-aristocrat she wanted the anonymity to be able to pass unimpeded. The children had no titles yet, but she would have Carlos do the same.

Chapter Fourteen

"**P**apá . . ."

At his desk Alfonso held his breath at the sound of her voice. It had been five months.

"Papá, may I come home?"

"Oh, Lord, of course, child. Where are you?"

"I'm at the tearoom on the corner of Ayala and La Castellana."

"Don't move. I'm on my way. I'll be there in minutes. And, Elena, I love you, I love you, I love you."

He went directly to the garage, not wanting to waste time looking for his chauffeur. When Elena was safely in his car he drove toward their home, having difficulty seeing clearly through the tears in his eyes.

"I'm sorry for what I said to you about not having a father, Papá"

"Don't even think about it. In fact, don't talk at all unless you want to."

"I do. But that was the first thing I wanted to say. I've wanted to say it for months. I want to tell you everything, starting with how right you and Mamá and José Maria—everybody—was. I don't know how I could have been so stupid. I was in love and I wasn't willing to see the obvious."

"Did he leave you?"

"No, Papá, I left him. Five hours ago. I was so embarrassed that it took me all that time to call you."

"Did you stop loving him?"

"Not really. But he's not a man. I mean he's a man in the normal sense, but he has no guts. When I started having morning sickness he always left the apartment. Then as I got bigger and didn't feel up to staying out all night he went out by himself. It was exactly what you said: he was irresponsible. He couldn't take care of me when I needed him. And I started thinking, 'I'm just having a baby. What if I were really sick?' I knew that if the pains were to start coming I would have to get myself to the hospital alone. I knew I had to get him behind me."

"Thank God you never got married."

"I would have. For the baby. But Van kept putting it off. He couldn't face the responsibility of officially having to take care of me."

"Your baby won't need him. And you still have your whole life ahead of you."

"With a baby."

"It will probably be healthy and beautiful. And we will all bring it up together until you find the right husband or the right husband finds you."

Alfonso worried that with a growing vindictive atmosphere in Spain physical harm might come to him, and if so then it was necessary to prepare José Maria to take over the bank. At lunch with Magdalena he said, "We've been lucky with our children. To have not one disaster among eight is miraculous. Well, there was one minor problem, but not a disaster. And I'm extremely pleased with José Maria. Luis and Rafael show the same promise. The twins have married well. I'm proud of them all. You've been a wonderful mother."

"You've been a wonderful father."

"I'm always away."

"Often, lately. But not always. And when you were here you were really here. With José Maria, Luis, Rafael, the twins. Even Alfonso. Not so with Trini and obviously not with Elena. She came back, though. And she loves you. Don't blame yourself too much. Even children with two attentive parents can make mistakes."

"You're generous Magda. I'm sorry that I haven't been able to be what I might have been to you."

She gazed into the air, "A red hot love perhaps would have been wonderful. I can't really know." She turned back to her husband, "But the friendship that we have . . . I wouldn't change. You have been all that you promised. I hope I've been as much for you."

"Eight wonderful children. A distinguished member of *La Grandeza de España,* a charitable, constructive, valuable citizen. The valiance to tolerate the gossip. What more could I ask you to do for me?"

Alfonso did not have the heart to answer his own question: *Let me leave you. Let us separate, so that I can enjoy my remaining years with America.*

As if reading his mind Magdalena said, "I'm frightened by your love for America. I would like to let you free, but I can't." Magdalena looked at the floor as she spoke, "I had always thought that we would grow old together. But now America is devoting her life to you." She raised her eyes to look at her husband, "Perhaps she needs you even more than I do. I have eight children, there will be grandchildren . . ." she looked at him imploringly, "but, please, never leave me, Alfonso. Please."

He couldn't stand the terror in her eyes. She had earned better. He reached across the table and took her hand. "Never. I promise," and he was rewarded by seeing his wife look as if she had awakened from a nightmare.

Alfonso broke the silence, "I'm thinking it's time for José Maria to become President of the bank. I'll remain as Chairman but he should be prepared to take control. And Luis is ready to be Executive Vice President."

"Nepotism," she joked.

"They are not *vagos* or *chulos.* As long as they are bright and hard workers, why not? It's their bank, no?"

Cayetana called from Marbella. "Fonso, Cristina told me about that shithead at the ski lift. Why didn't you tell him to get fucked and walk right past him? You should have said, 'You are a fool, you idiot. I have a pass, you know I have a pass, I'm going onto the lift with my party and if you wish to stop us then call the *Guardia Civil*.' That of course he wouldn't have dared. The owners would sack him if they knew he'd been bothering you. If it had been me, I'd have offered the asshole one of my ski poles and told him to try it for size."

"And I would have applauded you. But I abhor scenes."

"You need a change. I'm taking you out of this country for five days."

"My darling, I appreciate your concern but . . ."

"Forget the bank. Let José Maria start running it."

"Amazing. I've just discussed that with Magdalena."

"Then it's settled."

"I can't possibly."

"Fonso, you need to get away. I have already hired a wonderful jet that seats seven comfortably. I've invited America so it will be just three of us, even more comfortable. We'll meet you at the strip for private planes in Madrid. It's now four P.M. Be there at nine o'clock this evening. Bring your passport, black-tie, city clothes, ski clothes and a bathing suit. We begin in Paris; I have two suites booked for us at the Ritz tonight—then we'll fly over to 'Moritz.' The season is just starting and we can look at the pretty people, run into friends at the Corviglia Club . . ."

"Cay . . ."

She rolled over him like a tank, "A massive tin of caviar and a case of *cava* is iced and on the plane awaiting us. There's no turning back."

To his amazement, at nine o'clock that evening Alfonso found himself at Barajas Airport in Madrid, being driven to a small jet on which Cayetana and America had just arrived from Málaga. Cay was standing outside the plane with the two pilots. Alfonso kissed her hello, "You realize, of course, that you're completely crazy."

"It's one's only defense." She gestured for him to board, "Your delightful friend is waiting for you. Take the long back seat for the two of you. I'm going to stay up front with the pilots. They are—not accidentally—insupportably good-looking boys."

As the plane lifted into the air Cayetana drew closed the curtain between the cockpit and the cabin.

America was dressed in her most provocative, while still acceptable-in-public, clothes. Alfonso took her in his arms, "What was that you were telling me one day about the Thirty Thousand Feet in the Air Club?"

Cayetana gave them an hour before she announced over the loudspeaker system, "This is your stewardess speaking. Get dressed. A snack of caviar and *cava* is about to be served."

They were limousined from Orly to the Ritz and elevatored to their suites. Alone with Alfonso, noting the bucket of champagne, the chicken sandwiches and pâté de fois gras that Cayetana had ordered for them, America said, "I feel badly for her, all by herself."

"Trust Cay. She isn't going to suffer unless it pleases her. She may have General de Gaulle or Napoleon in there with her."

They lunched at Maxim's and then went on an "indulge-yourself-in-anything" tour of Hermes, Sulka, Yves St. Laurent, Pierre Cardin and Christian Dior. While the girls were raiding Chanel, Alfonso walked to Cartier and selected a large emerald ring surrounded by diamond baguettes.

Returning to the Ritz, Cayetana announced, "Tea is being served in my suite, lest we perish." A waiter was standing at a long room-service table laden with finger sandwiches, petits fours, chocolates, champagne, whiskey and even a pot of tea. As Alfonso indicated what he wanted, Cayetana gestured for America to follow her to the bedroom, where she handed her a box from Dior. "One thing that even The Woman Who Has Everything never has enough of is great lingerie." America opened it and held up a luscious green satin and lace brassiere and bikini. Cayetana pointed to the bathroom, "Go put it on so you can take it off."

As they returned to the living room Alfonso was holding the telephone, giving the operator a number that Cayetana recognized to be his bank. She rushed over, grabbed the phone from his hand, and exclaimed, "Forbidden!" She then spoke into the phone, "Excuse us, it was an error," and hung up the phone.

"But I have responsibilities."

"For these few days your only responsibility is to be irresponsible. Your sons who are past voting age . . ." she rolled her eyes, "¡votar! God help us . . . will see to it that the Bank of the Castle of Tarifa survives."

"You act like I'm one of your slaves." He shrugged, "But you're right, the boys can handle it."

In their own suite Alfonso gave America a small blue leather box. She quickly unwrapped it and stared at the ring.

"My religion and my commitment to Magdalena won't permit me to divorce and remarry, but there's no rule that we cannot be engaged to love each other forever."

He saw something in her eyes that he had not expected. Hesitation, a hint of displeasure. America looked at the ring and held it up. "You see that hole? For my finger? That is how empty the gesture is."

Alfonso sat down, jolted.

"I don't want jewelry. I want more of *you*. I know that I agreed that you could never leave Magdalena. That the children needed you. But years have passed and now most of them need you less than I do. Magdalena has a large family and a full life in Madrid. She'll soon have a grandchild to play with . . ."

He nodded unhappily. "I have thought the same thing. And I need more of you. But it would humiliate Magda in the life she's made for herself. How can I do that to someone who has always been true to our agreement? She's been a perfect mother and a perfect wife to a most imperfect husband."

She placed the ring on a table. "Excuse me," she said, "I need to be alone," and she went into the bedroom and closed the door. She sat down on a chaise longue, angered, heart-broken. It wasn't acceptable. As she turned her head toward the living room, in which Alfonso remained, her glance fell on a magazine next to her. Eager to clear her thoughts of "sacred Magdalena" she picked up a copy of *Paris Match*. Quickly she put it down. *I don't believe it. She's following me. Haunting me!* Again she looked at the cover. It featured four women. One was Magdalena Soto. The cover story in French was "Europe's Leading Ladies." Hating to look at it yet unable to resist she opened the magazine and flipped pages until she came to a full-page photo of Magdalena. The story covered another full page, with a small picture of the eight children and one of Alfonso. Her high-school French was still good enough for her to be able to understand the text:

BORN NOBLE, MARRIED NOBLE, THE DUCHESS OF THE CASTLE OF TARIFA HAS BEEN DECORATED BY THE SPANISH GOVERN- MENT WITH THE MEDAL OF ISABELA LA CATÓLICA FOR HER EXEMPLARY DEDICATION TO GOOD WORKS. AND THIS YEAR SHE'LL BE INDUCTED INTO THE FRENCH LEGION OF HONOR IN RECOGNITION OF HER MANY SUCCESSFUL EFFORTS TOWARD BETTER UNDERSTANDING BETWEEN SPAIN AND FRANCE.

EVEN WHILE BRINGING UP EIGHT CHILDREN AND MANAG- ING A SIZEABLE HOUSEHOLD THE DUCHESS FINDS TIME TO SERVE AS PRESIDENT OF THE SPANISH RED CROSS, AS A BOARD MEMBER OF THE SPANISH CANCER SOCIETY AND THE SPANISH- AMERICAN HOSPITAL, AND SUBDIRECTOR OF CÁRITAS, A MAJOR SPANISH CHARITY DEVOTED TO AIDING THE POOR. NOT SURPRISINGLY THE DUCHESS HAS A SPECIAL PLACE IN HER HEART FOR CHILDREN, AND WORKS TWO HOURS A DAY, FIVE DAYS EACH WEEK, TEACHING SPANISH GRAMMAR, ARITH- METIC AND COOKING TO ORPHANED GIRLS AT THE HOGAR DE SAN JERÓNIMO IN MADRID. "THE HOME IS UNDERSTAFFED, AS THERE ARE MORE ORPHANS THAN NUNS TO CARE FOR THEM. BUT THEY MUST BE TAUGHT TO BE LITERATE, CAPABLE CITI- ZENS SO THAT WHEN THEY COME OF AGE THEY ARE PREPARED

TO FEND FOR THEMSELVES. IT'S A PRIVILEGED PERSON'S DUTY TO HELP THE HELPLESS."

THE DUCHESS WAS UNWILLING TO SPEAK OF HER FINANCIAL AID TO THE HOME BUT THIS REPORTER INQUIRED OF THE MOTHER SUPERIOR WHO SAID, "I MUST RESPECT THE DUCHESS' WISHES IN TERMS OF NUMBERS BUT I CAN TELL YOU THAT WITHOUT HER ABUNDANT HELP FEW OF THE CHILDREN WOULD BE SO WELL NOURISHED AND HAVE FRESH CLOTHES EVERY YEAR."

THE DUCHESS DOES NOT HAVE MUCH FREE TIME TO ENJOY SPORT BUT SHE PLAYS GOLF WHENEVER THERE'S A CHARITABLE TOURNAMENT THAT WILL BENEFIT BY HER PRESENCE AND NAME VALUE . . .

America studied the photo of Magdalena. She was lovely. Kindness and humanity were reflected in her eyes. This was no ordinary person to be shoved aside, to humiliate, to cloud the pleasure of her worth that she should enjoy. America experienced a glow of admiration for Alfonso, also for not being ordinary. She knew that she would never again think of coming between them. She would enjoy him with the original ground rules. But no more than that. She checked her makeup and her hair and walked into the living room. He was still seated where she had left him, staring at the floor, still appearing dazed.

"Please forget what I said. I feel like a character in a cheap movie." She stepped out of her dress and stood before him in the green silk lingerie. She slipped the emerald onto her finger. "Thank you, Alfonso." Provocatively she placed her hand on her bikini'd hip. "They go well, don't you think?"

The three dined at Lasserre in the Boise du Bologne, and as they returned to their hotel Cayetana said, "Leave a wake-up for nine."

"Cay! I thought this was a pleasure trip."

"We're not in Spain so we must sacrifice the leisurely three o'clock lunch today and leave Paris by noon."

"But, we just got here."

"Fonso, we've had lunch and dinner here. Let's not risk boredom. Besides, I'm yearning for one of those little legs of baby lamb at the Hotel de Paris in Monaco. Even in Spain we don't do lamb so well."

After Monaco it was necessary to see the tulips that would just be blooming in Holland and then ". . . visit Mallorca to warm us up before freezing in Moritz," where Alfonso and America would skim along the snow as Cayetana enjoyed lunch with friends at the Corviglia Club.

On Sunday evening the plane dropped Alfonso off in Madrid and continued on to Málaga. Cayetana's car was waiting for them and at 11:00 P.M. America was delivered to *La Finca de la Tejana*, exhausted and happy.

Encarna was awaiting her with a telegram.

TRIED REACHING YOU BY PHONE SINCE MONDAY NIGHT. DAD HAD MASSIVE HEART ATTACK, RALLIED BUT DIED ON THURSDAY. BURIED HIM YESTERDAY. GAT

America was on the connecting flight to Madrid when Alfonso called from the office on Monday morning. Encarna told him what had happened and gave him the message that America did not know when she would be back but would call him from Texas.

Feeling numb on the Iberia flight to JFK, America wondered how she could have let herself be out of touch, for the only time in her life?

Gat was waiting for her at the gate in San Antonio. Stiffly, he accepted her embrace. "I want to get something out of my system before we're with Mom. She's suffered enough without seeing friction between us. You promised never to be out of touch. If we had found you, you might have been able to get over in time to see Dad and say goodbye before he died."

It brought tears to her eyes. How she would have loved to have kissed her father goodbye, to have told him how much she appreciated him.

"Where the hell were you, Ame?"

"I'd be too embarrassed to say."

"Dad asked for you till the end. You should have been here."

"I know, Gat. I'm sorry. I'll say it a hundred times if you like."

"Look, Ame, I'm not trying to beat you up. But I hope you'll stay home for awhile until Mom gets on her feet."

"I will, of course, I will."

It was past midnight when they arrived at the ranch. Her mother was standing at the door. She kissed her daughter and hugged her strongly. After Gat left she spoke firmly, "Let's clear the air. I know Gat's a hothead so you need to hear this. Do not feel guilty about missing your father's funeral. He was proud that you could make a comeback from hell and find your own way safely in a whole different ballpark. He loved you and he knew that you were happy. That is everything he wanted for you or from you. He did not suffer. The good Lord made it a short illness.

"Gat's been a darling staying over with me, but I'm glad that he's gone home. I really do not need anyone to sleep over with me. And I do not want you to sacrifice yourself futilely. I enjoyed nearly fifty perfect years with your daddy. He and I talked about this, that one day it would happen to one of us, and we agreed that the monument we could build to our years together would be to let them end; to go on with a different phase of life without weeping about the better one before. My plan is to continue with my work at the Garden Club, the Governor's Mansion Restoration Committee, the Cancer Society, the Arts and Music Council— all the things I did when your father was living. I have so many appointments scheduled that I will have no time for weeping."

"I'll stay on for a while, Mom. I'm so sorry I wasn't here."

She put her arm around her daughter's shoulder, "I told you your daddy wouldn't like that. Stay on as long as you like, but not for my sake. Thank the Lord, I was wrong in my misgivings about your lifestyle so I'll be delighted knowing that you are back with the man you love."

In the morning America visited her father's grave, just a few yards away from Angel's. She stayed with them both for an hour or more, lunched with her mother, then she walked alone over a few acres of the Harvey Ranch and remembered her father calling it "this little piece of land we love and call home." Yet, really, this wasn't home anymore. Now her *finca* was the little piece of land she loved and called home. Later, as they were finishing dinner, Alfonso called and Margaret, understanding a bit of Spanish, heard America saying, "I miss and love you, too, but I want to stay with my mom at least another week."

The following morning America expected to have breakfast with her mother but instead there was a note:

DARLING,
I'M GLAD YOU'RE SLEEPING. HAVE LEFT FOR AUSTIN FOR A MEETING AT THE GOVERNOR'S MANSION AND WILL BE GONE ALL DAY. LET'S SHOOT FOR THIS SUMMER IN SPAIN. MY SEC-RETARY HAS RESERVED YOUR FLIGHT BACK TO NEW YORK TODAY TO CONNECT WITH THE EIGHT P.M. TO MÁLAGA. DO NOT WASTE A DAY OF HAPPINESS WHILE IT'S YOURS TO ENJOY. HAPPY LANDINGS, ALWAYS, IN EVERYTHING. I LOVE YOU.
                                                          MOTHER

Clipped to the note was her plane ticket to New York and the connecting flights to Madrid and Málaga. She packed and asked the ranch manager to stop at the burial grounds. She left the car and walked alone, first to Angel's grave. "My eternal love." She kissed the headstone, *"Hasta siempre, mi queridísima."*

She knelt on the grass at her father's simple plot as she spoke to him. "So long, Daddy. I would have loved to have kissed you goodbye and let you know how much I appreciate all that you have been to me, all that you have given me. It's too late now so I'll just have to bite the bullet and take my losses on that. I'm going to miss you more now than I had the sense to miss you when I had you. And I'm going to cry for the loss of you. I know you would try to stop me but I'll be crying for me, not for you. Because after what you were on this earth I know that God already has His arms around you . . ."

Chapter Fifteen

merica called Alfonso from New York, "My mom's a giant. She booked me on flights that will get me home in time for this weekend. I'll be waiting for you at the airport on Friday."

When he called on Thursday he said, "*Mi amor,* stay at home and rest. I'll be coming in around 1:15, on the *golfo* this time. It's the only flight I haven't taken recently. I'm sorry, I hate to wait so long to see you . . ."

"Security first. I long to see you. I'll be there."

"No, stay at home. There are plenty of taxis . . ."

As Alfonso was being driven to the Madrid airport he was anticipating the moment of having America in his arms. Though it had only been their usual five days apart, her being away, the grief she had suffered, it all made it seem longer. She had sounded strong but he knew that guilt would add to her suffering. The traffic was unusually heavy for that hour. He looked at his watch. He had just enough time to make it, as he had no luggage. Everything was at America's house. Everything.

As he entered the airport an attractive Iberia Air Lines public relations girl in her red-jacketed uniform hurried to him. "Sr. Duque, this way, please. We have a car. It will be faster." She was gesturing toward the exit to the street from which he had just arrived.

Alfonso was surprised by the offer of a car outside at the arrival entrance. In the old days he had always been given the courtesy of an Iberia car, but always inside, from the gate to the plane. The VIP treatment had been discontinued for a year or more, and pleased by the renewed courtesy, he did not question it.

"We are late, Sr. Duque. We can drive around the terminal more quickly than walking through. We are holding the flight but time is short. And this is the last flight tonight to Málaga."

He followed her outside to an Iberia car. An Iberia driver was at the wheel. In the back seat was another uniformed P.R. woman. The girl opened the back door for Alfonso, followed him in, and the car started moving. It seemed that there were too many people attending him. Something was wrong. Yet, having nothing to base it on, how could he say, "Stop the car. Let me out."

A second later it was clear that he should have. Also that it wouldn't have mattered.

Though America was exhausted, anything but seeing him the first minute possible was out of the question. She began dressing earlier than necessary. Even after seven years the anticipation of seeing Alfonso, the joy of being with him always amazed her. Primavera and Al were chasing each other across her bed and rolling on the floor, wrestling. They always sensed Alfonso's arrival. America kissed them both and rubbed their stomachs. She put on her cassette player and selected one of Julio Iglesias' tapes.

Drawing her bath with the mixture of perfumed oils Alfonso liked, jasmine, verbena and tuberose, she let herself luxuriate in the warm water for twenty minutes.

Making up her face was difficult. She had to work for half an hour to cover her puffy eyes and use eye drops to remove the red. She put on white cotton gloves in order for a fingernail not to snare her hose, especially these from Fogal that had been horrendously expensive. But worth it. They were sheer black, of satin yarn with lace tops and a matching satin and lace garter belt. It was the lingerie she had worn every Friday night since the first time she had met his flight; always, driving him home from the airport, she had guided his hand onto her stocking'd leg, then under her skirt to her exposed body.

She selected a Black Watch plaid Escada dress with a white Peter Pan collar, and pinned on a Chanel camelia. Finally, black, low-heel Robert Clergerie shoes.

After much scrutiny, satisfied that she could do nothing more with herself, she went to the kitchen to check on the supper of smoked salmon and caviar sandwiches. She had gone to Marbella, to Semon, a new, small restaurant from Barcelona with a take-out department. Semon carried fresh triple-A Beluga caviar and out-standing smoked salmon. While Miguel had prepared the salmon, cutting paper-thin slices like a surgeon, Manolo had spooned the large, crisp, grey eggs of Beluga from a two-kilo tin into one of a quarter kilo. Then, a waiter had accompanied her to her car and placed the package in the back. *"Muchas gracias, Alfredo,"* she had said, thinking, *Like the old days in Madrid,* remembering stories Alfonso had told her of how life used to be in Spain.

The table in front of the fireplace was perfectly set. Encarna never required checking on. She was always perfect. It was just America's desire to feel that she had participated in the preparation of their snack. The stand for the champagne bucket was in place. In the pantry the silver serving tray was ready for the smoked salmon. In fact she had participated to some extent. When Encarna had first come to work for her at seventeen, from her *pueblo,* Istán, she hadn't known to wrap gauze on halves of lemon.

Encarna's face conveyed her happiness that America was home safely from Texas, that it was Friday and the Sr. Duque would be arriving. Later she would add another log to the fireplace, bring out the champagne bucket and put on the music. Rafael had brought the Range Rover to the front door and he ruffled the dogs as they soared into the back seat.

The star-filled, cloudless sky promised the clear warm weather Alfonso loved. There was no traffic on the road to Málaga, and, despite driving slowly, she arrived at the airport thirty minutes early. Finally the flight was announced. She always stood on the edge of the tarmac so that she could see Alfonso as soon as he appeared in the doorway. And he made a point of having an aisle seat in the first row so that he could be the first person off.

A chubby, pink-faced man in a plaid jacket stepped through the doorway. She rationalized that probably there were regular *golfos* who liked the front seats and they'd boarded earlier. There were no assigned seats on that flight. She watched another stranger appear, and another. She felt her smile fading. Alfonso wasn't among the people coming toward her, passing her and going into the terminal. Then there were no more passengers. Primavera and Alegría were beginning to whimper.

The crew was walking in her direction.

"Excuse me, but is that all of the passengers?"

The pilot, in his late forties, with a thin mustache in the tradition of Spanish military officers, replied, "All the passengers have disembarked, *Señora.*"

Futilely, she said, "But I'm expecting a friend . . ."

"He must have missed the flight. May we assist you in any way?"

"Thank you. No. You're very kind."

She stood in front of the public phones. But where could she call him? His home? Impossible. The airport in Madrid? The public relations desk? She imagined herself asking, "Do you know if the Duke of the Castle of Tarifa missed the last flight to Málaga?" and the P.R. woman requesting, "Your name, please?"

America dialed her house. "Encarna, have there been any telephone calls?"

"None, *Señorita.*"

Still, she couldn't stop herself from asking, "*El Sr. Duque* did not call?"

"No, *Señorita.*"

She sat down on a bench with Primavera and Alegría at her feet and watched the last of the travelers lifting luggage from the carousel. Then she was alone. It was 1:40 A.M. The airport was slowing for the night. A cleaning woman came out of the men's room and went into the ladies' room. A porter pushed his cart toward her.

"*Señora,* there's no more luggage. Give me your stubs and I will help you report them lost."

"Thank you, but I'm not waiting for luggage."

America stood up. Now what? Alfonso wasn't someone who fails to show up. Nor call. He was meticulous, punctual and considerate. She was certain that he would suddenly appear before her or behind her. Yet she knew that it wasn't possible. Something important must have happened. But why hadn't he called?

She phoned home again. "Encarna, I'm sorry, but since we spoke, has anyone called?"

"Nobody, *Señorita.*"

"I'm still at the airport. The *Sr. Duque* hasn't arrived. May I trouble you to wait up until I get home in case he calls while I'm on the road?"

She drove through the darkness with her radio on, listening to the news, dreading to hear his name. Primavera and Al were quiet. She had an instinct that something bad had happened. She felt it in her stomach, in her arms and legs as if the blood had stopped coursing through them.

Her headlights picked up the plaque *La Tejana* The front door was opening. America felt a flash of hope that Alfonso would be standing there, that he had made an earlier flight.

Encarna's eyes were sympathetic. America hugged her and sent her off to sleep.

She sat on the sofa, staring blankly at the champagne bucket and the table set for two. The dogs, wilted, silent, sat at her side. She stroked their heads, consoling them. It was after three in the morning. She could call Cristina or Marisa. Wake them up and alarm them. What would she say? Precisely what did she fear?

I'm panicking. Something has happened, but it does not have to be so serious. More than likely it's not. When you don't know something and begin guessing you always come up with the wrong answer. Just get into bed and read and wait. She couldn't concentrate on a novel that had engrossed her the week before, or on a magazine she usually enjoyed. What possibly could have happened that was so serious as to prevent him from calling her by now? Knowing that she was waiting and couldn't call him?

By four A.M. the phone still had not rung. She felt a surge of hope. Maybe it's out of order and he's been calling for hours unable to get through. She heard the dial tone. Of course. Hadn't she gotten through to Encarna?

When fear seemed to be closing her lungs, she dialed Cristina's number in Madrid and waited as it rang, three, four, five times.

"America? What's wrong?"

"Alfonso was due here on the last flight but he wasn't on it, nor has he called. I'm frantic. I was thinking that as his sister you could call the police department, the emergency hospitals, or his home."

"You will hear from me the second we know anything. Meanwhile keep yourself busy. Wash some stockings or something."

America got out of bed and began washing the stockings she had worn for their reunion. But the splashing water made her fear that she might not hear the phone ring in the bedroom.

She tried reading again. She walked around her room. She breathed deeply and kept walking, crying to herself, *Oh, God, please . . .*

The telephone rang.

"Miss Harvey?" It was a woman whose voice she had never heard before.

"Yes."

"I am Magdalena Soto. The wife of Alfonso."

In a moment she regained her composure and greeted her lover's wife. Magdalena continued, "I have just spoken with Paco. There's no trace of Alfonso. He left here in time to make the twelve-fifteen flight. The police have no record of anything. He's not in any hospital or emergency ward in Madrid. I'm calling you directly because we are both suffering. Let us do it together, and think together, and be civilized with our realities. I'm sympathetic to you at this moment."

"You are extremely generous."

"I worry that this is serious. People do not disappear like smoke. Least of all Alfonso. There's the possibility that he was robbed, possibly struck on the head, and is walking around Madrid amnesic. But this is remote and his face is so well known that someone would have helped him. The police have put forth the more likely possibility of an ETA kidnapping."

America lowered herself to the bed. Speaking to Magdalena had frozen her, but the thought of Alfonso kidnapped undid her muscles and she all but lost control of her spine and her arms. It was an effort to keep the phone to her ear.

"He is an appropriate victim. There's money for the ransom and he's so well known in Spain that it would result in a lot of publicity for them. As you're known to be a friend of his the *Guardia Civil* is sending men to your house in case contact is made through you. However, if it's an ETA kidnapping their usual technique is to maintain silence for several days to weaken us with worry." America heard a car approaching and said as much. Magdalena cautioned her: "Don't hang up. See who it is and let me know."

America peered through the peephole in the front door, opened it and offered her hand to each of the two *Guardias*. "Please come in and sit down."

Picking up the receiver she said, "*Sra. Duquesa*, it's the *Guardia Civil*."

"I'll hang up then. My private number is 261-0209. We will keep in close contact. And please, call me Magdalena."

One of the *Guardias* said, "With your permission, *Señorita*, I'll attach this earpiece to your phone and if someone calls I will listen to what is said. If it should be a person claiming to have kidnapped the Duke of the Castle of Tarifa, your posture is to be cooperative. Say yes to anything and encourage them to speak for as long as they will. For your information, until this matter is resolved, everything said on your line will be recorded."

"Then you believe he has been kidnapped?"

"It's possible. He's being searched for throughout Spain by a thousand policemen and detectives. Considering their expertise, the informers available to them, his famous face, if he hasn't been kidnapped he'll be found.

"Go to sleep, *Señorita*. It's five in the morning. I'll awaken you if the phone rings. At eight, two men will replace us. There will be two of us here around the clock."

Magdalena and America were in touch every few hours. "Have you heard anything?"

"Nothing."

"Then let's hang up and keep the lines open."

Friday night.

Saturday.

On Saturday afternoon Marisa arrived from Madrid.

Sunday.

Sunday night.

On Monday morning Alfonso's photograph appeared on the front page of the Madrid daily newspaper, *ABC*. There was no story. Just a caption:

KIDNAPPED. AN ANONYMOUS TELEPHONE CALL TO THE EDITOR OF THIS DAILY STATED THAT THE DUKE OF THE CASTLE OF TARIFA HAS BEEN KIDNAPPED BY THE MILITANT WING OF ETA AND IS BEING HELD FOR RANSOM. INFORMED SOURCES SAY THAT THE DUKE, DON ALFONSO GARCÍA DE LAS ARENAS HAS BEEN MISSING FROM HIS HOME SINCE FRIDAY NIGHT.

America and Magdalena were now yearning to hear from a kidnapper, wanting to pay anything to bring Alfonso back. But all they heard was:

"Anything, Magdalena?"

"No, dear, nothing."

America was grateful for Marisa's company, appreciating that she had left Carlos and the twins in order to be with her, but too close to make polite conversation they lived together in a semi-silent vacuum of fear. America feared for Alfonso both lovingly and selfishly because she did not know how she could go on living without the man who had brought her back to life. Primavera and Alegría lay on the side of her bed all but lifeless, as they had been from the night they returned from the airport.

In Madrid, a few minutes before eight A.M., Magdalena's private telephone rang. Dozing beside it she awoke expecting to hear America. Instead she heard a female voice with a Basque accent. "*La Sra. Duquesa, por favor.*"

"I am she."

"We have your husband."

"I will do anything you say."

"If you want to see him alive follow instructions."

"Anything." Magdalena asked a question she had been briefed on. "But how do I know he's alive and well now?"

"Listen." A tape of Alfonso's voice was played into the telephone: "Magda, they are treating me well. They want a lot of money. Give it to them. I send my love to you all."

Magdalena asked another question designed to prolong the conversation while the police attempted to locate the telephone being used by the caller. "How do I know when that was recorded? Of course I'll pay what you demand, but prove to me that my husband is alive and well now."

"Before payment you will have proof. This conversation is being recorded by the police and they are trying to trace the phone I'm using. Futile. Your husband and I are not in the same city. Prepare two hundred million pesetas in five-thousand-peseta notes. Keep the police out of our business. I warn you, we are fanatical and their interference will guarantee your husband will suffer miserably, then die."

Chapter Sixteen

Alfonso lay on his back on a mattress within a pup tent that had been set up in a bare room, he knew not where. It was dark in the tent, which served as a blindfold so that he couldn't see his captors' faces. Music was playing so that he couldn't hear their voices, loud, incessant rock.

His left ankle was chained to a bolt in the floor. His hands were not cuffed together. "Unless you make an attempt to escape or to attack one of us," he had been told by an unseen voice, "we have no objection to allowing you to be comfortable." And he was reasonably so, able to change position to whatever side he wished, or to lay on his stomach or back.

He mentally re-lived his *mecánico's* driving him to the airport, the anticipation of seeing America, his desire to comfort her, entering the Iberia car, then two sharp blades pressing against his neck, one from either side, the bogus Iberia P.R. girls holding knife tips like fangs against his throat. Then he felt hard steel snapped shut around his wrists. The car was exceeding normal speed limits. When it should have turned right toward the runways, it turned left and accelerated, speeding out of the airport to the highway.

The driver announced, "You are a prisoner of ETA." There was a sharp sting in his right arm. He heard, "Don't move," and he felt another sting in his left arm and he understood that something had been injected into him.

Waking had been difficult. There was no light. He couldn't move. He fell back into sleep again. Three times it happened and he wondered if it were a process of dying.

Then he heard, "Sr. *Duque*," a man's voice, close to him, "you're a prisoner of ETA. Are you awake enough to understand what I'm saying?"

"Yes."

"Then repeat what I said."

"I'm a prisoner of ETA."

"You were put to sleep by us, you are chained hand and foot, you cannot see, you don't know where you are. Nobody can help you. We can piss on you, we can amuse ourselves by slitting your nostrils open, or slicing off your ears, by sticking needles into your eyes; we can cut off your prick and send half to your wife and half to your girl friend in Marbella; we can skin you alive and burn you to death, slowly, or, we can treat you well. Do you follow me?"

"Yes."

"Good. We are not Communists or Socialists. We are Basque patriots. We do not hate you for having money. We are pleased by it because we expect you to give a lot of that money to us to finance our war for freedom from the Spanish government. For our own purposes we would prefer to treat you well, to have you return home in good condition. That would be publicized and give confidence to the families of our future hostages and expedite their ransoms. Therefore, if you cooperate you will be as comfortable as possible and back in your normal life in a few weeks. If not, you will be executed and we will easily find someone more intelligent to help finance our war."

"I will cooperate. Tell me what you want."

"Two hundred million pesetas."

"I'll pay."

"It isn't done so easily. Your wife will want to know that you're alive. The police will try to prevent payment. But don't despair. It takes time but we always win. Just continue to cooperate."

Hands touched his head and removed the blindfold from across his eyes. When his vision adjusted to the light he saw a figure standing over him wearing a stocking mask and a long robe. The man stepped back, allowing Alfonso to see the others. There were seven of them. Five held pistols. They all wore masks and billowing floor-length gowns that concealed their size. One of them was holding a cassette recorder. Alfonso appraised his situation. He was on a wooden bench. His wrists were handcuffed and drawn over his head. His feet were bound together and tied down to the bench.

"Now we will make you more comfortable."

The handcuffs were removed. Alfonso touched his face and felt a growth of beard. He had shaved just before leaving. "How long have I been here?"

"We took you on Friday night. Today is Monday. We did not need you until now, so we kept you sleeping."

"Three days?" *America has been waiting for me, agonizing for three days!*

"Now we need you to record a message to your wife." He held a tape recorder and after Alfonso had read the few lines they gave him, the man handed him a copy of Monday's *ABC* with his picture on the front page. The chain was removed from his ankles, and he was helped to his feet. His knees buckled and he would have fallen if he had not been held steady on both sides. "Sit on that chair, hold the newspaper up so that we can photograph you and show that you are alive today."

They helped him toward the chair, steadying him. There was a flash and he watched the camera expelling the photograph.

"Are there any medications you require?"

"No. Thank you."

"Most of the time that you're here you will be horizontal inside that tent, one foot chained. You will be let out to relieve yourself and take exercise."

In the pup tent again Alfonso thought about America, waiting for him at the airport, and his children and Magdalena. *Do they know? Of course. From the cover of* ABC. He realized that while he had been unconscious, oblivious to everything, they had all been suffering for days. He touched his face. Even in the war he had never had a three-day growth of beard. He noted that he still had his wristwatch and the new chain and cross that Magdalena had had made for him. His money was still in his pocket. Obviously this operation wasn't interested in minor jewelry or pocket money.

And how capable they were. Despite the change of routine they had caught him. Obviously they had tapped his or America's phone and heard him tell her the flight he was taking. He had told no one else and had not made a reservation. His stupidity in the airport now seemed incredible. He had sensed that something wasn't right. Why had he gone along with it? Incredibly: his good manners.

He was sickened by his crashing immorality. The spokesman had clearly stated that ETA wanted his money to continue their "war," that's what he had called it, a war, for "freedom" from Alfonso's own government, and to accomplish their desire by terrorism. And he, without a moment's hesitation, to save his own life, had agreed to give them two hundred million pesetas. How many plastic bombs, how many submachine guns, how many more killings would that finance?

Now, aware of what he had agreed to, he was also aware that he could rescind it by calling out, "Terrorists, assassins, kill me if you will, but I won't contribute a single peseta to your filthy work."

Tears fell from his eyes, for he did not hear himself saying it.

* * *

Alfonso needed to go to the bathroom. Following instructions he called out. His foot was unlocked. There were three guards now. He noted they had been playing cards at a table in front of a black cloth curtain that seemed to be covering a window.

The bathroom smelled of stale water. The door had been removed so that he could be watched. The paint was old. The tiles broken. There was a cake of soap and a towel.

He continued washing his hands and face longer than necessary to delay returning to the pup tent. Then he called out, "Would it be possible for me to shave?"

One of his captors brought him a throwaway razor.

When he came out he was told, "Exercise. Walk around the room, five laps to the right, clockwise, then five to the left."

Alfonso began walking. Despite the spokesman's benign tone the three hooded, robed figures held pistols pointed at him. One remained at the blacked-out window, two stood near the door leading out of the room.

"Do you customarily do calisthenics? Sit-ups, push-ups?"

"No. Just active sport."

"After you've walked for a while more do some stretching exercises. Touch your toes, stretch your waist. Then you may shower."

Alfonso reflected, *when you have been kidnapped, had knives at your throat, been drugged and chained, you do what you are told to do.* He was assaulted by the memory of a sixteen-year-old boy who had sat fearlessly behind a rock and killed his enemies, shooting them between the eyes, then, risking his life by creeping up to a machine-gun nest and wiping it out. Over and over again he had run boldly into the face of death because his life was less meaningful than the cause he was supporting.

What had happened to that boy? A lot, obviously. He had a wife, eight children, America, and José Maria, who was about to get married, Elena, who was due to give birth in a few weeks . . . *Stop. It's bad enough to be a coward, don't deceive yourself, also. No one needs you. Yes, they will cry, miss the pleasure of your company, but you're not needed. Think about all those* Guardias Civiles *who are going to be killed by your money. Think about their wives and children who are not adequately provided for.*

He prayed for his children, for America and Magdalena. He had little hope of ever being freed. He would pay the two hundred million. But he couldn't imagine how they would get their hands on it with the police watching and either capturing them or causing his death while trying.

Even if ETA successfully collected the ransom he could hardly believe they would let him go free, despite the logical "good business" reason they had given. True, the Valencia meatpacker and a wealthy army officer had been returned to their homes. Also, he did not know who his kidnappers were, what they looked like, or where he was, but probably they worried that he knew more than even he at that moment realized he knew. Why would they take that risk? For the good publicity of a prisoner being released? But were they that smart? Random killings, bombings, and taking on the entire Spanish government wouldn't indicate sound and conservative thinking. So, even performing as a coward, he was almost surely going to die.

He thought of the vault of the Duke of the Castle of Tarifa. He wondered once again how—after it was constructed, with the secret known to the men who had made the ingenious lock—how did his ancestor assure himself of their silence? A man who would build that vault, and have a plaque made that admonishes, "A secret between two people isn't a secret," that isn't a man who would trust a team of stone masons. Had he waited to use it until after they had died? Most likely he had killed them. Eliminated the risk. As ETA would.

Then Alfonso thought of the leather pouch and the sewing lessons he had given José Maria. He thanked God that within his son's first year he had deposited the sealed pouch in the strongbox at his lawyer's office, finding that more anonymous and safer than a bank. José Maria's name was burned onto it. At least he had not broken that long line.

The butler in the palace of *Los Duques del Castillo de Tarifa* gaped when the chef, Don Gregorio, appeared in the main hall.

"I must see *La Sra. Duquesa.*"

"Don Gregorio, have you gone mad?"

Pushing past the butler he whispered, *"¡Urgente!"* and propelled his white-clad hulk up the staircase. The Duchess' maid reacted as the butler had but Don Gregorio ignored her too and went to the sitting room where the Duchess was with Trini, Elena and her sister-in-law, the *Condesa de los Escalones.*

"Forgive me," he said, "but I must speak with the *Sra. Duquesa* privately." He turned to the maid and motioned toward the door, ordering her out. Cristina, Trini and Elena were on their feet, leaving the room. When the door had closed Don Gregorio said, "*Señora Duquesa,* when I returned home from the market and removed the vegetables from my baskets I found this."

Opening the envelope addressed: *Excma. Sra. Duquesa del Castillo de Tarifa,* Magdalena looked at the photograph of Alfonso, unshaven, with the newspaper in his hands, and read a ransom note from ETA with detailed instructions, among them a dire warning not to notify the police of anything.

* * *

Marisa at her side, America moved mindlessly through the tasks of life, paying her farmhands, listlessly testing fruits and vegetables. On Palm Sunday, Marisa brought her to church and they prayed. Sitting on the terrace together on Wednesday they saw a regatta, some twenty sailboats with mostly white sails and spinnakers of blue and yellow and orange gliding across the sea. People living their normal lives. Then a white Rolls was coming up the driveway to the house.

Pulling the front seat forward, Cayetana said, "Let's take a drive. I need to speak with you both, urgently and privately."

"We can talk inside."

"There are *Guardias Civiles* on duty, no?"

"But we have no secrets from the police."

"Yes, we have." Cayetana started up the engine, "That is why Magdalena hasn't told you that ETA made contact. Alfonso is safe . . ."

It was like hearing the doctor say, "All of your tests are negative."

". . . she begs you to understand that she had to lie to you and say she had heard nothing. She dared not let you know she had received the ransom demand because she knows the police are listening to your phone as well as to hers."

When they had gone a few hundred yards to an untraveled road Cayetana stopped the car and told them about the ransom note in the shopping basket. "Our problem is that since the anti-ransom law, banks are required to report all withdrawals of ten million pesetas or more. We need two hundred million. The treasurer of Alfonso's bank told Magdalena that he could 'not notice' checks in the amount of nine million pesetas. Magdalena has given me twenty-two checks for that amount and one for two million, the total that we need. They are all made out *al portador*, to the bearer. Magdalena won't leave the house for fear of missing a contact. So I've cashed four. Cristina knows nothing. As Paco's wife she's useless to us. José Maria, Luis and Rafael and Maria del Mar and Carmen have each cashed one. But the sister and children of a kidnapped man shouldn't cash them all. Will you therefore both come back to Madrid with me?"

They agreed instantly.

Cayetana addressed America; "We need you to deliver the money to ETA." She paused, aware of the enormity of the statement. "It was ETA's stipulation because Magdalena, José Maria and Luis and all of the children, I—even Marisa and Carlos—are scrupulously watched by the police. But the Madrid police do not know you. Of course we will completely understand and explain to ETA if you feel you do not want . . ."

"Tell me what to do."

"Forgive me. I knew that you wouldn't want an out, but I had to offer it."

Cayetana got out of the car and held the seat for them to step down. Once certain they were not being observed, she opened the trunk, which contained a golf bag. Then, reaching into the top of the bag, she tugged on the clubs and they came out in one cluster. But they were just the heads. The shafts had been cut off and the heads were stuck into a clump of putty. In the bag they saw a mass of banknotes. "Ten thousand bills of five thousand pesetas each. Fifty million pesetas concealed by the putty. ETA's instructions.

"We are to use three more bags of clubs in the same way. The plan is to go to Madrid and in the next two days cash the remaining checks. Then, America . . ."

. . . driving a rented Renault station wagon, dressed in golf clothes, the four golf bags in the rear, at exactly two-thirty P.M. left the city and drove to the luxurious suburb, *Puerta de Hierro,* to the country club of the same name. There she followed the road to the golf course, entered its parking lot and stopped in a space that had an opening for a car on either side. The lot was quiet as it was the middle of the week, when most of the members were in the city.

Turning off the ignition she angled her mirror as instructed so that she had no rear vision. She got out, unlocked the hatchback and returned to her seat behind the wheel. She had nothing more to do except wait, then if she heard a car pull up alongside and sound its horn lightly, she was to bend down as if tying her shoelace and remain looking down until she heard the car leave. If no car arrived inside of thirty minutes she was to take a room in the Hotel Villa Magna, and await new instructions.

Staring ahead at the trees beginning to bud in springtime, America prayed that Alfonso would return to see his favorite time of year, to enjoy it with her. Though less than a month had passed since last she had seen him, any one of those days since he had not arrived at the airport could be called a year, a lifetime. She thought, *in fact, an eternity, for life had stopped for her. But, no, it had not stopped, that would have been less torturous.*

Five minutes. Six minutes. She kept glancing at the clock, Seven minutes. Eight . . .

She heard a car draw up alongside of her and the light touch of its horn. America bent down as if tying her shoelace. She heard the other car's door open. Then she heard her hatchback open, the bags being dragged out, the hatchback close, then the door to the other car close, and then the sound of the motor as it drove away.

Chapter Seventeen

America saw him step off the plane first.

Primavera and Alegría were bouncing all over him, licking his face, his hands, the back of his neck as Alfonso got into the Range Rover.

They spoke little. The past was too awful, and the present did not want words.

Arriving at the *finca* she did not trouble to put the car in the garage, stopping instead at the front door. She led him toward her room, undoing her clothes. In the bedroom as she removed his necktie, undid his shirt buttons and lowered his zipper, he ran his hands up and down the shape of her body, reveling again in what had recently been so remote from his life. He stroked her breasts as she worked him out of his clothes, yearning to have her body show how much she loved him, soothingly, tenderly, filling him with so much joy that all memory of the past month would be cleansed from his mind and spirit.

In bed, their mouths met. Alfonso was hardened almost to the point of pain. Then, as he was about to enter her body his erection fell away to nothing.

"What happened?"

"I don't know." He returned to making love to her, trying to become hard again but nothing happened.

Whereas since his release, at least twenty times he had only to think of her to feel a thrill, and often needed to conceal the physical reaction, now holding her in his arms, feeling her strong legs, her firm breasts, still he couldn't get an erection. Unaccountably, his penis knew nothing of what he was thinking and feeling.

After an hour of making love he said, "It's not going to happen. I'm sorry."

"I was too eager. I rushed you." He shook his head. At any other time her excitement would have doubled his lust. She said, "Your nervous system has had a terrible shock. This will straighten out."

He looked at her ruefully, "An appropriate description of what did not happen just now."

"You haven't lost your sense of humor. The rest will return."

In Marbella the sublime obscures the realities of life. A dozen golf courses, an armada of luxury boats—some costing tens of millions of dollars—gluts of Middle Eastern oil money creating a spectacle for window-shoppers: boutiques with garish, obscenely expensive designer dresses, shops offering card-table-sized sterling silver serving trays with gold encrusted domes, gold studded silver ice buckets made to hold six bottles of champagne; Regine's discotheque, charging $350 for a bottle of Dom Perignon and selling plenty of it; Mercedes-Benzes, Lamborghinis, Rolls-Royces too wide for the narrow *pueblo* streets; private houses on the scale of small palaces, used for only the month of August, one with a movie theater that seats five hundred; bars filled with people who were there to forget what life was like where they had come from.

Even the Spaniards on holidays could lose themselves. Unless they turned on television: "Two *Guardias Civiles* were killed last night in Pamplona when a bomb concealed under their patrol car exploded, shattering glass in a nearby office building and wounding fifteen . . ."

On the terrace at *La Tejana* Alfonso listened to the news, indicting himself for the murder of those two policemen, the making of two more widows and how many fatherless children? His desire to live had provided the funds that caused them to become orphans— as he and his sisters and Paco had become so long ago—left to fend for themselves and grow up without a father. True, they had mothers, but the situations were not comparable. These children would grow up without the "guardian" of unlimited money.

He asked himself, not for the first time, "Who wouldn't have saved his own life to return to the woman he loved?" Only Don Quijote, and he was a madman. Also, the crazy knight had never been a prisoner of ETA. Then he thought of Beltran El Bueno, who had sacrificed his only son. And General Moscardó, who had, centuries later, done the same at the *Alcázar* in Toledo. Then he tried to stop thinking about anything.

Alfonso arrived in Pamplona a day after the funerals of the *Guardias*. The Ministry of the Interior had provided him with the addresses of the two families. The apartment door was open. A dozen women, all dressed in black, were seated on wooden folding chairs in the small living room. Alfonso stood in the doorway. His elegance and his famous face commanded everyone's attention.

All of the women rose and respectfully filed past him into the hall. One remained. "May I sit down?" he asked the widow. A woman of around forty, she gestured to the sofa.

Though it wasn't necessary, he introduced himself, "I'm the Duke of the Castle of Tarifa and I offer you my deepest sympathy for your enormous loss." She nodded her appreciation and though her face looked as if she were crying, no tears came forth. He said, "I, too, am an enemy of ETA." He handed her a check for one hundred thousand pesetas. "I hope to ease the sudden burden for you to take care of yourself and your children. At the end of every month, for the rest of your life, you will receive a cashier's check from the Bank of the Castle of Tarifa for fifty thousand pesetas, increasing with the annual rise in the cost of living. Additional monies will be provided for the university education of your children. Urge them to study well. When they finish their schooling I will assist them in obtaining jobs with futures commensurate with their educations. If you should have any problem or change your address please notify me at the principal office of the bank in Madrid."

The widow tried to speak. Alfonso gestured for her not to tire herself. He stood, took her hand to shake it, then raised it to his lips and kissed her hand. *"¡Y que vaya con Dios, Señora!"*

Outside he gave a taxi driver the second address.

America was awakened by the sound of Primavera growling. She heard her bedroom door opening. The light from a full moon shining through the windows illuminated the figure of a man walking toward her, the moonlight reflecting off the blade of a knife he held. She sat up, "What do you want?"

"You, *guapa*. I'm going to fuck your ass off. . . ."

An eighty-pound streak of fur, bone and muscle soared from the floor toward the man's chest. The combination of surprise and the dog's weight and forward motion knocked him over onto his back. Primavera pounced on top of him, clamping his jaws firmly on the man's throat.

Gasping, he cursed, "You fucking mutt! I'll kill you!"

The blade rose in the air, but Alegría leaped for the wrist of the hand that held it and sank his teeth into the flesh and bone, the man screamed in pain and the knife fell to the floor. Alegría chewed on the intruder's wrist, while Primavera, growling murderously, kept his jaws clamped firmly around the man's throat.

"Get them off me," he choked, "I'll go! Call them off!"

America had pressed the panic button that rang in Encarna's apartment and Rafael arrived, a shotgun in his hands. Training the gun on the man on the floor he did not order the dogs off him. He told Encarna, *"La Guardia Civil,* tell them there's an armed intruder."

Then, to America, *"Señorita,* the knife on the floor, quickly." When she had the knife and had backed away from the scene, Rafael said, "Alegría, down," and the dog released his hold on the man's wrist and backed away slightly, watching.

Rafael warned the rapist, "If you move one centimeter you get both barrels." Then he ordered, "Primavera, down," and the smaller dog loosened his grip on the man's neck but stayed on top of his chest, growling. "Primavera, here," Rafael said, and the dog backed away from the man on the floor, but never took his eyes off him.

Rafael held the shotgun three feet from the man's chest, out of his reach but close enough to blow away half his body. Now with the lights on, America recognized the redheaded poacher who had leered at her, whom Santiago had struck.

Two *Guardias Civiles* came into the house with Encarna and led him away. Then, the Sergeant of the *Guardias* listened to the story as America told it, writing down the details. She had forgotten to turn on the alarm before going to sleep.

Primavera and Alegría were positioned on both sides of America, guarding her. He asked, "Have these dogs been trained to attack?"

"No. They are pets."

He scratched Primavera behind the ears and patted his chest. "This is the one who went for his throat?" He turned to Alegría, "And this one disarmed him?" He shook his head. "It's incredible how an animal's love can make him smarter and braver than many humans."

* * *

Alfonso rushed across the tarmac and took America into his arms. They did not notice paparazzi photographing the moment. In the car to the house he was unable to keep his hands off her, needing to physically feel her body safe and sound, cherishing her, grateful to God that the rapist had failed.

When they arrived at the *finca* at eight P.M. the sun was still warm, they changed into bathing suits and dove into the pool. Then they lay on beach chairs feeling the sun and enjoying the simple fact of being together without a calamity having occurred. As the sun set below the mountains and the air cooled against their bodies America said, "I think we need to go someplace warm."

He took her outstretched hand and followed her to the bedroom. They touched each other gently, kissed as if for the first time, each longing for their bodies to unite and bring back the past. But again at the crucial moment Alfonso couldn't perform and he rolled away from her, despondent, embarrassed.

America pleaded, "My darling, it's not important. There's been too much stress, too much emotion. Don't worry. Please. It will happen again. I guarantee it."

On Saturday, watching him pace back and forth on the terrace America remembered the man on the flying trapeze gliding above the Marbella Club all those carefree years ago. Despite his impotency she knew that he did not love her less, yet she found herself unable to distract him as in the past. Hoping to entertain him this weekend she had planned a luncheon party, inviting Cayetana and some of the Marbella people he enjoyed. Cristina and Paco had flown from Madrid. Marisa and Carlos couldn't make it because they were going to Geneva. America had some trepidation about the political disagreements between the half brothers, that were constant, but so was their love, and a good argument might even be diverting.

Dressed in tight white jeans, white chukka boots and a billowing yellow and orange Emilio Pucci blouse and large orange ceramic earrings, she awaited her guests. Alfonso had appeared on the terrace, turned out beautifully as always, in shirt and trousers and with a cashmere sweater over his shoulders, all of the same tone of powder blue. Understanding what America was trying to do, he joked with Cayetana and the friends. After lunch he organized a game of *Mus* and seated at the card table gave the impression of being his buoyant self.

The telephone rang. America answered and her voice reflected pleasure, "Carlos, it's so nice to hear you." Abruptly her face became a frightened white. "Yes, Paco is right here. I'm so sorry." Everyone in the room was silent, waiting.

"Paco, Marisa has been arrested at Customs in Madrid."

He listened as Carlos explained, ". . . on the edge of panic for weeks, she had us change our diplomatic passports in case we needed to flee the country. Ever since staying with America during the kidnapping she's told me she wanted to get away, that she needed a rest, somewhere she could feel safe. We don't fly together so I was booked on the next flight. I took her to the airport and accompanied her as far as security. She put her carry-on bag and purse on the conveyer belt and walked through the metal detector. When she was on the other side I saw the police ask her to open her carry-on. The fluoroscope had shown it to be filled with paper. They found three million pesetas in cash."

Paco telephoned the General in charge of the Customs Division of the *Guardia Civil* and asked the favor of Marisa's release in his custody. It was granted.

"What will happen to her?" America asked.

Being the Undersecretary of the ministry that would prosecute her, Paco could answer with authority. "Removing pesetas from Spain is a felony. The maximum penalty is confiscation of the three million, a fine of three times that amount, and ten years in prison. However, as she's a first offender the government will waive prison and most likely the fine. But they will impose a period of probation. And they will publicize the confiscation and probation as a warning to others. It will come out in the papers, on the radio news and *Telediario*."

Within minutes the guests left the family alone.

Cristina was exasperated with her friend for having exposed herself to humiliation, financial loss and possible imprisonment. "How foolish!"

Alfonso was staring toward the sea, thinking aloud. "Yes, the way she did it. Unlucky to be caught. But I don't know how foolish it was to try to get some money to where you know it's safe. Marisa remembers 1936. The loss of three brothers. And Carlos' father. And she understands Spaniards. Of late I'm seeing myself as the foolish one. In 1950 I had five million American dollars that I could have left in New York or put in a Swiss bank. I believed that with Franco in charge '1936' could never happen again. So I brought it home and changed it into pesetas."

He looked at the others, "As you all know, I did not need that money here. I acted as a patriotic Spaniard should, especially a privileged nobleman. But that was a different Spain. Lately I find that I'm not a nobleman anymore, I'm a *Señorito*. And these days I don't feel so euphorically patriotic. I feel instead that I'm an irresponsible father of eight without a dollar or a Swiss franc outside of Spain. If *Banco del Castillo de Tarifa* gets nationalized tomorrow my children will be left with no means of support in Spain beyond paltry salaries, and not a penny outside if they must flee. I'm a billionaire in Spain, but beyond her borders I'm a pauper. I, for one, am never leaving my country. I did that as a child. I'll die here this time, if I must. But if I see another civil war coming, my children and Magdalena must get out. But on what money?"

Paco tried to console him, "We are not going to nationalize anything. That was never our platform."

"Who said anything about you? I'm talking about when your Centrist Party gets voted out of office and the Socialists come in. You know that will happen. Yours is a transitional government, from the extreme right to the moderate center. But in your heart you know that the majority will next vote for Felipe's working man's image: the statesman who won't wear a necktie! Even when he had an audience with His Majesty the King, he arrived in a windbreaker and a shirt with no tie! How many times has Felipe González told all those people who do not own neckties, but each have a vote, that the first thing he'll do is nationalize the banks and the utilities? That happens to be virtually everything we have. I invested heavily in *Telefónica* and electric companies. He will surely take our lands as well, in the name of agrarian reform. We would become only salaried employees at the bank. Until they fire us."

"*If* they come in. And even then we can't be sure what they'll do."

"Paco, Paco, Paco! Your 'Government of the Center' has little time left. You won because Spain wasn't emotionally ready for such a pendulum swing as from *Franquismo* to *Socialismo*. And the

Socialists needed time to organize. But they'll be ready by the next elections and they'll sweep in. Or worse, they may come in together with the Communists, a coalition like in 1936. Possibly there will be death in the streets again. And they will nationalize the banks and the utilities. They say it openly. That's how they'll get the votes. By promising to take from the rich." He half-smiled, sardonically, his voice softened as though thinking aloud, "But they never do give it to the poor, do they? Not in Russia, not in China, Africa, nowhere. They just take it from the rich and keep it for themselves, they confiscate our homes our lands and live in them. But the poor never catch on to that. They believe because they want to believe, they need to believe in something that might better their lives. That's why they buy lottery tickets. They are buying hope. Next, they'll be voting hope."

He looked up resignedly. "So the rich had better take care of themselves by being rich someplace other than in Spain."

"Alfonso!" Paco's voice snapped sharply in a tone he had never used with his half brother. "Do not say such a thing in my presence. I have taken an oath to uphold the laws of this government. Marisa was acting against Spain's best interests by taking our currency outside. There are too many like her, thinking of themselves above their country. Obviously I remember '36 and I understand their fears, but I also see them as traitors, draining our economy. I have forgotten what you just said. But if any evidence of evasion of capital comes through my department I won't be able to help you. Nor would I want to."

Cristina stood up. "I agree with Paco."

"Do you now? And if I were to tell you how to move a few million dollars in pesetas to Switzerland or New York?"

"I wouldn't do it." Her voice softened. "I know that we are probably alive today only because Tio Guillermo had money outside and could send us to Biarritz. But, Alfonso, we have been privileged from the day we were born. That has all come from our country. We must not weaken her. I believe that we must put the interests of Spain ahead of our own."

"And if the Communists come in and attack you on the streets, confiscate everything?"

"So be it."

"And your child? Without money?"

"She's a Spaniard. Her country comes first." She stood up and kissed him goodnight.

Alfonso was looking at his half brother, hoping Paco would say something that might lift the sadness he felt.

Paco said nothing.

Alfonso called out. "Don't worry, Paco. I only talk. I won't break any laws."

Paco returned. "Promise me that. Please."

"Of course."

When they had left, sitting with America, Alfonso felt alone in the world except for her. Yes, he had Magdalena and his children, but they were responsibilities, not companions.

America said, "You didn't mean what you said to Paco."

"In his position, and misplaced faith in the future . . ." he shook his head. "I was sorry to learn that I'm more his brother than he is mine. On the other hand he hasn't had the experience of being kidnapped. He saw his parents shot down and killed. Who knows if that is worse or less bad than finding your parents' corpses in a morgue? I know only that if today he were to get into trouble I would lie for him, cheat for him."

They were pensive for a while. Then, Alfonso asked, "How much money would you say a large family needs to live comfortably in the States?"

"You could never live there the way you live here, with the friends, the homes, the position you enjoy and the doors it opens for you."

"And lately slams in my face."

"Well, let's just say that there's nowhere in the world you could live as you live here, but you could be comfortable in the States on two million dollars. Even in Certificates of Deposit—that isn't much of a way to invest money—but even in C.D.'s you could live comfortably on a hundred and fifty or two hundred thousand dollars a year."

"Comfortably on two hundred thousand? Eight pampered children and a wife who's accustomed to the life of a Duchess. A rich Duchess. She gives more than that to charity every year." He dismissed the question of the amount necessary. "The trick is to get the capital out of Spain without being caught."

"Like poor Marisa."

"The result of hysteria. Naïveté."

"How else?"

"I'm embarrassed to say that I don't know, I've never thought about it before. But now I must. I don't believe I'm being melodramatic remembering '36 and seeing a similarity developing in the present."

And he worried, what if they think to loot law offices for *testimentos* to search out where assets are hidden? The looters might not be so rushed or unthinking as to dismiss a sealed leather envelope as "love letters."

* * *

On Monday morning Alfonso was dressing to go to the bank when he heard the screeching of automobile tires, three gunshots, then the front door slammed closed and bolted. He rushed out of his bedroom, to the hall at the top of the stairs and saw José Maria and Luis with their bodyguards Pedro and Manolo. Pedro was holding a pistol.

Breathlessly, his voice tremulous, José Maria explained, "We left the driveway and halfway down the street a car was stalled, blocking our way. As we stopped, another came up behind us. Two men got out of the second car and one from the first. They all had guns. Obviously they had been waiting for us. Pedro threw our car into reverse, smashing into the car behind us, pushing it back far enough to make room for a quick U-turn. Then, driving along the sidewalk, we escaped."

Alfonso rushed down the stairs and hugged his sons, his heir and his second son, gripping them to him with all of his strength, his hands pulsating from the relief of feeling the young men's shoulders and backs, his own flesh and blood.

He let go of the boys and gave the bodyguard a powerful *abrazo*. "Thank you, Pedro. Who shot at whom?"

"It was I, Sr. Duque. I thought a few shots into the grass would show we were armed and convince them they had failed and should get away. Shall I call the police, Sr. Duque?"

"Yes. Report an attempted kidnapping." He told José Maria, "Rest awhile, then you and Luis should go see Uncle Paco at the Ministry."

Returning to his bedroom, he found his hands were shaking as he made the knot in his necktie. ETA was growing still bolder to attempt a double kidnapping in broad daylight. But how smart of them! What would a man not pay for two sons?

Alfonso had lunch in a private dining room upstairs at Jockey with the Swiss manager of the Madrid branch of a significant Zurich bank. Though they were alone in the room, having dismissed the waiter and captain who had served the meal, the banker spoke in a low voice in German, and cryptically, "If any of your friends wish to send a parcel, and if you personally identify them as people of confidence, I will happily oblige. Naturally, I cannot give a receipt for it but in one week's time the parcel will be at their disposal in the main office."

"And the transportation charges?"

"20 percent."

Alfonso told America, "No receipt runs the risk that he could embezzle it and disappear."

"A reputable banker?"

"The only bankers who can get close enough to substantial money in order to embezzle it are 'reputable.' But he's not a banker as I am a banker. I'm a *banquero*, I own a bank. He's a *bancario*, an employee of a bank. Let's suppose I were to give him a hundred and fifty million pesetas. That's over a million dollars.

A man of his income level could retire on that in luxury. What recourse would I have? Call the police and denounce him?"

"I'll help you in any way I can," America said.

It was what he would have expected, but it could be dangerous for her. "Let us study this thoroughly. 'If you want to do something badly, do it fast.' We won't make Marisa's mistake."

Alfonso walked through *El Museo del Prado,* passing the masterworks of Goya, Velázquez, Titian, Rubens, Tiepolo, Zurbarán. But what interested him at the moment were the unknown artists with easels set up here and there before a masterpiece, copying it. They were accomplished technicians who could make the colors and the brush strokes and the shadings of the great masters, but they were not originators so they eked out a living selling copies of pictures and techniques that great artists had created.

He stood behind a man of forty or so who was copying Rubens' "Maria de Medici." Brilliantly, Alfonso thought. The artist ignored him as he did all the tourists who paused, fascinated by his ability. He had no time for ego stroking. He needed to turn out pictures to sell. For five minutes Alfonso watched him. "Is your work for sale?"

"I'm not doing this for my health." There was no pause in the movement of his brush or a glance away from his canvas.

"However, enough money is good for the health. No?"

The artist looked up, appraising the clearly affluent man.

"When will you finish this one?"

"Today if you are in a hurry. And if you have a hundred thousand pesetas."

"I'll be pleased to buy your work, at your price."

The artist would gladly have settled for fifty thousand. He was behind in his rent, telephone bill, electricity, his wife was pregnant, his girlfriend was pregnant—a hundred thousand pesetas was unreal.

Alfonso counted out the money in five-thousand-peseta notes and gave them to the man. "Do you specialize in Rubens?"

"I specialize in whatever I can sell you."

"Tiepolo, Goya, Velázquez, Titian?"

"I do them all. Which would you like?"

"None that are here. I have some of my own. These days, with so many burglaries the cost of insurance is so high that I would like to make copies and put the originals in a bank vault."

The artist had heard of this before. It made sense to him.

And it made even better sense to Alfonso. If he could obtain excellent counterfeits of paintings that were known to be in his home, then, without provoking questions such as "Where is the marvelous Rubens that used to hang here?" he could replace them and spirit the originals out of Spain to be sold. For an investment of a hundred thousand pesetas, twelve to fifteen hundred dollars, he would have a picture that could be sold in the world art market of the moment for upwards of a million dollars.

* * *

America asked, "But, how do you sell a historically famous masterwork that is known to be catalogued in Spain?"

"Simple. Get it to London or New York and locate an unscrupulous art dealer. That's easy—it's the other kind who are difficult to find—and have him sell privately to a zealous collector, most of whose scruples would make even the dealers look like your George Washington."

"But how do you slip a catalogued great master out of the country?"

"The ETA method: rolled up in a tube within a golf bag."

Alfonso had devoted the week to studying the transfer of money from Spain to other countries. There were various possibilities but they all involved another person and the consequent vulnerability to theft or blackmail. Finally, the most viable solution was Marisa's, but more carefully planned: the methodical removal of cash, art and jewels by oneself or by an unquestioned friend or family member.

"I'm your best shot," America said. "I'm anonymous, I think you know you can trust me, I'm a foreigner so I'd have the right to be carrying foreign money that we could get from your own bank, the dollars, marks, pounds, whatever the tourists change into pesetas. And I'm sufficiently affluent to be the owner of anything I might be caught carrying."

"It could endanger you. There's always risk."

She shrugged it off. "I'm an unlikely suspect."

Alongside *La Tejana's* swimming pool, Alfonso lay beneath the Marbella sun, warmed even more by the pleasure of being with America, lightly outlining her body with his finger, delighting in her *buena facha,* listening to her speak as though he were hearing Mozart, regretting that in an hour she would be driving him back to the airport and they would be separated by another "month" of five days.

America switched from lovers' small talk. She had convinced Alfonso that she was the only possible courier. "I'll go to Zurich on Tuesday, ostensibly on my way to ski in St. Moritz. I'll open a numbered account for cash and rent a safe-deposit box for jewels and paintings." She became flirtatious, "By coincidence you could be in the same bank as a tourist changing travelers' checks and then you could sign the signature cards right then."

He shook his head. "There are Spanish detectives watching every bank in Switzerland. It would be best that there's never a record of me being in Switzerland or near a Swiss bank. If you wouldn't mind, take photocopies of Magdalena's and my passports, bring the card back here, she and I will sign it, then you go back and open the account."

Disappointed, but accepting the logic she agreed, "Then, once I have the account open I can go every week or two, but it would be imprudent for me to travel directly to Switzerland so often. I'll mix it up. One week Paris. Other times London or Rome. Nobody will be aware of the side trips to Zurich. I'll leave here on Iberia then make the side trips on BEA, Air France, Swiss Air. Then I'll return on the second half of the Iberia ticket. There'll be no record in

Spain of where I've really been. Of course my travels will be during the week. Nothing is going to take away our weekends together. With the single exception of José Maria and Puri's wedding next Saturday and Sunday."

Alfonso stroked her hair. "We have a technical problem that will delay us. The government, alarmed by the volume of flight money has issued new five-thousand-peseta banknotes implanted with a metallic thread that will trigger electronic detectors. So I need time to accumulate the old five-thousand-peseta notes that won't be detected."

* * *

In the air, destination Zurich, America felt the chill of fear, awareness that for the first time in her life she was about to break the law, and worse, the law of a country in which she was a guest. *But,* she thought, *under some circumstances, like being deeply in love and caring for that person's well being, you break the rules.*

She had chosen to leave on Thursday in order to be away from the *finca* that weekend, when Alfonso couldn't be there. She took care of her banking business on Friday and spent Saturday and Sunday skiing.

The new *¡HOLA!* came out with a sixteen-page coverage of *Boda del Año,* the wedding of the year, heralded on the cover with a photo of *"Purificación Notario Jiménez con José Maria García de Las Arenas de Soto y de Aragon, Los Futuros Duques del Castillo de Tarifa."*

Everyone she knew was there, her friends from Madrid, Marbella, Sierra Nevada, and many Grandees of whom she had only heard. And representing the royal family were Prince Felipe, the heir to the throne, and his sisters, Elena and Cristina, *Infantas de España.* There were photos showing Alfonso and Magdalena entering the cathedral, dancing at the reception, toasting the bride and the groom. She ached to have been there but understood that it was hardly a place for the mistress of the father of the groom.

On the following Friday afternoon the piece of paper she gave Alfonso was typed out with numbers only.

He said, "Let's have dinner somewhere special tonight." Normally they dined at home or in obscure restaurants where they were unlikely to bump into someone from Madrid. But he felt that it was bad enough that she had to be a weekend wife, to say nothing of volunteering to endanger herself for him. At least they could go someplace festive for a change.

They chose *La Meridiana*, a restaurant just opened by Paolo Ghirelli at whose small *Don Leone*, in the old town of Marbella, they had dined on their first night out together. Paolo had enjoyed great success in the Marbella boom and had built a magnificent restaurant in the hills above where the King of Saudi Arabia, when Crown Prince, had built a palace with two hundred rooms that is a replica, but larger, of the White House in Washington, D.C. *La Meridiana* was staffed with the best waiters and headwaiters lured from Madrid, and Paolo had decorated it with a collection of paintings and sculptures so that it had the ambience of being a private home, a multimillionaire's private home.

Alfonso ordered a bottle of Vega-Sicilia Unico, usually the best of Spain's red wines, and always the most expensive. He raised his glass to America, "Dining here, at another restaurant of Paolo, takes me back to our beginning. Who could have imagined where that night would have brought us, the incredible happiness you have given me? And that I pray I have returned in some small kind."

When they got back to the house, instead of having their customary nightcap on the terrace, Alfonso took America's hand and led her to the bedroom. Holding her in his arms he made love to her mouth, her breasts, to all of her body, prolonging the foreplay so as to remain at his most ardent, most sensual.

When the moment came he again heard his voice saying, "*I'll pay.*" and his erection fell, lifeless. Dismayed by another failure that he had really expected would not occur, he finally accepted the fact that that part of him had died. "What good am I to you?"

"Darling, you're everything to me. And don't blame yourself. The years have gone by, I know you love me but maybe I'm just not that alluring anymore."

"Oh no, no, no! Nothing could be further from the truth. You saw how I lusted for you."

Crushed with sorrow that she should suffer a moment with thoughts so far from the truth, he revealed what happened in his mind. "I'm starving for you, but in the depth of my soul I fear that I'll never again be able to make love to you. To combine your soul with mine requires your respect, and I know that I have it, but under false pretenses. I have lost respect for myself, which apparently manifests itself in impotency.

"To Magdalena, my children, my sisters and yourself I'm a hero who survived something terrible and unjust. But none of you understand the plot within the plot. I have betrayed my country, my heritage, I'm a coward who obeyed his captors like a schoolboy and then gave them two hundred million pesetas to continue killing more people, making more widows and orphans."

America was torn apart for him. "Darling, this is totally unreasonable. Every man in the world would have done exactly as you did. The only difference is they wouldn't give it a thought afterwards. To save one's life, self-survival, that's the most basic human instinct."

"There have been heroic men who have given their lives for what they believed in."

"In the heat of battle, when the drama becomes hypnotic, but not in a situation like yours. You are judging yourself far, far too harshly. Please, stop. My heart breaks for you. As for us, give yourself time. We've had our moments when 'the earth moved' and we'll have them again. Until then I love you more than I have ever loved you and there's a lot more for us in life besides sex."

At eight A.M. Monday morning Alfonso called from Madrid. "Esperanza died in her sleep last night. Her heart malfunctioned. The funeral is tomorrow."

America sat in the back of the church. The family gathered in the first and second rows with Paco and Cristina. Cayetana was conservative in navy blue. Alfonso was with Magdalena, their sons and stunning daughters and sons-in-law. She would have recognized José Maria even if she hadn't met him, because he looked so like his father. Puri was at his side. Marisa and Carlos sat behind them. The altar was burgeoning with flowers.

Cristina's and Paco's faces were chalk white as if they themselves had suffered heart attacks. They remained on their knees throughout the Mass. America imagined the torture they were experiencing, their probable conversations with God, asking His forgiveness for having married and had a child.

As the coffin passed America summoned up all the self-discipline she could find. *This is Esperanza's funeral, not Angel's,* but her eyes blurred in kaleidoscopic memory of Angel and of sweet, tragic Esperanza, and empathy for Cristina and Paco.

As she was leaving the church Cayetana caught up with her. "It was good of you to come."

"How not?"

"Hah! Very easy how not. Cristina and Paco are among Madrid's most popular young couples, and he's a powerful man. If this were a wedding the church would be full. But look around you. Too many of their friends who live right here in Madrid have spared themselves the sadness and just sent flowers. Yet you flew from Marbella. Aware, I'm sure, that this would provoke unhappy memories of your own. I know you were wonderful to Esperanza and that she loved you. I've hired a helicopter to take us to *Los Escalones* for the internment. There will be a seat for you."

America glanced toward Magdalena. Though she had been warm during the kidnapping she wouldn't enjoy the sight of her husband's lover at this tragic family affair. And certainly she did not want the children to see her and remember the unfortunate photo in *¡HOLA!* and resent her being there. Cayetana was kind and generous but her judgment was emotionally flawed.

"I would be out of place at this family gathering. I'll wait in Madrid. When Cristina and Paco return I'll visit them." She touched Cayetana's hand, "But thank you."

Two days later Alfonso's car drew up to the entrance of the Villa Magna to bring America to Cristina and Paco's house. It had been understood that they couldn't appear together there, and though she could have gone by taxi Alfonso had wanted to see her, if only for a few minutes because this was a moment when she needed extra support. As she sat beside him in the car he squeezed her hand and she knew it was for Angel. They rode in silence until Alfonso said, "If 1936 had never happened, if Spain had remained at peace, then every autumn Cristina would have returned to Madrid and Paco would have stayed at *Los Escalones,* they would never have gone together to Biarritz and fallen in love. I'm not saying I'm sorry they are married. On the contrary. I regret only what it has cost them, the guilt, the stress, and now this dreadful loss."

America left the car a block away from Cristina and Paco's home and walked the short distance alone. Their discretion was unnecessary. Few people were present. As Cayetana had pointed out, the house overflowed with flowers, sacks of telegrams kept arriving, but most people did not subject themselves to the pain of trying to alleviate the grief of two souls so deeply wounded.

Cristina's scar, normally barely noticeable because of her radiance, now protruded, the first thing you saw when you looked at her. Naturally slender, she had lost several kilos in just these few days and her clothes hung loosely from her. Paco was at her side. America sat down with them.

"Cayetana told me why you did not come to *Los Escalones,*" Cristina said. "I'm glad for your sake that you did not. That coffin . . . seeing it lowered into the ground with my whole life in it." She touched her husband's hand, "I'm sorry, I did not mean that literally. It's just that she filled my life, every day, that sweet child, she was so loving. But imagine how good God is; to call her to Him in her sleep. When I went in to wake her and I found her . . . gone . . . she was smiling as if she had seen an angel and the angel had said, 'Come with me, Esperanza, and I'll take you to a beautiful place where there's cake and ice cream and teddy bears' and she had gone with the angel to Heaven, where she isn't different from anyone else and where she'll always be happy."

"I fear I'm intruding, causing you to talk about it."

"Oh, no, I *must* talk about Esperanza. I cannot explain the vacuum after waking every morning thinking of her, planning what I could do to make her little life happy." She put her hand on America's, "You're the one person I know who can understand that. Paco used to call her from the Ministry two or three times a day, in the middle of searching out terrorists and running the nation's police forces, just to tell her how much he loved her. And she was so happy that Papá called just to speak to her."

Paco was staring at the floor and America feared that he might topple forward in a faint.

"I cannot imagine what I'm going to do with myself from now on when Paco goes to work. To be in this house without Esperanza . . ." She stopped. "What did you do, America? How did you survive?"

"What I did in the beginning will be no consolation to you because even as I did it I suffered, as you will. But you have Paco. Only Alfonso finally brought me back to life."

"I know I shall flee from here every day, flee from the emptiness, the memories . . ."

Paco said, "Let's move, take an apartment or build another house that will have no memories."

"The memories will come with us. As I look at you I see her speaking to you on the telephone. As I look at America I see her listening to Alice in Wonderland. When Alfonso was here this morning I remembered him swinging her in the air, 'Love of my life, Queen of England, Princess of Austria, Queen of Spain . . .'"

Perhaps it was premature, America thought, but Cristina was screaming for help. Even in his absence she felt Alfonso giving her support to raise the idea she had discussed first with him the day after the funeral. She prayed she would say this well. "Cristina, there are many children who need somebody to love them, who have no mothers or fathers. Now you could adopt a child." She paused, prepared to withdraw the idea if she saw that Cristina and Paco were not ready to hear of such a thing. But they were looking at her with interest, so she continued, "You and Paco have so much love to give. Nobody can ever replace your own precious daughter, Esperanza will always be first in your hearts, but you might use what you have learned as parents to bring happiness to some lonely, perhaps hungry child who would come to love you as if you were his or her true parents. Just because a child does not come from your own body does not mean that love doesn't grow. Love begets love."

"We wouldn't be betraying Esperanza," Paco said.

Cristina thought aloud, "She's too sweet to be jealous. From Heaven she hears our hearts and she knows that no one will ever replace her, that she will be with us forever, and one day when God calls us we will all be together again, maybe with the brother and sister she could never have. And now there's no reason, no fear to prevent us from adopting a child, or two or three."

Cristina's constricted face was relaxing. "How nice it would be to give a home to a child who doesn't have one. A child who needs help, love."

Paco said, "That is exactly what happened to me."

Chapter Eighteen

The Duke of the Castle of Tarifa locked the door of his cellar. The racks were again burgeoning with the best Spanish wines, thousands of bottles of Vega-Sicilia, Conde de Los Andes and Cune's Imperial. Often he had enjoyed browsing among them but now he went directly to the vault. Inserting the stiff wires into the tiny holes he waited for the monolithic door to stop its slow, silent movement.

As always he carried a lantern because he, like his father and grandfather, would never have trusted an electrician to install electricity and learn of the vault's existence. It gave the scene a slightly medieval feeling. Alfonso had always felt wonderful inside the vault. Powerful, protected, secure. He thought of Paco and admired his brother's patriotism. But what did Paco have to protect? A single *finca*? With a single castle. And now, he thought, not even a child. And his wife was more than financially secure. He wasn't responsible for a large family and a fortune that had taken a thousand years to accumulate. If '36 were to return he would have to get Cristina to safety, but he really did not believe it would happen.

Alfonso stared at the stone plaque, the mandate for secrecy made by the Duke of the Castle of Tarifa, carved and mounted on that wall in the year 1715, more than two and a half centuries ago.

The trunks of cash were gone, some of it spent, most of it invested. Alfonso looked at the ancient coin collections, the tiaras, the diamonds, emeralds and rubies and he felt nothing for them. His heart was breaking for love of his family's history, for his country that had changed.

He was disconsolate to be breaking the chain of succession. So many times he had imagined his heir opening this vault and experiencing the delight that he, Alfonso, had enjoyed on that amazing day. But now he prayed that by the time José Maria's inheritance occurred the vault would be empty, that when he opened it he would find only their ancestors' desk and a letter of introduction to a bank in Switzerland, a number and a sum of money deposited there that would be his to administer for his sisters and brothers. A quantity of money, art and properties that was dizzying, beyond José Maria's imagining, for Alfonso, like his father before him, never denied their affluence, but neither did he hint at the immensity of the family fortune that he, Alfonso, had multiplied by at least fifty times.

But it tugged at him. Seven generations of the Duke of the Castle of Tarifa had managed to keep faith in their country.

"Ah, yes," he said aloud, speaking to his father, to all of them, "but let me say that it was easier for you. What had you to fear? The French? The Moors? Even you, Papá, you did not understand Soviet Russia's plans before you died, you had not learned to fear her or you and Mamá would never have been on the streets of Madrid in the early morning. But this is 1980. Russia has Cuba, most of Africa and South America. Eventually she'll get Spain and to dismantle her, to enslave us, she will, again, expertly turn Spaniards against Spaniards and return us to the past, to the barbarism of '36. We will revert from a reasonably unified, civilized, cultured people to a mindless mass, killing and hating again.

"The rules have changed; Papá, I cannot leave this here now. I'm taking it out, all of it."

He stared fondly at the plaque. "My beloved ancestors, you were splendid when it was possible to be splendid. But that time has passed."

* * *

José Maria entered his father's office at the bank. He had not asked Alfonso's secretary to announce him; he did not knock, nor did he even apologize for bursting in. His face and eyes blazed with anger. He slapped a copy of the scandal magazine *Interviú* onto his father's desk, open to a picture of Alfonso and America kissing in the Málaga airport. Alfonso remembered the moment. The feeling of relief that the rapist had failed, that she was safe, had overwhelmed his normal sense of discretion. "How can you continue doing this to Mamá? Have you any idea the grief you cause her, the humiliation? And for what? Because you continue to amuse yourself with this cheap woman."

"José Maria! She isn't a cheap woman."

"I have nothing against her. It's you."

"My son, I'm not amusing myself with America. You are old enough for me to tell you that your mother and I made a marriage of convenience. It was understood before we married that we were not in love with each other. We hoped that a love might grow but, lamentably, it did not. Just friendship. Now, after over twenty-five loveless years it happens, for the good of it and for the bad of it, that I'm in love with America."

"I've cleared my desk. Make Luis your President."

"Please, José Maria, don't leave me. I love you. I need you."

"Well, thank God, I don't need you. I was always so proud of you. When you set the agrarian reform in motion, I thought if those farmers didn't build a statue to you, I would. Frankly, I now have trouble looking at you for fear that I've inherited your genes."

The words closed Alfonso's eyes as if they had been fists striking him. "José Maria, please don't act hastily. Yes, I was indiscreet. But please reconsider."

"Never! Not as long as you continue with that woman."

The door closed between them.

He did not mention it to America on the phone, refusing to lay his grief on her, hoping that she might never see the article or hear about it. But of course America saw the photo. It was a magazine she did not read, but whenever there's bad publicity, there's always someone who is glad to show it to those involved or tell about it.

"Alfonso, I've seen *Interviú*. It's horrendous. What is the reaction at home?"

"José Maria has left me, left the bank. He can't look at me. He's worried that he's inherited my genes."

She yearned to hold him close and stroke away the pain he was feeling. "Surely he'll come back."

"I wouldn't bet on it. He's not entirely wrong. I miss him, already. I'll do anything in the world to get him back—except give you up." He felt drained of strength as he understood that he held the key to be reunited with his eldest son, whom he loved the most, but that he would never use it.

America felt that she wouldn't really mind if a bolt of lightning were to strike her dead.

Maria del Mar had come back from London to be present on Carmen's and her birthday the following day. Her husband, Cristóbal, was unable to be absent from the Embassy. At dinner she said, "Let's have a family lunch at Jockey tomorrow."

"You're on," Alfonso agreed.

Magdalena was surprised, "I have a party dinner organized, a beautiful cake . . ." The dinner was a tradition, held just after they had received their birthday presents.

"Can't we do both?"

"Of course," Magdalena said. "Why not?"

"Let me organize lunch. I'll call Puri and invite them."

Magdalena said, "I don't think they will join us. José Maria isn't acting well. He has appointed himself as the family's social arbiter."

Obviously it was something no one wanted to discuss further, so Maria del Mar did not ask. After dinner, in their old bedroom in which she was staying, Carmen filled her in. Maria del Mar was furious, "Where does that dumb kid come off making such judgments?"

The twins, dressed in matching sable coats they had received as part of their trousseaus, swept into Jockey with their mother and father, Rafa and all of their brothers and sisters except one, whom Maria del Mar had not called.

Perhaps it was being connected with the diplomatic service, or maybe it was living in a foreign country, but Maria del Mar had developed command and she took over the party. She had called Carmelo and described the table she wanted. A *mesa real,* a royal table, long with seats on both sides and two seats at one end. "Mamá and Papá together at the heads of the table, please. Our being on earth did not happen without some help. The birthday girls will have the honor of sitting on either side of their parents. The rest boy-girl-boy-girl."

At the end of the wonderful lunch they had champagne with their dessert and Alfonso stood up, "Happy birthday to Carmen and Maria del Mar. Your mother and I appreciate and love you both. We love you all. All of our children. All."

When they were back at the house and alone upstairs Maria del Mar told Carmen, "I could wring that damned José Maria's neck. In fact, I will."

She dialed her brother's apartment. Puri answered and they chatted together as the friends they had become. Finally, she asked if she could speak with her brother.

"Mari," he shouted, "Happy birthday. Are you calling from London? We were going to call you."

"I'm calling from the house in which we all grew up so comfortably and safely."

He let that go by. "How long are you staying? When can we see you?"

"You could have seen me this afternoon. We all had lunch at Jockey. But now you can't see me because I do not associate with judgmental, pompous asses who have the audacity to decide how their parents should live. Boy, you'd better be the straightest of all straight arrows or you'll be a hypocrite as well as a sanctimonious fool. I don't know about *your* religion, but in mine it's a sin not to honor your mother and father."

"Mari, listen . . ."

"I did not call you to *listen*. I called to let you know that I think you're a jerk and a twerp, one who is certainly not making Mamá any happier by abandoning your family. Also, you're a lousy business man. I suppose you'll be looking for a job somewhere, probably in a bank because banking is what you know, thanks to your father, who started teaching you since the first day you were in short pants. You're really brilliant, José Maria. You don't even have the brains to know that *working* for a bank isn't nearly as good as *owning* one. Goodbye until you grow up." She hung up the phone.

Carmen cried out, "Gorgeous! Aunt Cay couldn't have done better."

The door had been open and they had not heard their parents come in to give them their birthday presents.

They had never before seen their father crying, though he was smiling at the same time.

* * *

Alfonso called America, "Elena has just had healthy twin girls. How do you feel about running around with a grandfather?"

On Sunday in Marbella, as together they packed her suitcase, Alfonso tucked an envelope under some shoes. It contained two hundred of the old five thousand peseta banknotes without electronic bars. Then, into each corner of the suitcase he put a small package, a catalogued collection of eight ancient, Roman Empire coins. Beautiful, but crude by modern standards, they had been made more than two thousand years ago: they were round but not perfectly so, half an inch thick and bore the image of Caesar Augustus stamped on both sides. They were pure gold and consequently a brilliant yellow. They had not changed ownership in four hundred years, and depending on the zeal of the collector were worth in excess of a million dollars. He kept that from her, not wanting to add to her tension. Though she was trying to conceal it, despite all of her courage and her love and desire to help him, he saw that she was frightened.

Even more valuable was a golf bag containing a normal set of clubs, but rolled up in a cardboard tube lodged among them were a Titian and an El Greco that had hung in Alfonso's palace for centuries.

The least dangerous item was in her purse, an envelope containing twenty thousand dollars in American, German and British currency that Alfonso had been able to skim off what his Foreign Department took in for exchange. Any wealthy woman could be carrying that much cash.

Camouflaging her nerves she joked, "The airport staff will think I'm a great sportswoman. On my last trip I carried skis to Zurich. Now golf clubs to London." Her air tickets were to Gatwick and a connecting flight to Scotland. Once in London she would cancel the Glasgow flight and buy a ticket from London to Zurich.

Taking maximum precaution, Alfonso wasn't going to drive her to the airport. He would wait at *Finca de la Tejana.* She kissed him goodbye. "I won't call you from London. Getting ticketed on the flight to Zurich will be cutting it close. I'll call you the minute I get to Switzerland."

"Say nothing on the phone. Only that you landed safely and how the weather is." She looked at him wryly. "Well," he apologized, "you're not a professional smuggler."

"Yet."

Rafael was at the wheel of the Range Rover and America was wearing a Pértegaz suit, carrying a lynx coat, her golf bag, a single piece of King Ranch luggage and her Hermès handbag: the stereotypical wealthy tourist.

At the airport she was grateful for the first-class check-in counter. Economy had a line of at least twenty people and her nerves couldn't have survived it. She watched her suitcase get tagged and waddle away on the conveyer belt until it passed through the rubber flaps and out of sight. Then she watched the golf bag go. To be noticed? Inspected? Not noticed?

She went into the cafeteria and prayed against hearing her name on the loudspeaker. *Will passenger A. Harvey kindly report to*

Information? And then, *Would you mind unlocking your suitcase, Miss Harvey?*

Her mind reeled with a series of questions.

Why are you carrying so much cash when you must surely have excellent credit cards, Miss Harvey?

We accept your word on owning the foreign money, but surely you are aware it's illegal to take Spanish pesetas out of this country.

Also, these remarkable old masters rolled up in your golf bag? From whom did you purchase them? Do you happen to have the documents with you? Do you have certified Ministerial permission to remove these catalogued art treasures from Spain?

Feeling her clothes sticking to her body America was thinking that she definitely wasn't a professional smuggler. And Alfonso was just as much an amateur or they would have thought to trump up some story, even some false papers that an overworked Customs man might not challenge.

For fifty minutes she waited for her flight to be called before her name. Every announcement was a jolt to her nervous system. Then, finally: "Iberia announces the departure of Flight 304 to London. Passengers will please proceed to Gate 3."

Seated in the plane she found herself looking pleasant, innocent, smiling at everyone, again waiting for an announcement, *Will passenger Harvey please make herself known to any member of the crew?*

From the moment Alfonso calculated she would have arrived at the Málaga Airport he recognized the peril in which he had placed her. When more than enough time had passed for the plane to be in the air he made a gin and tonic. He looked at his watch. When an hour had passed he downed the rest of his drink. She was in the air.

Or was she? The plane, yes. But if she had been removed from the flight she might not be allowed to call anyone. And certainly she wouldn't call her house and risk involving him. But how could she talk away a million pesetas and an ancient million-dollar coin collection? And the rolled-up Titian and El Greco? All catalogued in his name. He thought, *when you're nervous you read meaning into the silliest things.* He found himself comforted by Primavera and Alegría chasing around the garden and wrestling with each other as if they knew that America was safe.

Though it was December the Marbella weather was spring-like. Alfonso changed into a bathing suit and dove into the pool. He went back to the house and looked at the telephone. He went out onto the terrace and sat in the sun. He got up and walked around the pool.

Encarna served lunch. He left most of it and poured a hooker of scotch. He tried to take a siesta. His eyes closed but his mind would not. Four hours with America always passed in a flash. These few hours limped along, minute . . . . by . . . . minute . . . . by . . .

The phone was ringing.

Alfonso lifted the receiver as though it were a serpent. "*¿Sí?*"

"Darling, I found this wonderful sports shop with a marvelous dark green Alpine sweater. Would a 44 be a good size for you?"

* * *

Cristina called America from Madrid on Monday morning. "Paco and I are thinking of passing a few days in Marbella. Some time convenient for you." Her voice was animated, a giant step from the condition in which America had last seen her.

"You are always convenient for me. Your room is ready. Let me know when your plane comes in and I'll be there."

"No, how boring for you! There are plenty of taxis."

"Cristina! I *want* to meet you and Paco at the airport."

They had a little boy of about four years old, each of them holding onto one of his hands. "This is our son, Marco," Paco said to America as he and Cristina watched for her reaction. She knelt down and hugged him, then kissed him on both cheeks, then on his forehead, then on both cheeks again. She hugged him once more. She held him at arms length, beaming at him and he beamed back. He had gorgeous brown hair and brown eyes and he wasn't the least bit shy. He was scrawny, but that would soon be fixed.

After dinner, when Marco had been put to bed, they sat in the living room and had a nightcap.

"Paco and I would feel honored if you would be the *madrina* of Marco."

Taken completely by surprise, thrilled, eager to accept, America asked, "Can a Presbyterian be the godmother of a Catholic child?"

"Our priest saw no problem at all."

"Then it's I who feel honored." She was ecstatic, and as if speaking to herself, "I'm a *madrina*. I have an *ahijado*."

Paco said, "We have named him Marco Americo, as close as we could come to America for a boy. He was baptized as Marco at the home for orphans when he was brought in as a newborn baby. And as he knows his name to be Marco we don't want to confuse him by changing it."

"Marco Americo is a beautiful name. I'm flattered and grateful."

Chapter Nineteen

America delighted in Alfonso's rapt attention as she set up the metal casting set that she had asked Gat to send her from the States. It was just like the one they had used as children making lead soldiers, but it had been wired for Spain's 220 volts. There were two parts: a cauldron with an eight-ounce capacity, and a steel mold with an opening at the top into which one poured molten metal.

She and Alfonso had bought objects in pawn shops and in flea markets, paying only the value of the gold. Placing some beat-up old rings and cuff links in the cauldron, America waited. When they were in a liquid state she poured it into the mold. A few minutes later she opened the mold and removed a solid gold infantryman of the U.S. Army.

When it had cooled America painted his uniform, hat and shoes, his canteen, web belts and rifle. In its freshly cast state, had it been polished it would have looked at home in Tiffany's window. Thus camouflaged, it appeared to be from Toys 'R' Us.

Alfonso was gleeful. "We could make dozens of these, wrap them as gifts and at Christmas time you could be taking them to nieces and nephews in Texas. We can put them in a safe-deposit box in your bank there. I'll come along and we can ski and enjoy the holidays together."

"What about your family?"

Sadness covered his face. "José Maria wouldn't even call me with the joyous news that Puri is expecting. Nor will he come back to the bank."

"How can you be so sure?"

"He applied for a job at *Banco Coca*. Naturally, Ignacio called and asked what I wanted him to do. I told him he would be lucky to have a born banker in his employ." Alfonso waved his hands in the air as if to disperse unpleasant smoke, a gesture she had seen too many times before. "Luis, Rafael and Alfonso are now adults and have *novias* with whom they would much rather pass time than with their father. Trini, Mari and Cristóbal won't be here for Christmas. As Administrator of our family's foundation, Trini will be in New York for several days starting December 15, coordinating our Spanish Cancer Society with the American one. Then she plans to visit a friend in Peru. Mari and Cristóbal must stay in London, as he cannot leave the Embassy. Another factor: Carmen drives her racing-green Jaguar to the Hippodrome every day, where she rides the most wonderful horses that money can buy. Elena has passed her hippy phase and spends more money on couture clothes than you spend on farm machinery. Magdalena has furnished a nursery for Elena's twins fit for two princesses and dresses them accordingly. They are all adorable and I'm happy to pamper them, but knowing it's you who are ensuring that life will continue so sweetly for my family, I feel no guilt. Nor will Magda object. She knows what we owe you. Also, she has Elena and the new twins and I think she'll enjoy her grandchildren more than her husband. And, if I'm not there, surely José Maria and Puri will be with her."

They went to dinner in a small restaurant in the old part of Marbella. As they sat down at a banquette table their legs touched and America felt it like a series of mild electric shocks, as in putting on a wool sweater in winter and there's a crackling of static electricity. Alfonso took her hand under the table and their bodies responded as they had on the first night they had touched each other. She put his hand on her leg and her ears began burning.

There was a clap of thunder and it started to rain torrentially. They had not yet ordered their meal, only a drink. America said, "I'm not hungry anymore."

"Nor I." He put a thousand pesetas on the table.

She looked him in the eyes. "We are going out into the rain and then we are going to your house. Like the first time." They stepped out into the rain, and arms around each other allowed themselves to become soaked, a wonderful, refreshing, cleansing wetness.

The fireplace was blazing. Alfonso brought in two Turkish towels with his initial and crown. America had removed her clothes and Alfonso bent over her gently drying her, adoring her. She looked up into his face. "It's time for us to make the earth move, *mi amor*. The past is gone. We're taking the next plane out of purgatory. It's going to work tonight."

"Yes, I know it is."

* * *

Alfonso watched her on the ski slope in Vail, Colorado. They stayed at Galatyn Lodge, a project her brother had developed. America wore a golden ski suit and the crisp cold air caused her complexion to glow even more than it usually did. He thought there was no place America looked more beautiful than she did in the snow. But then he realized he thought the same when she was in her riding clothes, bathing suits, and lingerie. What had he done, he wondered, to have received the gift of this beautiful, loyal and courageous woman? And to have her fully again, but with far deeper love and passion than they had shared on the first night?

Margaret Harvey greeted Alfonso as if he were her son-in-law, comfortable in calling him Alfonso, seating him next to her at the dinner table.

Alfonso was as impressed with the beauty and modernity of the Harvey Ranch as he was with the warm reception Margaret Harvey had given him.

327

Alfonso and America went to Angel's grave. She was awed by the fact of not feeling the hollowness. Instead, she had a sense of well being, of contentment for bringing him there. Speaking to the headstone she said, "My Angel, it's time you and Alfonso got to know each other . . ."

At the Dallas–Fort Worth airport Gat kissed America good-bye, held out his hand to Alfonso, then hugged him with all his strength.

When they returned to Spain and were at her *finca* Alfonso said, "You have been taking too many risks. I think it prudent to make one last removal."

"I admit I won't mind ending my career as a smuggler."

"I will begin accumulating the cash." He sensed her restrained silence. "Something is wrong?"

"Not really. I was just wondering why you feel you need more money outside. Four million dollars is better than beer money."

"Not today in the 1980's. Nor is it really four million because half of it's in art and I have come to learn that a coin collection or a picture may be worth a million dollars but when it cannot be auctioned publicly with documentation, when the buyer knows it's illegally out of its country of origin he'll offer a fraction of its value. Magdalena and the children wouldn't starve, but they wouldn't have capital for the boys to be able to invest and go into business. And when you speak of municipal bonds, or Certificates of Deposit, they have no growth factor. Inflation would eventually eat up the principal. Capital needs to be spread out in a variety of investments because nothing is certain. Today New York City is broke; tomorrow maybe General Motors will stop paying dividends, who knows? We need one more large removal. Three hundred million added to what is already out will give us around a seven million dollar liquidity for investment. With that done—*¡basta!*—we can relax and watch the political situation without desperation."

"Darling," she asked reflectively, "aren't you being obsessive over the possibility of a return to '36? Spain is a different country today. As Paco said, today's middle class doesn't want to fight, they want to enjoy their cars and TV sets. Democracy is taking hold here. If Spain finally joins the Common Market and NATO then your whole fear will have been for nothing. This will all have been a passing phase."

Alfonso replied softly, "When Hitler came into power there were eighth-generation German Jews who loved their country, their homes, their family histories, their lands and businesses in Germany, hundreds of years of their roots. When he made them wear yellow stars, when he confiscated their properties, some fled but many couldn't bring themselves to run from their fatherland. They said, 'Hitler won't last. It's a passing phase . . .'"

* * *

In his office Alfonso instructed his treasurer, "Tell the Bank of Spain that we want two hundred million pesetas in five-thousand-peseta notes. Old bills. Then, internally, charge them to me personally."

At the Bank of Spain, the counterpart of the United States' Federal Reserve, the clerk in charge of providing currency to banks received the order and thought it odd: only the day before he had sent the principal Madrid office of the Bank of the Castle of Tarifa their weekly ten million pesetas. For them to require an additional sum, twenty times their regular use, was abnormal. And "old notes"? Usually banks returned old, worn bills and asked for them to be replaced with new ones. His orders were to report anything irregular.

His superior couldn't deny funds to a bank that could afford them, so he initialed the order. But he reported the "old bills" request to the Ministry of the Interior.

Alfonso's secretary said, "Sr. Duque, there's a Mr. Köhler on the telephone. He says he represents the Swiss and German group that has been trying to buy the beachfront property situated in front of *Finca de la Tejana.*"

"Mari Sol, I made it patently clear to their representative in Marbella that that land isn't for sale, in person and on the two occasions when she called me here to repeat the offer. Do you remember that after her second call I told you to say I wasn't in if she called again?"

"*Sí*, Sr. Duque, and I told Mr. Köhler of your disinterest. He said that he was aware of your earlier responses but that there are circumstances that have changed and he would be grateful for ten minutes of your time to present them to you. He's most persistent."

Exasperated, Alfonso said, "Very well, to get him off your back, give him a ten-minute appointment. At the end of a day so that I have an excuse to leave him quickly."

When she had gone Alfonso called the treasurer. "Notify the Bank of Spain that we require another hundred million in old bills."

At the Ministry of the Interior, in the Anti-Terrorist Division, the news set into motion the following modus operandi: a member of the ATD went to the Bank of Spain and asked to see the two orders. "Is this the signature and code from the Bank of the Castle of Tarifa?" he asked the clerk who had received the order.

"It is."

"Do you know this man well?"

"For years."

"Call him and say that you need the name of the bank's client who ordered this much currency."

When the answer came back that it was for the President of the bank himself, the Duke of the Castle of Tarifa, the Subminister of the Interior was called and he attended an ATD meeting.

The Director summed up, "We know that they attempted a kidnapping of the Duke's sons. It's logical to suspect that they have communicated a threat to the Duke that one day they will succeed with one of his children, or his wife, or his sisters, girlfriend or himself again, and that if he wishes to avoid their suffering or their possible death, he must pay the ransom in advance. A "revolutionary tax.""

This theory was further supported by the request for old bills. ETA buys their arms and explosives outside of Spain; they house their head people and many of their commandos in France. That means they have to get large sums of money out of Spain.

Paco went to Alfonso's office. "Do not keep anything secret from me. Has there been a kidnapping threat?"

"No."

"Are the children all right?"

"Eight children are never all right. But they are all safely accounted for."

Paco called Cayetana, "Has anyone threatened you with kidnapping?"

"I've been threatened with extraordinary things. But fortunately kidnapping isn't among them."

Believing them would be imprudent, Paco thought. He needed to protect them, from themselves, from the notion that they should obey a warning not to allow police intervention, that they could trust ETA. Alfonso's experience supported that idea. Paco called in the Director of the ATD and gave him the phone numbers of all the family and of America. "Tap their lines. Destroy transcripts of any personal conversations. Bring me only what might pertain to a kidnapping or other threat.

"And I want a covert around-the-clock protection of both the Duke and Duchess, and the Countess. Two men each, following them wherever they go. And two men each on all of the children of the family.

"Provide the same security for my wife. She'll be advised of what is happening."

The blockbuster news story from Barcelona appeared on all of Spain's front pages and on every radio and TV news broadcast, stunning the country. A major figure in Catalan society, a leading industrialist, had been detained at Irún-Hendaye, on the Spanish-French border in the Pyrenees, while attempting to smuggle a hundred million pesetas in cash out of the country in the trunk of his car. It was incredible because rarely, if ever, were cars stopped there, even to show passports. But they had had a tip. Spanish Customs had been watching him for months and they had located a Swiss bank and a Cayman Island bank in which he had deposits amounting to the equivalent of twenty million dollars. It was announced that the government would act according to the letter of the law: complete confiscation, a sixty-three-million-dollar fine that would take more than everything he owned, and a stiff prison term. He and his family were ruined.

Alfonso shuddered. "Your 'business travel' days are over."

"But you've got all that cash out of the bank. What can you do with it?"

"An excess of money, here, is no problem. I'll return it to the bank. It will be uncomfortable, but so be it."

The next day, breakfasting on the terrace America said, "I had a brilliant idea while I was sleeping, the solution to removing all that cash!"

"*Mi amor*, your smuggling days are over. Period!"

"No, Alfonso, listen to me. You've taken great risk getting all those old bills to your house, and now getting them back will be difficult. You would have to do it slowly, briefcase by briefcase. You can't have an armored truck arrive at your house to do it in one go and give someone the idea that there are fortunes in your house. You're in danger. People talk. Even without bad intent a clerk at the bank would find it glamorous to tell someone that his boss has three hundred million pesetas in his house. The wrong person could overhear and come after it. Please hear me out."

Determined not to put her in jeopardy again, but not wishing to frustrate her, he listened.

"As a member of a flight crew I have passed international Customs at least twenty times, in and out of Mexico, Canada, the Bahamas, the Virgin Islands, all over the place and not once have I been asked to open my luggage. Usually there's not even passport or security control. Fortunately, I've maintained my certifications, so I can hire a Lear out of London and fly it to Málaga with empty suitcases, as if I'm planning a shopping spree for Spanish clothes and boots that are inexpensive."

He took her in his arms, grateful that she had such love for him that she was reopening the subject, willing to continue to endanger herself. Disappointed, she asked, "Don't you like my idea?"

"There has been enough risk and thanks to God nothing has happened, you're safe. I want you to stay that way."

"I think the risk is minimal."

He shook his head. "A pilot wouldn't fly in and out of Spain in a private plane for no reason other than to go shopping. The cost of the fuel alone would mitigate any savings on just a few suitcases of clothes."

"Right on!" she chortled. "But don't underestimate me. To make it appear legitimate I'll hire four models to play the roles of socialites who've chartered a plane to take them out of rainy London to the Costa del Sol sunshine for a few days."

"*Mi amor,* I do not want your beautiful hair to turn gray before its time. Forget it."

"It will turn gray far faster knowing that you're in danger. I realize that my estimates of what you need outside of Spain, considering your large family, have been tremendously unrealistic. $150,000 for Magdalena plus eight children plus husbands who are too young to be secure and whose families can't help them a great deal. And Elena and her two children to support. Hah! I can't believe I ever said that. Really, darling, there's no risk. There's no Customs for leaving the country. And flight crews don't go through metal detectors or get our bags fluoroscoped. It's a piece of cake."

She was right that bringing it back to the bank himself would be a slow process and in the meanwhile someone could break in and if he again felt a knife at his throat he knew he would refuse to open the vault for them and possibly – probably they would kill him.

* * *

Paco had been informed of the cash in Alfonso's house. He feared that something life-threatening was close to happening. Or at the very least someone was going to arrive at Alfonso's home to pick up the "revolutionary tax." He ordered a covert sixteen-man surveillance of Alfonso's palace and a police helicopter ready to pursue the terrorists in case they should slip through the ground forces net. There were Anti-Terrorist commandos in eight cars parked on the street on both sides of the house. Other commandos in an abandoned building across the street from Alfonso's palace were seated in darkness at windows on the third floor from which they could see over the wall surrounding the mansion and into the courtyard.

Chapter Twenty

Mr. Köhler said, "I'm grateful to you for receiving me." He was expensively dressed and carried himself with a rich man's self-confidence. "Sr. Duque, our representative in Marbella is a Spaniard and it would have been inappropriate to confide in her what I'm about to suggest to you." He paused, "For high visibility Spaniards such as yourself, these are dangerous times. Your bank might be nationalized, your fortune confiscated. Nobody knows what might happen once the Communist and Socialist passions are aroused. You, better than I, understand that Spaniards are by nature a vengeful, anarchistic people. You're a husband and also a father of eight children, so perhaps you will give some thought to the following: sell us the land we want, we will pay you its appraised value in pesetas in Spain and additionally ten million American dollars in Swiss francs or German marks in any bank of your choice in either of those countries, or in American dollars. The transaction will be secret for our mutual security."

"But why that land in particular? I have any number of other properties that are also waterfront land and closer to the red-hot center of the touristic boom."

"Sr. Duque, we have studied the Costa del Sol for the past year, invested a great deal of effort and money on this research, and we have concluded that the property most appropriate for us to build a luxury development for today, and the future, is the land we are hoping to acquire from you."

Alfonso was thinking that if he could obtain ten million dollars outside, in a single, risk-free transaction, then with the four million already outside, his family's future was assured. And America's trip would be cancelled. It was heaven sent.

Her house and land would hardly be affected. Obviously Köhler wasn't going to build a giant wall to block her view of the sea. She would simply be deprived of the luxury of an unobstructed view. Surely, weighing all that was involved she would not only agree, she would urge him to do it.

Alfonso stood up. "Give me a day to think about it."

"But of course."

Alfonso ran a check on Köhler's group. Rock solid.

The following afternoon, entering Alfonso's office, Mr. Köhler smiled in the way a man would, surmising that as the appointment had been granted the deal was as good as made. "It's a pleasure to see you again, Sr. Duque. As you are a busy man shall we, as they say in Hollywood, 'cut to the chase'? Do you prefer Swiss francs, Deutschmarks, or American dollars?"

"Swiss francs in Switzerland."

When the payment was made Magdalena and the family would be secure and rich, as he and Paco and his two sisters had been, thanks to Tio Guillermo. And America would be safe.

Alfonso asked, "What is your time frame with regard to construction?"

"As part of our cost research we have had the basic plans drawn and, prior to making you a firm offer, we secured assurance of building permits from the Town Hall. We need only to show the change of title and we can begin preparing the land."

As a businesswoman, the numbers alone would convince America it was the only thing to do. Her option to buy was at one thousand pesetas a meter, which, multiplied by the three hundred thousand meters of waterfront property, would come to three hundred million pesetas. Less than three million dollars. She wouldn't allow him to accept that in place of the fortune he was being paid, and under the conditions it was being done.

Then why did he dread telling her?

Chapter Twenty-One

In the way that it's often the good swimmers who drown, so it was with Alfonso on the snow. Having become adept and wanting to amuse America he tried to do something spectacular, and he fell. Alfonso knew he would have accomplished the stunt if his mind had been on it. But he had been preoccupied with not yet having told America about Mr. Köhler. All weekend he had been looking for an opportunity, the right moment to tell her. But he kept imagining her face: hurt, offended that he had acted without first consulting her, angered that he had violated her legal right to exercise her option. Yes, he believed that she would agree with what he had done. But he couldn't find the moment—or was it the courage?—to tell her.

The foot had swollen to half again its size and turned purple. The doctor at the ski station bandaged it and told him to stay off it for a week or ten days. En route to the airport in Granada, wearing a bedroom slipper with the toes cut away, Alfonso told America, "The doctor has this way out of proportion. Plus he doesn't know that I'm a terrible patient. I would much prefer a little pain than to endure a week away from you. I'll call you tomorrow from the bank as usual."

But it was Mari Sol who called, "Sta. Harvey, el Sr. Duque won't be ringing you from the office because the accident he had, according to his own doctor, resulted in a broken bone in his foot that has been put in a plaster cast. He's advised to remain at home immobilized for a few days. He says he'll submit to that but will be in Marbella on schedule this Friday. He will call you from his home at the first opportunity."

America understood that to mean that he would call when Magdalena was out of the house.

She was in bed reading the morning paper when she heard Alegría barking strangely. Or was he moaning? It wasn't his usual bark; it was as if he were calling to her. And crying. He came running into her bedroom. His tail was between his legs. He sat down by the side of her bed looking plaintively into her eyes. He *was* crying. But why? She slid out of bed and sat on the floor, examining his paws to see if he might have stepped on a thorn. There was nothing. He continued crying, then lay down on the floor and put his paws on top of his head as if to cover his eyes.

At that moment Rafael called out to her from the hallway. His manly voice conveyed an urgent sadness. His face was streaked with tears. He was holding Primavera in his arms. The dog's head hung lifelessly, blood was all over Rafael's shirt and dripping from Primavera's body.

America took Primavera from his arms. Holding him she sat on her bed and her tears fell onto his blood-matted fur. On the floor at her feet Alegría was still crying, still covering his eyes as if he found it as unbearable as she did to look at Primavera's mortally wounded body. His stomach was torn open. Encarna came in and stood with Rafael. America clutched Primavera to her chest and cried. They all grieved wordlessly and felt the dreadful helplessness one suffers when something terrible has happened and there's nothing you can do, nothing you can pay, nothing you can beg of anyone to undo it, to make it not have occurred. It was final. Primavera was dead and nothing could bring him back to life to sidle up to her and kiss her, to run and wrestle with Alegría, not even once more.

She needed Alfonso. She was bursting apart and she needed his strength. She prayed that Magdalena had a charity meeting or something that would take her out of the house and he would be able to call.

Eventually it occurred to her to ask Rafael how it had happened. "He was run over by one of two bulldozers working near the beach. A man there says the dogs were barking at the machines. The driver says he couldn't hear anything over the roar of the motor. He did not realize that he had run over Primavera until he saw the other driver waving to him to stop."

She kissed the dog's head, which had not been touched and was as beautiful as ever, except that now the eyes did not see her and would never see her again. She kissed his eyes and wet them with her tears. She wrapped him in a linen sheet, put him on her bed, asked Rafael to go to their carpenter and have him make a coffin. She asked Encarna to stay close to the telephone in case Alfonso called. Then she went outside to select the spot to bury Primavera, someplace close to the house that she could see every day, and where he would never be disturbed even after her lifetime. She called to Alegría to come with her but for the first time ever he did not respond. He remained in the bedroom with Primavera.

Rafael returned with a small wooden coffin that he'd had lined with tin. "Señorita, you cannot help Primavera by suffering more. Allow me to place him in this box and close the lid. Sit in the living room and I'll take care of this, then I'll dig his grave where you tell me."

By ten o'clock in the evening, when Alfonso had not called, she understood that Magdalena had probably not left his side. What if she stayed with him all week? America wondered, what if Alfonso were to arrive on Friday and learn that Primavera was dead and buried? He would have a heart attack.

She waited, praying for his call, but the phone did not ring. Exhausted she fell asleep in her clothes with Alegría on the bed at her side.

In the morning the bulldozers were working back and forth, a mile below *Finca de la Tejana*. America was on her terrace having coffee. She had no desire to rebuke the man who had killed him. What would that accomplish? Now she idly watched the earthmoving machines, wondering why they were digging such a large, deep cavity. Why would anyone be making *any* excavation on Alfonso's waterfront property? She ran to her car and drove down the hill. A small trailer served as an office. She said good morning to the man at the desk and asked what was happening, what the bulldozers were doing.

"Something marvelous, Señora." He gestured across the trailer and showed her a mock-up of a high-rise apartment building. "This is phase one." He looked at her shrewdly, "If you move quickly you can still have your choice, perhaps a penthouse overlooking the sea. It will double in price by the time we start phase two." There was no mock-up of a second building but he gestured as to where it would be in relation to the first.

Reeling from the surprise, from not knowing what to say or to ask, America looked more closely at the mock-up. On it was the name "*Alemain-Suiza del Sol.*"

"Who are these people?"

"The proprietors, Señora. Germans and Swiss." He rubbed his thumb against his index and middle finger, a gesture she disliked. "Very rich. This will be a top quality development. The facade will be completely marble. There will be three swimming pools, one for children, removed, to keep their noise from disturbing the adults. All the electrical equipment is coming from Germany, the infrastructure will be second to none."

"But this is the property of the Duke of the Castle of Tarifa."

He shrugged and pointed to the name: *Alemain-Suiza del Sol.* "These are the only owners I know, Señora. They are the ones who have the building permits and who pay me for my men and machinery."

She returned home but remained behind the wheel of her car, too weakened to move. Encarna came out the front door, "Señorita, el Sr. Duque is calling."

"What's happened?" Alfonso asked as soon as he heard her voice. "You sound terrible. What's wrong?"

"Primavera is . . . gone." She couldn't bear to pronounce the word dead and shock Alfonso.

"Gone? Where? Do you mean he's disappeared, run away?"

Suddenly she *wanted* to startle him. "He's dead. He was run over by a bulldozer working on your property down below."

"Oh, my God. Oh, *mi amor*, I'm so sorry."

Hoping against hope, leaving room for some outlandish circumstance that she couldn't imagine, something akin to force majeure, she asked, "Have you any idea why those tractors are there, Alfonso? That is your land, is it not?"

He hesitated. "We need to talk about it this weekend."

She felt ill. "No. Right now. I want a simple answer to a simple question. The land you own in front of my property, on which I have an option: are you aware that someone is developing it with high-rise buildings?"

"Well, I wasn't informed what they were going to put . . ."

"Then you sold it?"

"Yes. It was more money than you can imagine. Really, America, please, wait until Friday. This isn't for the telephone."

She put down the receiver, incapable of saying goodbye.

The phone rang. "*Mi amor,* I know how you must feel but you have to understand more about it. I beg you, we have trusted each other so much and so successfully, please wait until Friday."

"You didn't even give me the opportunity to exercise my option to buy that land. That was my legal right. But someone offered you a better deal."

"Extraordinarily so. And when I explain it to you, you will agree that I did the only thing possible. For us both."

"Wrong! The only thing possible was to have spoken first to the person who has the legal right to that property."

"Absolutely! I was stupid. Then, after it was done I was afraid. But, please, wait to have this conversation on Friday. Will you? Please!"

"All right." She forced the words out from her diaphragm, sounding hollow, as she now felt, and hung up the phone.

I'll never sell that strip of land in my lifetime. If only to protect your property. Those had been his words. Now: *It was more money than you can imagine.* She had caught the inference that most of it had been paid outside of Spain. And he was so sure of her love for him that he was certain she would understand and accept what he had done as being for the best. Never mind for whom.

However she rationalized it, he had betrayed her. Working behind her back, not consulting her, not even attempting to convince her that it was the right thing to do, he had gone ahead and done it. He had violated her right to buy that land and maintain what she valued so greatly. She had cut her roots in the United States; her father had died while she was having an affair with Alfonso; she had abandoned her mother and Gat, the business she had founded. Alfonso had a large and ever-growing family without her. Whereas she, without him, was alone, with nothing but this little piece of land she called home.

She walked out onto her terrace and stared below at the view. Already it was changing. The serenity she had prized was lost in the roar of the earthmoving machines. Dust from the excavation was floating through the air, coating her terrace, her house, entering even through closed windows. She could imagine the noise from the swimming pools, the automobiles. And phase two would completely obscure her view of the sea. But far above all that was the pain of the inconceivable yet undenied betrayal by the man to whom she would have entrusted her life and for whom she had been endangering her own.

She visualized Primavera, his body broken open, sprawled on that dust.

Alfonso and she, too, had died. Whatever joy, trust, intimacy, all they had shared was ruptured. It wasn't a mental decision, it was entirely emotional. But mentally she knew that for too long now she had looked away from the changed man, his gradual but eventual interest in nothing but this obsession for financial security, more than security, even. The Alfonso with whom she had fallen in love was gone. America emphatically did not want him to visit her again.

No one at the bank had ever seen the Duke of the Castle of Tarifa come out of his office hurrying, despite the cast on his foot, to personally greet a visitor. It was Wednesday and entering his outer office America offered her hand to Mari Sol. "Having spoken on the telephone so many times I'm happy to see you, Mari Sol."

Alfonso led her into his office and closed the door. She backed away from his attempted kiss. There was a sofa and a coffee table across from his desk. He gestured for them to sit there. "I cannot tell you how sorry I feel over Primavera. I loved him very, very much."

She questioned at that moment that he was capable of loving anybody very, very much except his own self. Nor was she going to allow herself to say anything along the lines of how it was he who had inadvertently caused the dog's death. Whatever he had done, as cavalier as it was, he certainly had not meant for that to happen.

America couldn't bring herself to slip into the intimacy of the Spanish language in which they had for so long spoken in the familiar "*tu.*" Nor could she suddenly begin calling him *Usted* as if they were strangers. She spoke to him in English for the first time in eleven years. "I'm here to tell you that I can no longer see you because I'm in love with someone else and I cannot sleep with two men at the same time."

"No, *mi amor,* that isn't true. I'm mortally sorry that I shocked you. I handled it badly. I betrayed you. On top of that, the tragedy of Primavera. But try to understand that I'm not a young man anymore. I'm mentally and emotionally exhausted. I need peace. *Cuantos Primaveros más tengo?* How many more springtimes have I? But there's no one else in your life. One cannot turn off love so quickly."

"Yes, you betrayed me. But, no, I do not love you. That has ended. There's someone else." She did not explain that the someone else was herself, that she couldn't tolerate any further justifying of what should never have happened, of something she knew she would never have done to him. "In any event, there's nothing more for us. I feel no rancor. Only terminal disillusionment. I thank you for the twelve best years of my life. I will never forget them. Nor you. For that reason I won't sue to nullify your deal."

"If you did you would win. And I would go to prison because it would become known that ten million dollars was paid outside of Spain."

"I have no wish to see you harmed. On the contrary, I wish you well. I wish us both well." She stood up to leave.

Alfonso rose also. "I'm not going to say goodbye because this isn't the end. It cannot be."

"It is, Alfonso. Do not contact me again. And, need I say, forget about my flying for you. Solve your own problems."

As she was walking through the bank she felt faint. A man who had been admiring her caught and supported her until the dizziness had passed.

"Should you not sit down, Señora?"

"You're very kind. I feel better now. But I would be grateful if you would accompany me to the street until I have a taxi."

On the road to the airport her faintness turned to tears. For herself. For the loss of the past and the loss of the future. But more for Alfonso. She couldn't shut from her mind his face and the words "How many more springtimes have I?" She thought of how many wonderful springtimes he had given her. He wasn't thinking of springtimes like those anymore. He was tired beyond his years. Overburdened by the past, by the responsibility to his heritage, for his family, his heartbreak with José Maria. He only wanted peace. Needed peace. But that was *his* problem.

She remembered the conversation with him regarding Cayetana and Cristina and their scars from the war. Yet he was the one who had suffered the most, the cloistered fourteen year old whose heart and soul and mind were forever scarred by the sight of the harshest reality. It had become an ever-present, inescapable malady that for years he had masked by being bigger than life. But no one really is. She saw that he suffered an incurable illness and a voice from her school days, Nietzsche's, rang in her mind: *I am trying now to remember, not to give of myself to the dead. Never. Not the tiniest shred.* She saw that Alfonso was on the *Titanic*—and her sense of survival wasn't going to let her go down with him.

She felt she had acted badly about the money after having convinced him how easily she could help him. She could do him that last favor. They were nearing Barajas. "Driver, please turn around when you can and return me to the Bank of the Castle of Tarifa?"

Again in Alfonso's office she said, "I'm sorry that I told you I wouldn't fly for you. Of course I will. We've meant too much to each other to end badly. We must set a date and time when you and I will meet at your house in Marbella. I'll have flown a jet to Málaga. Once you have given me the final shipment I'll fly it to London and from there take a commercial flight to Zurich, make the deposit for you and then we will each go about our own lives."

"I don't want you to do this. I have more than enough now."

"I want to. You have put yourself in serious physical danger. I'll fly it out for you."

"A last kiss before dying?"

"I want us to say goodbye gently, kindly, as we have always been to each other."

"Until I went mad."

"No. Until the scars of your childhood overwhelmed your love for me. But that's irrelevant. I would like to finish our relationship as soon as possible. I can go to London today. I'm not sure how long it will take. A day or two I would think. I'll know after I'm there. I'll call and tell you when I'm 'coming home.' The hour I name will be the code for when we can meet at your house and fill my empty suitcases."

"I'll go to *your* house."

"No. I don't want you in my home again. I will go to your house in Marbella."

He saw tears in her eyes.

"How much will you need for expenses, the plane, the actors?"

She did not at that moment have the heart or the mentality for calculating expenses. "Forget it," she said. "That will be my farewell gift to you."

* * *

Despite being told "no calls" because of an important meeting with several bankers that he was holding, Mari Sol rang Alfonso's phone, "La Sra. Duquesa on line one."

"Alfonso, I'm on my way to *La Luz*. José Maria called. Puri's begun having labor pains."

"I'll join you there. I'm going to sit and wait with him. Let him try to evict me. I'm his father."

"I agree. Puri does, too."

"I'll leave here shortly." Being the father of eight he knew that it took hours from arrival at hospital to birth. He had waited six hours for José Maria to enter the world. They had all taken at least that.

He turned to the three bankers with whom he had been meeting, "Gentlemen, I'll leave you shortly as I'm about to become a grandfather again. However, we still have time to go over the fundamentals . . ." and they touched on the key points of a four-bank merger into one entity that would bear the name *Banco Castillo de Tarifa*.

Half an hour later he was driven to *La Luz* where he went directly to the Maternity Ward waiting room. Magdalena was elated. "It's a boy. A healthy boy. And Puri is fine."

"Where's José Maria? In the room?"

At that moment the waiting room door opened. They looked up. It was José Maria, looking at his father. Alfonso stood up.

José Maria was biting his lower lip but it did not turn off the valves behind his eyes.

Alfonso bit his lower lip. It didn't work for him either.

His son stepped forward, arms open and hugged his father, then kissed him on both cheeks, then hugged him again.

"It's a boy," he said haltingly. "We would like to call him Alfonso."

Chapter Twenty-Two

America walked into the office of JetLon, a small charter company flying out of London's Loton Airport. "I'd like to lease a Lear-35A to go London-Málaga-London on the same day. I'll pay the full price, but I won't require a captain."

The man behind the desk looked at her as if she thought she were at a Hertz or Avis counter. A logical reaction on his part. You charter a jet airplane, you get the services of pilots familiar with the aircraft. She anticipated him. "I'm leasing not renting. And I'm type rated in most private aircraft, also 737 and 727. And I'm certified for flight in England." She produced the documents.

"But why must you fly the aircraft? We'll get you there just as fast."

She couldn't reveal that she needed to be a member of the flight crew going through passport control and escaping baggage detectors. She had deliberately chosen a small charter company because they would find it more difficult to turn away the business. But he was hesitating too long and she did not want to provoke curiosity. "Look," she lied, "we all have different needs and mine is to impress a certain man."

That made some sense to him. Still, he was reluctant. "I'm normally not interested in renting out a four-million-dollar machine to a stranger."

She was counting on him liking her looks, and needing the business that all small charters did. "You could come along as copilot to look after your equipment." And, aware that money is the champion negotiator, she placed her credit cards on the counter. "Check me out and then make the decision."

He made two phone calls and agreed to the charter with her as pilot, himself copilot.

Next hurdle. "Can I buy a Jetlon uniform?"

Everyone in aviation was aware that it was less of a hassle to enter and leave a foreign country as a crew member and she correctly counted on him to be sympathetic.

Then she went shopping and came back with three aluminum suitcases. "Would you mind letting me use your stencil to paint the JetLon logo onto my luggage?"

This was less okay. "Look, Miss, I don't know what it is you want to move past Spanish Customs, and I'm not asking, but I'm not prepared to let you get our airplane impounded in Málaga."

"No problem. Before take-off I'll expect you to check my bags. They'll be empty."

"Then, why . . . ?"

"Because Spanish clothes are beautiful and cheap. Especially their boots and leather pants and skirts. I'm going to pick up next year's wardrobe. Also, I will have four passengers who will be paying for the trip."

As long as he could be sure she wasn't trying to bring narcotics or arms into the country then it wasn't his business who paid for what or how she spent her money. He agreed to paint the logos for her.

She set the flight from London to Málaga for Sunday, to arrive at three-thirty in the afternoon. There were no jumbo overseas flights coming in at that time so it was unlikely there would be a lot of police and Customs personnel at the airport. And there would be less Customs vigilance during the lunch hour. Even though there would be nothing to hide, the less attention on the plane the better.

* * *

It was Friday afternoon and Alfonso was in his office, longing for his trip to Marbella when Mari Sol rang him on the intercom. "La Señorita Harvey. *Linea una.*"

"*¡Mi amor!*"

There was a silence. Then he heard America say, "I'll be home at five in the afternoon on Sunday."

The English, the flat coldness killed his hope.

Magdalena was at Tio Guillermo's *finca* with Elena and the twins. Alfonso spent a lonely Friday evening in Madrid, the second in twelve years. Could she turn off love so quickly? A candle can be snuffed out, but not the raging flame they'd had.

As he wondered if indeed she had another man, he tried to retrace the past. How long since he had become unprotective of her, so consumed with his own problems as to have been completely selfish? Long enough so that being left alone five days a week, waiting for a different Alfonso, a less-thoughtful, less-concerned Alfonso, so absorbed in himself that he no longer sang to her, no longer thought of ways to amuse her, that he left her empty, hungry. With that to expect on the weekend, she could well have needed and turned to someone else.

He remembered the Alfonso with whom she had fallen in love. How he wanted to be that man again! But leaves that have fallen from a tree do not turn green again.

He slept badly, dreams, nightmares, waking constantly, only half sleeping. A gnawing doubt began suggesting that something was wrong. Why was she doing this for him now? He had a lightly vibrating fear—or it was more like a question: was she deceiving him? Impossible. America was a thoroughbred. It was exactly in character for her to finish the race no matter what. Or would she? Does one betrayal deserve another? How much abuse can even a thoroughbred tolerate? Longing for America's love he was painfully aware of how cruel his betrayal had been.

Still, he couldn't imagine revenge. Not from her. Yet, if she could have come to Madrid, look him in the eye and say, "I cannot sleep with two men at the same time," if she could do that then she had another, tougher side to her that he had never seen.

For the first time in years he went to work on Saturday. It was better than hanging around his house. Long after the bank had closed and Mari Sol had gone, he sat at his desk, sensing that something was wrong but unable to pin it down. Finally, despondently, he went home. He brought down into the vault the three brown canvas suitcases that he had bought the day before. Sitting at his ancestors' desk, with a paper and pencil he figured backwards: on the occasions when he had driven a car to Marbella it had taken seven hours, pushing hard, going straight through. But now, allowing for heavy weekend traffic, he decided on nine hours. So he would leave the house at eight A.M. He'd had new tires put on his car and it was completely serviced and filled with gasoline. He would tell Gregorio to prepare a few sandwiches. But he would bring nothing to drink. With luck nothing would cause him to have to stop along the way. What an irony it would be to stop at a filling station, go to the men's room, return and find that a thief had stolen his beat-up car, hoping to quick-sell it for a handful of pesetas, not imagining that its trunk contained three hundred million in cash.

He opened the three suitcases and began filling them with five-thousand-peseta banknotes. Sixty thousand pieces of paper. Even to a banker it was an awesome sight. He had calculated well. The three bags had exactly enough space for the money. He zipped them shut, locked them and stood them on the inside of the vault near the entrance. Then he stepped out and watched the stone wall slide into place.

Alfonso had dinner in bed. Tired from the bad night's sleep and desperate to stop thinking, he turned the light off at ten P.M.

At ten-fifteen, wide awake, it came to him like a bullet. There *was* another man. And most likely she had told him their story. This would be *his* idea. He reheard her saying, "I can't sleep with two men at the same time." She *had* wanted to hurt him. And she was going to avenge herself. Why else had she insisted so? She would take the money out of the country, but it would never arrive in Zurich, certainly not in his name. Her "farewell gift" would be a gift of revenge.

Her mistake had been not letting him pay the expenses. The costly rental of a jet airplane? The hiring of actors? Twenty or thirty thousand dollars to "say goodbye gently, kindly"? To someone who had betrayed you? No. She had known that she wouldn't be seeing him again to collect the expenses.

His heart was beating rapidly. He had to change plans. He would drive to Marbella but not to his house, nor would he arrive at five. He would get to Puerto Banus at three. He would load the suitcases onto his boat and bring them to Gibraltar. The British banks there would charge a heavy commission for exchanging the pesetas into a free currency, but, in fact, the Swiss were not offering bargains, and he wouldn't lose three hundred million. Nor be made a fool.

So he would leave at six A.M. He set an alarm clock, put out the light and fell into a saddened sleep.

Across the street, at the third-story windows overlooking Alfonso's courtyard, ATB commandos were aware of the fact that the Duke of the Castle of Tarifa was nearly never at home over weekends. That alone had them on the ready. Then they saw the light in his bedroom go on at five-thirty in the morning. Surely that signaled whatever it was they had been waiting for. They radioed to the other policemen in cars surrounding the area.

Alfonso shaved and dressed. He drank no water, no coffee.

At six A.M. he opened the service door of the palace. It was next to the garage. He looked around him and listened. He heard nothing. He saw none of the sixteen ATB commandos.

Each of the three canvas bags weighed about sixty pounds. Although he was strong, he struggled with all that dead weight. When they were hefted into the trunk of his car he eased it quietly closed, locked it, and again searched the night around him. Satisfied that he was alone and unseen he opened the front gates, and without starting up the engine pushed the car into the street.

He drove slowly without making the noise of completely closing his door, or putting on the headlights, until he was well into the next block.

Six unmarked cars, also without lights, followed a block behind. In the lead car a policeman radioed to the Ministry of the Interior. "The Duke of the Castle of Tarifa has loaded three heavy suitcases into the trunk of his car. He has left his house alone, covertly. He's crossing Madrid. All cars are in pursuit according to plan. Inform the Sub Ministro."

Awakened by the phone call, Paco listened and hung up. Cristina had put on the lights. Her husband said, "He's on his way to make the payoff." He got out of bed and began dressing. "The fool! I have sixteen men behind him. Wherever he stops to rendezvous they'll surround him and apprehend whoever meets him to receive the money. Just pray that the arrest is made without violence."

"If only he would have cooperated, worked with you."

"Terror." He kissed her and rushed out to the car the Ministry had sent for him. One of the two policemen in the front seat reported, "Apparently he isn't making the rendezvous in Madrid. He has turned onto *Carretera Nacionál* 4, headed toward Andalucía. Four cars have turned back, as ordered, *Sr. Ministro*. They will be replaced in relays along the way. Our two cars remaining with him are in radio contact with the *Guardia Civil* along the route. Wherever he turns off, the local *Guardias* will join our cars."

Though normally he enjoyed high speed, Alfonso kept to the limit, 80 kilometers per hour. The last thing he wanted was to be stopped by a pair of *Guardias Civiles*. Not that they would find any cause for suspicion. The car was registered in his name, he had the documents, his driver's license was in order, he was going to his resort home in Marbella and leaving early to avoid traffic. Nor would they inspect his luggage. He wasn't crossing a frontier. But who needed such an encounter? Satisfied that he had studied everything carefully and made his plans well, he settled down to the drive.

Was he imagining her fragrance? Or was it left over from the last time she had sat beside him in this car? He did not feel happy over outsmarting America. He felt profoundly sad. About everything: about losing his dearest love; that his country had changed; that he and she and life had changed.

He made an effort to overcome his sense of loss over what mattered the most to him. The worst loss: the loss of love. Shaking himself out of debilitating nostalgia he reassured himself what her "farewell present" would have been. She would have smuggled the money out of the country but not to his bank account. No, she wouldn't keep his money. That was completely out of character. Possibly she would drive it to Málaga to *Hogar San Carlos*. Of course! For those children she loved. That would be more her style. In any event he would never hear from her again.

It was the ideal hour for him to arrive in Marbella, three o'clock on a Sunday afternoon in early June, when people were at lunch, or on the beach, and there were few cars on the road. As he neared the port he felt a chill in his stomach and vibration around the edges of his mouth. Once on the dock he and all that cash were technically out of the country. If the police were to catch him removing pesetas from Spain he would be arrested, the money would be confiscated, he would be fined three times the amount he had attempted to remove, an additional nine hundred million pesetas, and because of the quantity involved and his prominence he would surely be imprisoned. Instead of bringing security to his family he would cause them disgrace.

Within minutes he arrived at the marina. As a boat owner he had a pass that permitted him to drive onto the dock, whereas the unmarked police cars were stopped. Of course the policemen's credentials would have quickly opened the barrier to them but they preferred to follow on foot toward the Renault.

Alfonso drove as close as possible to his boat but other cars were there ahead of him and so he had to park at a distance of about twenty yards. Removing the first suitcase, locking the trunk, he proceeded toward *La Primavera*.

A blue-uniformed Customs officer was walking in his direction. This young man wasn't an inspector, he performed other duties, but if he sensed contraband or flight money he would know what to do about it. Too late it occurred to Alfonso that he had made a bad mistake. Desiring secrecy, he had not called Manolo. If Manolo were there, a gentleman, especially one so well known, wouldn't be seen struggling with the weight of this bag. His sailor should have been carrying it and Alfonso should have been on the boat changing into a bathing suit.

The officer reached out toward the suitcase, "Allow me to help el Sr. Duque."

"No . . . well, thank you very much," he recovered his demeanor and relinquished the bag.

"El Sr. Duque shouldn't be struggling so on such a warm day."

Alfonso smiled, looking into the Customs man's face, keeping his eyes away from the suitcase that the officer swung so casually. He prayed that it wouldn't unaccountably split open and spill a hundred million pesetas onto the dock.

With the bag safely on board Alfonso waited until the officer was out of sight before returning to his car, then made a single hurried trip lugging the remaining two suitcases. With all three pieces on board he started up the engines. He did not wait to change into a bathing suit, he could do that at sea. Then he saw the gasoline meter. NO! It was only a quarter full. The sudden change of plan. He'd done everything too fast. He cursed Manolo for failing to have the boat always ready for use. Now he would have to stop at the *gasolinera*.

The commandos were confused. They had expected him to be met by somebody and hand the money over. Or to stash it somewhere for it to be picked up by the recipient. But apparently there was a different plan. Was he going to meet another boat and transfer the suitcases? They did not have orders on this. The ranking officer hurried into a shop, commandeered the telephone and called his superior in Madrid.

"Detain him. Open his bags and if they contain pesetas then they are illegally out of Spain. Impound them and place him under arrest."

The boat was filling its second tank as the four policemen, at a half run, neared the *gasolinera*. Seeing them, immediately understanding who they were and what was about to happen, Alfonso couldn't bolt away and escape; a police helicopter would overtake him.

Two policemen stepped onto the boat. They showed their credentials and, looking at the three suitcases, one of them said, "Unlock those, please."

Alfonso handed him the keys. The policeman unzipped the first bag, exposing the fortune in five-thousand-peseta notes. He opened the other two.

"Sr. Duque, you are under arrest. Raise your hands." The other man frisked Alfonso and found no weapon. The first said, "There are numerous *Guardias Civiles* backing us up. We are all armed. If I have your word that you won't attempt to escape I won't handcuff you."

Alfonso nodded. "Thank you. I give you my word."

"Then you may sit down and wait. My superior is en route to take charge."

Hearing the words in his mind, *You're under arrest . . .* , looking at the policeman seated watchfully across from him, at the other standing at the gangplank, at the two others on the dock, Alfonso recognized that his life was over, life, that is, as he had known and enjoyed it for so many years.

Calm, as one is when there's absolutely nothing to do, he sat on the back of his boat, staring out at the water, at the past, the happiness the port had always represented, the beginning of wonderful days, loading the boat with *cava, tapas,* then water-skiing, singing, the two of them standing at the windshield of the small cruiser jumping the waves, speeding into the sunset.

He stared down at the planked deck, remembering twelve years ago when his life had begun for the second time. Had he really destroyed that wonderful, heavenly relationship, as she said he had? No, she didn't understand. Surely she thought she did but she could not, nor could any stranger to 1936. He began to wonder if in fact she would have taken revenge on him, betrayed him with money as he had betrayed her—for money. He wondered if in fact she would have tried to hurt him at all?

As if looking through a musty window that had been cleaned and was clear he saw reality. He knew, categorically, that she would not. Revenge wasn't her style. Nor would she ever reveal to another man what she had done for him, not to anybody. Emotion, confusion, hysteria, all had caused him to make his life's worst misjudgment, disastrous to himself and, sadder still, cruel, unjust to her.

Abruptly Alfonso remembered that within a few hours she would arrive at his house with empty suitcases. If he had been followed all the way from Madrid, then certainly his house was being watched. When America arrived there she would be questioned, her empty suitcases would be found. They wouldn't know how she fit into the plan. He was on his boat; she was at his house. But they would suspect a connection and they would question her: eventually she would slip and say something that would open a window to the truth, then another slip and the window would open a bit wider until she would implicate herself in having conspired to commit a felony. Maybe even admit to having committed numerous others before. And there was no way he could be in touch with her, to warn her. He felt a leaden weight in his stomach and around his heart, helplessness to save the woman he loved.

The Subminister of the Interior boarded the boat.

At the controls of the Lear, leaving the Seville region and nearing her destination, she was told by the FIR center, "JetLon 101C, you are cleared to thirteen thousand. Contact Málaga approach 125.7."

The word "approach" almost undid her. She had to will herself out of the total freeze it cast over her mind and body. Out of love for him she had overstated the "no risk." She had convinced him and herself. But when you break the law there's always risk. Then she admonished herself, *As you're not going to turn back you have no alternative but to go forward.*

One more change of radio frequency in sight of Málaga gave America to the Málaga tower. "JetLon 101C, turn left to 180, you are cleared for visual runway 3 . . ."

She taxied to the parking area until ordered to stop. She cut the engines.

As Paco stepped onto the boat the two policemen guarding Alfonso saluted. "*Sr. Ministro*," one said, "we have impounded three suitcases containing great quantities of pesetas. They have been brought past the Customs barrier and onto this boat. As this puts them technically out of the country we are holding el Sr. Duque for attempted evasion of capital."

Paco told them to wait on the dock.

"*You!*" Alfonso gasped, disbelievingly. "You meant it? You really wanted to catch me removing money, to ruin me. Why?"

"No." Paco's face pleaded to be believed. "We thought it was another kidnapping. We thought we were protecting you. Please! Believe me! Despite what I said to you, if I had known what you were really doing I would have looked the other way. And I would have warned you that the Ministry was on to the fact that you were doing something. Somehow I would have gotten them off your back. At least I would have tried. But now . . . sixteen police officers saw you remove this money from the house. Four of them followed you here and along with local *Guardias Civiles* saw you take it onto the boat."

I would have looked the other way. Hardly having listened to the rest, Alfonso asked, "Paco? Truly? Would you have looked the other way?"

His brother gazed into his eyes and into the past. "Alfonso, would you bring me a horse, to my *choza,* and teach me to ride into your world? Would you give me a noble title? Would you share your fortune with me? Would you tolerate, forgive the sin I committed with your sister?"

Alfonso was silent.

"Yes. I would have covered for you to the end. But, now . . ." He raised his arms in a gesture of helplessness, ". . . what can I do?"

"There's something that would mean everything to me. America is arriving in a private jet to fly the money out of the country for me. At the last minute, insanely, I lost trust in her and changed my plan."

"You lost trust in America? But how?"

"She said she has another man. I acted irrationally, as I have for some time. In any event I believed I could no longer trust her. I should have returned the money to the bank but I wasn't thinking well, so I decided to take it to Gibraltar. America will be landing at Málaga airport, at any moment, expecting to rendezvous with me at my house at five o'clock this afternoon. With three empty suitcases."

"Your house is under surveillance. Until an hour ago it was to protect you. If the policemen encounter America with empty suitcases she'll be detained and questioned."

"Don't let her go to my house, Paco. Stop her. Keep her out of this."

Paco rushed to the tower that controls all boat traffic in and out of the port. Identifying himself he called the Ministry in Madrid and had them transfer him and officially identify him to the captain of the *Guardia Civil* at the Málaga airport.

"*¿Sí, Sr. Ministro?* At your orders."

"A private jet, piloted by a foreign woman, Miss America Harvey, who speaks Spanish fluently, may have just landed or is due to land at any moment. Miss Harvey is to be temporarily detained. With courtesy. This is an action at the convenience of the government. I will personally arrive in an hour to take over her case."

* * *

"Permit me to help you, Señorita." The captain of the *Guardia Civil* was standing at the entrance to the plane. "You are Miss Harvey? Miss America Harvey?"

"That's right."

He snapped handcuffs onto her wrists.

The room in the offices of the *Guardia Civil* was comfortable enough. The officer had unlocked the handcuffs as soon as she was inside and he had told her that someone would bring coffee.

There had been no talk of questioning her. But they would. And what would she say? Of course they knew everything. The police of a civilized country do not handcuff you for nothing. If she answered truthfully, those answers would destroy Alfonso. Yet to lie and commit perjury would be to destroy herself.

She thought of her mother and Gat and how this would hurt them. She thought of Alegría. His warm, furry body beside her at night. Encarna and Rafael would take care of him, and the *finca*, but, oh, how she would miss them. She thought of the almonds just coming out, and this year in September the eight acres of avocados should be at peak quality . . .

Staring at a blank, whitewashed wall that might have been a movie screen on which she watched her idyllic experience pass by in detail—the good, the happy, the wonderful. Why did she see only that?

* * *

Alfonso was seated in the rear of the boat, a glass of whiskey in his hand. Paco sat down beside him. "I'll go to the airport and sign her release, reporting it as an error. There will be no charges against her."

"Don't tell her I've been arrested. I don't want her to feel sorry for me and come back. She's waited too long to start her life. Advise her to get on with it. A better life than what she can have with me."

"I will take care of everything."

Paco's love for Alfonso was a shield, fending off the arrows of his mistakes, a net to help him fall more softly. He put his hand on Paco's. To express gratitude was impossible, to say anything was unnecessary.

"You are another story. Those four policemen on the dock have three of your suitcases filled with pesetas. If I could take those away from them I would . . ."

Then, thinking aloud he said, "No, it's really quite simple. We will pursue the original suspicion that you were paying off kidnappers. It has been suspected that you were acting on ETA's orders to deliver a "revolutionary tax," and I'll steer the Ministry to believe that you were to make the delivery to ETA by rendezvous with another boat. Having been the victim of a political kidnapping, plus an attempt on your sons, the Ministry will be receptive and compassionate. The penalty for attempting to pay ransom will be nothing compared to fiscal evasion. And there's no confiscation. Your money will be returned to you. Bank records will prove that you brought five million American dollars into Spain in 1950. Also strongly in your favor is the millions of meters of land you gave to the people in Guadalajara and here in Andalucía. Nobody has ever made such a gesture and it's been invaluable to Spanish agriculture. The Ministry won't be looking to find fault with you. On the contrary."

"You're willing to perjure yourself for me?"

"God forgive me, but given the necessity, I would kill for you."

Alfonso couldn't speak.

"But do not make another mistake," Paco urged. "Please. I won't be able to help you again. As soon as this is safely resolved I will resign from the Ministry."

"I'm very sorry."

Paco put his arm around Alfonso's shoulder. "If one cannot be a brother and also a *Sub Ministro,* then I choose to be your brother." He stood up. "I'll inform the policemen that you are free on your own recognizance, that I assume full responsibility for you. Stay in Marbella for a few days. When you feel rested go back to Madrid and wait until we can work this out."

* * *

Paco was taken to the room in which America was being held. Alone with her they hugged. "Everything will be all right." He led her outside the detention room, to the captain's desk. "Miss Harvey was detained in error. There are no charges against her."

"*Sí, Sr. Ministro.*" The captain handed over a paper that Paco signed. "You're free to leave, Señorita. *Y que vaya con Dios.*"

Outside, she and Paco walked to the main terminal. America looked at him, "Alfonso?"

"The Anti-Terrorist Division was advised that he had removed three hundred million pesetas from the bank in old bills. That aroused suspicion of another kidnap threat and that he planned to pay ransom. I had him protected by a force of police who followed him. He was caught in an attempt to take three suitcases of pesetas out of the country on his boat."

America was stunned.

"I know that wasn't the plan. That you were going to help him. He foolishly feared that you would betray him."

She couldn't grasp how it would be possible for Alfonso to imagine that. "And now? What will happen to him?"

"At the moment he's a bit worse for wear. And remorse. But we have a plan to get him out of this." Paco paused. "He says you have someone else."

"There's nobody else. Something happened and I was deeply hurt by him. I wanted to cut it off without recourse."

"May I offer you advice?"

"I definitely need some."

"Try to forget Alfonso. He will never leave Magdalena. What can the future bring you?"

"I'm not leaving Alfonso because we have no future. I'm leaving him because we have no present. You have said that 1936 will never happen again and that is obvious to me, too. Maybe Alfonso will also begin to see that and return to being the man we used to know."

Paco understood what she was saying but he felt constrained to counsel her as Alfonso had asked him to. "You are still a young woman. There's a lot of life still to be enjoyed. Do not remain in Spain. If you do you will again be seduced by her. And by him. Go home, to your family. You need time and distance. Reflect on the possibilities of life available to you. If you decide that happiness means returning to Alfonso—under the conditions that will always prevail—then come back. I would give anything to be able to offer you some solution to spare you more pain, as you did for Cristina and me, but that is the best I have."

He kissed her on both cheeks and held her hands in his. "Find happiness, my dear friend."

As the taxi drove along the Costa del Sol toward *Finca de la Tejana* her spent body swayed with the curves. She made the decision not to even think about anything until the morning.

When the car stopped in front of the door, Encarna stepped out holding Alegría by the collar. Seeing it was America she let go and he leaped into her arms and she caught him and held him, stroking his silky hair as he kissed her over and over again, whimpering with happiness. She rubbed his chest, calming him down and carried him into the house, speaking to him gently, "Come on, Al. From now on it's just you and me."

When she woke and looked at the clock on her night table she saw that it was eleven A.M. Alegría was on the bed at her side, watching her, but he had not moved to disturb her. Now he stretched with pleasure at seeing her awake. She had not slept that late ever in her life. And still she was tired. Looking around her lovely bedroom, actively seeing it, she rejoiced that she wasn't in a gray prison cell. She was free.

Having coffee on the terrace she saw the excavation going on below, the truckloads of building materials that were arriving and being unloaded. She turned and looked at the beauty of the mountains.

America thought that she would make a visit to see her mother and brother, bring Al and spend a month or two with them. But she wasn't going to flee from the life she had made. She wouldn't run away from Alfonso. She did not want to see him, to remember his voice, not the good of him, not the bad. She would see what life could be like without him. And if in the end she decided to go back to him, and if he still wanted her, that would be a mental decision.

And she wouldn't give up her *finca*. She had put years of work and passion into it. So, the view was lost. Tough! Maybe love was lost. Tough! But she wouldn't lose the *finca*. She had given up part of Jetways for love. She wouldn't sacrifice a square meter of *La Tejana* for loss of love. And she thought of Marco Americo, her *ahijado*. And her children at the *Hogar*. Her roots were planted too deeply in Spain for her to leave.

Her eyes fell on Alfonso's cassette player on the coffee table. She pressed the play button. The pleading voice, singing in English, belonged to Julio Iglesias, but whose heart, whose soul was that? Her own? Alfonso's?

I'D LIKE TO RUN AWAY FROM YOU
BUT IF I WERE TO LEAVE YOU . . . I WOULD DIE.
I'D LIKE TO BREAK THE CHAINS YOU PUT AROUND ME
. . . AND YET I'D NEVER TRY.

YOU MAKE ME SAD, YOU MAKE ME STRONG,
YOU MAKE ME MAD, YOU MAKE ME . . . LONG FOR YOU.
YOU MAKE ME HATE, YOU MAKE ME DIE,
YOU MAKE ME LAUGH, YOU MAKE ME . . . CRY FOR YOU.
YOU TREAT ME WRONG, YOU TREAT ME RIGHT,
YOU LET ME BE, YOU MAKE ME FIGHT . . . WITH YOU.
YOU MAKE ME HIGH, YOU BRING ME DOWN
YOU SET ME FREE YOU HOLD ME BOUND . . . TO YOU.

I HATE YOU AND I LOVE YOU AND I HATE YOU
AND I LOVE YOU MORE. FOR . . .
WHATEVER YOU DO, I NEVER, NEVER, NEVER . . .
WANT TO BE IN LOVE
WITH ANYONE BUT YOU.

She sensed Encarna standing beside her. Opening her eyes she was amazed that she had dozed off again, merely an hour after a long night's sleep.

Encarna was looking at her with concern. Then, with the wonderfully homey, old-fashioned belief that food can cure anything, she asked, "Would the Señorita care for a *tortilla?*"

"I would love to have a *tortilla!*"

"And perhaps a bit of *chorizo?*"

"*Mucho chorizo.* And some *jamon serrano* and a glass of *tinto.*"

Beaming, Encarna said, "The Señorita has an appetite."

As she left for the kitchen America closed her eyes tightly. She did not want, couldn't stand, for another tear to fall.

Chapter Twenty-Three

She realized it was one of the few times in the last two years that she had checked-in at a Spanish airport without fear and ice in her stomach. Holding Alegría on a leash she followed the porter to the check-in counter. Paco had arranged with an official of Iberia to allow the dog to travel in the main cabin and not be consigned to the fear and loneliness of a box in the baggage hold.

The ticket agent returned her passport and boarding pass. "We have a new first-class lounge where you may wait if you like. It's just past Security."

America and Alegría walked through the metal detector, she retrieved her purse from the fluoroscope and walked to the VIP lounge.

Suddenly she felt a strong tug on Alegría 's leash. He was yelping, wagging his tail and pulling on his leash with all his strength. It wasn't like him at all.

"Al," she scolded, "behave or they won't let you travel with me." But nothing could stop him. Whimpering, he pulled powerfully. Rather than create a scene she followed him and he dragged her toward the far corner of the room, to a couch on which a man sat with his back to her. She recognized the back of his head, his shoulders, the brown, Harris tweed jacket he was wearing. She let go of the leash.

Alegría jumped up on Alfonso, licking his hands, his face, squealing with happiness, then curled up in his lap to have his head and stomach stroked.

Lifting him, holding him in his arms, Alfonso rose to his feet. "I saw you come in. I tried to avoid your seeing me. If not for Al I might have succeeded."

"Just one question: how could you have thought I would ever have betrayed you?"

His pained eyes looked back at hers and he shook his head slightly, unable to explain the impossible, nor wishing to justify it. He loved her too much to want to be forgiven.

She said, "You know, at least now, that I would never have done that?"

He nodded, all the sadness a human being can suffer expressed in his face, his eyes.

She changed the subject, chatting lightly, "Amazing. The coincidence of us both going to Madrid on this flight."

He yearned to say, "Perhaps it was meant to be," but instead he small-talked that indeed it was a remarkable coincidence. "You're looking well," he said, noting that she was rested and lightly tanned. He longed to caress her hair.

"*Tú tambien,*" she replied, unaware that she had spoken to him affectionately, aware only of wishing she could reach out and touch the bronzed skin of his face.

"Well," he said, as if they had nothing more in the world they could talk about, "I will change to the next flight. It was very good to see you once more. Have a lovely trip . . . home . . ." and he thought, . . . *mi amor.*

He put Alegría down and stroked his head, hating to let go of him. Then he kissed him and without looking at America he walked away.

She sat down in the seat he had vacated. It was still warm and she felt his body against hers.

Y volver, volver, volver . . . she thought, but she knew, as he had known, whatever life might bring later, now it was the time for distance.

He was halfway across the room, halfway to the exit, halfway out of her life . . .

Distance? Why? I'll always love him. And he loves me. We're adults, not children. Why waste months of pondering what I already know? Why waste a single day? We've already wasted too many. She looked down at Alegría, who was staring longingly at Alfonso's back as he neared the exit to the lounge. She dropped his leash, "Go get him, Al."

The dog bounded across the room and leaped up against Alfonso's back with his front paws. As Alfonso turned around he saw America standing, looking at him. They met in the middle of the lounge.

She said, "Al and I are going to miss this flight and the connection to the States."

He had to physically restrain himself from showing the elation that surged through his being. "Are you sure?"

"Very. And we're also going to miss tomorrow's flight, and tomorrow's and tomorrow's."

She reached out her arms. "It's springtime, Alfonso."

The End